· *THE STOLEN CHILD* ·

NAN A. TALESE

*New York   London   Toronto   Sydney   Auckland*

· THE ·

# Stolen Child

A NOVEL

*Keith Donohue*

PUBLISHED BY NAN A. TALESE
AN IMPRINT OF DOUBLEDAY
a division of Random House, Inc.

DOUBLEDAY is a registered trademark of Random House, Inc.

Excerpt from "Night" from *The Blue Estuaries* by Louise Bogan, © 1968.
Reprinted by permission of Farrar, Straus & Giroux.

Book design by Maria Carella

ISBN-13: 978-0-7394-7498-3

PRINTED IN THE UNITED STATES OF AMERICA

*For Dorothy and Thomas, wish you were here*

*"We look at the world once, in childhood.*
*The rest is memory."*
"NOSTOS" BY LOUISE GLÜCK

· *THE STOLEN CHILD* ·

## · CHAPTER 1 ·

on't call me a fairy. We don't like to be called fairies anymore. Once upon a time, *fairy* was a perfectly acceptable catchall for a variety of creatures, but now it has taken on too many associations. Etymologically speaking, a fairy is something quite particular, related in kind to the naiads, or water nymphs, and while of the genus, we are sui generis. The word *fairy* is drawn from *fay* (Old French *fee*), which itself comes from the Latin *Fata,* the goddess of fate. The fay lived in groups called the faerie, between the heavenly and earthly realms.

There exist in this world a range of sublunary spirits that *carminibus coelo possunt deducere lunam,* and they have been divided since ancient times into six kinds: fiery, aerial, terrestrial, watery, subterranean, and the whole class of fairies and nymphs. Of the sprites of fire, water, and air, I know next to nothing. But the terrestrial and underground devils I know all too well, and of these, there is infinite variety and attendant myth about their behavior, custom, and culture. Known around the world by many different names—Lares, genii, fauns, satyrs, foliots, Robin Goodfellows, pucks, leprechauns, pukas, *sídhe,* trolls—the few that remain live hidden in the woods and are rarely seen or encountered by human beings. If you must give me a name, call me hobgoblin.

Or better yet, I am a changeling—a word that describes within its own name what we are bound and intended to do. We kidnap a human child and replace him or her with one of our own. The hobgoblin becomes the child, and the child becomes a hobgoblin. Not any boy or girl will do, but only those rare souls baffled by their young lives or attuned to the weeping troubles of this world. The changelings select carefully, for such opportunities might come along only once a decade or so. A child who becomes part of our society might have to wait a century before his turn in the cycle arrives, when he can become a changeling and reenter the human world.

Preparation is tedious, involving close surveillance of the child, and of his friends and family. This must be done unobserved, of course, and it's best to select the child before he begins school, because it becomes more complicated by then, having to memorize and process a great deal of information beyond the intimate family, and being able to mimic his personality and history as clearly as mirroring his physique and features. Infants are the easiest, but caring for them is a problem for the changelings. Age six or seven is best. Anyone much older is bound to have a more highly developed sense of self. No matter how old or young, the object is to deceive the parents into thinking that this changeling is actually their child. More easily done than most people imagine.

No, the difficulty lies not in assuming a child's history but in the painful physical act of the change itself. First, start with the bones and skin, stretching until one shudders and nearly snaps into the right size and body shape. Then the others begin work on one's new head and face, which require the skills of a sculptor. There's considerable pushing and pulling at the cartilage, as if the skull were a soft wad of clay or taffy, and then the malicious business with the teeth, the removal of the hair, and the tedious re-weaving. The entire process occurs without a gram of painkiller, although a few imbibe a noxious alcohol made from the fermented mash of acorns. A nasty undertaking, but well worth it, although I could do without the rather complicated rearrangement of the genitals. In the end, one is an exact copy of a child. Thirty years ago, in 1949, I was a changeling who became a human again.

I changed lives with Henry Day, a boy born on a farm outside of town.

On a late summer's afternoon, when he was seven, Henry ran away from home and hid in a hollow chestnut tree. Our changeling spies followed him and raised the alarm, and I transformed myself into his perfect facsimile. We grabbed him, and I slipped into the hollowed space to switch my life for his. When the search party found me that night, they were happy, relieved, and proud—not angry, as I had expected. "Henry," a red-haired man in a fireman's suit said to me as I pretended to sleep in the hiding place. I opened my eyes and gave him a bright smile. The man wrapped me in a thin blanket and carried me out of the woods to a paved road, where a fire truck stood waiting, its red light pulsing like a heartbeat. The firemen took me home to Henry's parents, to my new father and mother. As we drove along the road that night, I kept thinking that if that first test could be passed, the world would once again be mine.

It is a commonly held myth that, among the birds and the beasts, the mother recognizes her young as her own and will refuse a stranger thrust into the den or the nest. This is not so. In fact, the cuckoo commonly lays its eggs in other birds' nests, and despite its extraordinary size and voracious appetite, the cuckoo chick receives as much, indeed more, maternal care, often to the point of driving the other chicks from their lofty home. Sometimes the mother bird starves her own offspring because of the cuckoo's incessant demands. My first task was to create the fiction that I was the real Henry Day. Unfortunately, humans are more suspicious and less tolerant of intruders in the nest.

The rescuers knew only that they were looking for a young boy lost in the woods, and I could remain mute. After all, they had found *someone* and were therefore content. As the fire truck lurched up the driveway to the Days' home, I vomited against the bright red door, a vivid mess of acorn mash, watercress, and the exoskeletons of a number of small insects. The fireman patted me on the head and scooped me up, blanket and all, as if I were of no more consequence than a rescued kitten or an abandoned baby. Henry's father leapt from the porch to gather me in his arms, and with a strong embrace and warm kisses reeking of smoke and alcohol, he welcomed me home as his only son. The mother would be much harder to fool.

Her face betrayed her every emotion: blotchy skin, chapped with salty tears, her pale blue eyes rimmed in red, her hair matted and disheveled. She reached out for me with trembling hands and emitted a small sharp cry, the kind a rabbit makes when in the distress of the snare. She wiped her eyes on her shirtsleeve and wrapped me in the wracking shudder of a woman in love. Then she began laughing in that deep coloratura.

"Henry? Henry?" She pushed me away and held on to my shoulders at arm's length. "Let me look at you. Is it really you?"

"I'm sorry, Mom."

She brushed away the bangs hiding my eyes and then pulled me against her breast. Her heart beat against the side of my face, and I felt hot and uncomfortable.

"You needn't worry, my little treasure. You're home and safe and sound, and that's all that matters. You've come back to me."

Dad cupped the back of my head with his large hand, and I thought this homecoming tableau might go on forever. I squirmed free and dug out the handkerchief from Henry's pocket, crumbs spilling to the floor.

"I'm sorry I stole the biscuit, Mom."

She laughed, and a shadow passed behind her eyes. Maybe she had been wondering up to that point if I was indeed her flesh and blood, but mentioning the biscuit did the trick. Henry had stolen one from the table when he ran away from home, and while the others took him to the river, I stole and pocketed it. The crumbs proved that I was hers.

Well after midnight, they put me to bed, and such a comfort may be the greatest invention of mankind. In any case, it tops sleeping in a hole in the cold ground, a moldy rabbit skin for your pillow, and the grunts and sighs of a dozen changelings anxious in their dreams. I stretched out like a stick between the crisp sheets and pondered my good fortune. Many tales exist of failed changelings who are uncovered by their presumptive families. One child who showed up in a Nova Scotia fishing village so frightened his poor parents that they fled their own home in the middle of a snowstorm and were later found frozen and bobbing in the frigid harbor. A changeling girl, age six, so shocked her new parents when she opened her mouth to speak that, thus frightened, they poured hot wax into each other's ears and never heard another sound. Other parents, upon learning that their child had been replaced by changelings, had their hair turn white overnight, were stunned into catatonia, heart attacks, or sudden death. Worse yet, though rare, other families drive out the creature through exorcism, banishment, abandonment, murder. Seventy years ago, I lost a good friend after he forgot to make himself look older as he aged. Convinced he was a devil, his parents tied him up like an unwanted kitten in a gunnysack and threw him down a well. Most of the time, though, the parents are confounded by the sudden change of their son or daughter, or one spouse blames the other for their queer fortune. It is a risky endeavor and not for the fainthearted.

That I had come this far undetected caused me no small satisfaction, but I was not completely at ease. A half hour after I had gone to bed, the door to my room swung open slowly. Framed against the hallway light, Mr. and Mrs. Day stuck their heads through the opening. I shut my eyes to mere slits and pretended to be sleeping. Softly, but persistently, she was sobbing. None could cry with such dexterity as Ruth Day. "We have to mend our ways, Billy. You have to make sure this never happens again."

"I know, I promise," he whispered. "Look at him sleeping, though. 'The innocent sleep that knits up the ravell'd sleeve of care.'"

He pulled shut the door and left me in the darkness. My fellow changelings and I had been spying on the boy for months, so I knew the contours of

my new home at the edge of the forest. Henry's view of their few acres and
the world beyond was magical. Outside, the stars shone through the window
above a jagged row of firs. Through the open windows, a breeze blew across
the top of the sheets, and moths beat their wings in retreat from their perches
on the window screen. The nearly full moon reflected enough light into the
space to reveal the dim pattern on the wallpaper, the crucifix above my head,
pages torn from magazines and newspapers tacked along the wall. A baseball
mitt and ball rested on top of the bureau, and on the washstand a pitcher and
bowl glowed as white as phosphorous. A short stack of books lay propped
against the bowl, and I could barely contain my excitement at the prospect of
reading come morning.

The twins began bawling at the break of day. I padded down the hallway,
past my new parents' room, following the sound. The babies hushed the moment they saw me, and I am sure that had they the gifts of reason and speech,
Mary and Elizabeth would have said "You're not Henry" the moment I walked
into the room. But they were mere tots, with more teeth than sentences, and
could not articulate the mysteries of their young minds. With their clear wide
eyes, they regarded my every move with quiet attentiveness. I tried smiling,
but no smiles were returned. I tried making funny faces, tickling them under
their fat chins, dancing like a puppet, and whistling like a mockingbird, but
they simply watched, passive and inert as two dumb toads. Racking my brain
to find a way to get through to them, I recalled other occasions when I had
encountered something in the forest as helpless and dangerous as these two
human children. Walking along in a lonesome glen, I had come across a bear
cub separated from its mother. The frightened animal let out such a godfor-
saken scream that I half expected to be surrounded by every bear in the
mountains. Despite my powers with animals, there was nothing to be done
with a monster that could have ripped me open with a single swat. By croon-
ing to the beast, I soothed it, and remembering this, I did so with my new-
found sisters. They were enchanted by the sound of my voice and began at

once to coo and clap their chubby hands while long strings of drool ran down their chins. "Twinkle, Twinkle" and "Bye, Baby Bunting" reassured or convinced them that I was close enough to be their brother, or preferable to their brother, but who knows for certain what thoughts flitted through their simple minds. They gurgled, and they gooed. In between songs, for counterpoint, I would talk to them in Henry's voice, and gradually they came to believe—or abandon their sense of disbelief.

Mrs. Day bustled into the babies' room, humming and tra-la-la-ing. Her general girth and amplitude amazed me; I had seen her many times before, but not quite at such close quarters. From the safety of the woods, she had seemed more or less the same as all adult humans, but in person, she assumed a singular tenderness, though she smelled faintly sour, a perfume of milk and yeast. She danced across the floor, throwing open curtains, dazzling the room with golden morning, and the girls, brightened by her presence, pulled themselves up by the slats of their cribs. I smiled at her, too. It was all I could do to keep from bursting into joyous laughter. She smiled back at me as if I were her only son.

"Help me with your sisters, would you, Henry?"

I picked up the nearest girl and announced very pointedly to my new mother, "I'll take Elizabeth." She was as heavy as a badger. It is a curious feeling to hold an infant one is not planning to steal; the very young convey a pleasant softness.

The girls' mother stopped and stared at me, and for a beat, she looked puzzled and uncertain. "How did you know that was Elizabeth? You've never been able to tell them apart."

"That's easy, Mom. Elizabeth has two dimples when she smiles and her name's longer, and Mary has just one."

"Aren't you the clever one?" She picked up Mary and headed off downstairs.

Elizabeth hid her face against my shoulder as we followed our mother.

The kitchen table groaned with a huge feast—hotcakes and bacon, a jug of warm maple syrup, a gleaming pitcher of milk, and china bowls filled with sliced bananas. After a long life in the forest eating what-you-can-find, this simple fare appeared a smorgasbord of exotic delicacies, rich and ripe, the promise of fullness.

"Look, Henry, I made all your favorites."

I could have kissed her right on the spot. If she was pleased with herself for taking the trouble to fix Henry's favorite foods, she must have been extremely gratified by how I tucked in and enjoyed breakfast. After four hotcakes, eight strips of bacon, and all but two small glassfuls of the pitcher of milk, I complained of hunger, so she made me three eggs and a half loaf of toast from home-baked bread. My metabolism had changed, it seemed. Ruth Day saw my appetite as a sign of love for her, and for the next eleven years, until I left for college, she indulged me. In time, she sublimated her own anxieties and began to eat like me. Decades as a changeling had molded my appetites and energies, but she was all too human, growing heavier with each passing season. Over the years, I've often wondered if she would have changed so much with her real firstborn or whether she filled her gnawing suspicion with food.

That first day she kept me inside the house, and after all that had occurred, who could blame her? I stuck closer than her own shadow, studying intently, learning better how to be her son, as she dusted and swept, washed the dishes, and changed the babies' diapers. The house felt safer than the forest, but strange and alien. Small surprises lurked. Daylight angled through the curtained windows, ran along the walls, and cast its patterns across the carpets in an entirely different geometry than beneath the canopy of leaves. Of particular interest were the small universes comprised of specks of dust that make themselves visible only through sunbeams. In contrast to the blaze of sunlight outside, the inner light had a soporific effect, especially on the twins. They tired shortly after lunch—another fête in my honor—and napped in the early afternoon.

My mother tiptoed from their room to find me patiently waiting in the same spot she had left me, standing like a sentinel in the hallway. I was be-witched by an electrical outlet that screamed out to me to stick in my little finger. Although their door was closed, the twins' rhythmic breathing sounded like a storm rushing through the trees, for I had not yet trained myself not to listen. Mom took me by the hand, and her soft grasp filled me with an abiding empathy. The woman created a deep peace within me with her very touch. I remembered the books on Henry's washstand and asked her if she would read me a story.

We went to my room and clambered into bed together. For the past century, adults had been total strangers, and life among the changelings had distorted my perspective. More than twice my size, she seemed too solid and stout to be real, especially when compared to the skinny body of the boy I had assumed. My situation seemed fragile and capricious. If she rolled over, she could snap me like a bundle of twigs. Yet her sheer size created a bunker against the outer world. She would protect me against all my foes. As the twins slept, she read to me from the Brothers Grimm—"The Story of the Youth Who Went Forth to Learn What Fear Was," "The Wolf and the Seven Young Kids," "Hansel and Gretel," "The Singing Bone," "The Girl Without Hands," and many others, rare or familiar. My favorites were "Cinderella" and "Little Red Riding Hood," which she read with beautiful expression in her mezzo timbre, a singsong much too cheerful for those awful fables. In the music of her voice, an echo sounded from long ago, and as I rested by her side, the decades dissolved.

I had heard these tales before, long ago, but in German, from my real mother (yes, I, too, had a mother, once upon a time), who introduced me to Ashenputtel and Rotkäppchen from the *Kinder- und Hausmärchen*. I wanted to forget, thought I was forgetting, but could hear quite clearly her voice in my head.

*"Es war einmal im tiefen, tiefen Wald."*

Although I quit the society of the changelings long ago, I have remained, in a sense, in those dark woods, hiding my true identity from those I love. Only now, after the strange events of this past year, do I have the courage to tell the story. This is my confession, too long delayed, which I have been afraid to make and only now reveal because of the passing dangers to my own son. We change. I have changed.

CHAPTER 2

I am gone.

This is not a fairy tale, but the true history of my double life, left behind where it all began, in case I may be found again.

My own story begins when I was a boy of seven, free of my current desires. Nearly thirty years ago, on an August afternoon, I ran away from home and never made it back. Certain trivial and forgotten matters set me off, but I remember preparing for a long journey, stuffing my pockets with biscuits left over from lunch, and creeping out of the house so softly that my mother might not know I had ever left.

From the back door of the farmhouse to the creeping edge of the forest, our yard was bathed in light, as if a borderland to cross carefully, in fear of being exposed. Upon reaching the wilderness, I felt safe and hidden in the dark, dark wood, and as I walked on, stillness nestled in the spaces among the trees. The birds had stopped singing, and the insects were at rest. Tired of the blazing heat, a tree groaned as if shifting in its rooted position. The green roof of leaves above sighed at every rare and passing breeze. As the sun dipped below the treeline, I came across an imposing chestnut with a hollow at its base big enough for me to crawl inside to hide and wait, to listen for the seekers. And when they came close enough to beckon, I would not move. The grown-ups kept shouting "Hen-ry" in the fading afternoon, in the half-light of dusk, in the cool and starry night. I refused to answer. Beams from the flashlights bounced crazily among the trees, and the search party crashed through the undergrowth, stumbling over stumps and fallen logs, passing me by. Soon their calls receded into the distance, faded to echoes, to whispers, to silence. I was determined not to be found.

I burrowed deeper into my den, pressing my face against the inner ribs of the tree, inhaling its sweet rot and dankness, the grain of the wood rough against my skin. A low rustle sounded faraway and gathered to a hum. As it drew near, the murmur intensified and quickened. Twigs snapped and leaves crackled as it galloped toward the hollow tree and stopped short of my hiding place. A panting breath, a whisper, and footfall. I curled up tight as something scrambled partway into the hole and bumped into my feet. Cold fingers wrapped around my bare ankle and pulled.

They ripped me from the hole and pinned me to the ground. I shouted once before a small hand clamped shut my mouth and then another pair of hands inserted a gag. In the darkness their features remained obscure, but their size and shape were the same as my own. They quickly stripped me of my clothes and bound me like a mummy in a gossamer web. Little children, exceptionally strong boys and girls, had kidnapped me.

They held me aloft and ran. Racing through the forest at breakneck speed on my back, I was held up by several pairs of hands and bony shoulders. The stars above broke through the canopy, streaming by like a meteor shower, and the world spun away swiftly from me in darkness. The athletic creatures moved about with ease, despite their burden, navigating the invisible terrain and obstacles of trees without a hitch or stumble. Gliding like an owl through the night forest, I was exhilarated and afraid. As they carried me, they spoke to one another in a gibberish that sounded like the bark of a squirrel or the rough cough of a deer. A hoarse voice whispered something that sounded like "Come away" or "Henry Day." Most fell silent, although now and then one would start huffing like a wolf. The group, as if on signal, slowed to a canter along what I later discerned to be well-established deer trails that served the denizens of the woods.

Mosquitos lit upon the exposed skin on my face, hands, and feet, biting me at will and drinking their fill of my blood. I began to itch and desperately wanted to scratch. Above the noise of the crickets, cicadas, and peeping frogs, water babbled and gurgled nearby. The little devils chanted in unison until the company came to a sudden halt. I could hear the river run. And thus bound, I was thrown into the water.

Drowning is a terrible way to go. It wasn't the flight through the air that alarmed me, or the actual impact with the river, but the sound of my body knifing through the surface. The wrenching juxtaposition of warm air and cool water shocked me most. The gag did not come out of my mouth; my hands were not loosed. Submerged, I could no longer see, and I tried for a moment to hold my breath, but then felt the painful pressure in my chest and sinuses as my lungs quickly filled. My life did not flash before my eyes—I was only seven—and I did not call out for my mother or father or to God. My last thoughts were not of dying, but of being dead. The waters encompassed me, even to my soul, the depths closed round about, and weeds were wrapped about my head.

Many years later, when the story of my conversion and purification evolved into legend, it was said that when they resuscitated me, out shot a stream of water a-swim with tadpoles and tiny fishes. My first memory is of awakening in a makeshift bed, dried snot caked in my nose and mouth, under a blanket of reeds. Seated above on rocks and stumps and surrounding me were the faeries, as they called themselves, quietly talking together as if I were not even there. I counted them, and, including me, we were an even dozen. One by one, they noticed me awake and alive. I kept still, as much out of fear as embarrassment, for my body was naked under the covers. The whole scene felt like a waking dream or as if I had died and had been born again.

They pointed at me and spoke with excitement. At first, their language sounded out of tune, full of strangled consonants and static. But with careful concentration, I could hear a modulated English. The faeries approached cautiously so as not to startle me, the way one might approach a fallen fledgling or a fawn separated from its doe.

"We thought you might not make it."

"Are you hungry?"

"Are you thirsty? Would you like some water?"

They crept closer, and I could see them more clearly. They looked like a tribe of lost children. Six boys and five girls, lithe and thin, their skin dusky from the sun and a film of dust and ash. Nearly naked, both males and females wore ill-fitting shorts or old-fashioned knickerbockers, and three or four had donned threadbare jerseys. No one wore shoes, and the bottoms of their feet were calloused and hard, as were their palms. Their hair grew long and ragged, in whirls of curls or in knots and tangles. A few of them had a complete set of original baby teeth, while others had gaps where teeth had fallen out. Only one, who looked a few years older than the rest, showed two new adult teeth at the top of his mouth. Their faces were very fine and delicate. When they scrutinized me, faint crow's feet gathered at the corners of their dull and vacant eyes. They did not look like any children I knew, but ancients in wild children's bodies.

They were faeries, although not the kind from books, paintings, and the movies. Nothing like the Seven Dwarfs, Munchkins, midgets, Tom Thumbs, brownies, elves, or those nearly naked flying sprites at the beginning of *Fantasia*. Not little redheaded men dressed in green and leading to the rainbow's end. Not Santa's helpers, nor anything like the ogres, trolls, and other monsters from the Grimm Brothers or Mother Goose. Boys and girls stuck in time, ageless, feral as a pack of wild dogs.

A girl, brown as a nut, squatted near me and traced patterns in the dust near my head. "My name is Speck." The faery smiled and stared at me. "You need to eat something." She beckoned her friends closer with a wave of her hand. They set three bowls before me: a salad made from dandelion leaves, watercress, and wild mushrooms; a hill of blackberries plucked from the thorns before dawn; and a collection of assorted roasted beetles. I refused the last but washed down the fruit and vegetables with clear, cold water from a hollowed gourd. In small clusters, they watched intently, whispering to one another and looking at my face from time to time, smiling when they caught my eye.

Three of the faeries approached to take away my empty dishes; another brought me a pair of trousers. She giggled as I struggled beneath the reed blanket, and then she burst out laughing as I tried to button my fly without revealing my nakedness. I was in no position to shake the proffered hand when the leader introduced himself and his cronies.

"I am Igel," he said, and swept back his blonde hair with his fingers. "This is Béka."

Béka was a frog-faced boy a head taller than the others.

"And this is Onions." Dressed in a boy's striped shirt and short pants held up by suspenders, she stepped to the front. Shielding her eyes from the sun with one hand, she squinted and smiled at me, and I blushed to the breast-bone. Her fingertips were green from digging up the wild onions she loved to eat. When I finished dressing, I pulled myself up on bent elbows to get a better look at the rest of them.

"I'm Henry Day," I croaked, my voice raw with suffering.

"Hello, Aniday." Onions smiled, and everyone laughed at the appellation. The faery children began to chant "Aniday, Aniday," and a cry sounded in my heart. From that time forward I was called Aniday, and in time I forgot my given name, although on occasion it would come back part of the way as Andy Day or Anyway. Thus christened, my old identity began to fade, much as a baby will not remember all that happened before it is born. To lose one's name is the beginning of forgetting.

As the cheering faded, Igel introduced each faery, but the jumble of names clanged against my ears. They walked away in twos and threes, disappeared into hidden holes that ringed the clearing, then reemerged with ropes and rucksacks. For a moment, I wondered whether they planned to tie me up to be baptized yet again, but most of them took scant notice of my panic. They milled about, anxious to begin, and Igel strode over to my bedside. "We're going on a scavenger hunt, Aniday. But you need to stay here and rest. You've been through quite an ordeal."

When I tried to stand up, I met the resistance of his hand upon my chest. He may have looked like a six-year-old, but he had the strength of a grown man.

"Where is my mother?" I asked.

"Béka and Onions will stay with you. Get some rest." He barked once, and in a flash, the pack gathered by his side. Without a sound, and before I could raise a word of protest, they disappeared, fading into the forest like ghostly wolves. Lagging behind, Speck turned her head and called out to me, "You're one of us now." Then she loped off to join the others.

I lay back down and fought tears by staring into the sky. Clouds passed beneath the summer sun, rolling their shadows through the trees and across the faery camp. In the past, I had ventured into these woods alone or with my father, but I had never wandered so deeply into such a quiet, lonesome place. The familiar chestnut, oak, and elm grew taller here, and the forest rimming the clearing appeared thick and impenetrable. Here and there sat well-worn stumps and logs and the remnants of a campfire. A skink sunned itself on the rock that Igel had sat upon. Nearby, a box turtle shuffled through the fallen leaves and hissed into its shell when I sat up to take a closer look.

Standing proved to be a mistake and left me woozy and disoriented. I wanted to be home in bed, near the comfort of my mother, listening to her sing to my baby sisters, but instead I felt the cold, cold gaze of Béka. Beside him, Onions hummed to herself, intent on the cat's-cradle in her busy fingers. She hypnotized me with her designs. Exhausted, I laid my body down, shivering despite the heat and humidity. The afternoon drifted by heavily, inducing sleep. My two companions watched me watching them, but they said nothing. In and out of consciousness, I could not move my tired bones, thinking back on the events that had led me to this grove and worrying about the troubles that would face me when I returned home. In the middle of my drowse, I opened my eyes, sensing an unfamiliar stirring. Nearby, Béka and Onions wrestled beneath a blanket. He was on top of her back, pushing and grunting, and she lay on her stomach, her face turned toward mine. Her green mouth gaped, and when she saw me spying, she flashed me a toothy grin. I closed my eyes and turned away. Fascination and disgust clawed at one another in my confused mind. No sleep returned until the two fell quiet, she humming to herself while the little frog snored contentedly. My stomach seized up like a clenched fist, and nausea rolled into me like a fever. Frightened, and lonesome for home, I wanted to run away and be gone from this strange place.

CHAPTER 3

I taught myself how to read and write again during those last two weeks of summer with my new mother, Ruth Day. She was determined to keep me inside or within earshot or in her line of vision, and I happily obliged her. Reading, of course, is merely associating symbols with sounds, memorizing the combinations, rules and effects, and, most important, the spaces between words. Writing proved more difficult, primarily because one had to have something to say before confronting the blank page. The actual drawing of the alphabet turned out to be a tiresome chore. Most afternoons, I practiced with chalk and an eraser on a slate, filling it over and over with my new name. My mother grew concerned about my compulsive behavior, so I finally quit, but not before printing, as neatly as possible, "I love my mother." She was tickled to find that later, and the gesture earned me an entire peach pie, not a slice for the others, not even my father.

The novelty of going to second grade quickly eroded to a dull ache. The schoolwork came easily to me, although I entered somewhat behind my classmates in understanding that other method of symbolic logic: arithmetic. I still tussle with my numbers, not so much the basic operations—addition, subtraction, multiplication—as the more abstract configurations. Elementary science and history revealed a way of thinking about the world that differed from my experience among the changelings. For example, I had no idea that George Washington is, metaphorically speaking, the father of our country, nor did I realize that a *food chain* is the arrangement of organisms of an ecological community according to the order of predation in which each uses the next, usually lower, members as a food source. Such explanations of the natural order felt most unnatural at first. Matters in the forest were far more existential. Living depended on sharpening instincts, not memorizing facts. Ever since the last wolves had been killed or driven off by bounty hunters, no enemy but man remained. If we stayed hidden, we would continue to endure.

Our struggle was to find the right child with whom to trade places. It couldn't be a random selection. A changeling must decide on a child the same age as he was when he had been kidnapped. I was seven when they took me, and seven when I left, though I had been in the woods for nearly a century. The ordeal of that world is not only survival in the wild, but the long, unbearable wait to come back into this world.

When I first returned, that learned patience became a virtue. My schoolmates watched time crawl every afternoon, waiting an eternity for the three o'clock bell. We second graders sat in the same stultifying room from September to mid-June, and barring weekends and the glorious freedom of holidays, we were expected to arrive by eight o'clock and behave ourselves for the next seven hours. If the weather cooperated, we were let out into the playground twice a day for a short recess and at lunchtime. In retrospect, the actual moments spent together pale to our time apart, but some things are best measured by quality rather than quantity. My classmates made each day a torture. I expected civilization, but they were worse than the changelings. The boys in their grubby navy bow ties and blue uniforms were indistinguishably horrid—nose-pickers, thumbsuckers, snorers, ne'er-do-wells, farters, burpers, the unwashed and unclean. A bully by the name of Hayes liked to torture the rest, stealing lunches, pushing in line, pissing on shoes, fighting on the playground. One either joined his sycophants, egging him on, or would be slated as a potential prey. A few of the boys became perpetually oppressed. They reacted badly, either by withdrawing deep inside themselves or, worse, crying and screaming at every slight provocation. At an early age, they were marked for life, ending up, doubtlessly, as clerks or store managers, systems analysts or consultants. They came back from recess bearing the signs of their abuse—black eyes and bloody noses, the red welt of tears—but I neglected to come to their rescue, although perhaps I should have. If I had ever used my real strength, I could easily have dispatched the bullies with a single, well-placed blow.

The girls, in their own way, suffered worse indignities. They, too, displayed many of the same disappointing personal habits and lack of general hygiene. They laughed too loudly or not at all. They competed viciously among themselves and with their opposites, or they faded into the woodwork like mice. The worst of them, by the name of Hines, routinely tore apart the shyest girls with her taunts and shunning. She would humiliate her victims without mercy if, for instance, they wet their pants in class, as happened right before recess on the first day to the unprepared Tess Wodehouse. She flushed as if on fire, and for the very first time, I felt something close to sympathy for another's misfortune. The poor thing was teased about the episode until Valentine's Day. In their plaid jumpers and white blouses, the girls relied upon words rather than their bodies to win their battles. In that sense, they paled next to the female hobgoblins, who were both as cunning as crows and as fierce as bobcats.

These human children were altogether inferior. Sometimes at night, I wished I could be back prowling the forest, spooking sleeping birds from their roosts, stealing clothes from clotheslines, and making merry, rather than enduring page after page of homework and fretting about my peers. But for all its faults, the real world shone, and I set my mind to forgetting the past and becoming a real boy again. Intolerable as school was, my home life more than compensated. Mom would be waiting for me every afternoon, pretending to be dusting or cooking when I strode triumphantly through the front door.

"There's my boy," she would say, and whisk me to the kitchen for a snack of jam and bread and a cup of Ovaltine. "How was your day today, Henry?"

I would make up one or two pleasant lies for her benefit.

"Did you learn anything new?"

I would recite all that had been rehearsed on the way home. She seemed inordinately curious and pleased, but would leave me at last to the dreadful homework, which I usually managed to finish right before suppertime. In the few moments before my father came home from work, she would fix our meal, my company at tableside. In the background, the radio played her favorite ballads, and I learned them all upon first hearing and could sing along when the records were invariably repeated. By accident or ignorance, I mimicked the balladeers' voices perfectly and could sing tone for tone, measure for measure, phrase for phrase, exactly like Bing Crosby and Frank Sinatra, Rosemary Clooney or Jo Stafford. Mom took my musical ability as a natural extension of my general wonderfulness, charm, and native intellect. She loved to hear me, often switching off the radio to beg me to sing it one more time.

"Be a dear boy and give us 'There's a Train Out for Dreamland' again."

When my father first heard my act, he didn't respond as kindly. "Where did you pick that up? One day you can't carry a tune, now you sing like a lark."

"I dunno. Maybe I wasn't listening before."

"You're kidding me? She has that racket on day and night with your Nat Cole King and all that jazz, and 'Can you take me dancin' sometime?' As if a mother of twins . . . What do you mean, you weren't listening?"

"Concentrating, I mean."

"You should be concentrating on your homework and helping your mother with the chores."

"If you pay attention and listen instead of merely hearing the song, you can pick up the tune in no time."

He shook his head and lit another Camel. "Mind your elders, if you please, Caruso."

I took care not to be such a perfect mimic around my dad.

Mary and Elizabeth, on the other hand, were too young to know any better, and they accepted without question my budding talent for impersonation. Indeed, they begged for songs all the time, especially in their cribs, where I'd trot out all the novelty tunes like "Mairzy Doats" or "Three Little Fishies." Without fail, however, they fell asleep as if knocked unconscious every time I sang "Over the Rainbow." I did a mean Judy Garland.

My days with the Days quickly fell into a comfortable routine, and as long as I stayed inside the house or inside the classroom, all went well. The weather suddenly grew cooler, and almost at once the leaves turned garish shades of yellow and red, so bold that the mere sight of trees hurt my eyes. I hated those bright reminders of life in the forest. October proved a riot to the senses and climaxed those giddy last weeks before Halloween. I knew that parties were involved, begging for nuts and candies, bonfires in the square, and playing tricks on the townsfolk. Believe me, we hobgoblins did our share of mischief—unhinging gates, smashing pumpkins, soaping the library windows with cartoon demons. What I had not experienced was the folderol among the children and the way that even the schools had gotten into the act. Two weeks before the big day, the nuns began planning a classroom party with entertainment and refreshments. They hung orange and black crepe paper along the tops of the chalkboards, pasted paper pumpkins and black cats on the walls. We dutifully cut out scary things from construction paper and glued together our own artistic efforts, pitiable though they were. Mothers were enlisted to bake cookies and brownies, make popcorn balls and candy apples. Costumes were allowed—indeed, expected. I remember exactly my conversation on the matter with my mother.

"We're having a party for Halloween at school, and teacher says we come dressed in our trick-or-treat outfits instead of our uniforms. I want to be a hobgoblin."

"What was that?"

"You know, a hobgoblin."

"I'm not sure what that is. Is it anything like a monster?"

"No."

"Or a ghost? Or a ghoul?"

"Not those."

"Perhaps a little vampire?"

"I'm no bloodsucker, Mother."

"Perhaps it's a fairy?"

I howled. For the first time in nearly two months, I lost my temper and screamed in my natural wild voice. The sound startled her.

"For the love of God, Henry. You scared the wits out of me, raising the dead and howling like a banshee. There'll be no Halloweenin' for you."

Banshee keen, I wanted to tell her, they wail and weep, but they never howl. Instead, I turned on the tears, bawling like the twins. She drew me to her and hugged me against her stomach.

"There now, I was only kidding." She lifted my chin and gazed into my eyes. "I just don't know what a hobgoblin is. Listen, how about going as a pirate, you'd like that now, wouldn't you?"

And that's how I ended up dressed in pantaloons and a shirt with puffed sleeves, a scarf tied around my skull, and wearing an earring like Errol Flynn. On Halloween day, I stood before a class of ghosts, witches, and hoboes, the only pirate in the school, probably the whole county. Teacher had tapped me to sing "The Teddy Bears' Picnic" as part of the scary entertainment for our party. My normal speaking voice was a squeak like Henry Day's, but when I sang "If you go out in the woods tonight," I sounded exactly like the sonorous bass of Frank DeVol on the record. The imitation shocked nearly everybody. In a back corner, Caroline Hines sobbed in fear through the whole song. Most of the slack-jawed kids gaped through their masks and makeup, not quite knowing what to believe. I remember that Tess Wodehouse sat and stared without blinking, as if she realized a fundamental deception but could not unravel the trick. But the nuns knew better. At the end of the song, they whispered together in a conspiracy of penguins, then nodded in unison as they crossed themselves.

The actual trick-or-treating left much to be desired. My father drove me into town at dusk and waited for me as I walked the row of houses along Main Street, spying here and there another child in pathetic costume. No hobgoblin appeared, although a black cat did try to cross my path. I hissed at the creature in perfect cat, and it turned tail, running away in panic to hide beneath a honeysuckle bush. An evil grin crossed my face. It was good to know I had not yet lost all my tricks.

CHAPTER 4

In the gloaming, the crows flew in to gather for the night in a stand of bare oaks. Bird by bird, they soared to the rookery, black shadows against the fading light. My kidnapping, still fresh in my mind, left me timid and battered, not trusting a soul in the woods. I missed my family, yet days and weeks passed, marked by the routine appearance of the birds. Their arrival and departure provided reassuring continuity. By the time the trees lost their leaves and their naked limbs stretched to the sky, the crows no longer frightened me. I came to look forward to their graceful arrival, silhouetted against the wintry sky, a natural part of my new life.

The faeries welcomed me as their own and taught me the ways of the woods, and I grew fond of them all. In addition to Speck, Igel, Béka and Onions, there were seven others. The three girls were inseparable—Kivi and Blomma, blonde and freckled, quiet and assured, and their tagalong, Chavisory, a chatterbox who looked no more than five years old. When she grinned, her baby teeth shone like a string of pearls, and when she laughed, her thin shoulders shook and twitched. If she found something truly funny or exciting, she took off like a skittering bat, dancing in circles and figure eights across the clearing.

Apart from the leader Igel and the loner Béka, the boys formed two pairs. Ragno and Zanzara, as I remember them, reminded me of the two sons of the Italian grocers in town. Thin and olive-skinned boys, each had a thatch of dark curls on his head and was quick to anger and quicker to forgive. The other set, Smaolach and Luchóg, behaved as brothers, though they could not be more dissimilar. Towering over everyone but Béka, Smaolach concentrated on the task at hand, as oblivious and earnest as a robin tugging up an earthworm. His good friend Luchóg, smallest of us all, was forever pushing back an untamable lock of night-black hair that curled across his forehead like the tail of a mouse. His eyes, blue as the summer sky, gave away his fierce devotion to his friends, even when he tried to feign nonchalance.

Igel, the eldest and leader of the band, took pains to explain the ways of the forest. He showed me how to gig for frogs and fish, how to find water collected overnight in the hollow of fallen leaves, to distinguish edible mushrooms from deadly toadstools, and dozens of other survival tricks. But even the best guide is no match for experience, and for most of my early time, I was coddled. They kept me under constant watch by at least two others, and I was forced to stay around camp, with dire warnings to hide away at any hint of other people.

"If they catch you, they will think you a devil," Igel told me. "And lock you away, or worse, they will test to see if they are right by throwing you in a fire."

"And you will burn up like kindling," said Ragno.

"And be nothing more than a puff of smoke," said Zanzara, and Chavisory demonstrated by dancing around the campfire, circling away to the edge of darkness.

When the first hard frost hit, a small party was sent away for an overnight excursion, and they came back with armloads of sweaters, jackets, and shoes. Those of us who had stayed behind were shivering beneath deerskins.

"Since you are the youngest," Igel told me, "you have first choice of the clothes and boots."

Smaolach, who stood over the pile of shoes, beckoned me. I noticed that his own feet were bare. I poked through the assortment of children's saddle shoes, square-toed brogues, canvas tennis shoes, and the odd unmated boot, choosing at last a pair of brand new black-and-white wingtips that seemed to be my size.

"Those'll cut your ankles off."

"How about these?" I asked, holding up the tennis shoes. "I might be able to squeeze into these." My feet felt damp and chilled on the cold ground.

Smaolach rooted around and picked out the ugliest brown shoes I had ever seen. The leather creaked when he flexed the soles, and the laces looked like coiled snakes. Each toe was tipped with a small steel plate. "Trust me, these will keep you warm and toasty all winter long, and a long time in the wearing."

"But they're too small."

"Don't you know you've been shrinking yourself?" With a sly grin, he reached into his trousers pocket and pulled out a pair of thick woolen socks. "And I found these especially for you."

The whole crowd gasped in appreciation. They gave me a cableknit sweater and an oilskin jacket, which kept me dry on the wettest days.

As the nights lengthened and grew colder, we exchanged our grass mats and solitary beds for a heap of animal skins and stolen blankets. The twelve of us slept together in a tangled clump. I rather enjoyed the comfort of the situation, although most of my friends had foul breath or fetid odors about them. Part of the reason must be the change in diet, from the bounty of summer to the decay of late fall and the deprivation of winter. Several of the poor creatures had been in the woods for so long that they had given up all hope of human society. Indeed, a handful had no such desire at all, so they lived like animals, rarely taking a bath or cleaning their teeth with a twig. Even a fox will lick its hindquarters, but some of the faeries were the dirtiest beasts.

That first winter, I yearned to go with the hunter-gatherers on their morning forage for food and other supplies. Like the crows that convened at dusk and dawn, those thieves enjoyed freedom away from the roost. While I was left behind, I had to suffer babysitters like that toad Béka and his companion Onions, or old Zanzara and Ragno, who squabbled all day and threw nutshells and stones at the birds and squirrels poking around our hidden hoard. I was bored and cold and lonesome for adventure.

On a gray morning, Igel himself chose to stay behind to watch over me, and as luck would have it, my friend Smaolach kept him company. They brewed a pot of tea from dried bark and peppermint, and as we watched a cold rain fall, I pressed my case.

"Why won't you let me go with all the others?"

"My great fear is that you'll run away and try to return whence you came, but you cannot, Aniday. You are one of us now." Igel sipped his tea and stared at a point far off. After a decent interval, letting his wisdom sink into my mind, he continued. "On the other hand, you have proved yourself a valuable member of our clan. You gather the kindling, husk the acorns, and dig a new privy hole when asked. You are learning true obedience and deference. I have watched you, Aniday, and you are a good student of our ways."

Smaolach stared into the dying fire and said something in a secret language, all vowels and hard consonants full of phlegm. Igel pondered over that secret sentence, then chewed on his own thoughts before spitting them out. Then, as now, I was eternally puzzled over how people think, by what process they solve life's riddles. Their consultation over, Igel resumed his study of the horizon.

"You're to come with Luchóg and me this afternoon," Smaolach informed me with a conspiratorial wink. "We'll show you the lay of the land around these parts as soon as the rest of them get back."

"You better dress warmly," Igel advised. "This rain will changeover soon."

On cue, the first snowflakes started mixing with the raindrops, and within minutes, a heavy snow began to fall. We were still sitting in our places when the faery troop meandered back to the camp, chased home by the sudden inclemency. Winter sometimes came early to our part of the country, but usually we did not get a snowfall until after Christmas. As the squall blew in, I wondered for the first time whether Christmas had passed altogether, or perhaps at least Thanksgiving had slipped by, and most certainly Halloween was gone. I thought of my family, still looking for me every day in the woods. Perhaps they thought me dead, which made me feel sorry and wish that word could be sent concerning my welfare.

At home, Mom would be unpacking boxes of decorations, putting out the stable and the manger, running garland up the stair rail. The past Christmas, my father took me out to chop down a small fir tree for the house, and I wondered if he was sad now, without me to help him choose the right one. I even missed my little sisters. Were they walking and talking and dreaming of Santa Claus, wondering what had become of me?

"What day is it?" I asked Luchóg as he changed into warmer clothes.

He licked his finger and held it into the wind. "Tuesday?"

"No, I mean what day of the year? What day of the month?"

"I have no idea. Judging by the signs, could be late November, early December. But memory is a tricky thing and unreliable when it comes to time or weather."

Christmas had not passed after all. I resolved to watch the days from then on and to celebrate the season in an appropriate fashion, even if the rest of them did not care about holidays and such things.

"Do you know where I can get a paper and a pencil?"

He struggled into his boots. "Now, what would you want them things for?"

"I want to make a calendar."

"A calendar? Why, you would need a store of paper and any number of pencils to keep a calendar out here. I'll teach you how to watch the sun in the sky and take notice of the living things. You'll know time enough by them."

"But what if I want to draw a picture or write someone a note?"

Luchóg zipped up his jacket. "Write? To whom? Most of us have forgotten how to write entirely, and those that haven't, didn't learn in the first place. It is better to have your say and not be putting down in more or less a permanent way what you're thinking or feeling. That way lies danger, little treasure."

"But I do like to draw pictures."

We started across the ring, where Smaolach and Igel stood like two tall trees, conferring. Because Luchóg was the smallest of us all, he had trouble keeping up with me. Bouncing along at my side, he continued his dissertation.

"So, you're an artist, are ye? No pencil and paper? Do you know that the artists of old made their own paper and pens? Out of animal skin and bird feathers. And ink from soot and spit. They did, and further back still, they scratched on stones. I'll teach you how to leave your mark, and get you that paper if you want, but in due time."

When we reached the leader, Igel clapped me on the shoulder and said, "You've earned my trust, Aniday. Listen and heed these two."

Luchóg, Smaolach, and I set off into the woods, and I looked back to wave goodbye. The other faeries sat together in bunches, huddled against the cold, and let the snow coat them, mad and exposed stoics.

I was thrilled at being out of that camp, but my companions did their best to control my curiosity. They let me stumble about on the trails for a time before my clumsiness flushed a covey of doves from their rest. The birds exploded into the air, all pipes and feathers. Smaolach put a finger to his lips, and I took the hint. Copying their movements, I became nearly as graceful, and we walked so quietly that I could hear the snowfall over the sound of our footsteps. Silence has its own allure and grace, heightening all the senses, especially hearing. A twig would snap in the distance and instantly Smaolach and Luchóg would cock their heads in the direction of the sound and identify its cause. They showed me the hidden things silence revealed: a pheasant craning its neck to spy on us from a thicket, a crow hopping from branch to branch, a raccoon snoring in its den. Before the daylight completely faded, we tramped through the wet grounds to the mucky bank of the river. Along the water's edge ice crystals grew, and listening closely, we heard the crack of freezing. A single duck paddled further down the river, and each snowflake hissed as it hit the water's surface. The sunlight faded like a whisper and vanished.

"Listen"—Smaolach held his breath—"to this."

At once, the snow changed over to sleet, which ticked against the fallen leaves and rocks and dripping branches, a miniature symphony of the natural world. We walked away from the river and took cover in a grove of evergreens. Ice encased each of the needles in a clear jacket. Luchóg pulled out a leather pouch hanging from a cord around his neck, first producing a tiny paper and then a fat pinch of dried and brown grasslike fibers that looked like tobacco. With deft fingers and a quick lick, he rolled a thin cigarette. From another section of the pouch, he extracted several wooden matches, counted them in his palm, and returned all but one to the waterproof compartment. His thumbnail struck the match, causing it to burst into flame, which Luchóg applied to the end of the cigarette. Smaolach had dug a hole deep enough to reach a layer of dry needles and cones. Carefully taking the burning match from his friend's fingertips, he set it in the bowl, and in short order we had a fire to toast our palms and fingertips. Luchóg passed the cigarette to Smaolach, who took a deep drag and held the smoke inside his mouth for a long time. When he exhaled at last, the effect was as sudden and percussive as the punchline to a joke.

"Give the boy a puff," Smaolach suggested.

"I don't know how to smoke."

"Do what I do," said Luchóg through clenched teeth. "But whatever you do, don't tell Igel about this. Don't tell anyone at all."

I took a drag on the glowing cigarette and began coughing and sputtering from the smoke. They giggled and kept on laughing well after the last scrap had been inhaled. The air beneath the evergreen boughs was thick with

a strange perfume, which made me feel dizzy, light-headed, and slightly nau-
seous. Luchóg and Smaolach fell under the same spell, but they merely seemed
content, simultaneously alert and peaceful. The sleet began to taper off, and
silence returned like a lost friend.

"Did you hear that?"

"What is it?" I asked.

Luchóg shushed me. "First, listen to see if you hear it." A moment later,
the sound came to me, and though familiar, its substance and origin mystified me.

Luchóg sprang to his feet and rousted his friend. "It's a car, little treasure.
Have you ever chased an automobile?"

I shook my head, thinking he must have me confused with a dog. Both
of my companions took hold of my hands and off we went, running faster
than I had ever imagined possible. The world whirred by, patches and blurs of
darkness where trees once stood. Mud and snow kicked up, mottling our
trousers as we sped on at an insanely giddy pace. When the brush grew thicker,
they let go of my hands and we raced down the trail one behind the other.
Branches slapped me in the face, and I stumbled and fell into the muck.
Scrambling to my feet, cold and wet and dirty, I realized I was alone for the
first time in months. Fear took hold, and I opened my eyes and ears to the
world, desperate to find my friends. Fierce pains of concentration shot across
my forehead, but I bore down and heard them running through the snow in
the distance. I felt a new and powerful magic in my senses, for I could see
them clearly, while realizing that they should be too far ahead and out of sight.
By visualizing my way, I gave chase, and the trees and branches that had confused me before now seemed no obstacle. I whipped through the woods the
way a sparrow flies through the openings in a fence, without a thought, fold-
ing up its wings at the right moment, gliding through.

When I caught up, I found they were standing behind the rough pines
short of the forest edge. Before us lay a road and on that road a car had
stopped, its headlights streaking through the misty darkness, broken pieces of

the metal grille glistening on the asphalt. Through the open driver's door, a small light shone in the empty cab. The anomaly of the car pulled me toward it, but the strong arms of my friends held me back. A figure emerged from the darkness and stepped into the light, a thin young woman in a bright red coat. She held one hand to her forehead, and bending slowly, she reached out with her free arm, nearly touching a dark mass lying in the road.

"She hit a deer," Luchóg said, a note of sadness in his voice. She agonized over its prostrate form, pulling her hair back from her face, her other hand pressed against her lips.

"Is it dead?" I asked.

"The trick," said Smaolach in a quiet voice, "is to breathe into its mouth. It's not dead at all, but in shock."

Luchóg whispered to me. "We'll wait until she's gone, and you can inspire it."

"Me?"

"Don't you know? You're a faery now, same as us, and can do anything we can do."

The notion overwhelmed me. A faery? I wanted to know right away if it was true; I wanted to test my own powers. So I broke away from my friends, approaching the deer from the shadows. The woman stood in the middle of that lonesome road, scanning in both directions for another car. She did not notice me until I was already there, crouching over the animal, my hand upon its warm flank, its pulse racing alongside my own. I cupped the deer's muzzle in my hand and breathed into its hot mouth. Almost immediately, the beast lifted its head, shouldered me out of the way, and rocked itself up into a standing position. For an instant, it stared at me; then, like a white ensign, its tail shot up a warning, and the deer bounded into the night. To say that we—the animal, the woman, myself—were surprised by this turn of events would be the most severe understatement. She looked bewildered, so I smiled at her. At that moment, my comrades started calling to me in loud whispers.

"Who are you?" She wrapped herself tighter in that red coat. Or at least

I thought those were her words, but her voice sounded alien, as if she were speaking through water. I stared at the ground, realizing that I did not know the true answer. Her face drew close enough for me to detect the beginning of a smile on her lips and the pale bluegreen of her irises behind her glasses. Her eyes were splendid.

"We must go." From the darkness, a hand grasped my shoulder, and Smaolach dragged me away into the bushes, leaving me to wonder if it had all been a dream. We hid in a tangle while she searched for us, and at last she gave up, got in her car and drove off. I did not know it at the time, but she was the last human person I was to encounter for more than a dozen years. The taillights zigzagged over the hills and through the trees until there was no more to see.

We retreated back to camp in a cross silence. Halfway home, Luchóg advised, "You mustn't tell anyone about what happened tonight. Stay away from people and be content with who you are." On the journey, we created a necessary fiction to explain our long absence, invented a narrative of the waters and the wild, and once told, our story endured. But I never forgot that secret of the redcoated woman, and later, when I began to doubt the world above, the memory of that bright and lonely meeting reminded me that it was no myth.

Life with the Day family acquired a reassuring pattern. My father would leave for work before any of us stirred from our sleep, and that golden waking hour between his departure and my march to school was a comfort. My mother at the stove, stirring oatmeal or frying breakfast in a pan; the twins exploring the kitchen on unsteady feet. The picture windows framed and kept away the outside world. The Days' home had long ago been a working farm, and though agriculture had been abandoned, vestiges remained. An old barn, red paint souring to a dark mauve, now served as a garage. The split-rail fence that fronted the property was falling apart stick by stick. The field, an acre or so that had flushed green with corn, lay fallow, a tangle of brambles that Dad only bothered to mow once each October. The Days were the first to abandon farming in the area, and their distant neighbors joined them over the years, selling off homesteads and acreage to developers. But when I was a child, it was still a quiet, lonesome place.

The trick of growing up is to remember to grow. The mental part of becoming Henry Day demanded full attention to every detail of his life, but no amount of preparation for the changing can account for the swath of the subject's family history—memories of bygone birthday parties and other intimacies—that one must pretend to remember. History is easy enough to fake; stick around anyone long enough and one can catch up to any plot. But other accidents and flaws expose the risks of assuming another's identity. Fortunately we seldom had company, for the old house was isolated on a small bit of farmland out in the country.

Near my first Christmas, while my mother attended to the crying twins upstairs and I idled by the fireplace, a knock came at the front door. On the porch stood a man with his fedora in hand, the smell of a recent cigar mixing with the faintly medicinal aroma of hair oil. He grinned as if he recognized me at once, although I had not seen him before.

"Henry Day," he said. "As I live and breathe."

I stood fixed to the threshold, searching my memory for an errant clue as to who this man might be. He clicked his heels together and bowed slightly at the waist, then strode past me into the foyer, glancing furtively up the stairs. "Is your mother in? Is she decent?"

Hardly anyone came to visit in the middle of the day, except occasionally the farmers' wives nearby or mothers of my schoolmates, driving out from town with a fresh cake and new gossip. When we had spied on Henry, there was no man other than his father or the milkman who came to the house.

He tossed his hat on the sideboard and turned to face me again. "How long's it been, Henry? Your mama's birthday, maybe? You don't look like you've grown a whisker. Your daddy not feeding you?"

I stared at the stranger and did not know what to say.

"Run up the stairs and tell your mama I'm here for a visit. Go on now, son."

"Who shall I say is calling?"

"Why, your Uncle Charlie, a-course."

"But I don't have any uncles."

The man laughed; then his brow furrowed and his mouth became a severe line. "Are you okay, Henry boy?" He bent down to look me in the eye. "Now, I'm not actually your uncle, son, but your mama's oldest friend. A friend of the family, you might say."

My mother saved me by coming down the stairway unbidden, and the moment she saw the stranger, she threw her arms into the air and rushed to embrace him. I took advantage of their reunion to slip away.

A close call, but not as bad as the scare a few weeks later. In those first few years, I still had all my changeling powers and could hear like a fox. From any room in the house, I could eavesdrop on my parents during their un-guarded conversations, and overheard Dad's suspicions during one such pillow talk.

"Have you noticed anything odd about the boy lately?"

She slips into bed beside him. "Odd?"

"There's the singing around the house."

"He's a lovely voice."

"And those fingers."

I looked at my hands, and in comparison with other children's, my fin-gers were exceedingly long and out of proportion.

"I think he'll be a pianist. Billy, we ought to have him at lessons."

"And toes."

I curled up my toes in my bed upstairs.

"And he seems to have grown not an inch or put on not a pound all winter long."

"He needs some sun is all."

The old man rolls over toward her. "He's a queer lad, is all I know."

"Billy . . . stop."

I resolved that night to become a true boy and begin paying closer at-tention to how I might be considered normal. Once such a mistake had been made, nothing could be done. I couldn't very well shorten my fingers and toes and invite further skepticism, but I could stretch the rest of me a bit each night and keep up with all the other children. I also made it a point to avoid Dad as much as possible.

The idea of the piano intrigued me as a way to ingratiate myself with my mother. When she wasn't listening to crooners on the radio, she might dial in the classics, particularly on a Sunday. Bach sent my head spinning with buried reveries, conjuring an echo from the distant past. But I had to figure a way to mention my interest without Mom realizing that her private conversations could be heard no matter how quiet or intimate. Fortunately, the twins supplied the answer. At Christmas, my distant grandparents sent them a toy piano. No bigger than a bread basket, it produced but a tinny octave of notes, and from New Year's Day the keys gathered a dusty coat. I rescued the toy and sat in the nursery, playing nearly recognizable tunes from distant memory. My sisters, as usual, were enchanted, and they sat like two entranced yogis as I tested my memory on the piano's limited range. Dust rag in hand, my mother wandered by and stood in the doorway, listening intently. From the corner of my eye, I watched her watching me, and when I ended with a flourish, her applause was not completely unexpected.

In the fleeting time between homework and dinner, I picked out a tune of sorts, and gradually revealed my native talent, but she needed more encouragement than that. My scheme was casual and simple. I let drop the fact that a half-dozen of the kids in school took music lessons, when, in truth, there may have been one or two. On car trips, I pretended that the panel below my window was a keyboard and fingered measures until my father ordered me to cut that out. I made a point of whistling the first few bars of something familiar, like Beethoven's Ninth, when helping Mom dry the dishes. I did not beg, but bided my time, until she came to believe the idea as her own. My gambit played out when, on the Saturday before Henry's eighth birthday, my parents drove me into the city to see a man about piano lessons.

We left the twin toddlers with the neighbors, and the three of us sat up front in my father's coupe, embarking early that spring morning in our Sunday clothes. We drove past the town where I went to school, where we shopped and went to Mass, and onto the highway into the city. Shiny cars zipped along the asphalt as we picked up speed, joining a ribbon of pure energy flowing in both directions. We went faster than I'd ever gone in my life, and I had not been to the city in nearly one hundred years. Billy drove the '49 De Soto like an old friend, one hand on the wheel, his free arm thrown across the seat behind my mother and me. The old conquistador stared at us from the steering wheel's hub, and as Dad made a turn, the explorer's eyes seemed to follow us.

On our approach to the city, the factories on the outskirts appeared first, great smokestacks exhaling streams of dark clouds, furnaces within glowing with hearts of fire. A bend in the road—then all at once, a view of buildings stretched to heaven. The downtown's sheer size left me breathless, and the closer we came, the greater it loomed, until suddenly we were in the car-choked streets. The shadows deepened and darkened. At a cross street, a trolley scraped along, its pole shooting sparks to the wires above. Its doors opened like a bellows, and out poured a crowd of people in their spring coats and hats; they stood on a concrete island in the street, waiting for the light to change. In the department store windows, reflections of shoppers and traffic cops mingled with displays of new goods: women's dresses and men's suits on mannequins, which fooled me initially, appearing alive and posing perfectly still.

"I don't know why you feel the need to come all the way downtown for this. You know I don't like coming into the city. I'll never find parking."

Mom's right arm shot out. "There's a space, aren't we lucky?"

Riding up in the elevator, my father reached inside his coat pocket for a Camel, and as the doors opened on the fifth floor, he lit up. We were a few minutes early, and while they debated over whether or not to go in, I walked to the door and entered. Mr. Martin may not have been a fairy, but he was very fey. Tall and thin, his white hair long in a shaggy boy's cut, he wore a worn plum-colored suit. Christopher Robin all grown up and gone to genteel seed. Behind him stood the most beautiful machine I had ever seen. Lacquered to a high black finish, the grand piano drew all of the vitality of the room toward its propped-open lid. Those keys held in their serenity the possibility of every beautiful sound. I was too dumbstruck to answer his inquiry the first time.

"May I help you, young man?"

"I'm Henry Day, and I'm here to learn everything you know."

"My dear young man," he replied, sighing, "I'm afraid that's impossible."

I walked to the piano and sat at the bench. The sight of the keys unlocked a distant memory of a stern German instructor ordering me to increase the tempo. I stretched my fingers as far apart as possible, testing my span, and laid them upon the ivory without eliciting an accidental tone. Mr. Martin glided behind me, overlooking my shoulder, studying my hands. "Have you played before?"

"Once upon a time . . ."

"Find me middle C, Mr. Day."

And without thinking, I did, pressing the single key with the side of my left thumb.

My mother and father entered the room, announcing themselves with a polite *ahem*. Mr. Martin wheeled around and strode over to greet them. As they shook hands and made introductions, I played scales from the middle outward. Tones from the piano triggered powerful synapses, resurrecting scores that I knew by heart. A voice in my head demanded *heissblütig, heissblütig*—more passion, more feeling.

"You said he was a beginner."

"He is," my mother replied. "I don't think he's ever even seen a real piano."

"This boy is a natural."

For fun, I plinked out "Twinkle, Twinkle, Little Star," the way I would play it for my sisters. I was careful to use only one finger, as if the grand were but a toy.

"He taught himself that," Mom said. "On a tiny piano that you might find in a fairy orchestra. And he can sing, too, sing like a bird."

Dad shot me a quick sideways glance. Too busy sizing up my mother, Mr. Martin did not notice the wordless exchange. My mother rattled on about all of my talents, but nobody listened. In measures too slow and far apart, I practiced my Chopin, so disguised that even old Martin did not discover the melody.

"Mr. Day, Mrs. Day, I agree to take on your son. My minimum requirement, however, is for eight weeks of lessons at a time, Wednesday afternoons and Saturdays. I can teach this boy." Then he mentioned, in a voice barely above a whisper, his fee. My father lit another Camel and walked toward the window.

"But for your son"—he addressed my mother now—"for Henry, a born musician if I ever heard one, for him, I will require only half the tuition, but you must commit to sixteen weeks. Four months. We will know how far we can go."

I picked out a rudimentary "Happy Birthday." My father finished his smoke and tapped me on the shoulder, indicating we were to leave. He walked over to Mom and grabbed her lightly by the fleshy part of her arm above the elbow.

"I'll call you Monday," he said, "at three-thirty. We'll think it over."

Mr. Martin bowed slightly and looked me straight in the eye. "You have a gift, young man."

As we drove home, I watched the city recede in the mirror and disappear. Mom chattered incessantly, dreaming the future, planning our lives. Billy, hands locked on the wheel, concentrated on the road and said nothing.

"I'll buy some laying hens, that's what I'll do. Remember when you used to say you wanted to turn our place back into a real farm? I'll start a brood of chickens, and we'll sell the eggs, and that will pay the bill, surely. And imagine, we'll have fresh eggs ourselves every morning, too. And Henry can take the school bus to the streetcar, and the streetcar into town. You could drive him to the streetcar Saturdays?"

"I could do chores to earn the fare."

"You see, Billy, how much he wants to learn? He has a gift, that Mr.

Martin said. And he's so refined. Did you ever see such a thing in your life as that piano? He must shine it every day."

My father rolled down his window about an inch to let in a roar of fresh air.

"Did you hear him play 'Happy Birthday to You,' like he's been at it forever? It's what he wants; it's what I want. Sweetheart."

"When would he practice, Ruth? Even I know you have to play every day, and I might be able to afford piano lessons, but I certainly can't afford a piano in the house."

"There's a piano at school," I said. "Nobody uses it. I'm sure if I asked, they'd let me stay after. . . ."

"What about your homework and those chores you said you would do? I don't want to see your grades slipping."

"Nine times nine is eighty-one. *Separate* is spelled S-E-P-A-R-A-T-E. Oppenheimer gave us the bomb, which took care of the Japs. The Holy Trinity is the Father, Son, and the Holy Ghost, and it is a holy mystery that no one can figure out."

"All right, Einstein. You can try it, but for eight weeks. Just to be sure. And your mother will have to raise the egg money, and you have to help care for the chickens. They teach you that in that school of yours?"

Ruth studied his face, a rare look of love and wonder in her gaze. Both grinned a private, sheepish half-smile, the meaning of which eluded me. Sitting between them, I basked in the warmth of the moment, lacking any guilt over the fact that I was not their child. We drove on, the happiest of happy little families.

As we crossed a high bridge over the river not far from our house, a commotion flashed along the riverbank far below. To my horror, I saw a line of changelings walking through a clearing in single file, blending in with the budding trees and bushes, then vanishing in a blink. Those strange children moved like deer. My parents were oblivious, but at the thought of those creatures down there, I flushed and broke into a sweat, which as quickly turned to a chill. That they still existed alarmed me, for I had nearly forgotten them. That they could expose my past made me ill, and I was about to beg my father to pull off the road. But he lit up another cigarette and opened his window wider, and the fresh air alleviated my nausea, if not my fear.

Mom broke the spell. "Didn't Mr. Martin ask us to commit to four months?"

"I'll call him Monday and work out a deal. Let's try two months, actually, at first. See if the boy likes it."

For the next eight years, I took piano lessons, and it was the happiest time of all my lives. If I came in early to school, the nuns were glad to let me practice at the upright in the lunchroom. Later on, they let me into the church to learn the organ, and I was the youngest substitute organist the parish ever had. Life became orderly, and the discipline a joy. Each morning, my hand went under the warm bellies of the chickens, collecting eggs, and each afternoon, my fingers upon the keyboard, perfecting my technique. On Wednesdays and Saturdays, the trip into the city proved a tonic, away from farm and family and into civilization. No longer something wild, but a creature of culture, on my way to becoming a virtuoso once again.

· *CHAPTER 6* ·

In setting down these recollections of my early years so far removed from their unfolding, I am fooled, as all are, by time itself. My parents, long gone from my world, live again. The redcoated woman, met only once, abides more persistently in mind than what I did yesterday or whether I had thistles and honey or elderberries for breakfast. My sisters, now grown into their middle years, are ever infants to me, two matching cherubs, ringlets of curls, chubby and helpless as cubs. Memory, which so confounds our waking life with anticipation and regret, may well be our one true earthly consolation when time slips out of joint.

My first nighttime foray into the woods left me exhausted. I burrowed beneath a heap of coats and blankets and furs, and by next midday, a fever burned. Zanzara brought me a cup of hot tea and a bowl of nasty broth, ordering me to "drink, drink, sip it." But I could not stomach a single swallow. No matter how many layers they heaped upon me, I could not get warm. By nightfall, I shook uncontrollably with chills. My teeth rattled and my bones ached.

Sleep brought strange, horrible nightmares where everything seemed to happen at once. My family invaded my dreams. Hands joined, they stand in a half circle around a hole in the ground, silent as stones. My father grabs me around the ankle and pulls me from the hollow tree where I lie hidden and sets me on the ground. Then he reaches in again and yanks each twin by the ankles and holds them aloft, the girls giggling in fear and pleasure. And my mother admonishes him: "Don't be so hard on the boy. Where have you been, where have you been?"

Then I am on the road, in the arclight streaming from an old Ford, the deer supine on the pavement, its breathing shallow, and I synchronize my respiration with its rhythms and the redcoated woman with the pale green eyes says: "Who are you?" And she bends to my face, taking my chin in her hands, to kiss me on the lips, and I am a boy again. Me. But I cannot remember my name.

Aniday. A wild child like myself, a girl named Speck, leans over to kiss my forehead, and her lips cool my hot skin. Behind her, the oak leaves turn into a thousand crows that take off in unison, flying away in a great twisting, singing tornado of wings. Silence returns after the drumming flock escapes to the horizon and morning breaks through. I give chase to the birds, running so fast and so hard that my skin splits a seam on both sides and my heart drums against my ribs until halted by the deathly appearance of a roiling black river. Concentrating with my entire mind, I see to the other side, and there on the bank, holding hands around a hole in the ground, are my father and mother, the woman in the red coat, my two sisters, and the boy who is not me. They stand like stones, like trees, staring into the clearing. If I summon courage to jump into the water, I may reach them. Blackwater once carried me away, so I stand on the bank, calling out in a voice that cannot be heard, with words no one can understand.

I don't know how long I was delirious with fever. Overnight, a day or two, a week, a year? Or longer? When I awakened under a damp steely sky, I felt snug and safe, although my arms and legs throbbed with stiffness and my insides felt scraped raw and hollow. Attending me, Ragno and Zanzara played cards, using my belly as a table. Their game defied logic, for they had not managed to swipe a full deck. Mixing remnants from many different packs, they ended up with nearly a hundred cards. Each of them held a fistful, and the remainder sat in a jumble on my stomach.

"Do you have any *cinque*?" Ragno asked.

Zanzara scratched his head.

Holding up five fingers, Ragno shouted at him, *"Cinque, cinque."*

"Go fish."

And fish he would, turning over card after card until he found a match, which he would then hold up triumphantly before ceding his turn to Zanzara.

"You are a cheater, Ragno."

"And you are a bloodsucker."

I coughed, making my consciousness known.

"Hey look, kid, he's awake."

Zanzara put his clammy hand against my forehead. "Let me get you something to eat. A cup of tea, maybe?"

"You been asleeping a long time, kid. That's what you get for going out with those boys. Those Irish boys, they're no good."

I looked around the camp for my friends, but as usual at midday, everyone else was gone.

"What day is it?" I asked.

Zanzara flicked out his tongue, tasting the air. "I'd say Tuesday."

"No, I mean what day of the month."

"Kid, I'm not even sure what month it is."

Ragno interrupted. "Must be getting toward spring. The days are growing longer, inch by inch."

"Did I miss Christmas?" I felt homesick for the first time in ages.

The boys shrugged their shoulders.

"Did I miss Santa Claus?"

"Who he?"

"How do I get out of here?"

Ragno pointed to a path obscured by two evergreens.

"How do I go home?"

Their eyes glazed over, and, holding hands, they turned around and skipped away. I felt like crying, but the tears would not come. A fierce gale blew in from the west, pushing dark clouds across the sky. Huddled under my blankets, I observed the changing day, alone with my troubles, until the others came skittering home on the wind. They took no more notice of me than any other lump on the ground one passes every day. Igel started a small fire by striking a flint until a spark caught the kindling. Two of the girls, Kivi and Blomma, uncovered the nearly depleted pantry and dug out our meager fare, neatly skinning a partially frozen squirrel with a few deft strokes of a very sharp knife. Speck crumbled dried herbs into our old teapot and filled it with water drawn from a cistern. Chavisory toasted pine nuts on a flat griddle. The boys who were not engaged in cooking took off their wet shoes and boots, exchanging them for yesterday's gear, now dry and hard. All of this domestic routine proceeded without fuss and with scant conversation; they had made a science of preparing for the night. As the squirrel cooked on a spit, Smaolach came over to check on me, and was surprised to discover me awake and alert.

"Aniday, you've come back from the dead."

He reached for my hand, pulling me to my feet. We embraced, but he squeezed me so hard that my sides ached. Arm around my shoulder, he led me to the fire, where some of the faeries greeted me with expressions of wonder and relief. Béka gave me an apathetic sneer, and Igel shrugged at my hello and continued waiting to be served, arms crossed at his chest. We set to the squirrel and nuts, the meal barely curbing the growling appetite of all assembled. After the first stringy bites, I pushed away my tin plate. The firelight made everyone's face glow, and the grease on their lips made their smiles shine.

After supper, Luchóg motioned for me to come closer, and he whispered in my ear that he had stashed away a surprise for me. We walked away from camp, the last rays of pink sunlight illuminating the way. Clamped between two large stones were four small envelopes.

"Take them," he grunted, the top stone heavy in his arms, and I whisked out the letters before he dropped the cap with a thud. Reaching inside his shirt to his private pouch, Luchóg extracted but the nub of a sharp pencil, which he presented with becoming modesty. "Merry Christmas, little treasure. Something to get you started."

"So it is Christmas today?"

Luchóg looked around to see if anyone was listening. "You did not miss it."

"Merry Christmas," I said. And I tore open my gifts, ruining the precious envelopes. Over the years, I have lost two of the four letters, but they were not so valuable in and of themselves. One was a mortgage stub with payment enclosed, and at his entreaty, Luchóg received the check to use as rolling paper for his cigarettes. The other lost piece of correspondence was a rabid letter to the editor of the local newspaper, denouncing Harry Truman. Covered both front and back with crabbed handwriting that scuttled from margin to margin, that paper proved useless. The other two had much more white space, and with one, the lines were so far apart, I was able to write between them.

*Feb. 2, 1950*

*Dearest,*

*The other night ment so much to me that I can't understand why you have not phoned or written since that night. I am confused. You told me that you loved me and I love you too, but still you have not answered my last three letters and nobody answers the telephone at your home or even your work. I am not in the habit of doing what we did in the car, but because you told me that you loved me and you were in such pain and agony as you kept saying. I wanted to let you know that I am not that kind of girl.*

*I am that kind of girl who loves you and that kind of girl who also expects a Gentleman to behave like a Gentleman.*

*Please write back to me or better yet call me on the phone. I am not angry so much as just confused, but I will be mad if I do not here from you.*

*I love you, do you know that?*

*Love,*
*Martha*

At the time, I considered this letter to be the truest expression of real love that I had ever known. It was difficult to read, for Martha wrote in cursive, but thankfully in big letters that resembled printing. The second letter baffled me more than the first, but it, too, used only three-quarters of the front side of the page.

*2/3/50*

*Dear Mother and Father,*
*Words cannot begin to express the sorrow and sympathy I send to you at the loss of dear Nana. She was a good woman, and a kind one, and she is now in a better place. I am sorry that I cannot come home, but I've not enough money for the trip. So, all my heartfelt grief must be shared by this most insufficient letter.*

*Winter draws to a cold and unhappy close. Life is not fair, since you have lost Nana, and I, near everything.*

*Your Son*

When they learned of the two messages, the girls in camp insisted they be shared aloud. They were curious not only about their substance but about my professed literacy, for almost no one in camp bothered to read or write any longer. Some had not learned, and others had chosen to forget. We sat in a ring around the fire, and I read them as best I could, not fully comprehending all of the words or understanding their meanings.

"What do you think of Dearest?" Speck asked the group after I had finished.

"He is a cad; he is a rotter," Onions said.

Kivi pushed back her blonde curls and sighed, her face bright in the firelight. "I do not understand why Dearest will not write back to Martha, but that is nothing compared to the problems of Your Son."

"Yes," Chavisory jumped in, "perhaps Your Son and Martha should get married, and then they will both live happily ever after."

"Well, I hope Mother and Father find Nana," added Blomma.

Into the night the bewildering conversation flowed. They fabricated poetical fictions about the other world. The mysteries of their sympathies, concerns, and sorrows perplexed me, yet the girls had a wellspring of empathy for matters outside our knowing. I was anxious, however, to have them go away, so that I might practice my writing. But the girls lingered until the fire collapsed into embers; then they nestled under the covers together, where they continued their discussion, pondering the fate of the writers, their subjects, and their intended readers. I would have to wait to use the pages. The night became bitterly cold, and soon all twelve of us were huddled together in a tangle of limbs. When the last of us wiggled under the mat, I suddenly remembered the day. "Merry Christmas!" I said, but my greetings brought only derision: "Shuddup!" and "Go to sleep." During the long hours before dawn, a foot hit me on the chin, an elbow knacked me in the groin, and a knee banged against my sore ribs. In a dark corner of the pack, a girl groaned when Béka climbed upon her. Enduring their fitfulness, I waited for morning, the letters pinned against my chest.

The rising sun reflected against a blanket of high cirrus clouds, coloring them in a spectrum that began in brightness on the eastern edge and fanned out in soft pastels. Branches of the trees broke the sky into fragments, like a kaleidoscope. When the red sun rose, the pattern shifted hues until it all dissipated into blue and white. Up and out of bed, I savored the light growing strong enough for drawing and writing. I took out my papers and pencil, put a cold flat stone in my lap, and folded the mortgage statement into quarters. I drew a cross along the folds and made panels for four drawings. The pencil was at once odd and familiar in my grasp. In the first panel, I created from memory my mother and father, my two baby sisters, and myself, full-body portraits lined up in a straight row. When I considered my work, they looked crude and uneven, and I was disappointed in myself. In the next panel, I drew the road through the forest with the deer, the woman, the car, Smaolach and Luchóg in the same perspective. Light, for example, was indicated by two straight lines emanating from a circle on the car and extending outward to opposite corners of the frame. The deer looked more like a dog, and I dearly wished for an eraser on the yellow pencil. In the third panel: a flattened Christmas tree, lavishly decorated, a pile of gifts spread out on the floor. In the final panel, I drew a picture of a boy drowning. Bound in spirals, he sinks below the wavy line.

When I showed my paper to Smaolach later that afternoon, he took me by the hand and made me run with him to hide behind a wild riot of holly. He looked around in all directions to make sure we were alone; then he carefully folded the paper into quarters and handed it back to me.

"You must be more careful with what you draw in them pictures."

"What's the matter?"

"If Igel finds out, then you'll know what's the matter. You have to realize, Aniday, that he doesn't accept any contact with the other side, and that woman . . ."

"The one in the red coat?"

"He's a-scared of being found out." Smaolach grabbed the paper and tucked it into my coat pocket. "Some things are better kept to yourself," he said, then winked at me and walked away, whistling.

Writing proved more painful than drawing. Certain letters—B, G, R, W—caused my hand to cramp. In those early writings, sometimes my K bent backward, S went astray, an F accidentally became an E, and other errors that are amusing to me now as I look back on my early years, but at the time, my handwriting caused me much shame and embarrassment. Worse than the alphabet, however, were the words themselves. I could not spell for beans and lacked all punctuation. My vocabulary annoyed me, not to mention style, diction, sentence structure, variety, adjectives and adverbs, and other such matters. The physical act of writing took forever. Sentences had to be assembled nail by nail, and once complete, they stood no better than a crude approximation of what I felt or wanted to say, a woebegone fence across a white field. Yet I persisted through that morning, writing down all I could remember in whatever words I had at my command. By midday, both blank sides of the paper contained the story of my abduction and the adventures as well as the vaguest memories of life before this place. I had already forgotten more than I remembered—my own name and the names of my sisters, my dear bed, my school, my books, any notion of what I wanted to be when I grew up. All that would be given back to me in due course, but without Luchóg's letters, I would have been lost forever. When I had squeezed the final word in the last available space, I went to look for him. Out of paper, my mission was to find more.

CHAPTER 7

*A*t age ten, I began to perform in front of ordinary people. In appreciation of the nuns who allowed me use of the school piano, I agreed to play as prelude to the annual Christmas show. My music would usher the parents to their seats while their children shed coats and scarves for their elf and wise-man costumes. My teacher, Mr. Martin, and I put together a program of Bach, Strauss, and Beethoven, ending with part of "Six Little Piano Pieces" in honor of Arnold Schoenberg, who had passed away the year before. We felt this last "modern" piece, while not overly familiar to our audience, displayed my range without being overly ostentatious. The day before the Christmas show, I went through the thirty-minute program for the nuns after school, and the choices brought nothing but frowns and scowls from beneath their wimples.

"That's wonderful, Henry, truly extraordinary," the principal said. She was the Mother Superior of the gang of crows that ran the joint. "But that last song."

"Schoenberg's?"

"Yes, very interesting." She stood up in front of the sisters and paced to and fro, searching the air for tact. "Do you know anything else?"

"Else, Mother?"

"Something more seasonal perhaps?"

"Seasonal, Mother?"

"Something people might know?"

"I'm not sure I understand."

She turned and addressed me directly. "Do you know any *Christmas* songs? A hymn? 'Silent Night' perhaps? Or 'Hark! The Herald Angels'—I think that's Mendelssohn. If you can play Beethoven, you can play Mendelssohn."

"You want carols?"

"Not only hymns." She walked on, hitching down her habit. "You could do 'Jingle Bells' or 'White Christmas.'"

"That's from *Holiday Inn*," one of the other nuns volunteered. "Bing Crosby and Fred Astaire and Marjorie Reynolds. Oh, but you're too young."

"Did you see *Bells of St. Mary's*?" the third-grade teacher asked her fellow sisters. "Wasn't he good in that?"

"I really liked that *Boys Town*—you know, the one with Mickey Rooney."

Rattling the beads on her rosary, Mother Superior cut them off. "Surely you know a few Christmas songs?"

Crestfallen, I went home that night and learned the fluff, practicing on a paper-cutout keyboard fashioned by my father. At the show the next evening, I trimmed half my original program and added a few carols at the end. I kept the Schoenberg, which, needless to say, bombed. I played the Christmas stuff brilliantly and to a thunderous ovation. "Cretins," I said under my breath as I accepted their adulation. During my repeated bows, loathing swelled over their loud clapping and whistling. But then, looking out at the sea of faces, I began to recognize my parents and neighbors, all happy and cheerful, sending me their sincere appreciation for the holiday warmth generated by the vaguely predictable strains of their old favorites. No gift as welcome as the expected gift. And I grew light-headed and dizzy the longer the applause went on. My father rose to his feet, a real smile plastered on his mug. I nearly fainted. I wanted more.

The glory of the experience rested in the simple fact that my musical talent was a human one. There were no pianos in the woods. And as my magic slowly diminished, my artistry increased. I felt more and more removed from those who had taken me for a hundred years, and my sole hope and prayer was that they would leave me alone. From the night of the first performance, it was as if I were split in two: half of me continuing on with Mr. Martin and his emphasis on the canon of classics, pounding out the old composers until I could hammer like Thor or make the keys whisper under the gentlest pressure. The other half expanded my repertoire, thinking about what audiences might like to hear, like the ballads crooned on the radio adored by my mother. I loved both the fugues from *The Well-Tempered Clavier* and "Heart and Soul," and they flowed seamlessly, but being adept at popular song allowed me to accept odd jobs when offered, playing at school dances and birthday parties. Mr. Martin objected at first to the bastardization of my talent, but I gave him a sob story about needing money for lessons. He cut his fee by a quarter on the spot. With the money we saved, the cash I earned, and my mother's increasingly lucrative egg and chicken business, we were able to buy a used upright piano for the house in time for my twelfth birthday.

"What's this?" my father asked when he came home the day the piano arrived, its beautiful machinery housed in a rosewood case.

"It's a piano," my mother replied.

"I can see that. How did it get here?"

"Piano movers."

He slid a cigarette from the packet and lit it in one swift move. "Ruthie, I know someone brought it here. How come it *is* here?"

"For Henry. So he can practice."

"We can't afford a piano."

"We bought it. Me and Henry."

"With the money from my playing," I added.

"And the chickens and eggs."

"You bought it?"

"On Mr. Martin's advice. For Henry's birthday."

"Well, then. Happy birthday," he said on his way out of the room.

I played every chance I could get. Over the next few years, I spent hours each day at the keys, enthralled by the mathematics of the notes. The music seized me like a river current pushing my conscious self deeper into my core, as if there were no other sound in the world but one. I grew my legs an inch longer than necessary that first summer in order to better reach the pedals on the upright. Around the house, school, and town, I practiced spreading my fingers as far apart as they would go. The pads of my fingertips became smooth and feather-sensitive. My shoulders bowed down and forward. I dreamt in wave after wave of scales. The more adept my skill and understanding grew, the more I realized the power of musical phrasing in everyday life. The trick involves getting people to listen to the weak beats and seemingly insignificant silences between notes, the absence of tones between tones. By phrasing the matter with a ruthlessly precise logic, one can play—or say—anything. Music taught me great self-control.

My father could not stand to hear me practice, perhaps because he realized the mastery I had attained. He would leave the room, retreat into the farthest corners of the house, or find any excuse to go outside. A few weeks after Mom and I bought the piano, he came home with our first television set, and a week later a man came out and installed an antenna on the roof. In the evenings, my father would watch *You Bet Your Life* or *The Jackie Gleason Show*, ordering me to keep it down. More and more, however, he simply left altogether.

"I'm going for a drive." He already had his hat on.

"You're not going drinking, I hope."

"I may stop in for one with the boys."

"Don't be too late."

Well after midnight, he'd stagger in, singing or muttering to himself, swearing when he stepped on one of the girls' toys or barked his shin on the piano bench as he passed. Weather permitting, he worked outdoors every weekend, replacing shutters, painting the house, rewiring the chicken coop. He was absent from the hearth, unwilling to listen. With Mary and Elizabeth, he played the doting father, still dandling them on his knees, fussing over their curls and dresses, fawning at the latest primitive drawing or Popsicle-stick hut, sitting down at the table for tea parties and the like. But he regarded me coldly, and while I cannot read minds, I suspect he felt at odds with my passion for music. Maybe he felt art corrupted me, made me less a boy. When we spoke, he would chastise me for a neglected chore or chide me for a less than perfect grade on a test or essay.

As he drove me home from the trolley station one Saturday, he made an effort to engage and understand. On the radio, a football game between the Fighting Irish of Notre Dame and Navy unfolded. One of the teams scored a touchdown in a spectacular fashion.

"How about that? Did you hear that?"

I looked out the window, tapping out with my right hand a melody on the armrest.

"Do you even like football?" he asked.

"I dunno. It's okay."

"Do you like any sport at all? Baseball? Basketball? Would you like to go hunting someday?"

I said nothing. The very thought of being alone with Billy Day and a shotgun frightened me. There are devils out in the woods. We let a few silent miles pass beneath us.

"How's come it's nothing but the piano night and day?"

"I like music. And I'm good."

"You are that, but honestly, did you ever stop to think you could try something else for a change? Don't you know there's more to life than music?"

If he had been my true father, I would have been eternally disappointed in him. The man had no vision, no passion for life, and I was grateful that we were not actually related. The car passed through the shadows of trees, and the glass in the window darkened. I saw in my own reflection the mirrored image of Henry's father, but I only appeared to be his offspring. Once upon a time, I had a real father. I could hear his voice: *"Ich erkenne dich! Du willst nur meinen Sohn!"* His eyes danced wildly behind his owlish spectacles, and then the phantom memory disappeared. I sensed Billy Day was watching me from the corner of his eye, wondering what on earth happened? How did I get this for a son?

"I'm thinking that I'm starting to like girls," I volunteered. He smiled and tousled my hair. He lit another Camel, a sure sign he was content with my answer. The subject of my masculinity never came up again.

A basic truth had escaped by accident. Girls hovered on the surface of every situation. I noticed them in school, ogled them in church, played to them at every concert performance. As if they jumped from the shadows, girls arrived, and nothing was ever the same. I fell in love ten times a day: an older woman, perhaps in her mid-twenties in a gray coat on a gray street corner; the raven-haired librarian who came every Tuesday morning to buy a dozen eggs. Ponytailed girls jumping rope. Girls with charming accents. Girls in bobby socks and poodle skirts. In the sixth grade, Tess Wodehouse trying to hide her braces behind her smiles. Blondie in the funny pages; Cyd Charisse; Paulette Goddard; Marilyn Monroe. Anyone curved. Allure goes beyond appearances to the way they grace the world. Some women propel themselves by means of an internal gyroscope. Others glide through life as if on ice skates. Some women convey their tortured lives through their eyes; others encircle you in the music of their laughter. The way they become their clothes. Redheads, blondes, brunettes. I loved them all. Women who flirt with you: where'd you get such long eyelashes? From the milkman. Girls too shy to say a word.

The best girls, however, were those who liked music. At virtually every performance, I could pick out from the crowd those who were listening, as opposed to the terminally bored or merely disinterested. The girls who stared back unnerved me, but at least they were listening, as were the ones with their eyes closed, chins cocked, intent on my playing. Others in the audience would be cleaning their teeth with their nails, digging in their ears with their pinkies, cracking their knuckles, yawning without covering their mouths, checking out the other girls (or boys), or checking their watches. After the performances, many in the audience invariably came up to have a few words, shake my hand, or stand near me. These post-performance encounters were most rewarding and I was delighted to receive compliments and answer questions for as long as I could while unmasking the enthusiasms of the women and girls.

Unfortunately, the concerts and recitals were few and far between, and the public demand for my performances of classical music at parties and shows diminished as I neared puberty. Many aficionados had been interested in a ten-year-old prodigy, but the novelty died when I was all elbows and acne as a teenager. And to be honest, I was sick of the Hanon and Czerny exercises and the same insipid Chopin étude that my teacher fussed over year after year. Changing yet again, I found my old powers ebbed as my hormones raged. As if overnight, I had gone from wanting to be just a boy to wanting to be a grown man. Midway through my freshman year in high school, following months of soul-searching and sullen fighting with my mother, it hit me that there was a way to combine my passion for music and my interest in girls: I would form my own band.

have something for you."

The last bitter days of winter imprisoned the whole band. A snowstorm and freezing temperatures made travel outside of camp impossible. Most of us spent night and day under cover in a drowse caused by the combination of cold and hunger. Speck stood above me, smiling, a surprise hidden behind her back. A breeze blew her long black hair across her face, and with an impatient hand, she brushed it aside like a curtain.

"Wake up, sleepyhead, and see what I found."

Keeping the deerskin wrapped tight against the cold, I stood. She thrust out a single envelope, its whiteness in relief against her chapped hands. I took it from her and opened the envelope, sliding out a greeting card with a picture of a big red heart on its front. Absentmindedly, I let the envelope slip to the ground, and she quickly bent to pick it up.

"Look, Aniday," she said, her stiff fingers working along the seams to carefully tear the seal. "If you would think to open it up, you could have two sides of paper—nothing but a stamp and address on the front, and on the back, you have a blank sheet." She took the card from me. "See, you can draw on the front and back of this, and inside, too, go around this writing here." Speck bounced on her toes in the snow, perhaps as much out of joy as to ward off the chill. I was speechless. She was usually hard as a stone, as if unable to bear interaction with the rest of us.

"You're welcome. You could be more grateful. I trudged through the snow to bring that back while you and all these lummoxes were nice and cozy, sleeping the winter away."

"How can I thank you?"

"Warm me up." She came to my side, and I opened the deerskin rug for her to snuggle in, and she wrapped herself around me, waking me alert with her icy hands and limbs. We slid in near the slumber party under the heap of blankets and fell into a deep sleep. I awoke the next morning with my head pressed against her chest. Speck had one arm around me, and in her other hand she clutched the card. When she woke up, she blinked open her emerald eyes to welcome morning. Her first request was that I read the message inside the card:

> But if the while I think on thee, dear friend,
> All losses are restored and sorrows end.
>> *Shakespeare, Sonnet 30*

There was no other signature, no addressee, and whatever names had been inked on the envelope had been smudged into oblivion by the wet snow.

"What do you think it means?"

"I don't know," I told her. "Who is Shakespeare?" The name seemed vaguely familiar.

"His friend makes all his troubles end, if he but thinks about him . . . or her."

The sun rose above the treetops, warming our peaceful camp. The aural signs of melting began: snow sloughing off firs, ice crystals breaking apart, the thaw and drip of icicles. I wanted to be alone with the card, and my pencil burned like an ember in my pocket.

"What are you going to write?"

"I want to make a calendar, but I do not know how. Do you know what day is today?"

"One day is like another."

"Aren't you curious about what day it is today?"

Speck wriggled into her coat, bidding me to do the same. She led me through the clearing to the highest point near the camp, a ridge that ran along the northwestern edge, a difficult passage over a steep slope of loose shale. My legs ached when we reached the summit, and I was out of breath. She, on the other hand, tapped her foot and told me to be quiet and listen. We were still and waited. Other than the thawing mountains, it was silent.

"What am I supposed to hear?"

"Concentrate," she said.

I tried, but save for the occasional laugh of a nuthatch and the creak of twigs and branches, nothing reached my ear. I shrugged my shoulders.

"Try harder."

I listened so intently that a fierce headache knocked inside my skull: her even, relaxed breathing, the beating of her heart, and a far-off rhythmic vibration that at first sounded like the rasp of a file but soon took on a more fixed character. A hum of alternating speeds, a low splash, the occasional horn, tires on pavement, and I realized we were listening to distant traffic.

"Neat," I told her. "Cars."

"Pay attention. What do you hear?"

My head was splitting, but I focused. "Lots of cars?" I guessed.

"Right." She grinned. "Lots and lots of cars. Traffic in the morning."

I still didn't get it.

"People going to work. In the city. Schoolbuses and kids. Lots of cars in the morning. That means it's a workday, not a Sunday. Sundays are quiet and not so many cars speeding by."

She held her bare finger to the air and then tasted it in her mouth for an instant. "I think it's a Monday," she said.

"I've seen that trick before. How can you tell?"

"All those cars make smoke, and the factories make smoke. But there aren't so many cars on the road and the factories are closed on Sundays. You hardly taste any smoke at all. Monday, a bit more. By Friday night, the air tastes like a mouthful of coal." She licked her finger again. "Definitely a Monday. Now, let me see your letter."

I handed over the valentine and envelope, which she inspected, pointing to the postmark over the stamp. "Do you remember what day is Valentine's Day?"

"February fourteenth." I felt proud, as if I had given the correct answer in math class. An image flashed of a woman, dressed in black and white, writing numbers on a chalkboard.

"That's right, and you see this?" She pointed to the date on the postmark, which ran in a semicircle: *MON FEB 13 '50 AM*. "That's when your Shakespeare put it in the mailbox. On a Mon. That means Monday morning is when they stamped it."

"So, today is Valentine's Day? Happy Valentine's Day."

"No, Aniday. You have to learn to read the signs and figure it out. Deduction. How could today be Valentine's Day if today is a Monday? How can we find a letter the day before it is lost? If I found the letter yesterday, and today is Monday, how could today be Valentine's Day?"

I was confused and tired. My head ached.

"February thirteenth was last Monday. If this card had been out for more than a week, it would be ruined by now. I found it yesterday and brought it to you. Yesterday was a quiet day—not many cars—a Sunday. Today must be the next Monday."

She made me question my ability to reason at all.

"It's simple. Today is Monday, February 20, 1950. You do need a calendar." She held out her hand for my pencil, which I gladly ceded her. On the back of the card, she drew seven boxes in a row and labeled S-M-T-W-T-F-S for the days of the week. Then she printed all the months of the year in a column on the side, and then on the opposite side, the numerals from 1 to 31.

As she drew them, she quizzed me on the proper number of days in each month, singing a familiar song to help me remember, but we forgot about leap years, which would throw me off in time. From her pocket, she took three round metal circles to demonstrate that if I wanted to keep track of time, all I would have to do would be to move the disks to the next space on the calendar each morning, remembering to start over at the end of the week and month.

Speck would often show me what proved to be the obvious answer, for which nobody else had the clarity of imagination and creativity. At such moments of insight, her eyes fixed on me, the tremor in her voice disappeared. A single hair escaped now, bisecting her face. She gathered her mane with her two rough red hands and pushed it behind her ears, smiling all the while at my stare. "If you ever forget, Aniday, come find me." She walked away, moving through the forest, across the ridge and away from camp, leaving me alone with my calendar. I spied her figure progressing among the trees until she blended into the natural world. When she vanished, all I could think of was the date: February 20, 1950. I had lost so much time.

Far below, the others in camp slumbered beneath a mat of stinking blankets and furs. By listening to the traffic and following the noise to its source, I could be back among the people, and one of those cars was bound to stop and take me home. The driver would see a boy standing by the side of the road and pull off on the berm ahead of me. I would wait for her, the woman in the red coat, to come save me. I would not run away, but wait there and try not to frighten her as before. She would lower herself to eye level, sweeping her hair back from her face. "Who are you?" I would summon up the faces of my parents and my little sister, tell the woman with the pale green eyes where I lived, how to get home. She would bid me climb into her car. Sitting beside her, I'd tell her my tale, and she would put her hand around the back of my head, saying everything would be all right. I'd jump from that car as we stopped before my house, my mother hanging laundry on the clothesline, my sister waddling toward me in her yellow dress, her arms aflutter. "I've found your boy," the woman would say, and my father would pull up in a red fire engine. "We've been looking all over for you for a long time." Later, after fried chicken and biscuits, we'd come back to the woods and rescue my friends Smaolach, Luchóg, and Speck, who could live with us and go to school and come home warm, safe, and sound. All I had to do was to concentrate and follow the sounds of civilization. I looked to the horizon as far as possible, but saw no sign. I listened, but heard nothing. I tried to remember, but could not recall my name.

Pocketing my three tokens, I turned over the calendar and read the Shakespeare aloud to myself: "But if the while I think on thee, dear friend . . ." The people sleeping down below in the hollow were my friends. I took out my pencil and began to write all I could remember. Many a year has passed between then and now, and I have written this story more than once, but that was the beginning, alone atop the ridge. My fingers stiffened in the cold. As I walked down to the camp, the bedcovers called out to me with the promise of warm dreams.

Not long after Speck's valentine, another gift landed in my lap. Luchóg brought it back from one of his pirating expeditions, unpacking his sack like Santa at the Christmas tree. "And this, little treasure, is for you. The sum-all and be-all of your earthly desires. Enough space here for your every dream. Miracle of miracles, and dry, too. Paper."

He handed me a bound black notebook, the kind schoolchildren use for their lessons, the pages lined to ensure the proper placement of words and sentences. On the front was the name of the school and the title RULED COMPO-SITION BOOK. On the back was a small box with this printed warning: *In the event of atomic attack: close the shades, lie down under your desk. Do not panic.* Inside, the author of the book, Thomas McInnes, had written his name on the flyleaf.

The weathered pages were filled with his virtually indecipherable penmanship, the ink a rusty brown. As far as I could tell, it was a story, or part of a story, because on the last page, the writing ends mid-sentence with the rather cryptic *See Other Book* written on the inside back cover. Over the years, I tried to read it, but the point of the story eluded me. The beauty of the composition book for me stemmed from McInnes's self-indulgence. He had written on only one side of the eighty-eight sheets of paper. I turned the book upside-down and wrote my contrary story in the opposite direction. While that journal is in ashes now with so much else, I can attest to its basic contents: a naturalist's journal recording my observations of life in the forest, complete with drawings of found objects—a diary of the best years of my life.

My chronicle and calendar helped me track the passing time, which fell into an easy rhythm. I kept up hope for years, but no one ever came for me. Heartbreak ran like an undercurrent of time, but despair would come and go like the shadow of clouds. Those years were mixed with the happiness brought by my friends and companions, and as I aged inside, a casual nothing drowned the boy.

The snows stopped by mid-March most years, and a few weeks later the ice would melt, green life would bud, insects hatch, birds return, fish and frogs ready for the catching. Spring instantly restored our energies, the lengthening light corresponding to our interest in exploration. We would throw off our hides and ruined blankets, shed our jackets and shoes. The first warm day in May, nine of us would go down to the river and bathe our stinking bodies, drown the vermin living in our hair, scrape off the caked dirt and scum. Once, Blomma had stolen a bar of soap from a gas station, and we scrubbed it away to a splinter in a single renewing bath. Pale bodies on a pebbly shore, rubbed pink and clean.

The dandelions blossomed from nowhere, and the spring onions sprouted in the meadows, and our Onions would gorge herself, eating the bulbs and grass, staining her teeth and mouth green, reeking, indolent, until her skin itself smelled pungent and bittersweet. Luchóg and Smaolach distilled the dandelions into a potent brew. My calendar helped track the parade of berries: strawberries in June, followed by wild blueberries, gooseberries, elderberries, and more. In a patch of forest over the ridge, Speck and I found a red army of raspberries invading a hillside, and we spent many a July day gathering sweetness among the thorns. Blackberries ripened last, and I am sad every time to see the first potful at our evening repasts, for those black jewels are a harbinger of summer's end.

The insect-eaters among us rejoiced at the abundance of the warm season, although bugs are a decidedly acquired taste. Each of the faeries had their own peculiar pleasures and preferred capturing techniques. Ragno ate only flies, which he plucked from spiderwebs. Béka was a gourmand, taking anything that crawled, flew, slithered, or wriggled his way. He would search out a colony of termites in a rotting log, a party of slugs in the mire, or a maggoty carcass, and dig in and eat those disgusting creatures raw. Sitting patiently by a small fire, he snatched moths out of the air with his tongue when they flew too close to his face. Chavisory was another notorious bug-eater, but at least she cooked them. I could tolerate the grubs and queens she baked on a heated rock until they popped, as brown and crispy as bacon. Cricket legs tend to stick in your teeth, and ants, if not roasted first, will bite your tongue and throat on the way down.

I had never killed a living thing before coming to the woods, but we were hunter-gatherers, and without an occasional bit of protein in the diet, all of us would suffer. We took squirrels, moles, mice, fish, and birds, although the eggs themselves were too great a hassle to steal from the nest. Anything bigger—such as a dead deer—we'd scavenge. I do not care for things that have been dead a long time. In late summer and early fall, in particular, the tribe would dine together on an unfortunate creature roasted on a spit. Nothing beats a rabbit under a starry night. But, as Speck would say, every idyll succumbs to desire.

Such a moment in my fourth year in the woods stands above all the rest. Speck and I had strayed from camp, and she showed me the way to the grove where honeybees had hidden their hive. We stopped at an old gray dogwood.

"Climb up there, Aniday, and reach inside, and you'll find the sweetest nectar."

As commanded, I shinnied up the trunk, despite the buzzing of the bees, and inched toward the hollow. From my purchase in the branches, I could see her upturned face, eyes aglow with expectation.

"Go on," she hollered from below. "Be careful. Don't make them mad."

The first sting startled me like a pinprick, the second and third caused pain, but I was determined. I could smell the honey before I felt it and could feel it before I saw it. Hands and wrists swollen with venom, my face and bare skin welted red, I fell from the limb to the forest floor with handfuls of honeycombs. She looked down at me with dismay and gratitude. We ran from the angry swarm and lost them on a hillside slanted toward the sun. Lying in the long new grass, we sucked every drop of honey and ate the waxy combs until our lips and chins and hands gummed up. Drunk on the stuff, the nectar heavy in our stomachs, we luxuriated in the sweet ache. When we had licked clean the honey, she began to pull the remaining stingers from my face and hands, smiling at my every wince. When she removed the last dagger from my hand, Speck turned it over and kissed my palm.

"You are such an idiot, Aniday." But her eyes betrayed her words, and her smile flashed as briefly as lightning rending the summer sky.

· *CHAPTER 9* ·

L isten to this." My friend Oscar put a record on the turntable and set down the needle with care. The 45 popped and hissed; then the melody line rose, followed by the four-part doo-wop, "Earth Angel" by The Penguins or "Gee" by The Crows, and he'd sit back on the edge of the bed, close his eyes, and pull apart those different harmonies, first singing tenor and so on through the bass. Or he'd put on a new jazz riff by Miles or maybe Dave Brubeck and pick out the counterpoint, cocking his ear to the nearly inaudible piano underneath the horns. All through high school we'd spend hours in his room, idly listening to his vast eclectic record collection, analyzing and arguing over the more subtle points of the compositions. Oscar Love's passion for music put my ambitions to shame. In high school, he was nicknamed "The White Negro," as he was so alien from the rest of the crowd, so cool, so in his head all the time. Oscar was such an outsider, he made me feel normal by comparison. And even though he was a year ahead of me, he welcomed me into his life. My father thought Oscar wilder than Brando, but my mother saw beneath the facade and loved him like a son. He was the first person I approached about forming a band.

Oscar stuck with me from its beginning as The Henry Day Five through every version: The Henry Day Four, The Four Horsemen, Henry and the Daylights, The Daydreamers, and lastly, simply Henry Day. Unfortunately, we could not keep the same group together for more than a few months at a time: Our first drummer dropped out of high school and enlisted in the Marine

Corps; our best guitarist moved away when his father was transferred to Davenport, Iowa. Most of the guys quit because they couldn't cut it as musicians. Only Oscar and his clarinet persisted. We stayed together for two reasons: one, he could play a mean lick on any horn, particularly his beloved stick; two, he was old enough to drive and had his own car—a pristine '54 red and white Bel Air. We played everything from high school dances to weddings and the occasional night at a club. Discriminating by ear and not by any preconceived notion of cool, we could play any kind of music for any crowd.

After a jazz performance where we particularly killed the crowd, Oscar drove us home, radio blaring, the boys in a great mood. He dropped off the others, and late that summer night we parked in front of my parents' house. Moths danced crazily in the headlights, and the rhythmic cricket song underscored the silence. The stars and a half-moon dotted the languid sky. We got out and sat on the hood of the Bel Air, looking out into the darkness, not wanting the night to end.

"Man, we were gas," he said. "We slayed them. Did you see that guy when we did 'Hey Now,' like he never heard a sound like that before?"

"I'm 'bout worn-out, man."

"Oh, you were so cool, so cool."

"You're not bad yourself." I hitched myself farther up on the car to stop skidding off the hood. My feet did not quite reach the ground, so I swung them in time to a tune in my head. Oscar removed the cigarette he had stashed behind his ear, and with a snap from his lighter he lit it, and into the night sky he blew smoke rings, each one breaking its predecessor.

"Where'd you learn to play, Day? I mean, you're still a kid. Only fifteen, right?"

"Practice, man, practice."

He quit looking at the stars and turned to face me. "You can practice all you want. Practice don't give you soul."

"I've been taking lessons for the past few years. In the city. With a guy named Martin who used to play with the Phil. The classics and all. It makes it easier to understand the music beneath it all."

"I can dig that." He handed me the cigarette, and I took a deep drag, knowing he had laced it with marijuana.

"But sometimes I feel like I'm being torn in two. My mom and dad want me to keep going to lessons with Mr. Martin. You know, the symphony or a soloist."

"Like Liberace." Oscar giggled.

"Shut up."

"Fairy."

"Shut up." I punched him on the shoulder.

"Easy, man." He rubbed his arm. "You could do it, though, whatever you want. I'm good, but you're out of this world. Like you've been at it all your life or you were born that way."

Maybe the dope made me say it, or maybe it was the combination of the summer night, the post-performance high, or the fact that Oscar was my first true friend. Or maybe I was dying to tell someone, anyone.

"I've got a confession, Oscar. I'm not Henry Day at all, but a hobgoblin that lived in the woods for a long, long time."

He giggled so hard, a stream of smoke poured out of his nostrils.

"Seriously, man, we stole the real Henry Day, kidnapped him, and I changed into him. We switched places, but nobody knows. I'm living his life, and I guess he's living mine. And once upon a time, I was somebody else, before I became a changeling. I was a boy in Germany or somewhere where they spoke German. I don't remember, but it comes back to me in bits and pieces. And I played piano there a long time ago, until the changelings came and stole me. And now I'm back among the humans, and I hardly remember anything about the past, but it's like I'm part Henry Day and part who I used to be. And I must have been one cool musician way back when, because that's the only explanation."

"That's pretty good, man. So where's the real Henry?"

"Out in the woods somewhere. Or dead maybe. He could be dead; it happens sometimes. But probably hiding out in the woods."

"Like he could be watchin' us right now?" He jumped off the car and whispered into the darkness. "Henry? Is that you?"

"Shut up, man. It's possible. But they're afraid of people, that much I know."

"The whosits?"

"The changelings. That's why you never see them."

"Why they so afraid of us? Seems like we should be afraid of them."

"Used to be that way, man, but people stopped believing in myths and fairy tales."

"But what if Henry's out there, watching us right now, wanting to get his body back, and he's creeping up, man, to get you?" And he reached out quickly and snatched my ankle.

I screamed, embarrassed to be fooled by such a simple joke. Oscar sprawled on the hood of the car, laughing at me. "You've been watching too many horror movies, man."

"No, the truth is . . ." I socked him on the arm.

"And there's pods in your cellar, right?"

I wanted to punch him again, but then I realized how ridiculous my story sounded, and I started laughing, too. If he remembered that night at all, Oscar never again brought up the matter, and maybe he thought I was hallucinating. He drove off, cackling to himself, and I felt empty after the truth had been told. My impersonation of Henry Day had succeeded so well that no one suspected the real story. Even my father, a natural skeptic, believed in me, or at least kept his doubts hidden deep in his soul.

The ground floor of our house was as dark and silent as a cave. Upstairs everyone slept soundly. I turned on the kitchen light and poured a drink of water. Attracted to the brightness, moths crashed and flapped up against the window screen. They scritched up and down, a sound menacing and foreboding. I turned off the lights, and they flew away. In the new darkness, I searched for a moving shadow, listened for footsteps among the trees, but nothing stirred. I crept upstairs to check on my sisters.

When the girls were young children, I often feared that Mary and Elizabeth would be snatched away by the hobgoblins and two changelings would be left in their place. I knew their ways, their tricks and deceptions, and also knew they could strike the same family twice, or, indeed, three times. Not far from here, the story goes, back in the 1770s, the Church family had seven children stolen and replaced by changelings, one by one, each at age seven, until there were no Churches at all, only simulacra, and pity those poor parents with an alien brood. My sisters were as susceptible, and I watched for the telltale changes in behavior or appearance—a sudden winsomeness, a certain detachment from life—that would reveal a possible switch.

I warned the twins to stay out of the woods or any shadowy places. "Dangerous snakes and bears and wildcats wait near our patch of land. Do not talk to strangers. Why go out to play," I'd ask, "when there is something perfectly good and interesting on television?"

"But I like exploring," Elizabeth said.

"How will we ever find our way back home if we never leave home?" Mary added.

"Did you ever see a timber rattler? Well, I have, and copperheads and water moccasins. One bite and you're paralyzed, your limbs go black, then you're dead. Do you think you can outrun or outclimb a bear? They climb trees better than cats, and they would grab your leg and gobble you up. Have you ever seen a raccoon foaming at the mouth?"

"I never get to see anything," Elizabeth cried.

"How can we ever avoid danger if we don't know what danger is?" Mary asked.

"It's out there. You could trip and fall over an old log and break your leg and nobody would ever find you. Or you could be caught in a blizzard with the wind blowing every which way until you can't find your own front door, and then they'd find you the next morning, frozen like a Popsicle, not ten feet from home."

"Enough!" They shouted in unison and went off to watch *Howdy Doody* or *Romper Room*. I knew, however, that while I was at school or rehearsing with the band, they would ignore my cautions. They'd come home with grass stains on their knees and bottoms, ticks on their bare skin, twigs in their curls, frogs in their overalls, and the smell of danger on their breath.

But that night they were sleeping lambs, and two doors down my parents snored. My father called out my name in his sleep, but I dared not answer at such a late hour. The house grew preternaturally still. I had told my darkest secret with no consequences, so I went to bed, safe as ever.

They say that one never forgets one's first love, but I am chagrined to admit that I do not remember her name or much else about her—other than the fact that she was the first girl I saw naked. For the sake of the story, I'll call her Sally. Maybe that actually was her name. After the summer of my confession to Oscar, I resumed my lessons with Mr. Martin, and there she was. She had departed at the end of the school year and returned a different creature— someone to be desired, a fetish, an obsession. I am as guilty of anonymous lust as anyone, but it was she who chose me. Her affections I gratefully accepted without pause. I had been noticing her curves for months, before she gathered the courage to speak to me at the winter recital. We stood together backstage in our formal wear, enduring the wait for our individual turns at the piano. The youngest kids went first, for agony is best served as an appetizer.

"Where did you learn to play?" Sally whispered over an achingly slow minuet.

"Right here. I mean with Mr. Martin."

"You play out of this world." She smiled, and, buoyed by her remarks, I gave my most inspired recital. In the weeks and months that followed, we slowly got to know each other. She would hang around the studio listening to me play the same piece over and over, Mr. Martin whispering gruffly, "Adagio, adagio." We arranged to have lunch together on Saturdays. Over sandwiches spread out on waxed paper, we'd chat about that day's lessons. I usually had a few dollars in my pocket from performances, so we could go to a show or stop for an ice cream or a soda. Our conversations centered around the kinds of subjects fifteen-year-olds talk about: school, friends, unbelievable parents, and, in our case, the piano. Or rather, I talked about music: composers, Mr. Martin, records, the affinities of jazz with the classics, and all sorts of nattering theories of mine. It was not a conversation, more like a monologue. I did not know how to listen, how to draw her out, or how to be quiet and enjoy her company. She may well have been a lovely person.

When the sun began to heat up the spring air, we took a stroll to the park, a place I normally avoided because of its resemblance to the forest. But the daffodils were in flower, and it seemed perfectly romantic. The city had turned on the fountain, another sign of spring, and we sat by the water's edge, watching the cascade for a long time. I did not know how to do what I wanted to do, how to ask, what to say, in what manner even to broach the subject. Sally saved me.

"Henry?" she asked, her voice rising an octave. "Henry, we've been taking walks and having lunch together and going to the movies for over three months, and in all that time, I've wondered: Do you like me?"

"Of course I do."

"If you like me, like you say, how come you never try to hold my hand?"

I took her hand in mine, surprised by the heat in her fingers, the perspiration in her palm.

"And how come you've never tried to kiss me?"

For the first time, I stared her straight in the eyes. She looked as if she were trying to express some metaphysical question. Not knowing how to kiss, I did so in haste, and regret now not having lingered awhile, if only to remember the sensation. She ran her fingers through my brilliantined hair, which produced an unexpected reaction, and I copied her, but a riddle percolated through my mind. I had no idea what to do next. Without her sudden discovery of a need to catch a streetcar, we might still be sitting there, stupidly staring into each other's faces. On the way back to meet my father, I took apart my emotions. While I "loved" my family by this point in my human life, I had never "loved" a stranger. It's voluntary and a tremendous risk. The emotion is further confused by the matter of lust. I counted the hours between Saturdays, anxious to see her.

Thank goodness she took the initiative. While we were necking in the dark balcony of the Penn Theater, she grabbed my hand and placed it on her breast, and her whole body fluttered at my touch. She was the one who suggested everything, who thought to nibble ears, who rubbed the first thigh. We rarely spoke when we were together anymore, and I did not know what Sally was scheming or, for that matter, if she was thinking at all. No wonder I loved the girl, whatever her name was, and when she suggested that I feign an illness to get out of Mr. Martin's class, I gladly complied.

We rode the streetcar to her parents' home on the South Side. Climbing the hill to her house in the bright sunshine, I started to sweat, but Sally, who was used to the hike, skipped up the sidewalk, teasing that I could not keep up. Her home was a tiny perch, clinging to the side of a rock. Her parents were gone, she assured me, for the whole day on a drive out to the country.

"We have the place to ourselves. Would you like a lemonade?"

She might as well have been wearing an apron, and I smoking a pipe. She brought the drinks and sat on the couch. I drank mine in a single swig and sat on her father's easy chair. We sat; we waited. I heard a crash of cymbals in my mind's ear.

"Why don't you come sit beside me, Henry?"

Obedient pup, I trotted over with a wagging tail and lolling tongue. Our fingers interlocked. I smiled. She smiled. A long kiss—how long can you kiss? My hand on her bare stomach beneath her blouse triggered a pent-up primal urge. I circled my way north. She grabbed my wrist.

"Henry, Henry. This is all too much." Sally panted and fanned herself with her fluttering hands. I rolled away, pursed my lips, and blew. How could I have misinterpreted her signals?

Sally undressed so quickly that I almost failed to notice the transition. As if pushing a button, off came her blouse and bra, her skirt, slip, socks, and underwear. Through the whole act, she brazenly faced me, smiling beatifically. I did love her. Of course, I had seen pictures in the museum, Bettie Page pinups and French postcards, but images lack breadth and depth, and art isn't life. Part of me pulled forward, desperate to lay my hands upon her skin, but the mere possibility held me back. I took a step in her direction.

"No, no, no. I've showed you mine; now you have to show me yours."

Not since a young boy at the swimming hole had I taken off my clothes in front of anyone else, much less a stranger, and I was embarrassed at the prospect. But it is hard to refuse when a naked girl makes the request. So I stripped, the whole time watching her watching me. I had progressed as far as my boxers when I noticed that she had a small triangle of hair at the notch of her, and I was completely bare. Hoping that this condition was peculiar to the female species, I pulled down my shorts, and a look of horror and dismay crossed her face. She gasped and put her hand in front of her mouth. I looked down and then looked back up at her, deeply perplexed.

"Oh my God, Henry," she said, "you look like a little boy."

I covered up.

"That's the smallest one I've ever seen."

I angrily retrieved my clothes from the floor.

"I'm sorry but you look like my eight-year-old cousin." Sally began to pick up her clothes off the floor. "Henry, don't be mad."

But I was mad, not so much at her as at myself. I knew from the moment she spoke what I had forgotten. In most respects, I appeared all of fifteen, but I had neglected one of the more important parts. As I dressed, humiliated, I thought of all the pain and suffering of the past few years. The baby teeth I wrenched out of my mouth, the stretching and pulling and pushing of bones and muscle and skin to grow into adolescence. But I had forgotten about puberty. She pleaded with me to stay, apologized for laughing at me, even saying at one point that size didn't matter, that it was actually kind of cute, but nothing she could have said or done would have relieved my shame. I never spoke to her again, except for the most basic greetings. She disappeared from my life, as if stolen away, and I wonder now if she ever forgave me or forgot that afternoon.

Stretching remedied my situation, but the exercise pained me and caused unexpected consequences. The first was the curious sensation that typically ended in the same messy way, but, more interestingly, I found that by imagining Sally or any other alluring thing, the results were a foregone conclusion. But thinking on unpleasant things—the forest, baseball, arpeggios—I could postpone, or avoid altogether, the denouement. The second outcome is somewhat more disconcerting to report. Maybe because the squeaking bedsprings were beginning to annoy him, my father burst into my room and caught me one night, red-handed so to speak, although I was completely under cover. He rolled his eyes toward the ceiling.

"Henry, what are you doing?"

I stopped. There was an innocent explanation, which I could not reveal.

"Don't think I don't know."

*Know what?* I wanted to ask.

"You will go blind if you keep at it."

I blinked my eyes.

He left the room and I rolled over, pressing my face against the cool pillow. My powers were diminishing over time. Farsightedness, distance hearing, speed of foot—all had virtually disappeared, and my ability to manipulate my appearance had deteriorated. More and more, I was becoming the human I had wanted to be, but instead of rejoicing in the situation, I sagged into the mattress, hid beneath the sheets. I punched my pillow and tortured the covers in a vain effort to get comfortable. Any hopes for pleasure subsided along with my erection. In pleasure's place, a ragged loneliness ebbed. I felt stuck in a never-ending childhood, doomed to living under their control, a dozen suspicious scowls each day from my false parents. In the forest, I had to mark time and take my turn as a changeling, but the years had seemed like days. In the anxiety of adolescence, the days were like years. And nights could be endless.

Several hours later, I woke in a sweat and threw off the covers. Going to the window to let in the fresh air, I spotted out on the lawn, in the dead of night, the red ash of a cigarette, and picked out the dark figure of my father, staring into the dark wood, as if waiting for something to spring out from the shadows between trees. When he turned to come back inside, Dad looked up at my room and saw me framed in the windowpanes, watching him, but he never said a word about it.

• *C H A P T E R   1 0* •

The full moon created a halo behind Igel's head and evoked the memory of saints and icons in the church I could barely remember. By his side stood Luchóg. Both were dressed for travel in jackets and shoes to ward off the frost.

"Aniday, get up and get dressed. You're coming with us this morning."

"Morning?" I rubbed the sleep from my eyes. "It's the middle of the night."

"The sun'll be up in no time. You'd best be quick," Luchóg advised.

We stole along the hidden trails through the forest, leaping like rabbits, scrambling through brambles, covering ground with great speed and no pause. Clouds passed beneath the moon, first hiding and then revealing the landscape. The trail led across empty roads, our feet sounding on the pavement. We darted through open spaces, through a field of cornstalks that rustled and hummed as we rolled between rows, past a barn big against the dark sky and a farmhouse yellow in the skittish moonlight. In her stall, a cow lowed at our fleeting presence. A dog barked once. Past the farm, another patch of trees, another road, and then we were crossing a stream from the dizzying height of a bridge. On the far side, Igel led us into a ditch that paralleled the road, and we crouched low in its cover. The sky began to lighten to a deep violet. An engine coughed and soon a milk truck passed by on the road above.

"We started too late," Igel said. "He'll have to be more careful now. Aniday, this morning we will test how far you've come to being one of us."

Looking down the road, I spied the milk truck stopping at a dreary bungalow on the outskirts of town. Next door stood a small general store with a single gasoline pump out front. The milkman, all in white, descended from his perch and carried his basket to the side door, returning briskly with two glass empties that clinked against the wire. Caught up in the scene, I nearly forgot to follow my comrades as they slithered ahead. I reached them in a culvert not ten yards from the gas station, and they were whispering and pointing in dire conspiracy. The object of desire began to take shape in the gathering light. Atop the pump, a coffee mug shone like a white beacon.

"Go get that cup," Igel ordered. "Don't be seen."

The rising sun pushed away the deeper hues of the night, and any hesitation on my part risked discovery. It was a simple task to sprint across the grass and pavement, grab the cup, and dash back to our hiding place. Fear held me back.

"Take off your shoes," Igel advised. "They'll never hear you."

I slipped off my brogans and ran to the pump, its red-winged horse vaulting toward the heavens, and I grasped the mug and turned to go, when an unexpected noise froze me to the spot. Glass on glass. I imagined the station owner reaching into the milk box, detecting a peculiar motion at the gas pump, and hollering to stop me. But no such thing happened. A screen door whined and closed with a bang. I swallowed and trotted back to my comrades, holding up the mug in triumph.

"You done well, little treasure."

"While you dallied in the open"—Igel stared down—"I went ahead for the milk."

The bottle was already open. Without shaking down the half-inch of cream, Igel poured me some first, and we washed down the half-gallon like three drunkards, toasting the dawn. Cold milk settled into my stomach, swelling my belly, causing me to swoon and drowse away the morning with my fellow thieves in a ditch.

At midday, we woke from our slumber and moved closer to town in measured steps, hiding among the shadows, halting at the hint of any people. Stopping only at places that appeared to be empty, homes with nobody inside, we pried, snooped, and hunted. The three of us clambered over a low stone wall and stole armloads of fruit from a pear tree. Each bite was a sweet sin, and we took far more than we could eat. I hated to abandon the pears, but we tossed most of them back over the wall and into the orchard, leaving them to rot in the sun. From a clothesline of drying laundry, we each took a clean, fresh shirt, and I swiped a white sweater for Speck. Luchóg pocketed one sock from a hanging pair. "Tradition." He grinned like the Cheshire Cat. "The mystery of the missing sock from every washing day."

As daylight began its slow fade, the children appeared with their books and satchels, and an hour or two later came the fathers in their big automobiles. We waited for sundown, and after that, lights on and lights out. Goodnights begot goodnights, and houses popped into darkness like bubbles in a chain. Here and there a lamp burned, betraying perhaps some lonesome soul reading past midnight or a wandering insomniac or forgetful bachelor. Like a battlefield general, Igel studied these signs of time before we moved out into the streets.

Years had passed since I'd last looked through the storefront window of the toy shop or felt the rough surface of brick corners. The town felt otherworldly, yet I could not pass by a single place without experiencing a flood of associations and memories. At the gates of the Catholic church, I heard Latin raised by a phantom chorus. The motionless candy cane in front of the barbershop brought back smells of witch hazel and the clip of scissors. Mailboxes on the corner reminded me of valentines and birthday cards. My school conjured a picture of children streaming out by the dozens from its doubledoors, screaming for summer. For all their familiarity, however, the streets unsettled me with their neat corners and straight lines, the dead weight of walls, the clear boundaries of windows. The repetitive architecture bore down like a walled maze. The signs and words and admonitions—STOP; EAT HERE; SAME DAY DRY CLEANING; YOU DESERVE A COLOR TV—did not illuminate any mystery, but only left me indifferent to reading their constant messages. At last, we came to our target.

Luchóg climbed up to a window and slipped through a space that seemed much too small and narrow. He collapsed like a mouse going under the door. Standing in the alleyway, Igel and I kept lookout until he heard the soft click of the front lock; he guided us up the stairs to the market. As he opened the door, Luchóg gave us a wan grin, and Igel tousled his hair. Silently, we proceeded down the row of goods, past the Ovaltine and Bosco, cereal in bright boxes, cans of vegetables, fruit, fish, and meat. Every new food tempted me, but Igel would not allow any delay, and he ordered me in a whisper to "come here right now." They crouched by bags on the bottom row, and Igel ripped one open with a slice of his sharp thumbnail. He licked his fingertip, dipped it in the powder, then tasted it.

"Bah . . . flour."

He moved a few paces and repeated the procedure.

"Worse . . . sugar."

"That stuff will kill you," Luchóg said.

"Excuse me," I interrupted, "but I can read. What are you looking for?"

Luchóg looked at me as if the question was the most preposterous thing he'd ever heard. "Salt, man, salt."

I pointed to the bottom shelf, observing that even without the gift of language, one might recognize the picture of the old-fashioned girl under her umbrella, leaving behind a trail of salt. "When It Rains, It Pours," I said, but they seemed unable to take my meaning. We loaded our rucksacks with as much as could be carried and left the store by the front door, a deflating departure, considering the smorgasbord inside. Our cargo made the journey home longer and more arduous, and we did not reach camp until daybreak. The salt, as I would later discover, was used to preserve meat and fish for the lean months, but at the time, I felt as if we had searched the wide seas for treasure and sailed into port with a chest filled with sand.

When she was handed the new sweater, Speck's eyes widened with surprise and delight. She peeled off the tattered jersey she had worn for months and lifted the sweater over her head, sliding her arms inside like two eels. The brief sight of her bare skin unsettled me, and I looked away. She sat on a blanket, curled up her legs beneath her bottom, and bade me sit beside her.

"Tell me, O Great Hunter, about your visit to the old world. Recount your mishaps and brave deeds. Give us a story."

"There's not much to say. We went to the store for salt. But I saw a school and a church, and we swiped a bottle of milk." I reached into my pocket and brought out a soft, overripe pear. "I brought this back, too."

She set the pear on the ground. "Tell me more. What else did you see? How did the world make you feel?"

"Like I was remembering and forgetting at the same time. When I stepped into lamplight, my shadow appeared, sometimes several shadows, but once outside the circle, they all disappeared."

"You've seen shadows before. Brighter lights throw harder shadows."

"It is a strange light, and the world is full of straight lines and edges. The corners of their walls looked as sharp as a knife. It is unreal and a bit scary."

"That's just a trick of your imagination. Write your impressions in your book." Speck fingered the hem of her sweater. "Speaking of books, did you see the library?"

"Library?"

"Where they keep the books, Aniday. You didn't see the library?"

"I had forgotten all about it." But as we talked, I could recall the stacks of well-worn books, the hushing librarian, quiet men and intent women bowing forward, reading. My mother had taken me there. My mother. "I used to go there, Speck. They let me take home books and bring them back when I was finished. I got a paper card and signed my name on a slip at the back of the book."

"You remember."

"But I don't remember what I wrote. I didn't write 'Aniday.'"

She picked up the pear and inspected it for soft spots. "Get me a knife, Aniday, and I'll cut this in half. And if you're good, I'll take you to the library to see the books."

Rather than leaving in the middle of the night as before, we walked out of camp at noon on a crisp October day without so much as a fare-thee-well. Luchóg, Speck, and I followed the same trail into town, but we took our time, as if strolling through the park, not wanting to reach the streets until dusk. A broad highway severed the woods, and we had to wait for a long break in the traffic. I scanned the cars on the chance that the lady in the red coat might drive by, but our vantage point was too far from the road to make out any of the drivers.

At the gas station on the edge of town, two boys circled the pump on their bicycles, tracing lazy arcs, enjoying their last fun in the remnant sunlight. Their mother called them for dinner, but before I could see her face, she vanished behind a closing door. Luchóg leading, we moved across the road in single file. Halfway across the asphalt, he froze and pricked his ears to the west. I heard nothing, but in my bones sensed the electric approach of danger moving quickly as a summer storm. A moment's indecision, and we lost our advantage. Springing from the darkness, the dogs were nearly upon us before Speck grabbed my hand and shouted, "Run!"

Teeth snapping, the pair split to chase us in a melee of barks and growls. The bigger dog, a muscular shepherd, went after Luchóg as he sprinted toward town. Speck and I raced back to the woods, a hound yelping in pursuit. When we reached the trees, she yanked me forward and up, so that I was six feet off the ground before realizing I was climbing a sycamore. Speck turned and faced the dog, which leapt for her, but she stepped to the side, grabbed the beast by the scruff of the neck, and flung it into the bushes. The dog cried in the air, snapped branches when it landed, and scrambled to its feet in great pain and confusion. Looking back over its shoulder at this girl, he tucked his tail between his legs and slunk away.

Coming down the road from the other direction, the German shepherd trotted alongside Luchóg as if he were a longtime pet. They stopped as one in front of us, and the dog wagged its tail and licked Luchóg's fingers. "Do you remember the last changeling, Speck? The German boy?"

"You're not supposed to mention—"

"He came in handy with this bloody canine. I was running for my life when I suddenly remembered that old lullaby our man used to sing."

" '*Guten Abend*'?"

He sang, *"Guten Abend, gut' Nacht, mit Rosen bedacht,"* and the dog whimpered. Luchóg stroked the shepherd between the ears. "Turns out music doth soothe the savage beast."

"Breast," she said. "The quote is: 'Music hath charms to soothe the savage breast.' "

"Don't tell him," Luchóg burst out. "*Auf Wiedersehen, Schatzi.* Go on home." The dog trotted off.

"That was scary," I said.

Feigning nonchalance, Luchóg rolled a cigarette. "Could have been worse. Could have been people."

"If we meet somebody, play dumb," Speck instructed. "They'll think we're a bunch of kids and tell us to go on home. Nod your head when I talk and don't say a word." I looked around the empty streets, half hoping for an encounter, but all the people seemed to be inside, at dinner, bathing the children, getting ready for bed. In many homes, an unearthly blue glow emanated from within.

The library squatted stately in the middle of a tree-lined block. Speck moved as if she had passed this way many times before, and the problem of locked doors was easily circumvented. Luchóg led us around the back to a staircase and pointed out a gap where the concrete had separated from the main wall.

"I don't think I can fit through that. My head's too big, and I'm not that skinny."

"Luchóg is a mouse," Speck said. "Watch and learn."

He told me the secret of softening one's bones. The gist is to think like a mouse or a bat, simply realizing one's own flexibility. "It will hurt the first time, lad, like every good thing, but there's no trick to it. A matter of faith. And practice."

He disappeared into the crack, and Speck followed him, exhaling a single drawn-out sigh. Pushing through that narrow space hurt more than I can say. The abrasions on my temples took weeks to heal. After softening myself, I had to remember to keep my muscles tense for a while or risk an arm or a leg going limp. But Luchóg was right—with practice, squeezing became second nature.

Underneath the library, the crawlspace was dark and foreboding, so when Speck struck a match, the flame glowed with hope. She touched the flame to a candlewick, and with the candle lit a hurricane lamp that smelled of must and kerosene. Each successive illumination brought the dimensions and features of the room into sharper focus. The back of the building had been built on a slight slope, so that the floor inclined from our entranceway, where one could stand quite comfortably, rising to the opposite wall, where one could rest only by sitting. I can't tell you how many times I bumped my head on the ceiling by that far wall. The chamber had been made accidentally, a sort of hollow beneath a new addition to the old library building. Since it did not rest on the same foundation, the room was hotter than outside during the summer and bone-cold in the winter. By lamplight I could see that someone had added a few homey touches—a brace of rugs, a few drinking vessels, and, in the northwest corner, a sort of easy chair fashioned from salvaged blankets. Luchóg began fiddling with his cigarette pouch, and Speck ordered him out, if he must smoke. Grumbling, he scooted through the crack.

"So what do you think, Aniday? A bit rustic, but still . . . civilization."

"It's grand."

"You haven't seen the best part. The whole reason I brought you here."

Speck motioned me to follow, and we scuttled up the incline to the back wall. She reached up, turned out a knob, and a panel dropped from the ceiling. In a flash, she hoisted herself up through the hole and was gone. I knelt on the spot, waiting for her return, looking up through the empty space. All at once, her face appeared in the frame.

"Are you coming or not?" she whispered.

I followed her into the library. The pale light from our chamber below dissipated in the room, but I could still make out—my heart leapt at the sight—row after row, shelf above shelf, floor to ceiling, a city of books. Speck turned to me and asked, "Now, what shall we read first?"

The end, when it arrived, proved both timely and apt. Not only had I learned everything Mr. Martin had to offer, but I was sick of it all—the practice, the repertoire, the discipline, and the ennui of eighty-eight keys. By the time I turned sixteen, I began looking for an excuse to quit, a way out that would not break my mother's heart. The truth is that while I am a very good pianist, great even, I was never sublime. Yes, by far the best in our remote hamlet, no doubt our corner of the state, maybe the best from border to border, but beyond that, no. I lacked the passion, the consuming fire, to be a world-class pianist. Looking forward, the alternative was dreadful. To end up like old Mr. Martin himself, teaching others after a second-rate career? I would rather play in a bordello.

Over breakfast one morning, I opened with this gambit: "Mom, I don't think I'm going to get any better."

"Better than what?" she asked, whipping eggs.

"At the piano, at music. I think it's as far as I can go."

She poured the mess into a skillet, the eggs sizzling as they hit butter and hot iron, and said nothing while she stirred. She served me a plate of eggs and toast, and I ate them in silence. Coffee cup in hand, she sat across the table from me. "Henry," she said softly, wanting my attention. "Do you remember the day when you were a little boy and ran away from home?"

I did not, but I nodded in the affirmative between bites.

"It was a bright day and hot, hotter than Hades. I wanted a bath to cool off. The heat's one thing I can't get used to. And I asked you to mind Mary and Elizabeth, and you disappeared into the forest. Do you remember that?"

There was no way I could remember, but I nodded my head as I swallowed the last slug of orange juice.

"I put the girls to bed and came back down, but you were gone." Her eyes welled up as she recounted the experience. "We looked over hill and yon but couldn't find you. As the day wore on, I called your father to come home, and then we telephoned the police and the firemen, and we were all looking for you for hours, calling out your name into the night." She looked past me, as if reliving the experience in her mind's eye.

"Any more eggs, Mom?"

She waved her spoon toward the stove, and I helped myself. "When it grew dark, I grew afraid for you. Who knows what lives out in that forest? I knew a woman once in Donegal whose baby was stolen from her. She'd gone out to pick blackberries and left her child sleeping on a blanket on a bright summer day, and when she came back, the baby was gone, and they never did find it, poor thing, not a trace. All that remained was an impression left on the grass."

I peppered my eggs and dug in.

"I thought of you lost and wanting your mother, and I couldn't get to you, and I prayed to God that you'd come home. When they found you, it was like a second chance. Quitting would be throwing away *your* second chance, your God-given gift. It's a blessing and you should use your talent."

"Late for school." I mopped the plate clean with a heel of bread, kissed the top of her head, and exited. Before I made it down the front steps, I regretted not being more forceful. Most of my life has been ruled by indecision, and I am grateful when fate intercedes, relieving me from choice and responsibility for my actions.

By the time of the winter recital that year, just the sight and sound of the piano made my stomach churn. I could not disappoint my parents by quitting

Mr. Martin altogether, so I pretended that all was well. We arrived early at the concert hall, and I left my family at the door to find their seats while I moped about backstage. The folderol surrounding the recitals remained unchanged. In the wings of the theater, students milled about, mentally preparing for their turns, practicing their fingering on any flat surface. Mr. Martin paced among us, counting heads, reassuring the stage-frightened, the incompetent, and the reluctant. "You are my prize pupil," he said. "The best I've ever taught. The only real piano player in the whole bunch. Make them cry, Henry." And with that, he pinned a carnation on my lapel. He swirled and parted the curtains to the brightness of the footlights to welcome the assemblage. My performance was the grand finale, so I had time to duck out the back and smoke a Camel pinched from my father's pack. A winter's night had fallen, clear and cold. A rat, startled by my presence in the alley, stopped and stared at me. I showed the vermin my teeth, hissed and glowered, but I could not scare it. Once upon a time, such creatures were terrified of me.

That frozen night, I felt entirely human and heartened at the thought of the warm theater. If this was to be my farewell performance, I resolved to give them something to remember me by. I moved like a whip, cracking the keys, thundering, floating, the right pressure on all the partial notes. Members of the audience began rising from their seats to lead the applause before the strings stopped humming. Enchanted, they showered their huzzahs, so much so that I almost forgot how much I hated the whole business. Backstage, Mr. Martin greeted me first, tears of joy in his eyes, squealing "Bravo," and then the other students, half of them barely masking their resentment, the other half consumed with jealousy, acknowledging with grudging graciousness that I had outshone their performances. In came the parents, siblings, friends, neighbors, and assorted music lovers. They clumped around the players, but I drew the largest crowd, and I did not notice the woman in the red coat until most of the well-wishers had vanished.

My mother was wiping lipstick from my cheek with a wet handkerchief when the woman meandered into my peripheral vision. She appeared normal and pleasant, about forty years old. Her deep brown hair framed an intelligent face, but I was perplexed at the way her pale green eyes had fixed upon me. She stared, scrutinized, studied, and pondered, as if dredging up an inner mystery. She was an utter stranger to me.

"Excuse me," she said. "But you're Andrew Day?"

"Henry Day," I corrected her.

"Right, Henry. You play wonderfully."

"Thank you." I turned back to my parents, who intimated that they were ready to go.

Maybe she saw my profile, or perhaps the simple act of turning away set off something in her brain, but she gasped and drew her fingers to her mouth. "You're him," she said. "You're the little boy."

I squinted at her and smiled.

"You are the one I saw in the woods that night. On the road? With the deer?" She started to raise her voice. "Don't you remember? I saw you on the road with those other boys. It must have been eight or nine years ago by now. You're all grown up and everything, but you're that little boy, no doubt. I was worried about you."

"I don't know what you are talking about, ma'am." I turned to go, but she grabbed my arm.

"It is you. I cracked my head on the dashboard when I hit the deer, and I thought you were a dream at first. You came out of the forest—"

I yelped a sound that hushed the room, a pure raw cry that startled everyone, myself included. I did not realize my capacity for such an inhuman noise still existed. My mother intervened.

"Let go of my son," she told her. "You're hurting his arm."

"Look, lady," I said, "I don't know you."

My father stepped into the middle of the triangle. "What is this all about?"

The woman's eyes flashed in anger. "I saw your boy. One night I was driving home from the country, and this deer jumped right onto the road in front of my car. I swerved to miss her, but I clipped her with my bumper. I didn't know what to do, so I got out of the car to see if I could help."

She shifted her attention from my father and began addressing me. "From the woods comes this boy, about seven or eight years old. Your son. And he startled me more than the deer did. Out of nowhere, walks right up to the deer like the most natural thing in the world; then he bent down to its mouth or nose or whatever you call it. Hard to believe, but he cupped his hand over her muzzle, and breathed. It was magic. The deer rolled off her side, unfolded her legs, stood, and sprang off. The most incredible thing that's ever happened to me."

I realized then that she had experienced an encounter. But I knew I had not seen her before, and while some changelings are willing to inspire wild animals, I never engaged in such foolishness.

"I got a real good look at the boy in my headlights," she said, "although not so good at his friends in the forest. It was you. Who are you really?"

"I don't know her."

My mother, riveted by her story, came up with an alibi. "It can't be Henry. Listen, he ran away from home when he was seven years old, and I didn't let him out of my sight for the next few years. He was never out by himself at night."

The intensity melted from the woman's voice, and her eyes searched for a sign of faith. "He looked at me, and when I asked him his name, he ran away. Since that night I've wondered . . ."

My father spoke in a gentle tone he seldom used. "I'm sorry, but you must be mistaken. Everybody has a double in the world. Maybe you saw someone who looked a bit like my son. I'm sorry for your troubles." She looked into his eyes, searching for affirmation, but he offered only the solace of his calm demeanor. He took the red coat from her arm and held it open for her. She slipped inside it, then left the room without a word, without looking back. In her wake trailed the remnants of anger and anxiety.

"Did you ever?" my mother asked. "What a story. And to think that she'd actually have the nerve to say it."

From the corner of my eye, I could see my father watching me, and the sensation unnerved me. "Can we go now? Can we get out of here?"

When we were all in the car and out of the city, I announced my decision. "I'm not going back there. No more recitals, no more lessons, no more strangers coming up to me with their wild stories. I quit."

For a moment, I thought my father would drive off the road. He lit a cigarette and let Mom take over the conversation.

"Henry, you know how I feel about quitting. . . ."

"Did you hear what that lady said?" Mary chimed in. "She thought you lived in the woods."

"You don't even like to stand next to a tree." Elizabeth laughed.

"This isn't about your feelings, Mom, but mine."

My father stared at the white line in the middle of the road.

"You are a sensitive boy," my mother continued. "But you can't let one woman with one story ruin your life. You don't mean to tell me you're going to quit eight years of work on the basis of a fairy tale."

"It isn't the woman in the red coat. I've had enough. Gone as far as I can go."

"Bill, why don't you say something?"

"Dad, I'm tired of it. Sick of practice, practice, practice. Tired of wasting my Saturdays. I think I should have a say over my own life."

He drew a deep breath and drummed his fingers on the steering wheel. The rest of the Days understood the signal. Quiet all the way home. That night I could hear them talking, make out the ebb and flow of a loud and emotional confrontation, but I had lost all ability to eavesdrop from a distance. Once in a while I'd hear a "goddam" or "bloody" explode from him, and she may have cried—I suppose she did—but that's it. Near midnight, he stormed out of the house, and the sound of the car pulling away left a desolation. I went downstairs to see if Mom had survived the ordeal and found her calmly sitting in the kitchen, a shoebox open on the table before her.

"Henry, it's late." She tied a ribbon around a bundle of letters and set it in the box. "Your father used to write once a week while he was over in North Africa." I knew the story by heart, but she unwound it again. Pregnant, with a husband overseas at war, all of nineteen at the time, she lived with his parents. She was still alone at the time of Henry's birth, and I was now almost as old as she had been through the whole ordeal. Counting my life as a hobgoblin, I was old enough to be her grandfather. Untamed age had crept into her heart.

"You think life's easy when you're young, and can take almost anything because your emotions run so strong. When you're up, you're in the stars, and when you're down, you're at the bottom of the well. But although I've grown old—"

She was thirty-five by my calculations.

"That doesn't mean I've forgotten what it's like to be young. Of course, it's your life to do with what you choose. I had high hopes for you as a pianist, Henry, but you can be whatever you wish. If it's not in your heart, I understand."

"Would you like a cup of tea, Mom?"

"That would be grand."

Two weeks later, during the afternoon before Christmas, Oscar Love and I drove into the city to celebrate my newly won independence. Ever since that episode with Sally, I'd had a question or two about my capability to have intercourse, so the trip was not without apprehension. When I lived in the forest, only one of those monsters could do the trick. He had been captured too late in his childhood, at the cusp of puberty, and he gave the poor females nothing but trouble. The rest of us were not ready physically to perform the act.

But I was ready to experience sex that night. Oscar and I tipped back a bottle of cheap wine. Thus fortified, we approached the house at dusk as the girls were opening up shop. I would like to report that losing my virginity was both exotic and erotic, but the truth is that it was mainly dark, rough, and over much more quickly than I had expected. She was fair-skinned and past her glory, the crown of platinum hair a come-on and a ruse, and among her several rules for the duration, no kissing. When I displayed a tentative uncertainty as to where and how to go about the act, she grabbed me with her hand and pushed me into position. A short time later, all that remained was to get dressed, pay the bill, and wish her merry Christmas.

When morning came with gifts around the tree and the family lounging in pajamas and robes, I felt on my way to a brand-new life. Mom and the twins were oblivious to any change as they went about their cheerful tasks, offering genuine affection and consideration of one another. My father, on the other hand, may have suspected my debauch of the night before. Earlier that morning, when I came home around two o'clock, the living room smelled of Camels, as if he had been waiting up for me and only gone to bed when Oscar's car pulled into the driveway. Throughout that drowsy holiday, my father moved about the house the way a bear moves through its territory when it smells the presence of another male. Nothing said, but wayward glances, brusqueness, a snarl or two. For the rest of our time together, we did not get along. A year and a half remained in my high school career before I could get away to college, so we circled one another, barely exchanging a sentence on our rare encounters. He treated me like a stranger half of the time.

I recall two occasions when he stepped out of his inner world, and both times were unsettling. A few months after the scene at the winter recital, he brought up the matter of the woman in red and her strange story. We were tearing down my mother's henhouse, having sold the birds and gotten out of the egg and chicken business after turning a handsome profit. His questions arrived in the intervals between the prying crowbar, squealing nails, and tearing lumber.

"So, you remember that lady and her story about the boy and the deer?" He ripped another plank from the frame. "What do you make of that? Do you think such a thing could happen?"

"Sounded incredible to me, but I suppose it might have happened. She seemed pretty sure of herself."

Grunting with effort, he tugged away at a rusty nail. "So it might be true? How do you explain her thinking it was you?"

"I didn't say it was true. She seemed convinced it happened, but it isn't likely, is it? And anyway, suppose something like that did happen to her, she is wrong about me. I wasn't there."

"Maybe it was someone who looked like you?" He threw his weight into it, and the rest of the wall crashed down, leaving only the skeleton stark against the sky.

"That's a possibility," I said. "I reminded her of someone she saw once upon a time. Didn't you tell her that everyone has a double in the world? Maybe she saw my evil twin?"

He eyeballed the frame. "This'll tumble down with a few good kicks." He knocked down the frame, loaded it up in the back of a truck, and drove away.

The second occasion occurred about a year later. His voice woke me at first light, and I followed the sound from my bedroom and through the back doorway. A feathery mist rose from the lawn and he stood, his back to me, in the middle of the wet grass, calling out my name as he faced a stand of firs. A dark trail of footsteps led into the woods ten feet in front of him. He was stuck to the spot, as if he had startled a wild animal that fled away in fear. But I saw no creature. By the time I drew near, the diminuendo of a few raspy calls of

"Henry" lingered in the air. Then he fell to his knees, bent his head to the ground, and quietly wept. I crept back into the house, and pretended to be reading the sports page when he came in. My father stared at me hunched over the newspaper, my long fingers wrapped around a coffee cup. The wet belt of his robe dragged along the floor like a chain. Soaked, disheveled, and unshaven, he seemed much older, but maybe I had not noticed before how he was aging. His hands trembled as if palsied, and he took a Camel from his pocket. The cigarette was too wet to light despite his repeated attempts, so he crumpled the whole pack and tossed it in the trash can. I set a cup of coffee in front of him, and he stared at the steam as if I had handed him poison.

"Dad, are you all right? You look a mess."

"You." He pointed his finger at me like a gun, but that's all he said. The word hung in the air all morning, and I do not think I ever heard him call me "Henry" again.

e entered the church to steal candles. Even in the dead of night, the slate and glass building asserted its prominence on Main Street. Bound by an iron fence, the church had been laid out in the shape of a cross, and no matter how one approached it, the symbols were inescapable. Huge chestnut doors at the top of a dozen steps, mosaics from the Bible in the stained-glass windows reflecting moonlight, parapets hiding angels lurking near the roof—the whole edifice loomed like a ship that threatened to swamp us as we drew near. Smaolach, Speck, and I crept through the graveyard adjacent to the eastern arm of the church and popped in through a side door that the priests left unlocked. The long rows of pews and the vaulted ceiling created a space that, in the darkness, pressed down on us; its emptiness had weight and substance. Once our eyes adjusted, however, the church did not seem as smothering. The threatening size diminished, and the high walls and arched ceilings reached out as if to embrace us. We split up, Smaolach and Speck in search of the larger candles in the sacristy to the right, I to find the smaller votive candles in an alcove on the other side of the altar. A fleeting presence seemed to follow me along the altar rail, and a real dread rose inside me. In a wrought iron stand, dozens of candles stood like lines of soldiers in glass cups. A coinbox rattled with pennies when I tapped my nails against its metal face, and spent matches littered the empty spaces. I struck a new match against the rough plate, and a small flame erupted like a fingersnap. At once, I regretted the fire, for I looked up and saw a woman's face staring down at me. I shook out the light and crouched beneath the rail, hoping to be invisible.

Panic and fear left as quickly as they had come, and what amazes me now is how much flows through the mind in such a short space of time. When I saw her eyes looking down on me, I remembered: the woman in red, my schoolmates, the people in town, the people in church, Christmas, Easter, Halloween, the kidnapping, drowning, prayers, the Virgin Mary, and my sisters, father, mother. I nearly had solved the riddle of my identity. Yet as quickly as it takes to say "Pardon me," they vanished, and with them, my real story. It seemed as if the eyes of the statue flickered in the match light. I looked upon the enigmatic face of the Virgin Mary, idealized by an anonymous sculptor, the object of untold adoration, devotion, imagination, supplication. As I stuffed my pockets with candles, I felt a pang of guilt.

Behind me, the great wooden doors at the center entrance groaned open as a penitent or a priest entered. We zipped out through the side door and zigzagged among the gravestones. Despite the fact that bodies lay buried there, the cemetery was not half as frightening as the church. I paused at a gravestone, ran my fingers over the incised letters, and was tempted to light a match to read the name. The others leapt over the iron fence, so I scurried to catch up, chasing them across town, until we were all safely beneath the library. Every close call thrilled us, and we sat on our blankets giggling like children. We lit enough candles to make our sanctuary shine. Smaolach crawled off to a dark corner and curled up like a fox, his nose buried under a cloaking arm. Speck and I sought out the brightness, and with our latest books, we sat side by side, the scrape of turning pages marking time.

Ever since she had introduced me to this secret place, I loved going to the library. Initially, I went for the books first encountered in my childhood. Those old stories—*Grimm's Fairy Tales* and *Mother Goose*, picture books like *Mike Mulligan*, *Make Way for Ducklings*, and *Homer Price*—promised another clue to my fading identity. Rather than help me recapture the past, the stories only alienated me further from it. By looking at the pictures and reading aloud the text, I had hoped to hear my mother's voice again, but she was gone. After my first few visits to the library, I shelved such childish things and never again looked at them. Instead, I embarked upon a journey mapped by Speck, who chose, or helped me choose, stories to hold my adolescent interest: books like *The Call of the Wild* and *White Fang*, tales of adventure and derring-do. She helped me sound out words I could not decipher and explained characters, symbols, and plots that ran too wild or deep for my imagination. Her confidence, as she moved through the stacks and countless novels, inspired me to believe in my own ability to read and imagine. If not for her, I would be the same as Smaolach, filching comic books like *Speed Carter* or the *Adventures of Mighty Mouse* from the drugstore. Or worse, not reading at all.

Cozy in our den, she held on her lap a fat volume of Shakespeare, the type set in a minuscule font, and I was midway through *The Last of the Mohicans*. The flickering candlelight conspired with the silence, and we only interrupted each other's reading to share a casual delight.

"Speck, listen to this: 'These children of the woods stood together for several moments pointing at the crumbling edifice, and conversing in the unintelligible language of their tribe.'"

"Sounds like us. Who are these people?"

I held up the book to show her its cover, the title in gilt letters on a green cloth. We receded back into our stories, and an hour or so passed before she spoke again.

"Listen to this, Aniday. I'm reading *Hamlet* here and these two fellows come in. Rosencrantz and Guildenstern. Hamlet greets them: 'Good lads, how do ye both?' And Rosencrantz says, 'As the indifferent children of the earth.' And Guildenstern says, 'Happy in that we are not over-happy. On Fortune's cap we are not the very button.'"

"Does he mean they were unlucky?"

She laughed. "Not that, not that. Don't go chasing after a better fortune."

I did not understand the half of what she said, but I laughed along with
her, and then tried to find my place again with Hawkeye and Uncas. As
morning threatened and we packed our things to go, I told her how much I
had enjoyed what she had read to me about Fortune.

"Write it down, boy. If you come across a passage in your reading that
you'd like to remember, write it down in your little book; then you can read
it again, memorize it, and have it whenever you wish."

I took out my pencil and a card from the stack I had filched from the
card catalog. "What did they say?"

"Rosencrantz and Guildenstern: the indifferent children of the earth."

"The last of the Mohicans."

"That's us." She flashed her smile before going to the corner to wake
our slumbering friend Smaolach.


We would snitch a few books to take home with us for the satisfaction of
lying abed on a chilled winter's morning under weak sunshine and slipping
out a slim volume to read at leisure. Between the covers, a book can be a sin.
I have spent many hours in such a waking dream, and once having learned
how to read, I could not imagine my life otherwise. The indifferent children
around me did not share my enthusiasm for the written word. Some might
sit for a good story well told, but if a book had no pictures, they showed scant
interest.

When a raiding party went to town, they often came back with a collection of magazines—*Time* or *Life* or *Look*—and then we would huddle together under the shade of an old oak to look at the photographs. I remember
summer days, a mass of knees and feet, elbows and shoulders, jockeying for a
choice viewing position, their bare skin damp against mine. We stuck together

like the slick pages clumped and wrinkled in the humidity. News and celebrity did not appeal to them. Castro or Khrushchev, Monroe or Mantle, none meant anything more than a passing fancy, an interesting face; but they were profoundly intrigued by images of children, particularly in fanciful or humorous situations, and any photographs of the natural world, particularly exotic animals from a zoo or circus or in the wild reaches of a faraway land. A boy on top of an elephant caused a sensation, but a boy with a baby elephant was talked about for days. Most beloved of all were shots of parents and children together.

"Aniday," Onions would plead, "tell us the story about the daddy and his baby."

A bright-eyed baby girl peeps up from a bassinet to stare at her delighted, grinning father. I read the caption to them. " 'Little bundle of joy: Senator Kennedy admires his new baby daughter, Caroline, in their Georgetown home.' "

When I tried to turn the page, Blomma stuck her palm on the photograph. "Wait. I want to see the baby again."

Chavisory chimed in: "I want to see the man."

They were intensely curious about the other world, especially at the distance photography allows, the place where people grew up, fell in love, had children, became old, and the cycle continued, unlike our relentless timelessness. Their ever-changing lives fascinated us. Despite our many chores, a persistent boredom hung around the camp. For long stretches, we did nothing but allow time to pass.

Kivi and Blomma could spend a day braiding each other's hair, unraveling the plaits and starting all over again. Or they played with the dolls they had stolen or made from sticks and scraps of cloth. Kivi, in particular, became a little mother, holding a rag doll to her breast, tucking her toy baby in a cradle fashioned from a forgotten picnic basket. One baby was composed of the lost or broken limbs of four other dolls. As Kivi and Blomma bathed their dolls at the creek's edge one humid morning, I joined them on the bank and helped to rinse the nylon hair till it lay plastered against the dolls' plastic scalps.

"Why do you like playing with your babies so much?"

Kivi did not look up from her task, but I could sense that she was crying.

"We are practicing," said Blomma, "for when our turn comes along to be changelings. We are practicing to be mothers someday."

"Why are you sad, Kivi?"

She looked at me, the brightness now drained from her eyes. "Because it takes so long."

Indeed it did. For while we all grew older, we did not change physically. We did not grow up. Those who had been in the forest for decades suffered most. The truly mischievous fought the monotony by creating trouble, solving imaginary problems, or by pursuing an enterprise that, on the surface, appeared worthless. Igel had spent the past decade in camp digging an elaborate system of tunnels and underground warrens for our protection. Béka, the next in line, was on a constant prowl to catch any unsuspecting female and drag her into the bushes.

Ragno and Zanzara attempted to cultivate grapes nearly every spring in hope of replacing our fermented mash with a homegrown wine. Of course, the soil resisted every enrichment, the days lacked sufficient sun, mites and spiders and insects invaded, and my friends had no luck. A vine or two would sprout, twist and meander along the trellis Ragno had built, but never a grape in all those years. Come September, they cursed their luck and tore down the remnants, only to begin again when March teased such dreams. The seventh time I saw them breaking the hard ground, I asked Zanzara why they persisted in the face of continued failures. He stopped digging and leaned against the cracked and ancient spade.

"When we were boys, every night we had a glass of wine at supper. I'd like to taste it again."

"But surely you could steal a bottle or two from town."

"My papa grew grapes and his before him and back and back and back." He wiped his brow with an earth-caked hand. "One day we'll get the grapes. You learn to be patient here."

I passed much time with Luchóg and Smaolach, who taught me how to fell a tree and not be crushed, the geometry and physics behind a deadfall trap, the proper angle of chase to catch a hare on foot. But my favorite days were spent with Speck. And the best of all were my birthdays.

I still kept my calendar and had chosen April 23—Shakespeare's birthday— as my own. In my tenth spring in the woods, the date fell on a Saturday, and Speck invited me to go to the library to spend the night quietly reading together. When we arrived, the chamber had been transformed. Dozens of small candles suffused the room with an amber glow reminiscent of the light from a campfire under the stars. Near the crack at the entranceway, she had chalked a birthday greeting in a scrolled design of her own devising. The general shabbiness—the cobwebs, dirty blankets, and threadbare rugs—had been cleared away, making the place clean and cozy. She had laid in a small feast of bread and cheese, locked away against the mice, and soon the kettle boiled cheerfully, with real tea in our cups.

"This is incredible, Speck."

"Thank goodness we decided today is your birthday, or I would have gone to all this fuss for nothing."

At odd times that evening, I would look up from my text to watch her reading nearby. Light and shadow flickered across her face, and like clockwork she brushed a stray lock from in front of her eyes. Her presence disturbed me; I did not get through many pages of my book and had to read many sentences more than once. Late that night, I awoke in her embrace. Instead of the usual kicking or shouldering away when I woke up with someone all over me, I nestled into her, wanting the moment to last. Most of the shorter candles had burned down, and sadly I realized that our time was nearly over.

"Speck, wake up."

She murmured in her sleep and pulled me closer. I pried away her arm and rolled out.

"We have to go. Don't you feel the air on your skin changing? The dawn's about to begin."

"Come back to sleep."

I gathered my things together. "We won't be able to leave unless we go right now."

She lifted herself up by the elbows. "We can stay. It's Sunday and the library's closed. We can stay all day and read. Nobody will be here. We can go back when it's dark again."

For a fleeting second, I considered her idea, but the very thought of staying in town during daylight hours, chancing discovery with people up and about, filled me with a holy terror.

"It's too risky," I whispered. "Suppose someone happens by. A policeman. A watchman."

She dropped back down to the blanket. "Trust me."

"Are you coming?" I asked at the door.

"Go. Sometimes you are such a child."

Squeezing through the exit, I wondered if it was a mistake. I did not like arguing with Speck or leaving her there by herself, but she had spent many days on her own away from camp. My thoughts bounced back and forth between the two choices, and perhaps my worries over Speck affected my sense of direction, for I found myself quite lost soon after abandoning her. Each new turn brought unfamiliar streets and strange houses, and in my haste to escape, I became more hopelessly disoriented. At an edge of town, a grove of trees invited me into its warm cloak, and there I picked a trail from three options, following its twists and turns. In hindsight, I should have stayed put until the sun had fully risen, so that it could serve as compass, but at the time, my thoughts were clouded by questions. What had she been thinking, planning, doing for my birthday? How was I to grow older, be a man, stuck eternally in this small, useless body? The waning sliver moon dipped and disappeared.

A small creek, not more than a trickle, bisected the path. I decided to follow the water. Tracing a creek at dawn can be a peaceful experience, and those woods had appeared so often in my dreams as to be as familiar to me as my own name. The creek itself ran beneath a stony road, and the road led me to a solitary farmhouse. From the culvert, I saw the roof and circled round to the back as the first sunrays bathed the porch in gold.

Some trick of light gave the house an unfinished appearance, as if caught in a dream between night and day. I half expected my mother to come through the door, calling me home for dinner. As the light brought it into focus, the house took on a more welcoming character, its windows losing their menacing stare, its door less and less like a hungry mouth. I stepped out of the forest and onto the lawn, leaving a dark wake behind me on the wet grass. The door swung open suddenly, petrifying me on the spot. A man came down the stairs, pausing on the next-to-bottom step to light a cigarette. Wrapped in a blue robe, the figure took one step forward, then lifted his foot, startled by the moisture. He laughed and cursed softly.

The specter still did not notice me, though we faced each other—he at the edge of the house, and I at the edge of the forest. I wanted to turn around and see what he was looking for, but I stood frozen as a hare as the daybreak lifted around us. From the lawn, a chill rose in wisps of fog. He drew closer, and I held my breath. Not a dozen steps between us, he stopped. The cigarette fell from his fingers. He took one more step toward me. His brow creased with worry. His thin hair blew in the breeze. An eternity passed as his eyes danced in their sockets. His lips trembled when he opened his mouth to speak.

"And we? Envy?"

The words coming to me did not make sense.

"Is a chew? Atchoo? Can a bee, Houston?"

The sounds he made hurt my ears. At that moment, I wished to be sleeping in Speck's arms again. He knelt on the damp grass and spread out his arms as if he expected me to run to him. But I was confused and did not know if he meant me harm, so I turned and sprinted, as fast as I could go. The monstrous gargle from his throat followed me deep into the forest until, as suddenly, the strange words stopped, yet I kept running all the way home.

CHAPTER 13

The ringing phone began to sound like a mad song before someone mercifully answered. Far down the hall, I was in my dorm room that night with a coed, trying to stay focused on her bare skin. Moments later, a rap on my door, a curious pause, and then the knock intensified to a thundering, which scared the poor girl so that she nearly fell off of me.

"What is it? I'm busy. Can't you see the necktie on the doorknob?"

"Henry Day?" On the other side of the door, a voice cracked and trembled. "It's your mother on the telephone."

"Tell her I'm out."

The voice lowered an octave. "I'm really sorry, Henry, but you need to take this call."

I pulled on pants and a sweater, opened the door, and brushed past the boy, who was staring at the floor. "Someone better've died."

It was my father. My mother mentioned the car, so naturally, in my shock, I assumed there had been an accident. Upon returning home, I learned the real story through a word here, raised eyebrows, and innuendo. He had shot himself in the head, sitting in the car at a stoplight not four blocks away from the college. There was no note, nothing explained. Only my name and dorm room number on the back of a business card tucked in a cigarette pack with one remaining Camel.

I spent the days before the funeral trying to make sense of the suicide. Since that awful morning when he saw something in the yard, he drank more heavily, though alcoholics, in my experience, prefer the long and slow pour rather than the quick and irreversible bang. It wasn't the drink that killed him, but something else. While he may have had suspicions, he could not have figured out the truth about me. My deceptions were too careful and clever, yet in my infrequent encounters with the man since leaving for college, he had acted cold, distant, and unyielding. Some private demons plagued him, but I felt no compassion. With one bullet, he had abandoned my mother and sisters, and I could never forgive him. Those few days leading up to the funeral, and the service itself, hardened my opinion that his selfishness had rotted our family to the roots.

With good grace, my mother, more confused than distraught, bore the brunt of making arrangements. She convinced the local priest, no doubt abetted by her weekly contributions over many years, to allow my father to be buried in the church's graveyard despite the suicide. There could be no Mass, of course, and for this she bore some resentment, but her anger shielded her from other emotions. The twins, now fourteen, were more prone to tears, and at the funeral home they keened like two banshees over the closed coffin. I would not cry for him. He was not my father, after all, and coming as it did in the spring semester of my sophomore year, his death was supremely ill-timed. I cursed the fair weather of the day we buried him, and a throng of people who came from miles around to pay their respects astonished me.

As was the custom in our town, we walked from the mortuary to the church along the length of Main Street. A bright new hearse crawled ahead of us, and a cortege of more than a hundred people trailed behind. My mother and sisters and I led the grim parade.

"Who are all these people?" I whispered to my mother.

She looked straight ahead and spoke in a loud, clear voice. "Your father had many friends. From the army, from his job, people he helped along the way. You only knew part of the story. There's more to a salmon than the fin."

In the shade of new leaves, we put him in the ground and covered him with dirt. Robins and thrushes sang in the bushes. Behind her black veil, my mother did not weep, but stood in the sunshine, stoic as a soldier. Seeing her there, I could not help but hate him for doing this to her, to the girls, to our friends and family, and to me. We did not speak of him as I drove my mother and sisters back to the house to receive condolences.

Women from church welcomed us in hushed tones. The house felt more cool and quiet than it did in the dead of night. On the dining room table lay tokens of community spirit—the noodle casseroles, pigs in blankets, cold fried chicken, egg salad, potato salad, Jell-O salad with shaved carrots, and a half-dozen pies. On the sideboard, new mixers and bottles of soda stood next to gin and scotch and rum and a tub of ice. Flowers from the funeral home perfumed the air, and the percolator bubbled madly. My mother chatted with her neighbors, asking about each dish and making gracious compliments to the particular cooks. Mary sat at one end of the sofa, picking at the lint on her skirt, and Elizabeth perched on the opposite end, watching the front door for visitors. An hour after we arrived, the first guests showed up—men who had worked with my father, stiff and formal in their good suits. One by one, they pressed envelopes filled with money into my mother's palm and gave her awkward hugs. My mother's friend Charlie flew in from Philadelphia, but he had missed the interment. He looked askance at me when I took his hat, as if I were a stranger. A couple of old soldiers dropped by, specters from a past that no one else knew. They huddled in the corner, lamenting good ole Billy.

I soon tired of them all, for the reception reminded me of those post-recital gatherings, only more somber and pointless. Out on the porch, I took off my black jacket, loosened my necktie, and nursed a rum and Coke. The greened trees rustled in the intermittent breeze, and the sunshine gently warmed the meandering afternoon. From the house, the guests produced a murmur that rose and fell consistent as the ocean, and every so often, a quick peal of laughter rose to remind us that no one is irreplaceable. I lit a Camel and stared at the new grass.

She appeared at my side, redolent of jasmine, her scent betraying her stealth. A quick sideways glance and an even briefer smile, then we both resumed our inspection of the lawn and the dark woods beyond. Her black dress was trimmed at the collar and cuffs in white, for she followed the smart fashion, twice removed from the haute couture of Mrs. Kennedy. But Tess Wodehouse managed to copy the style without looking foolish. Perhaps it was her quiet poise as we stood at the rail. Any other girl my age would have felt the necessity to speak, but she left it to me to decide the moment for conversation.

"It was nice of you to come. I haven't seen you since when? Grade school?"

"I'm so sorry, Henry."

I flicked my cigarette into the yard and took a sip from my drink.

"I heard you once at a recital downtown," she said, "four or five years ago. There was a big to-do afterward with a ranting lady in a red coat. Remember how gently your father treated her? As if she weren't crazy at all, but a person whose memory had come undone. I think my daddy would have told her to buzz off, and my mother probably'd have punched her on the nose. I admired your father that night."

While I remembered the woman in red, I had not remembered Tess from that night, had not seen or thought of her in ages. In my mind, she was still a little tomboy. I set down my glass and invited her, with a sweeping gesture, to a nearby chair. With a demure and becoming grace, she took the seat next to me, our knees nearly touching, and I stared at her as if in a trance. She was the girl who had wet her pants in second grade, the girl who had beaten me at the fifty-yard dash in sixth grade. When I went off to the public high school in town, she took the bus to the Catholic girls' school in the other direction. Vanished. Those intervening years had shaped her into a beautiful young woman.

"Do you still play piano?" she asked. "I hear you're up in the city at college. Are you studying music?"

"Composition," I told her. "For orchestra and chamber music. I gave up performing the piano. Couldn't ever get comfortable in front of people. You?"

"I'm nearly finished for my LPN—licensed practical nurse. But I'd like to get a master's in social work, too. All depends."

"Depends on what?"

She looked away, toward the door. "On whether I get married or not. Depends on my boyfriend, I guess."

"You don't sound too enthusiastic."

She leaned to me, her face inches from mine, and mouthed the words: *I'm not.*

"Why is that?" I whispered back.

As if a light clicked on behind her eyes, she brightened. "There's so much I want to do. Help those in need. See the world. Fall in love."

The boyfriend came looking for her, the screen door slapping the frame behind him. Grinning at having found her, he had an uncanny effect upon me, as if I had met him somewhere long ago, but I could not place his face. I could not shake the feeling that we knew each other, but he was from the opposite side of town. His appearance spooked me, as if I were seeing a ghost or a stranger drawn from another century. Tess scrambled to her feet and nestled into his side. He stuck out a paw and waited a beat for my handshake.

"Brian Ungerland," he said. "Sorry for your loss."

I muttered my thanks and resumed my observation of the unchanging lawn. Only Tess's voice brought me back to the world. "Good luck with your compositions, Henry," she said. "I'll look in the record store for you." She steered Brian toward the door. "Sorry we had to renew our friendship under these circumstances."

As they left, I called out, "I hope you get what you want, Tess, and don't get what you don't." She smiled at me over her shoulder.

After all the visitors had departed, my mother joined me on the porch. In the kitchen, Mary and Elizabeth fussed over the covered dishes and the empty glasses in the sink. The final moments of the funeral day, we watched crows gather in the treetops before evening fell. They flew in from miles away, strutted like cassocked priests on the lawn before leaping into the branches to become invisible.

"I don't know how I'll manage, Henry." She sat in the rocker, not looking at me.

I sipped another rum and Coke. A dirge played in the background of my imagination.

She sighed when I did not reply. "We've enough to get by. The house is nearly ours, and your father's savings will last awhile. I'll have to find work, though the Lord knows how."

"The twins could help."

"The girls? If I had to count on those two to help with so much as a glass of water, I would be dead of thirst. They are nothing but trouble now, Henry." As if the notion had just occurred to her, she quickened her rocking. "It will be enough to keep them out of ruining their reputations. Those two."

I drained the glass and fished a wrinkled cigarette from my pocket.

She looked away. "You might have to stay home for a while. Just until I can get on my feet. Do you think you could stay?"

"I guess I could miss another week."

She walked over to me and grabbed my arms. "Henry, I need you here. Stay for a few months, and we'll save up the money. Then you can go back and finish up. You're young. It will seem long, but it won't be."

"Mom, it's the middle of the semester."

"I know, I know. But you'll stay with your mother?" She stared till I nodded. "That's a good boy."

I ended up staying much longer than a few months. My return home lasted for a few years, and the interruption of my studies changed my life. My father hadn't left enough money for me to finish college, and my mother floundered with the girls, who were still in high school. So I got a job. My friend Oscar Love, back from a tour of duty with the navy, bought an abandoned store off Linnean Street with his savings and a loan from the Farmers & Merchants. With help from his father and brother, he converted the place into a bar with a stage barely big enough for a four-piece combo, and we moved the piano from my mother's house. A couple of guys from the area were good enough to round out a band. Jimmy Cummings played the drums, with George Knoll on bass or guitar. We called ourselves The Coverboys, because that's all we played, and when I wasn't pretending to be Gene Pitney or Frankie Valli, I would tend bar a few other nights of the week. The gig at Oscar's Bar got me out of the house; plus, the few extra dollars enabled me to help out the family. My old friends would drop in, applaud my return to playing piano, but I loathed performing. That first year back, Tess showed up with Brian or a girl-friend a couple of times. Seeing her there reminded me of the dreams I had deferred.

"You were a mystery man," Tess told me one night between sets. "Or mystery boy, I should say, back in grade school. As if you were somewhere totally different from the rest of us."

I shrugged my shoulders and played the first measures from "Strangers in the Night." She laughed and rolled her eyes. "Seriously, though, Henry, you were a stranger. Aloof. Above it all."

"Is that right? I certainly should have been nicer to you."

"Oh, go on." She was tipsy and grinning. "You were always in another world."

Her boyfriend beckoned, and she was gone. I missed her. She was about the only good thing that happened as the result of my forced homecoming, my reluctant return to the piano. Late that night, I went home thinking about her, wondering how serious her relationship was and how to steal her away from the guy with the déjà vu face.

Tending bar and playing piano kept me out late at night. My mother and sisters were long asleep, and I ate a cold dinner alone at three in the morning. That night, something stirred in the yard outside the kitchen window. A flash through the glass, visible for an instant, that looked sort of like a head of hair. I took my plate into the living room and turned on the television to *The Third Man* on the late, late movie. After the scene where Holly Martins first spies Harry Lime in the doorway, I fell asleep in my father's chair, only to wake up in the depths before dawn, sweating and cold, petrified that I was back in the forest again amid those devils.

ooking far ahead on the path, I spied her returning to camp, which set my mind at ease. She appeared between the trees, moving like a deer along the ridgeline. The incident at the library had left me eager to apologize, so I took a shortcut through the forest that would allow me to cut her off along her route. My mind buzzed with the story of the man in the yard. I hoped to tell her before the important parts vanished in the confusion. Speck would be mad, rightfully so, but her compassion would mollify any anger. As I drew near, she must have spotted me, for she took off in a sprint. Had I not hesitated before giving chase, perhaps I would have caught her, but the rough terrain defeated speed. In my haste, I snagged my toe on a fallen branch and landed facedown in the dirt. Spitting leaves and twigs, I looked up to see Speck had already made it into camp and was talking with Béka.

"She doesn't want to speak with you," the old toad said upon my arrival, and clamped his hand on my shoulder. A few of the elders—Igel, Ragno, Zanzara, and Blomma—had sidled next to him, forming a wall.

"But I need to talk to her."

Luchóg and Kivi joined the others. Smaolach walked toward the group from my right, his hands clenched and shaking. Onions approached from my left, a menacing toothsome smile on her face. Nine of them encircled me. Igel stepped inside the ring and jabbed a finger at my chest.

"You have violated our trust."

"What are you talking about?"

"She followed you, Aniday. She saw you with the man. You were to avoid any contact with them, yet there you were, trying to communicate with one of them." Igel pushed me to the ground, kicking up a cloud of rotten leaves. Humiliated, I quickly sprang back to my feet. My fear grew as the others hollered invectives.

"Do you know how dangerous that was?"

"Teach him a lesson."

"Do you understand we cannot be discovered?"

"So he won't forget again."

"They could come and capture us, and then we will never be free."

"Punish him."

Igel did not strike the first blow. From behind, a fist or a club smashed into my kidneys, and I arched my back. With my body thus exposed, Igel punched me squarely in the solar plexus, and I hunched forward. A line of drool spilled from my open mouth. They were all upon me at once like a pack of wild dogs bringing down wounded prey. The blows came from all directions, and initial shock gave way to pain. They scraped my face with their nails, ripped hunks of hair from my scalp, sank their teeth into my shoulder, drawing blood. A ropy arm choked my neck, shutting off the flow of air. I gagged and felt my gorge rise. Amid the fury, their eyes blazed with frenzy, and sheer hatred twisted their features. One by one, they peeled off, sated, and the pressure lessened, but those who remained kicked at my ribs, taunting me to get up, snarling and growling at me to fight back. I could not muster the strength. Before walking away, Béka stomped on my fingers, and Igel delivered a kick with each word of his final admonition: "Do not talk to people again."

I closed my eyes and stayed still. The sun shone down through the branches of the trees, warming my body. My joints ached from the fall, and my fingers swelled and throbbed. One eye was painted black and blue, and blood oozed from cuts and pooled beneath plum bruises. My mouth tasted of vomit and dirt, and I passed out in a rumpled heap.

Cool water on my cuts and bruises startled me awake, and my first vision was of Speck bent over me, wiping the blood from my face. Directly behind her stood Smaolach and Luchóg, their faces pinched with concern. Drops of my blood left a red patch on Speck's white sweater. When I tried to speak, she pressed the wet cloth to my lips.

"Aniday, I am so sorry. I did not want this to happen."

"We're sorry, too," Smaolach said. "But the law has a ruthless logic."

Chavisory poked out her head from behind Speck's shoulder. "I took no part in it."

"You should not have left me, Aniday. You should have trusted me."

I sat up slowly and faced my tormentors. "Why did you let them?"

"I took no part," Chavisory said.

Luchóg knelt beside Speck and spoke for all. "We had to do it, so that you will not ever forget. You spoke to the human, and if he caught you, you would be gone forever."

"Suppose I want to go back."

No one looked me in the eye. Chavisory hummed to herself while the others kept silent.

"I think that might have been my real father, Speck. From the other world. Or maybe it was a monster and a dream. But it wanted me to come into the house. I have been there before."

"Doesn't matter who he was," said Smaolach. "Father, mother, sister, brother, your Aunt Fanny's uncle. None of that matters. We're your family."

I spat out a mouthful of dirt and blood. "A family doesn't beat up one of its own, even if they have a good reason."

Chavisory shouted in my ear, "I didn't even touch you!" She danced spirals around the others.

"We were following rules," said Speck.

"I don't want to stay here. I want to go back to my real family."

"Aniday, you can't," Speck said. "They think you are gone these past ten years. You may look like you're eight, but you are almost eighteen. We are stuck in time."

Luchóg added, "You'd be a ghost to them."

"I want to go home."

Speck confronted me. "Listen, there are only three possible choices, and going home is not one of them."

"Right," Smaolach said. He sat down on a rotting tree stump and counted off the possibilities on his fingers. "One is that while you do not get old here, nor get deathly ill, you can die by accident. I remember one fellow who went a-walking a wintry day. He made a foolish calculation in his leap from the top of the bridge to the edge of the riverbank, and his jump was not jumpy enough. He fell into the river, went right through the ice, and drowned, frozen to death."

"Accidents happen," Luchóg added. "Long ago, you could find yourself eaten. Wolves and mountain lions prowled these parts. Did you ever hear of the one from up north who wintered out inside a cave and woke up spring-time next to a very hungry grizzly? A man can die by any chance imaginable."

"Two, you could be rid of us," Smaolach said, "by simply leaving. Just up and saunter off and go live apart and alone. We discourage that sort of attitude, mind you, for we need you here to help us find the next child. 'Tis harder than you think to pretend to be someone else."

"Besides, it is a lonesome life," said Chavisory.

"True," Speck agreed. "But you can be lonely with a dozen friends beside you."

"If you go that way, you're more likely to meet with a singular fate," Luchóg said. "Suppose you fell in a ditch and couldn't get up? Then where would you be?"

Said Smaolach, "Them fellows usually succumb, don't they, to some twist in the road? You lose your way in a blizzard. A black widow nips your thumb as you sleep. And no one to find the anecdote, the cowslip or the boiled frogs' eggs."

"Besides, where would you go that's any better than this?" Luchóg asked.

"I would go crazy being just by myself all the time," Chavisory added.

"Then," Luchóg told her, "you would have to make the change."

Speck looked beyond me, toward the treeline. "That's the third way. You find the right child on the other side, and you take her place."

"Now you're confusing the boy," said Smaolach. "First, you have to find a child, learn all about him. All of us watch and study him. From a distance, mind."

"It has to be somebody who isn't happy," Chavisory said.

Smaolach scowled at her. "Never mind that. We observe the child in teams. While certain people take down his habits, others study his voice."

"Start with the name," said Speck. "Gather all the facts: age, birthday, brothers and sisters."

Chavisory interrupted her. "I'd stay away from boys with dogs. Dogs are born suspicious."

"You have to know enough," Speck said, "so you can make people believe you are one of them. A child of their own."

Carefully rolling a cigarette, Luchóg said, "I've betimes thought that I'd look for a large family, with lots of kids and so on, and then pick the one in the middle that nobody'll miss or notice they're gone for a bit. Or if I forget some detail or am slightly off in my imitation, nobody is the wiser. Maybe number six of thirteen, or four of seven. Not as easy as it once was, now that mums and dads aren't having so many babies."

"I'd like to be a baby again," said Chavisory.

"Once you have made the choice," said Smaolach, "we go in and grab the child. He or she's got to be alone, or you'll be found out. Have you ever heard the tale of them ones in Russia or thereabouts, where they caught the lot of them stealing a tiny Cossack lad with pointy teeth, and them Cossacks took all our boys of the woods and burnt them up to a crisp?"

"Fire is a devil of a way to go," said Luchóg. "Did I ever tell you of the faery changeling caught snooping around the room of a girl she wished to replace? She hears the parents come in, and leaps in the closet, making the change right there in the room. At first, the parents thought nothing of it, when they opened the door and there she was, playing in the dark. Later that day, the real girl comes home, and what do you think? There's the two of them side by side, and our friend would have made it, but she hadn't yet learned how to speak like the little girl. So the mother says, 'Now which one of you is Lucy?' and the real Lucy says, 'I am,' and the other Lucy lets out a squawk to raise the dead. She had to jump out the second-floor window and start all over again."

Smaolach looked perplexed during his friend's story, scratching his head as if trying to recall an important detail. "Ah, there's a bit of magic, of course. We bind up the child in a web and lead him to the water."

Spinning on her heels, Chavisory shouted, "And there's the incantation. You mustn't forget that."

"In he goes like a baptism," Smaolach continued. "Out he comes, one of us. Never to leave except by one of three ways, and I would not give you my shoes for the first two."

Chavisory drew a circle in the dust with her bare toe. "Remember the German boy who played the piano? The one before Aniday."

With a short hiss, Speck grabbed Chavisory by the hair and pulled the poor creature to her. She sat on her chest and threw her hands upon her face, massaging and kneading Chavisory's skin like so much dough. The girl screamed and cried like a fox in a steel trap. When she had finished, Speck revealed a reasonable copy of her own sweet face on the visage of Chavisory. They looked like twins.

"You put me back," Chavisory complained.

"You put me back." Speck imitated her perfectly.

I could not believe what I was seeing.

"There's your future, little treasure. Behold the changeling," said Smaolach. "Going back to the past as yourself is not an option. But when you return as a changed person to their world, you get to stay there, grow up as one of them, live as one of them, more or less, grow old as time allows, and you'll do that yet, when your turn comes."

"My turn? I want to go home right now. How do I do it?"

"You don't," Luchóg said. "You have to wait until the rest of us have gone. There's a natural order to our world that mustn't be disturbed. One child for one changeling. When your time comes, you will find another child from a different family than what you left behind. You cannot go back whence you came."

"I'm afraid, Aniday, you're last in the line. You'll have to be patient."

Luchóg and Smaolach took Chavisory behind the honeysuckle and began to manipulate her face. The three of them laughed and carried on through the whole process. "Just make me pretty again," and "Let's get one of them magazines with the women's pictures," and "Hey, she looks like Audrey Hepburn." Eventually, they fixed her face, and she flew from their clutches like a bat.

Speck was unusually kind to me for the rest of that day, perhaps out of misplaced guilt for my beating. Her gentleness reminded me of my mother's touch, or what I thought I remembered. My own mother might as well have been the phantom, or any other fiction to be conjured. I was forgetting again, the distinction between memory and imagination blurring. The man I saw, could he be my father? I wondered. He appeared to have recognized me, but I was not his son, only a shadow from the woods. In the dead of night, I wrote down the story of the three ways in McInnes's notebook, hoping to understand it all in the future. Speck kept me company while the others slept. In the starlight, her cares had vanished from her face; even her eyes, usually so tired, radiated compassion.

"I am sorry they hurt you."

"It doesn't hurt," I whispered, stiff and sore.

"Life here has its compensations. Listen."

Low in a flyway, an owl swept between the trees, unrolling its wings on the hunt. Speck tensed, the fine hairs on her arms bristling.

"You will never get old," she said. "You won't have to worry about getting married or having babies or finding a job. No gray hair and wrinkles, no teeth falling out. You won't need a cane or a crutch."

We heard the owl descend and strike. The mouse screamed once; then life left it.

"Like children who never grow up," I said.

" 'The indifferent children of the earth.' " She let her sentence linger in the air. I fixed my eye upon a single star, hoping to sense the earth or see the heavens move. This trick of staring and drifting with the sky has cured my insomnia many times over the years, but not that night. Those stars were fixed and this globe creaked as if stuck in its rotation. Eyes lifted, chin pointing to the moon, Speck considered the night, though I had no idea what she was thinking.

"Was he my father, Speck?"

"I cannot tell you. Let go of the past, Aniday. It's like holding dandelions to the wind. Wait for the right moment, and the seeds will scatter away." She looked at me. "You should rest."

"I can't. My mind is filled with noises."

She pressed her fingers to my lips. "Listen."

Nothing stirred. Her presence, my own. "I can't hear a thing."

But she could hear a distant sound, and her gaze turned inward, as if transported to its source.

oving back home from college brought a kind of stupor to my daily
life, and my nights became a waking dread. If I wasn't pounding out yet
another imitation on the piano, I was behind the bar, tending to the
usual crowd with demons of their own. I had fallen into a routine at Oscar's
when the strangest of them all arrived and ordered a shot of whiskey. He slid
the glass against the rail and stared at it. I went on to the next customer,
poured a beer, sliced a lemon, and came back to the guy, and the drink was
sitting undisturbed. He was a pixy fellow, clean, sober, in a cheap suit and tie,
and as far as I could tell, he hadn't lifted his hands from his lap.

"What's the matter, mister? You haven't touched your drink."

"Would you give it to me on the house if I can make that glass move
without touching it?"

"What do you mean, 'move'? How far?"

"How far would it have to move for you to believe?"

"Not far." I was hooked. "Move it at all, and you have a deal."

He reached out his right hand to shake on it, and beneath him, the glass
started sliding slowly down the bar until it came to a halt about five inches to
his left. "A magician never reveals the secret to the trick. Tom McInnes."

"Henry Day," I said. "A lot of guys come in here with all sorts of tricks,
but that's the best I ever saw."

"I'll pay for this," McInnes said, putting a dollar on the bar. "But you
owe me another. In a fresh glass, if you please, Mr. Day."

He gulped the second shot and pulled the original glass back in front of him. Over the next several hours, he suckered four people with that same trick. Yet he never touched the first glass of whiskey. He drank for free all night. Around eleven, McInnes stood up to go home, leaving the shot on the bar.

"Hey, Mac, your drink," I called after him.

"Never touch the stuff," he said, slipping into a raincoat. "And I highly advise you not to drink it, either."

I lifted the glass to my nose for a smell.

"Leaded." He held up a small magnet he had concealed in his left hand. "But you knew that, right?"

Swirling the glass in my hand, I could now see the iron filings at the bottom.

"Part of my study of mankind," he said, "and our willingness to believe in what cannot be seen."

McInnes became a regular at Oscar's, coming in four or five times a week over the next few years, curiously intent on fooling the patrons with new tricks or puzzles. Sometimes a riddle or complicated math game involving picking a number, doubling it, adding seven, subtracting one's age and so forth, until the victim was right back where he'd started. Or a game involving matches, a deck of cards, a sleight of hand. The drinks he won were of small consequence, for his pleasure resulted from the gullibility of his neighbors. And he was mysterious in other ways. On those nights The Coverboys performed, McInnes sat close to the door. Sometimes between sets he'd come up to chat with the boys, and he hit it off with Jimmy Cummings, of all people, a fine example of the artless thinker. But if we played the wrong song, McInnes could be guaranteed to vanish. When we started covering The Beatles in '63 or '64, he would walk out each time at the opening bars of "Do You Want to Know a Secret?" Like a lot of drunks, McInnes became more himself after he'd had a few. He never acted soused. Not more loquacious or morose, merely more relaxed in his skin, and sharper around the edges. And he could consume mass quantities of alcohol at a sitting, more than anyone I have ever known. Oscar asked him one night about his strange capacity for drink.

"It's a matter of mind over matter. A cheap trick hinged upon a small secret."

"And what might that be?"

"I don't honestly know. It's a gift, really, and at the same time a curse. But I'll tell you, in order to drink so much, there has to be something behind the thirst."

"So what makes you thirsty, you old camel?" Cummings laughed.

"The insufferable impudence of today's youth. I would have tenure now were it not for callow freshmen and the slippery matter of publication."

"You were a professor?" I asked.

"Anthropology. My specialization was the use of mythology and theology as cultural rituals."

Cummings interrupted: "Slow down, Mac. I never went to college."

"How people use myth and superstition to explain the human condition. I was particularly interested in the pre-psychology of parenting and once started a book about rural practices in the British Isles, Scandinavia, and Germany."

"So you drink because of some old flame, then?" Oscar asked, turning the conversation back to its origins.

"I wish to God it was a woman." He spied the one or two females in the bar and lowered his voice. "No, women have been very good to me. It's the mind, boys. The relentless thinking machine. The incessant demands of tomorrow and the yesterdays piled up like a heap of corpses. It's this life and all those before it."

Oscar chewed on a reed. "Life before life?"

"Like reincarnation?" Cummings asked.

"I don't know about that, but I do know that a few special people re-member events from the past, events from too long ago. Put them under a spell, and you'd be amazed at the stories that come out from deep within. What happened a century ago, they talk about as if it were just yesterday. Or today."

" 'Under a spell'?" I asked.

"Hypnosis, the curse of Mesmer, the waking sleep. The transcendent trance."

Oscar looked suspicious. "Hypnosis. Another one of your party tricks."

"I've been known to put a few people under," said McInnes. "They've told tales from their own dreaming minds too incredible to believe, but with such feeling and authority that one is convinced that they were telling the truth. People do and see strange things when they're under."

Cummings jumped in. "I'd like to be hypnotized."

"Stay behind after the bar is closed, and I'll do it."

At two in the morning after the crowd left, McInnes ordered Oscar to dim the lights and asked George and me to stay absolutely quiet. He sat next to Jimmy and told him to close his eyes; then McInnes started speaking to him in a low, modulated voice, describing restful places and peaceful circumstances in such vivid detail that I'm surprised we all didn't fall asleep. McInnes ran a few tests, checking on whether Jimmy was under.

"Raise your right arm straight out in front of you. It's made of the world's strongest steel, and no matter how hard you try, you cannot bend it."

Cummings stuck out his right arm and could not flex it; nor, for that matter, could Oscar or George or I when we tried, for it felt like a real iron bar. McInnes ran through a few more tests, then he started asking questions to which Cummings replied in a dead monotone. "Who's your favorite musi-cian, Jimmy?"

"Louis Armstrong."

We laughed at the secret admission. In his waking life, he would have claimed some rock drummer like Charlie Watts of the Stones, but never Satchmo.

"Good. When I touch your eyes, you'll open them, and for the next few minutes you'll be Louis Armstrong."

Jimmy was a skinny white boy, but when he popped open those baby blues, the transformation came instantaneously. His mouth twisted into Armstrong's famous wide smile, which he wiped from time to time with an imaginary handkerchief, and he spoke in a gravelly skat voice. Even though Jimmy never sang on any of our numbers, he did a passing fair rendition of some old thing called "I'll Be Glad When You're Dead, You Rascal You," and then, using his thumb as a mouthpiece and his fingers as the horn, blatted out a jazz bridge. Normally Cummings hid behind his drums, but he jumped up on a table and would be entertaining the room still, had he not slipped on a slick of beer and fallen to the floor.

McInnes raced to him. "When I count to three and snap my fingers," he said to the slouching body, "you'll wake up, feeling refreshed as if you have slept soundly each night this week. I want you to remember, Jimmy, that when you hear someone say Satchmo, you'll have the uncontrollable urge to sing out a few bars as Louis Armstrong. Can you remember that?"

"Uh-huh," Cummings said from his trance.

"Good, but you won't remember anything else except this dream. Now, I'm going to snap my fingers, and you'll wake up, happy and refreshed."

A goofy grin smeared on his face, he woke and blinked at each one of us, as if he could not imagine why we were all staring at him. Upon serial questioning, he recalled nothing about the past half-hour.

"And you don't remember," Oscar asked, "Satchmo?"

Cummings began singing "Hello, Dolly!" and suddenly stopped himself.

"Mr. Jimmy Cummings, the hippest man alive," George laughed.

We all gassed Cummings over the next few days, working in "Satchmo" now and again until the magic words wore off. But the events of that night played over in my imagination. For weeks afterward, I pestered McInnes for more information on how hypnosis worked, but all he could say was that "the subconscious rises to the surface and allows repressed inclinations and memories free play." Dissatisfied with his answers, I drove over to the library in town on my days off and submerged myself in research. From the sleep temples of ancient Egypt through Mesmer and on to Freud, hypnosis has been around in one form or another for millennia, with philosophers and scientists arguing over its validity. A piece from *The International Journal of Clinical and Experimental Hypnosis* settled the debate for me: "It is the patient, not the therapist, who is in control of the depth to which the imagination reaches the subconscious." I tore the quote from the page and tucked it into my wallet, reading the words now and again as if repeating a mantra.

Convinced that I could manage my own imagination and subconscious, I finally asked McInnes to hypnotize me. As if he knew the way back to a forgotten land, McInnes could tap into my repressed life and tell me who I was, where I came from. And if it was merely truthful and revealed my German roots, the story would be derided by anyone who heard it as a fantastical delusion. We had all heard it before: In a former life, I was Cleopatra, Shakespeare, the Genghis Khan.

What would be harder to laugh off or explain was my life as a hobgoblin in the forest—especially that awful August night when I became a changeling and stole the boy away. Ever since my time with the Days, I had been carefully erasing every vestige of the changeling life. It could be dangerous if, under hypnosis, I would not be able to recall anything about Henry Day's childhood prior to age seven. My mother's tales of Henry's childhood had been so often repeated that I not only believed she was talking about me, but at times thought I remembered that life. Such created memories are made of glass.

McInnes knew my half-story, what he had gathered from hanging around the bar. He had heard me talk about my mother and sisters, my aborted college career. I even confessed to him my crush on Tess Wodehouse one night when she came round with her boyfriend. But he had no clue about the other side of my tale. Anything I accidentally divulged would have to be rationalized away. My desire for the truth about the German boy trumped my fear of being unmasked as a changeling.

The last drunk staggered away for the night, and Oscar closed the cash register and hung up his apron. On his way out, he threw me the keys to lock the doors while McInnes turned off all the lights except for a lamp at the end of the bar. The boys said their good-byes, and McInnes and I were alone in the room. Panic and apprehension clawed at me. Suppose I said something about the real Henry Day and gave myself away? What if he tried to blackmail me or threatened to expose me to the authorities? The thought crossed my mind: I could kill him, and nobody would even know he was gone. For the first time in years, I felt myself reverting to something wild, an animal, all instinct. But the moment he began, panic subsided.

In the dark and empty bar, we sat across from each other at a small table, and listening as McInnes droned on, I felt made of stone. His voice came from a distance above and beyond me, and he controlled my actions and feelings with his words, which shaped my very existence. Giving in to the voice was a bit like falling in love. Submit, let go. My limbs were pulled by tremendous gravity, as if being sucked out of space and time. Light disappeared, replaced by the sudden snap of a projected beam. A movie had begun on the white wall of my mind. The film itself, however, lacked both a narrative and any distinct visual style that would allow one to draw conclusions or make inferences. No story, no plot, just character and sensation. A face appears, speaks, and I am scared. A cold hand wraps around my ankle. A shout is followed by discordant notes from the piano. My cheek pressed against a chest, a hand hugging my head close to the breast. At some conscious level, I glimpsed a boy, who quickly turned his face from me. Whatever happened next resulted from the clash of inertia and chaos. The major chords were altogether ignored.

The first thing I did when McInnes snapped me out of the trance was to look at the clock—four in the morning. As Cummings had described the sensation, I, too, felt curiously refreshed, as if I had slept for eight hours, yet my sticky shirt and the matted hair at my temples belied that possibility. McInnes seemed totally worn and wrung-out. He pulled himself a draft and drank it down like a man home from the desert. In the dim light of the empty bar, he eyed me with incredulity and fascination. I offered him a Camel, and we sat smoking in the dead of morning.

"Did I say anything revealing?" I asked at last.

"Do you know any German?"

"A smattering," I replied. "Two years in high school."

"You were speaking German like the Brothers Grimm."

"What did I say? What did you make of it?"

"I'm not sure. What's a *Wechselbalg*?"

"I never heard of the word."

"You cried out as if something terrible was happening to you. Something about *der Teufel*. The devil, right?"

"I never met the man."

"And the *Feen*. Is that a fiend?"

"Maybe."

"*Der Kobolden*? You shrieked when you saw them, whatever they are. Any ideas?"

"None."

"*Entführend?*"

"Sorry."

"I could not tell what you were trying to say. It was a mash of languages. You were with your parents, I think, or calling out for your parents, and it was all in German, something about *mit, mit*—that's 'with,' right? You wanted to go with them?"

"But my parents aren't German."

"The ones you were remembering are. Someone came along, the fiends or the devils or *der Kobolden*, and they wanted to take you away."

I swallowed. The scene was coming back to me.

"Whoever or whatever it was grabbed you, and you were crying out for Mama and Papa and *das Klavier*."

"The piano."

"I never heard anything like it, and you said you were stolen away. And I asked, 'When?' and you said something in German I could not understand, so I asked you again, and you said, 'Fifty-nine,' and I said, 'That can't be. That's only six years ago.' And you said, clear as a bell, 'No . . . 1859.' "

McInnes blinked his eyes and looked closely at me. I was shaking, so I lit another cigarette. We stared at the smoke, not saying a word. He finished first and ground out the butt so hard that he nearly broke the ashtray.

"I don't know what to say."

"Know what I think?" McInnes asked. "I think you were remembering a past life. I think you may have once upon a time been a German boy."

"I find that hard to believe."

"Have you ever heard of the changeling myth?"

"I don't believe in fairy tales."

"Well . . . when I asked you about your father, all you said was, 'He knows.' " McInnes yawned. Morning was quite nearly upon us. "What do you think he knew, Henry? Do you think he knew about the past?"

I knew, but I did not say. There was coffee at the bar and eggs in a miniature refrigerator. Using the hot plate in the back, I made us breakfast, settling my wayward thoughts by concentrating on simple tasks. A kind of hazy, dirty light seeped in through the windows at dawn. I stood behind the counter; he sat in front on his usual stool, and we ate our scrambled eggs and drank our coffee black. At that hour the room looked worn and pitiful, and McInnes's eyes tired and vacant, the way my father had appeared the last time we met.

He put on his hat and shrugged into his coat. An awkward pause between us let me know that he would not be coming back. The night had been too raw and strange for the old professor. "Good-bye, and good luck."

As his hand turned the knob, I called out for him to wait. "What was my name," I asked, "in this so-called former life of mine?"

He did not bother to turn around. "You know, I never thought to ask."

CHAPTER 16

When a gun goes off on a cold winter's day, the retort echoes through the forest for miles around and every living creature stops to look and listen. The first gunshot of hunting season startled and put the faeries on alert. Scouts fanned out along the ridge, searching for orange or camouflage vests or hats, listening for the trudge of men seeking out deer, pheasant, turkey, grouse, rabbit, fox, or black bear. Sometimes the hunters brought their dogs, dumb and beautiful— mottled pointers, feathery setters, blueticks, black-and-tans, retrievers. The dogs could be more dangerous than their owners. Unless we masked our scent along every path, the dogs could smell us out.

My great fear in setting out alone is the chance of meeting up with a stray or worse. Years later, when we were fewer in number, a pack of hunting dogs picked up our trail and surprised us at rest in a shady grove. They raced our way, a stream of flashing sharp teeth and howling menace, and we moved as one by instinct, scrambling toward the safety of a bramble thicket. With each stride we took in retreat, the dogs gained two in pursuit. They were an army with knives drawn, hollering a primal battle cry, and we escaped only by sacrificing our bare skin to the tangle of thorns. We were lucky when they stopped at the edge of the thicket, confused and whimpering.

But on this winter day, the dogs were far away. All we heard was the yelp, the random shot, the muttered curse, or the kill. I once saw a duck fall out of the sky, instantly changing from a stretched-forward silhouette to a pinwheel of feathers that landed with a clap on the water. Poaching had disappeared from these hills and valleys by the middle of the decade, so we had to worry only during the hunting season, which corresponded roughly with the late fall and winter holidays. The brightness of trees gave way to bareness, then to bitter cold, and we began to listen for humans in the glens and the crack of the gun. Two or three of us went out while the other faeries hunkered down, buried beneath blankets under a coat of fallen leaves, or in holes, or hid in hollow trees. We did our best to become unseeable, as if we did not exist. The early arrival of night or dripping-wet days were our only respite from the tense boredom of hiding. The odor of our constant fear mingled with the rot of November.

Back to back to back in a triangle, Igel, Smaolach, and I sat watch upon the ridge, the morning sun buffered by low dense clouds, the air pregnant with snow. Ordinarily, Igel wanted nothing to do with me, not since that day years before when I nearly betrayed the clan by trying to speak with the man. Two sets of footsteps approached from the south; one heavy, crashing through the brush, the other soft. The humans stepped into a meadow. An air of impatience hung about the man, and the boy, about seven or eight years old, looked anxious to please. The father carried his shotgun, ready to fire. The son's gun was broken apart and awkward to carry as he struggled out of the brush. They wore matching plaid jackets and billed caps with the earflaps down against the chill. We leaned forward to listen to their conversation in the stillness. With practice and concentration over the years, I was now able to decipher their speech.

"I'm cold," said the boy.

"It'll toughen you up. Besides, we haven't found what we came for."

"We haven't even seen one all day."

"They're out here, Osk."

"I've only seen them in pictures."

"When you see the real thing," said the man, "aim for the little bugger's

heart." He motioned for the boy to follow, and they headed east into the shadows.

"Let's go," said Igel, and we began to trail them, keeping ourselves hidden at a distance. When they paused, we paused, and at our second such stop,
I tugged on Smaolach's sleeve.

"What are we doing?"

"Igel thinks he may have found one."

We moved on, resting again when the quarry paused.

"One what?" I asked.

"A child."

They led us on a circuitous route along empty pathways. No prey appeared, they never fired their weapons, and they hadn't said more than a few
words. Over lunch, they maintained an uncomfortable silence, and I could not
understand how these two were of any interest at all. The sullen pair headed
back to a green pickup parked on the slope beside the road, and the boy
stepped into the passenger's side. As he crossed the front of the truck, the
father muttered, "That was a fucking mistake." Igel scrutinized the pair with
savage intensity, and as the truck pulled away, he read out the license plate
numbers, committing them to memory. Smaolach and I lagged behind Igel as
he marched home, intent on his private ruminations.

"Why did we track them all day? What do you mean, he found a child?"

"Them clouds are ready to burst." Smaolach studied the darkening sky.
"You can smell it coming."

"What is he going to do?" I yelled. Up ahead, Igel stopped in his tracks
and waited for us to catch up.

"How long have you been with us, Aniday?" Igel asked. "What does
your stone calendar say?"

Ever since that day when they turned on me, I had been wary of Igel,
and had learned to be deferential. "I don't know. December? November?
1966?"

He rolled his eyes, bit his lip, and continued. "I've been looking and waiting since you arrived, and it's my turn now and that boy may be the one. When you and Speck are in town with your books, keep an eye out for that green truck. If you see it again, or the boy or the father, let me know. If you have the courage to follow them and find where he lives or goes to school, or where the father works, or if he has a mother, sister, brother, friend, you let me know."

"Of course I will, Igel. I'd be happy to spy on him at the library."

He bade Smaolach to walk with him, and I brought up the rear. A bitterly freezing rain began to fall, and I ran the last few moments to escape from being drenched. The warren excavated by Igel and Luchóg over the years proved an ideal shelter on such blustery nights, although most of the time claustrophobia forced me out. The cold and damp drove me into the tunnels, and with my palms I felt along in the darkness until I sensed the presence of others.

"Who's there?" I called out. No answer, only a furtive muffled sound.

I called out again.

"Go away, Aniday." It was Béka.

"You go away, you old fart. I've just come in from the rain."

"Go back the way you came. This hole is occupied."

I tried to reason with him. "Let me pass by, and I'll sleep somewhere else."

A girl screamed and so did he. "She bit my damn finger."

"Who is there with you?"

Speck shouted out in the darkness. "Just go, Aniday. I'll follow you out."

"Vermin." Béka cursed and let her go. I reached out in the darkness and she found my hand. We crawled back to the surface. Stinging rain gathered in her hair and flattened it against her skull. A thin layer of ice caked over her head like a helmet, and the drops collected on our eyelashes and streamed down our faces. We stood still, unable to say anything to each other. She looked as if she wished to explain or apologize, but her lips trembled and her teeth knocked and chattered. Grabbing my hand again, she led me to the shelter of another tunnel. We crawled in and crouched near to the surface, out of the rain, yet not in the cold earth. I could not stand the silence, so I yammered on about the father and son we had followed and Igel's instructions. Speck took it all in without speaking a word.

"Squeeze out that water from your hair," she said. "It will dry faster that way and stop dripping down your nose."

"What does he mean, he found a child?"

"I'm cold," she said, "and tired and sick and sore. Can't we talk about this in the morning, Aniday?"

"What did he mean that he's been waiting since I got here?"

"He's next. He's going to change places with that boy." She pulled off her coat. Even in the darkness, her white sweater threw back enough light to allow me a better sense of her presence.

"I don't understand why he gets to go."

She laughed at my naïveté. "This is a hierarchy. Oldest to youngest. Igel makes all the decisions because he has seniority, and he gets to go next."

"How old is he?"

She calculated in her mind. "I don't know. He's probably been here about one hundred years."

"You're kidding." The number nearly fried my brain. "How old are all the others? How old are you?"

"Will you please let me sleep? We can figure this out in the morning. Now, come here and warm me up."

In the morning, Speck and I talked at length about the history of the faeries, and I wrote it all down, but those papers, like many others, are in ashes now. The best I can do is re-create from memory what we recorded that day, which was far from truly accurate to begin with, since Speck herself did not know the full story and could merely summarize or speculate. Still, I wish I had my notes, for the conversation was years ago, and my whole life seems to be nothing more than reconstructing memories.

That my good friends could one day leave profoundly saddened me. The cast of characters, in fact, constantly revolves, but so slowly over time that they seemed permanent players. Igel was the oldest, followed by Béka, Blomma, Kivi, and the twins, Ragno and Zanzara, who came late in the nineteenth century. Onions arrived in the auspicious year of 1900. Smaolach and Luchóg were the sons of two families who had emigrated from the same village in Ireland in the first decades of the twentieth century, and Chavisory was a French Canadian whose parents had died in the great influenza epidemic of 1918. Besides myself, Speck was the baby, having been stolen as a four-year-old in the second year of the Great Depression.

"I was a lot younger than most of the others when I made the change," she said. "Except for the twins. From the beginning, there have been twins in this line, and they're impossible to take unless very young. And we never take babies. Too much trouble."

Vague memories stirred the sauce of my thoughts. Where had I known twins before?

"Luchóg named me, because I was a speck of a girl when they snatched me. Everyone else is ahead of me in line for the change, except you. You're the bottom of the totem pole."

"And Igel has been waiting for his turn for a whole century?"

"He's seen a dozen make the change and had to bide his time. Now we're all in line behind him." The mention of such a wait caused her to shut her eyes. I leaned against a tree trunk, feeling helpless for her and hopeless for myself. Escape was not a constant thought, but occasionally I allowed myself to dream of leaving the group and rejoining my family. Dejected, Speck hung her head, dark hair covering her eyes, her lips parted, drawing in air as if each breath was a chore.

"So what do we do now?" I asked.

She looked up. "Help Igel."

I noticed that her once-white sweater was fraying at the collar and the sleeves, and I resolved to look for a replacement as we searched for the boy.

In glowing red letters, the sign out front read OSCAR'S BAR, and alone in the lot behind the building, Béka found the hunter's green pickup. He and Onions jumped into its bed and rode, undetected by the drunken driver, to the man's house out in the country. She laughed when she read the name off the mailbox: LOVE'S. They memorized the location, sharing the good news with us later that night. With the information in hand, Igel set in motion our reconnaissance and assigned shifts of teams to watch the boy and his family to learn their movements and habits. He instructed us to pay close attention to the boy's character and demeanor.

"I want a detailed account of his life. Does he have any brothers or sisters? Uncles or aunts? Grammy and Gramps? Does he have any friends? What sort of games does he play? Any hobbies or spare-time activities? Find all there is to know about his relationship with his parents. How do they treat him? Is he inclined to daydream? To wander about by himself in the woods?"

I transcribed his words in McInnes's composition book and wondered how we might undertake such a task. Igel walked over and stood in front of me, glaring down at my scribbling.

"You," he said, "will be our scrivener. I want a complete record. You are to be his biographer. Everyone else can tell Aniday what they learn. Don't come pestering me with every detail. When the story is complete, you can tell it. This will be the most perfect change in our history. Find me a new life."

Before I saw the child again, I felt as if I knew him as well as myself. Chavisory, for instance, found out that he was named after his uncle Oscar. Smaolach could do a passing imitation of his voice, and Kivi had applied an unknown calculus to plot out his height, weight, and general body type. After years of mere self-preservation and maintenance, the faeries' industry and devotion to the task bordered on the fanatic.

I was assigned to watch for him at the library, but I rarely bothered to look for him there, and it is by chance that he appeared at all. His mother had dragged the poor child along and left him alone on the small playground out front. From my hiding place, direct observation was impossible, so I watched his reflection in the plate-glass windows across the street, which distorted his appearance, making him smaller and somehow transparent.

The dark-haired, beetle-browed boy sang quietly to himself as he climbed up and swooshed off the slide over and over again. His nose ran, and every time he mounted the stairs he'd wipe the snot with the back of his hand, then wipe his hand on his greasy corduroys. When he tired of the sliding board, he sauntered over to the swings to pump and pull himself into the clear blue sky. His blank expression never changed, and the song under his breath never faltered. I watched him for nearly an hour, and in that whole time, he expressed absolutely no emotion, content to play alone until his mother came. A thin smile creased his face when she arrived, and without a word he jumped down from the swing, grabbed her hand, and off they went. Their behavior and interaction baffled me. Parents and children take such everyday moments for granted, as if there is an endless supply.

Had my parents forgotten me completely? The man who cried after me that long-ago morning surely had been my father, and I resolved to go see him, my mother, and my baby sisters one day soon. Perhaps after we had abducted the poor misfortunate bastard from the playground. The swing stopped, and the early June day faded. A swallow appeared, chasing insects in the air above the iron bars, and all of my desires were tipped by the wings as the bird scissored away into the milky dusk. I felt sorry for the boy, although I knew that changing places was the natural order. His capture would mean Igel's release and one more step toward the head of the line for me.

The child was an easy mark; his parents would barely be aware of the change. He had few friends, caused neither excitement nor alarm as a student, and was so ordinary as to be almost invisible. Ragno and Zanzara, who had taken residence in the family's attic for months, reported that aside from peas and carrots, the boy ate anything, preferred chocolate milk with his meals, slept on rubber sheets, and spent a lot of time in the living room watching a small box that let one know when to laugh and how to schedule bedtime. Our boy was a good sleeper, too, up to twelve hours at a stretch on weekends. Kivi and Blomma reported that he liked to play outdoors in a sandbox by the house, where he had set up an elaborate tableau of small plastic dolls in blue and gray. The doleful fellow seemed satisfied to go on living life as it is. I envied him.

No matter how we pestered him, Igel refused to hear our report. We had been spying on Oscar for over a year, and everyone was ready for the change. I was running out of paper in McInnes's book, and one more dispatch from the field would not only be a waste of time, but a waste of precious paper as well. Haughty, distracted, and burdened by the responsibilities of leadership, Igel kept to himself, as if he both yearned for and flinched at the possibility of freedom. His normally stoic disposition changed to a general peevishness. Kivi came to dinner once with a red welt under her eye.

"What happened to you?"

"That son of a bitch. Igel hit me, and all I asked him was if he was ready. He thought I meant ready to go, but all I meant was for dinner."

No one knew what to say to her.

"I can't wait till he leaves. I am sick and tired of the old crab. Maybe the new boy will be nice."

I stood up from the meal and stormed through the camp, looking for Igel, resolving to confront him, but he was not to be found in his usual places. I poked my head into the entranceway of one of his tunnels and called out, but no answer. Perhaps he had gone out to spy on the boy. Nobody knew where he might be found, so I spent several hours walking in circles, until chancing upon him alone down by the river, where he was staring at his reflection in the broken surface of water. He looked so alone that I forgot my anger and quietly crouched down beside him.

"Igel? Are you all right?" I addressed the image on the water.

"Do you remember," he asked, "your life before this life?"

"Vaguely. In my dreams, sometimes my father and mother and a sister, or maybe two. And a woman in a red coat. But no, not really."

"I have been gone so long. I'm not sure I know how to go back."

"Speck says there are three choices but only one ending for us all."

"Speck." He spat out her name. "She is a foolish child, almost as foolish as you, Aniday."

"You should read our report. It will help you make the change."

"I will be glad to be rid of such fools. Have her come see me in the morning. I don't want to talk to you, Aniday. Have Béka make your report."

He stood up, brushed dirt from the seat of his pants, and walked away. I hoped he would disappear forever.

CHAPTER 17

M y long-forgotten history peeked out from behind the curtains. The questions McInnes posed during hypnosis had dredged up memories that had been repressed for more than a century, and fragments of those subconscious recollections began intruding into my life. We would be performing our second-rate imitation of Simon and Garfunkel when an unexpected Germanism would leap out of my mouth. The boys in the band thought I was tripping, and we'd have to start over after a brief apology to the audience. Or I'd be seducing a young woman and find that her face had morphed into the visage of a changeling. A baby would cry and I'd wonder if it was human or a bundle of holy terror that had been left on the doorstep. A photograph of six-year-old Henry Day's first day of school would remind me of all I was not. I'd see myself superimposed over the image, my face reflected in the glass, layered over his face, and wonder what had become of him, what had become of me. No longer a monster, but not Henry Day either. I suffered trying to remember my own name, but that German boy stole away every time I drew near.

The only remedy for this obsession was to substitute another. Whenever my mind dwelled on the distant past, I would force myself to think of music, running alternative fingerings and the cycle of fifths in my mind, humming to myself, pushing dark thoughts away with a song. I flirted with the notion of becoming a composer again even as college aspirations faded while another two years slipped by. In the seemingly random sounds of everyday life, I began to abstract patterns, which grew to measures, which became movements. Often I would go back to Oscar's after a few hours' sleep, put on a pot of coffee, and scribble the notations resonating in my head. With solely a piano available, I had to imagine an orchestra in that empty barroom, and those early scores echo my chaotic confusion over who I am. The unfinished compositions were tentative steps back to the past, to my true nature. I spent ages looking for the sound, reshaping it, and tossing it away, for composition was as elusive at the time as my own name.

The bar was my studio most mornings. Oscar arrived around lunchtime, and George and Jimmy usually showed up midafternoon for rehearsal and a few beers—barely enough time for me to cover up my work. Halfheartedly, I plunked away at the piano before our practice was to begin on an early summer afternoon in '67. George, Jimmy, and Oscar experimented with a few chord changes and rhythms, but they were mostly smoking and drinking. The area kids had been out of school for two weeks and were already bored, riding their bicycles up and down Main Street. Their heads and shoulders slid across the view through the windowpanes. Lewis Love's green pickup truck pulled up outside, and a moment later the bar door swung open, sending in a crush of humid air. His shoulders slumped with exhaustion, Lewis stopped in the threshold, numb and dumb. Setting down his horn, Oscar walked over to talk with his brother. Their conversation was too soft to be overheard, but the body gives away its sorrows. Lewis hung his head and brought his hand to the bridge of his nose as if to hold back tears, and George and Jimmy and I watched from our chairs, not knowing quite what to say or do. Oscar led his brother to the bar and poured him a tall shot, which Lewis downed in a single swig. He wiped his mouth on his sleeve and bent over like a question mark, his forehead resting on the rail, so we crowded around our friends.

"His son is missing," Oscar said. "Since last night. The police and fire and rescue are out looking for him, but they haven't found him. He's only eight years old, man."

"What does he look like?" George asked. "What's his name? How long has he been gone? Where did you last see him?"

Lewis straightened his shoulders. "His name is Oscar, after my brother here. About the averagest-looking kid you could find. Brown hair, brown eyes, about so high." He held out his hand and dropped it roughly four feet above the ground.

"When did he disappear?" I asked.

"He was wearing a baseball shirt and short pants, dark blue—his mother thinks. And high-top Chuck Taylors. He was out back of the house, playing after dinner last night. It was still light out. And then he vanished." He turned to his brother. "I tried calling you all over the place."

Oscar pursed his lips and shook his head. "I'm so sorry, man. I was out getting high."

George began walking to the door. "No time for recriminations. We've got a missing kid to find."

Off we went to the woods. Oscar and Lewis rode together in the cab of the pickup, and George, Jimmy, and I sat in the bed, where there was the residual odor of manure baking in the heat. The truck bumped and rattled along a firebreak cut through the timberline, and we ground to a stop in a cloud of dust. The search and rescue team had parked in a glen about a mile due west from my house, about as far into the forest as they could manage to drive the township's sole fire engine. The captain of the fire department leaned against the big rig. He pulled on a bottle of cola in enormous gulps, his face like an alarm against his starched white shirt. Our party got out of the pickup, and I was overwhelmed by the sweet smell of honeysuckle nearby. Bees patrolled among the flowers, and as we walked toward the captain, they lazily inspected us. Grasshoppers, panicked by our footfall, whirred ahead in the tall grass. Along the edge of the clearing, a tangle of wild raspberries and poison ivy reminded me of the double-edged nature of the forest. I followed the boys down a makeshift path, looking over my shoulder at the captain and his red truck until they vanished from sight.

A bloodhound bayed in the distance, taking up a scent. We trudged along single file for several hundred yards, and the dark shade cast by the canopy gave the appearance of dusk in the shank of the afternoon. Every few moments, someone would call out for the boy, and his name hung in the air before dissipating in the warm half-light. We were chasing shadows where no shadows could be seen. The group halted when we reached the top of a small rise.

"This is getting us nowhere," Oscar said. "Why don't we spread out?"

Though I loathed the idea of being alone in the forest, I could not counter his logic without seeming a coward.

"Let's meet back here at nine." With an air of determined sobriety, Oscar studied the face of his watch, following the sweep of the second hand, counting off moments to himself. We waited and watched our own time go by.

"Four thirty," he said at last.

"I've got four thirty-five," said George.

And almost simultaneously, I said, "Twenty after."

"Twenty-five of five," said Jimmy.

Lewis shook his wrist, removed his watch, and held the timepiece to his ear. "That's funny—my watch has stopped." He stared at its face. "Seven thirty. That's right around when I saw him last."

Each of us looked at the others for the way out of this temporal confusion. Oscar resumed his clock watching.

"Okay, okay, on my signal, set your watches. It is now four thirty-five."

We fiddled with the stems and dials. I wondered if the time was such an issue after all.

"Here's the plan. Lewis and I will go this way. Henry, you go in the opposite direction. George and Jimmy, you head off opposite to each other." He indicated by means of hand signals the four points of the compass. "Mark your trail to find your way back. Every couple hundred feet, break a branch on the same side of your path, and let's meet back here at nine. It'll be getting dark by then. Of course, if you find him before that, go back to the fire truck."

We went our separate ways, and the sound of my friends tramping through the brush receded. I had not dared enter the woods since changing lives with Henry Day. The tall trees hemmed in the pathway, and the humid air felt like a blanket that smelled of rot and decay. With each step I took, cracking twigs and crunching leaves, my sound reinforced my solitude. When I stopped, the noise ceased. I'd call for the boy, but halfheartedly, not expecting a reply. The stillness brought back a forgotten sensation, the memory of my wildness, and with it the ache of being trapped, timeless, in this perilous world. Twenty minutes into my search, I sat down on the fallen trunk of a scrub pine. My shirt, damp with perspiration, clung to my skin, and I took out a handkerchief to mop my brow. Far away, a woodpecker hammered on a tree, and nuthatches scrabbled down tree trunks, pipping their staccato signals. Along one limb of the dead pine, a file of ants raced back and forth, carrying a mysterious cargo in one direction as others headed back to the food source. Amid the litter of fallen leaves, small red flowers poked their pin-size heads from clusters of silvery moss. I lifted a log, and a rotting wetness lay beneath it, pill bugs curled into balls and long-legged spiders maddened at the sudden disruption of their lives. Fat, glistening worms burrowed into holes on the bottom of the log, and I tried to imagine what hidden chambers existed in the decay, what life was going on unbeknownst to me. I lost track of the time. A glance at my watch startled me, for nearly two hours had wasted away. I stood up, called out the boy's name once, and, hearing no reply, resumed my hunt. Moving deeper into the darkness, I was entranced by the random arrangement of trunks and limbs, green leaves as plentiful as raindrops. My every step was new yet familiar, and I expected to be startled by something sudden, but it was as quiet as a deep sleep. There was nothing in the woods, no sign of my past, scant life beyond the growing trees and plants, the occasional stir of the inscrutable tiny animals hidden in the rot and decay. I stumbled upon a small creek gurgling over stones, meandering nowhere. Suddenly very thirsty, I dipped my hands into the water and drank.

The current rolled over a bed dotted with stones and rocks. On the surface, the stones were dry, dull, and impenetrable, but at the waterline and below, the water changed the stone, revealing facets and extraordinarily rich colors and infinite variety. Millennia of interplay had worn and polished the rocks, made them beautiful, and the stones had changed the water as well, altered its flow and pace, made turbulent its stilled predisposition. Symbiosis made the creek what it was. One without the other would change everything. I had come out of this forest, had been there for a long, long time, but I also lived in the world as a very real person. My life as a human and my life among the changelings made me what I was. Like the water and the rock, I was this and that. Henry Day. As the world knows him, there is no other, and this revelation filled me with warmth and pleasure. The rocks along the bottom of the creek suddenly appeared to me as if a line of notes, and I could hear the pattern in my head. Searching my pockets for a pencil to copy it down before the notes disappeared, I heard a stirring among the trees behind me, footsteps racing through the brush.

"Who's there?" I asked, and whatever it was stopped moving. I tried to make myself short and inconspicuous by crouching in the culvert cut by the creek, but hiding made it impossible to see the source of danger. In the tension of anticipation, sounds that had gone unnoticed became amplified. Crickets sang under rocks. A cicada cried and then went silent. I was at odds whether to run away or stay and capture the notes in the water. A breeze through the leaves, or something breathing? Slowly at first, the footsteps resumed, then the creature bolted, crashing through the leaves, running away from me, the air whispering and falling quiet. When it had departed, I convinced myself that a deer had been startled by my presence, or perhaps a hound that had picked up my scent by mistake. The disturbance unnerved me, so I quickly traced my way back to the clearing. I was the first one there, fifteen minutes ahead of our planned rendezvous.

George arrived next, face flushed with exertion, his voice less than a rasp from calling for the boy. He collapsed in exhaustion, his jeans emitting puffs of dust.

"No luck?" I asked.

"Do you think? I am dragging and didn't see a damn thing. You don't have a square on you?"

I produced two cigarettes and lit his, then mine. He closed his eyes and smoked. Oscar and Lewis showed up next, similarly defeated. They had run out of ways to say so, but the worry slackened their pace, bowed their heads, clouded their eyes. We waited for another fifteen minutes for Jimmy Cummings, and when he failed to appear, I began to wonder if another search party was in order.

At 9:30, George asked, "Where is Cummings?"

The residual twilight gave way to a starry night. I wished we had thought to bring flashlights. "Maybe we should go back to where the police are."

Oscar refused. "No, someone should wait here for Jimmy. You go, Henry. It's a straight shot, dead on."

"C'mon, George, go with me."

He raised himself to the standing position. "Lead on, Macduff."

Up the trail, we could see red and blue lights flashing against the treetops and bouncing into the night sky. Despite his aching feet, George hurried us along, and when we were nearly there, we could hear the static shout over the walkie-talkies, sense something wrong in the air. We jogged into a surreal scene, the clearing bathed in lights, fire engines idling, dozens of people milling about. A man in a red baseball cap loaded a pair of bloodhounds into the back of his pickup. I was startled to see Tess Wodehouse, her white nurse's uniform glowing in the gloom, embracing another young woman and stroking her hair. Two men lifted a dripping canoe to the roof of a car and strapped it down. Patterns emerged as if time stood still, and all could be seen at once. Firemen and policemen, their backs to us, formed a half ring around the back of the ambulance.

The chief pivoted slowly, as if averting his gaze from the somber paramedics invalidated reality, and told us carefully, "Well . . . we have found a body."

Mistakes were made, despite our careful planning. I am troubled to this day by my part, however minor, in the series of misfortunes and errors that led to his death. I am even more sorry about the changes wrought by those two days in June, which consequences confounded us for years. That none of us intended any harm matters not at all. We are responsible for our actions, even when accidents occur, if only for the steps we omitted or neglected. In retrospect, perhaps we overplanned. They could have sneaked into the Loves' house, snatched Oscar while he slept, and innocently tucked Igel under the covers. The boy always was left alone to play for hours at a time. We could have grabbed him in broad daylight and sent in a changed Igel for dinner. Or we could have skipped the purification by water. Who still believes in that old myth? It did not have to end in such a heartbreaking way.

Oscar Love came out to play on a June evening, dressed in blue shorts and a shirt with writing across the chest. He wore sandals, dirt caked between his toes, and kicked a ball back and forth across the lawn. Luchóg and I had climbed a sycamore and sat in the branches for what felt like hours, watching his mindless game and trying to attract him into the woods. We broadcast a menagerie of sounds: a puppy, a mewing kitten, birds in distress, a wise old owl, a cow, a horse, a pig, a chicken, a duck. But he took scant notice of our imitations. Luchóg cried like a baby; I threw my voice, disguised as a girl's, then a boy's. Oscar was deaf to all that, hearing instead the music in his mind.

We called out his name, promised him a surprise, pretended to be Santa Claus. Stumped, we descended, and Luchóg had the bright idea to sing, and the boy immediately followed the melody into the forest. As long as the song continued, he sought its source, dazed by curiosity. In my heart, I knew that this is not the way fairytales should be, bound for an unhappy ending.

Hidden behind trees by a creek, the gang lay in ambush, and Luchóg lured the boy deeper into the woods. Oscar stood on the bank considering the water and the stones, and when the music stopped he realized how lost he was, for he began to blink his eyelids, fighting back the urge to weep.

"Look at him, Aniday," Luchóg said from our hideaway. "He reminds me of the last one of us to become a changeling. Something wrong with him."

"What do you mean, 'wrong'?"

"Look in his eyes. It's as if he's not really all there."

I studied the boy's face, and indeed he seemed detached from his situation. He stood motionless, head bowed to the water, as if stunned by his own reflection. A whistle signaled the others, and they rushed from the bushes. Birds, alarmed by the sudden violence, cried out and took wing. Hidden among the ferns, a rabbit panicked and bounded away, cottontail flashing. But Oscar stood impassive and entranced and did not react until the faeries were nearly upon him. He brought his hand up to his mouth to cover his scream, and they pounced on him, tackling him to the ground with swift ferocity. He all but disappeared in the swirl of flailing limbs, wild eyes, and bared teeth. Had the capture not been explained beforehand, I would have thought they were killing him. Igel, in particular, relished the assault, pinning the boy to the ground with his knees and cramming a cloth in his mouth to muffle his cries. With a vine, he cinched the boy around the middle, pinning his arms to his sides. Pulling Oscar down the trail, Igel led us all back to camp.

Years later, Chavisory explained to me how out of the ordinary Igel's behavior had been. The changeling was supposed to model his own body and features to match the child before the kidnapping. But Igel let the boy see him as he was. Rather than making the switch immediately, he taunted the child. Zanzara tied Oscar to a tree and removed the gag from the boy's mouth. Perhaps the shock silenced him, for all Oscar could do was watch in dumb amazement the happening before him, his dark eyes moist yet fixed on his tormentors. Igel tortured his own face into a replica. I could not bear the painful grimaces, could not stomach the cracking cartilage, the wrenching bone. I vomited behind a tree and stayed away until Igel had finished molding himself into a copy of the boy.

"Do you understand, Oscar?" Igel taunted him, standing nose-to-nose. "I am you and will take your place, and you will stay here with them."

The child stared at him, as if looking in the mirror yet not recognizing his own reflection. I fought back the urge to go to Oscar, to offer kindness and reassurance. Speck sidled up to me and spat out, "This is cruel."

Stepping away from his victim, Igel addressed us: "Boys and girls. I have been with you for too long and now take my leave. My time in this hell is done, and you may have it. Your paradise is vanishing. Every morning, I hear the encroaching roar of cars, feel the shudder of planes overhead. There's soot in the air, dirt in the water, and all the birds fly away and never come back. The world is changing, and you must go while you can. I am not pleased to be trading places with this imbecile, but better that than to remain here." He swept his arms to the trees and the star-filled skies. "For this will soon be gone."

Igel walked over to Oscar and untied him and held his hand. They were identical; it was impossible to tell who was real and who was the spit and image. "I'm going down below to the tunnel now to tell a story to this poor idiot. I'll take his clothes and those disgusting shoes, then you may perform the ablution. He could do with a bath. I will crawl out on the other side. Adieu. Come away, human child."

As he was being led off, Oscar looked back once more, his gaze disguising all emotion. Soon after, the faeries went to the tunnel entry to pluck out

Oscar's naked body. They wrapped him in a caul of spider's silk and vines. He remained placid during the process, but his eyes appeared more alert, as if he deliberately was trying to be calm. Hoisting him atop our shoulders, we ran, crashing through the undergrowth toward the river. Until we reached the edge of the water, I did not notice that Speck had stayed behind. Béka, our new leader, proclaimed the incantation as we lifted our package high into the air and threw it. In midair, the body jack-knifed and fell headfirst into the water. Half of the group split off to chase and retrieve the body, as the ceremony required. They were expected to pull it ashore, as they had done with me years before, as had been done with us all. I stood there, determined to be helpful to the boy, to be understanding and patient as he made the transition.

All such hopes were washed away. The retrievers waited ashore, ready to fish the body from the water, but it never floated to the surface. Despite their severe fear of drowning, Smaolach and Chavisory waded into the river. Soon all of the faeries were in waist-deep, frantically searching for our bundle. Onions dived again and again, until, exhausted and gasping for breath, she could barely climb to the riverbank. Béka charged downstream to a ford where the body would most likely be snagged in the shallows. But Oscar could not be found. We kept vigil there all night and well into the morning, examining the stones and tree limbs where his body might have been caught, looking for any sign, but the water did not yield its secrets. The boy was gone. Around midday, below in the valley, a dog yowled with excitement. Kivi and Blomma were sent to look out for the intruders. Red-faced and panting, they came back a half hour later, collecting us from our scattered posts along the riverbank.

"They're coming," said Blomma, "with a pair of bloodhounds."

"The firemen and policemen," said Kivi.

"They'll find our camp."

"Igel brought the boy's scent to our home."

The sound of baying dogs echoed in the hills. The rescuers drew near. In his first crisis as our new leader, Béka commanded our attention. "Quick, back to camp. Hide everything. We'll stay in the tunnels until they leave."

Kivi spoke sharply to the rest of us. "There's too many coming."

"The dogs," Blomma added. "They've gone to ground and won't be tricked by a few sticks of brush thrown over the tunnels' entrances."

Béka looked perplexed and began to pace, fists clenched behind his back, a vein of anger throbbing on his forehead. "I say we hide and wait."

"We need to run." Smaolach spoke with quiet authority. Most of us fell in behind him. "They have never been this close in all my years."

Luchóg stepped up and confronted Béka. "That mob is already deeper into the woods than any human has come. You're wrong to think—"

Béka raised his arm to strike him, but Onions grabbed his hand. "But what about the boy?"

Our new leader turned from the crowd and announced, "Oscar is gone. Igel is gone. What's done is done, and we must save ourselves. Gather what you can carry and hide the rest. But be quick, for we will have to outrun them."

Abandoning Oscar's body to the waters, we raced home. While others stashed useful items—burying pots or knives, caching food and clothing—I gathered my papers and fashioned a sack to put them in. While a few of my possessions were safe beneath the library, I still had my journal and collection of pencil stubs, my drawing of my family and the dream lady in the red coat, and some treasures—gifts from Speck. I was ready quickly and hurried to find her.

"Where were you?" I asked. "Why didn't you come to the river?"

"What happened?"

"We never found it. What happened with Igel?"

"He crawled out and started to cry."

"He cried?" I began helping her pile brush over the tunnel openings.

"Like a baby," she said. "He crawled out dazed, and when he saw that I had stayed behind, he ran off. He may be hiding nearby still."

We gathered our belongings and joined the others, climbing the ridge, now a band of refugees. Below us lay a simple clearing that might fool the men, if not the dogs.

"We will never come back," Speck said.

Béka sniffed the air. "Dogs. Humans. Let's go."

Now eleven in number, we raced away, the mournful bays of the blood-hounds echoing through the hills, drawing nearer and nearer. We could smell them approaching and heard the excited voices of the men. As the sun set bloodred on the horizon, the searchers came close enough for us to make out two burly fellows, straining at the leashes, gasping to keep up with the dogs. Stumbling on the trail, Ragno dropped his pack and scattered his possessions in the leafy debris. I turned to watch him gathering up his garden spade and saw a red cap flash behind him, the man oblivious to our presence. Zanzara reached out and grabbed Ragno by the hand, and off we sped to the others, leaving behind those few clues.

We ran for hours, crossing a creek like a hunted fox to mask our scent, cloaking ourselves at last behind a tangle of nettles. The sun dipped below the treeline as the sound of the men and dogs faded. They were circling back. We bivouacked there for the night, laying down our burdens, taking up our anxieties. No sooner had I stashed my papers than Béka strode up to me, his chest puffed out, ready to command.

"Go back to check when it is safe to return."

"By myself?"

"Take someone with you." He surveyed his charges, then leered at me. "Take Speck."

We waded in the winding creek back toward our pursuers, stopping now and then to listen and look ahead for trouble. Halfway to the river, Speck hopped out midstream onto a large rock.

"Aniday, do you still want to leave?"

"Leave? Where would I go?"

"Just leave, right now. We could go. I don't know. West to California and stare at the deep blue sea."

Another noise in the water silenced us. Perhaps a person wading in the stream, or the splashing dogs as they crossed, or perhaps a deer quenching an evening's thirst.

"You're not going to leave, are you, Speck?"

"Did you hear that?" she asked.

We froze and listened hard. Creeping along through the brush, we carefully investigated the noise. A few hundred yards downstream, a most peculiar odor—neither human nor animal, but something in between. My stomach pained me as we moved along the banks of the water. Around a bend and in the fading light through the trees, we were nearly upon him before we saw the man.

"Who's there?" the figure said, then ducked down, trying to hide.

"Speck," I whispered. "That's my father."

She stood on her tiptoes and peeked at the crouching man; then she held her finger to her lips. Her nostrils flared as she breathed in deeply. Speck grabbed my hand and led us away as quietly as a fog.

· *CHAPTER 19* ·

D espite being underwater for a day, the body was identified as that of young Oscar Love. The sheet pulled back, the shocking bloat of the drowned, and sure enough, it was him, although the truth is, none of us could bear to look closely. Had it not been for the strange netting around the waterlogged corpse, maybe no one would have thought it anything other than a tragic accident. He would have been laid to rest under two yards of good earth, and his parents left to their private grief. But suspicions were raised from the moment that they gaffed him from the river. The corpse was transported twelve miles to the county morgue for a proper autopsy and inquest. The coroners searched for cause but found only strange effects. To all outward appearance he was a young boy, but when they cut him open, the doctors discovered an old man. The weirdness never made the papers, but Oscar later told me about the atrophied internal organs, the necrosis of the heart, the dehydrated lungs, liver, kidneys, spleen, and brain of a death-defying centenarian.

The strangeness and sorrow surrounding this discovery were compounded by the vanishing act of Jimmy Cummings. With the rest of the searchers, he had gone into the woods that night but had not returned. When Jimmy did not show up at the hospital, we all assumed he had gone home early or found another exit, and not until the next evening did George begin to worry. By the third day, the rest of us were all anxious about Jimmy, desperate for any news. We planned to go back to the woods that evening if the weather held, but just as I sat down with my family for dinner, the phone rang in the kitchen. Elizabeth and Mary both sprang from their chairs, hoping a boy might be trying to reach them, but my mother ordered them to sit.

"I don't like your friends calling in the middle of meals." Mom picked up the receiver from its cradle on the wall, and after she said hello, her face was a palette of surprise, shock, disbelief, and amazement. She half turned to finish her discussion, leaving us to stare at the back of her head. As she hung up the phone with her left hand, she crossed herself with her right, then turned to share the news.

"It's a miracle. That was Oscar Love. Jimmy Cummings is okay, and he found him alive."

My sisters stopped mid-bite, their forks suspended in the air, and stared at her. I asked my mother to repeat the message, and in so doing, she realized the implications of her sentences.

"They walked out of the woods together. He's alive. He found him in a hole. Little Oscar Love."

Elizabeth's fork fell and clattered on the plate.

"You're kidding. Alive?" Mary said.

"Far out," said Elizabeth.

Distracted, Mom fretted with the bobby pins at her temples. She stood behind her chair, thinking.

"Isn't he dead?" I asked.

"Well . . . there must be a mistake."

"That's a helluva mistake, Mom," Mary said.

Elizabeth asked the not-so-rhetorical question we were all wondering about. "So who's that in the morgue?"

Mary asked her twin, "There's another Oscar Love? That's so cool."

My mother sat hard in the chair. Staring at the plate of fried chicken, she seemed lost in abstraction, reconciling what she knew to be true with what she had just heard. The twins one-upped each other with hypotheses too absurd to believe. Too nervous to eat, I retired to the porch for a smoke and contemplation. On my second Camel, I heard the noise of an approaching car. A cherry red Mustang veered off the road and barreled up our drive, kicking up gravel and fishtailing to a stop. The twins rushed out to the porch, the screen door slapping shut twice, before Cummings got out of the car. Hair pulled back into a ponytail, a pair of rose-colored glasses perched on his nose, he flashed the two-finger V and broke into a broad grin. Mary and Elizabeth greeted him with their own peace signs and smiled coyly back at him. Jimmy loped across the yard, took the porch stairs in two bounds, and stood directly in front of me, expecting a hero's welcome. We shook hands.

"Welcome back from the dead, man."

"Man, you know already? Have you heard the news?" His eyes were bloodshot, and I could not tell if he was drunk or stoned or just worn-out.

Mom burst through the door and threw her arms around my friend, bear-hugging him until his face turned red. Not able to restrain themselves a moment longer, my sisters joined in, nearly tackling him in their enthusiasm. I watched them unpeel one by one.

"Tell us all about it," my mother said. "Would you like a drink? Let me get you an iced tea."

While she busied herself in the kitchen, we arranged ourselves on the rattan. Unable to decide upon a sister, Jimmy slumped onto the settee, and the twins bunched together on the porch swing. I kept my post at the railing, and when she returned, Mom sat beside Jimmy, beaming at him as if he were her own son.

"Have you ever seen anyone come back from the dead, Mrs. Day?"

"Oh, angels and ministers of grace defend us."

"That's what the Loves thought when they saw him," Jimmy said. "As if Oscar might have come from the airs of heaven, or been blasted out of hell. They couldn't believe what their own eyes were telling them. 'Cause they were all set to take the body to the funeral home, thinking Little Oscar was dead and fit to be buried, when I come in with their son, holding his hand. Lewis looked as if he was having a heart attack, man, and Libby walked up and said, 'Are you real? Can I touch you? What are you? Can you speak to me?' And the boy ran to her and wrapped his arms around her waist, and she knew he was no ghost."

Two identical beings, one dead, the other living—the changeling and the child.

"All the doctors and nurses freaked out, too. Speaking of nurses, Henry, there's a nurse there who said she saw you the other night when they brought up that other boy."

That was no boy.

"Lew starts shaking my hand, and Libby says 'Bless you' about a thousand times. And Oscar, big Oscar, came in a few minutes later, then he goes through the whole routine with his nephew, and man, is he glad to see me, too. The questions start flying, and of course I already told the whole story to the firemen and the cops. They brought us to the hospital on account of him being out there for three days. Near as they can tell, there isn't a thing wrong with the boy. A little strung out, like he'd been tripping, and we were pretty tired and dirty and thirsty."

A big storm darkened in the western skies. In the forest, the creatures would be scrambling for cover. The hobgoblins had created an underground warren in their ancient campsite, a maze of tunnels that sheltered them from the rough weather.

"But you had to know, man, so I got in my ride and drove right over here."

He drank his iced tea in a single gulp, and my mother refilled his glass at once. She, like the rest of us, grew anxious for the beginning, and I was wondering if his story would beat the rain. No longer able to wait, she asked, "So, how did you find little Oscar?"

"Hey, Henry, did I tell you that I saw that nurse, Tess Wodehouse? You should give her a call, bro. That night, I got so caught up looking for that kid that I lost track of the time. My watch stopped dead around half past seven. Which freaked me out because it must have been after nine. Not that I believe in ghosts or anything like that, just that it was dark."

I checked my watch and studied the approaching storm, trying to calculate its tempo. If one or two of them were away from camp when the rain hit, they would have to look for a cave or a hollow tree to wait out the worst.

"So I was really, really lost. And at that point, I'm concerned about finding my own way out. I come to this clearing in the woods, and it's starlit and spooky. There's these mooshed-down places in the grass and leaves, like maybe deer bed down there. Then I see these flat ovals in a ring around the edges of the clearing, and I figure this is where a herd sleeps for the night, right?"

On fair summer nights, we slept above ground. We read the skies each morning for any hint of foul weather. As Jimmy paused for a breath, I thought I heard the notes from the stones in the river again.

"There's this circle of ashes and burnt sticks from a campfire that some freakin' hunters or backpackers left, and if I have to stay the night in the woods, this might be a good place since, obviously, someone had stayed here before. I made myself a small fire, and the flames hypnotize me, for next thing I know, I'm asleep and having the strangest dreams. Hallucinations. Bad acid. A voice from far away, a little boy calling and calling 'Mama,' but I can't see him, and I'm too tired to get up. You ever have one of those dreams where you think your alarm clock is going off in your dream, but it's really going off beside your bed? Only you think it's just a dream, so you don't get up to shut if off, then you oversleep, and then you remember when you do get up that you had a dream about it ringing?"

"I think I have that dream every morning," said Mary.

"Dig it. I can't see him, but I can hear little Oscar crying out for his Mama, so I start looking for him. 'Oscar? Your mama and daddy sent me here to find you.' So he starts calling out, 'I'm under here!' Under where? I can't see him, and what he's under? 'Keep calling me' . . . and I try to follow the sound of his voice. That's when I fall into the freakin' hole. Crashing right through branches and stuff that someone had laid over the opening like it's a trap. I'm stuck in this hole up to my armpits in the dead dark of night with the boy crying his eyes out nearby. A bad scene, man, a bad scene."

The girls stopped swinging. My mother leaned forward. I forgot about the gathering storm and concentrated on the elusive melody, but it receded in the swale of talk.

"I was jammed inside, man. My arms are trapped up against the sides of the hole. Worse is, my feet aren't on the bottom of the pit, but dangling there, at the top of a bottomless pit. Or maybe something's down at the bottom, going to get me." He lunged out at the girls, who screamed and giggled.

"I stayed still, considering my situation, Mrs. Day, and I shout out to Little Oscar to be cool with the yelling 'cause he was getting on my nerves. And I says, 'I'm stuck in a hole, but I will get you as soon as I can figure out a way to get out.' And he says he thinks it's a tunnel. So I tell him to crawl around and if he sees a pair of big feet in the middle of the air, they're mine and could he help me get out?"

In the distance, the low rumble of thunder. I hopped off the porch and ran down to roll up the windows of his car. The hobgoblins would be huddled, all elbows and knees, worried about a sudden wrack of lightning. The song had slipped my mind again.

"Morning comes, so now I see where I am, which is still stuck in a hole. But give myself a skosh more room on the left, all I have to do is twist and down I go. Turns out I was only a foot or two off the bottom. But my feet are asleep, and my arms are aching, and I have to take a leak—pardon my French, Mrs. Day. I was dog-tired, but that boy—"

We jumped at a loud boom of thunder and a wraith of light that filled the horizon. The air smelled of electricity and the coming deluge. When the first fat drops lashed the ground like coins, we scurried inside. Cummings sat between Mary and Elizabeth on the sofa, and Mom and I perched in the uncomfortable chairs.

"At the bottom of this hole," Jimmy continued over the rumbling, "tunnels in three different directions. I shouted down each one, but no reply. I was beginning to wonder whether Oscar was at the other end of any one of them or did I dream up the whole thing. You should see these tunnels, man, unbelievably cool. Lord knows who or what made them. Or why. As you crawl along, they get real skinny, like maybe kids made them. You snake on your belly until you come to the end and another chamber, sometimes big enough where even I could squat. And at each of the chambers, there were more tunnels. It just now occurs to me that I saw something like this on TV with Cronkite. Like the VC. Maybe it's a Vietnamese camp?"

"Do you really think," I asked, "that the Vietcong have invaded America and set up camp in the middle of nowhere?"

"No, man. Do you think I'm crazy? Maybe it's where they train our guys to go into the tunnels to find their guys? Like a beehive. A freakin' maze. I went back and forth, trying not to get lost, when suddenly I realized that I hadn't heard from Oscar all day. Just when I think maybe he's dead, here he crawls in like a mole and pops his head up. The thing of it is—and I didn't notice this at first because of all the dirt and grime—he was naked as a jaybird."

"What happened to his clothes?" Mom asked.

The changelings stripped him, wrapped him in a caul of spiderwebs, and threw the body in the river to make him their own. That's what they thought they were doing.

"Mrs. Day, I have no clue. First thing we had to do was get up out of the earth, and he showed me these holes along each of the walls where these handgrips and foot ledges had been carved. I didn't notice them before, but up he scooted, like climbing a ladder."

I had spent the better part of a month carving out those handholds, and

I could almost picture the hobgoblin who was constantly digging in the warren.

"It was late when I found him, and the kid was tired and hungry, and in no condition to tramp back through the woods. And I was sure everyone was still looking for us. So we're sitting there wondering what to do next, when he asks me if I'm hungry. He marches right over to the edge of the ring and rolls back an old dirty blanket that's lying there. Underneath is a whole stash of food. Like a grocery store in the middle of the freakin' woods. Peas, pears, applesauce, baked beans, a bag of sugar, a box of salt, dried-out mushrooms, raisins, apples. Like finding a buried treasure."

I looked out the window. The storm had abated. Where had they gone?

"As I'm fixing up dinner, Oscar starts poking around the edges of this camp, exploring while I'm trying to find a way to open the cans. The kid comes back wearing these groovy old-time pants like knickerbockers and a dingy white sweater. He says he found a whole pile of things. You wouldn't believe the stuff that's out there—clothes and shoes, and gloves, hats, mittens. We go around uncovering all this junk—buttons, a pouch of primo weed—excuse me, Mrs. Day—a rock collection, and old cards and newspapers with stuff written on them, like a kid practicing his ABCs. Someone had saved a ball of string, a hair comb, a pair of rusty scissors. This freakin' mixed-up doll baby. Like a commune out there, man. When I told the cops, they said they were going to go up and investigate, because they don't want those types around our town."

"I should say not." My mother pursed her lips.

Elizabeth barked at her. "What's wrong with communing with nature?"

"I didn't say anything about nature."

"Whoever lives out there," Jimmy continued, "must have split before I got there, because they were gone, man. Over supper, Oscar tells me how he came to be naked in a hole in the ground in the middle of the forest. This group of children, pretending to be pirates, kidnapped him and tied him to a tree. Another boy put on a mask that looked exactly like him and made him jump into a hole. He took off all his clothes, and then he made Oscar take off all his clothes. I'm getting kind of freaked out, but the other kid says for Oscar to forget it all happened, and he climbs out, puts a lid on the tunnel."

He chose not to go through with the change. I tried to remember who that might be.

"All the kids ran away, except for one girl, who said she would help him home. But when she heard a dog barking, she ran away too. When nobody came for him in the morning, he was scared and all freaked out, and that's when he heard me. I don't believe a word of it, but it does explain a lot of things. Like the children's old clothes."

"And that boy they found in the river," Mom said.

"Maybe that's what he thought he saw," Elizabeth said. "Maybe that boy kinda looked like him, and that's why Oscar thought he was wearing a mask."

Mary put forward her own theory. "Maybe it was his double. Daddy used to say that everybody has one."

Mom had the last word on the subject. "Sounds like the fairies to me."

They all laughed, but I knew better. I pressed my forehead against the cool windowpane and searched the landscape for those I have tried to forget. The puddles in the yard were sinking slowly into the earth.

CHAPTER 20

We lost our home and never went back. Trackers and dogs arrived first, poking about the camp, uncovering what we had left behind in our evacuation. Then men in black suits came to take photographs of the holes and our footprints left in the dirt. A helicopter hovered over the site, filming the oval perimeter and well-trod pathways into the woods. Dozens of soldiers in green uniforms collected every discarded possession and carted them off in boxes and bags. A few souls shinnied underground, crawled through the network of burrows and emerged blinking at the sky as if they had been beneath the sea. Weeks later, another crew arrived, their heavy machinery rumbling up the hill, cutting a swath through the old trees to collapse the tunnels, dig them up, and bury them again, turning the earth over and over until the top ran orange with thick wet clay. Then they doused the ring with gasoline and set the field afire. By the end of that summer, nothing remained but ashes and the blackened skeletons of a few trees.

Such destruction did not temper the urge to return home. I could not sleep without the familiar pattern of stars and sky framed by branches overhead. Every night-sound—a snapped twig or a woodrat scrabbling through the brush—disturbed my rest, and in the mornings my head and neck ached. I heard, too, the others moaning in their dreams or straining behind the bushes to relieve the growing pressure in their guts. Smaolach looked over his shoulder a dozen times each hour. Onions chewed her nails and braided intricate chains of grass. Each swell of restlessness was followed by a swale of listlessness. Knowing our home was gone, we kept looking for it still, as if hope alone could restore our lives. When hope faded, a morbid curiosity set in. We would go back time and again to worry over the bones.

Hidden in the top of tall oaks or scattered in pockets along the ridge, we'd witness and whisper among ourselves, descrying the loss and ruin. The raspberries crushed under the backhoe, the chokecherry felled by a bulldozer, the paths and lanes of our carousals and mad ecstasies erased as one might rub away a drawing or tear up a page. That campsite had existed since the arrival of the first French fur traders, who had encountered the tribes at their ancestral territory. Homesick, we drifted away, huddling in makeshift shelters, lost for good.

We wandered rough country into early autumn. The influx of men, dogs, and machines made moving about difficult and unsafe, so we spent hard days and nights together, bored and hungry. Whenever someone roamed too far from the group, we ran into danger. Ragno and Zanzara were spotted by a surveyor when they crossed in front of his spyglass. The man hollered and gave chase, but my friends were too fast. Dump trucks brought in loads of gravel to line the dirt road carved from the highway to our old clearing. Chavisory and Onions made a game of finding gems among the rubble; any unusual stone would do. By moonlight, they picked over each newly spread load, until the night when they were discovered by a driver sleeping in his rig. He sneaked up on them and grabbed the girls by their collars. They would have been caught if Onions hadn't snapped free and bitten him hard enough to draw blood. That driver may be the only man alive with a faery's scars lined up like beads in the web of skin between his thumb and finger.

On the construction site where the men dug cellars, Luchóg spotted an open pack of cigarettes resting on the front seat of an empty truck. Quiet as a mouse, he skittered over, and as he reached inside to steal the smokes, his knee hit the horn. He grabbed the Lucky Strikes as the door to a nearby outhouse burst open, and the man, tugging up his trousers, swore and cursed as he came looking about for the trespasser. He hustled over to the truck, searched about the cab, and then ducked his head behind the dashboard. From the edge of the forest, Luchóg could not resist any longer and struck a match in the lingering darkness. After the very first drag, he had to duck when birdshot peppered the air above his head. The man fired the shotgun again, long after my friend had disappeared, laughing and coughing, into the heart of the forest.

After these incidents, Béka clamped down on our freedoms. We were not allowed to travel alone, nor could we be on any road during the daylight. He restricted any forays into town for supplies out of fear of detection. By day, the hum of engines, the staccato of hammers echoing from our old home to wherever we had camped. By night, a haunting stillness invaded. I longed to run away with Speck to the library and its comforting privacy. I missed my books and papers, and my materials were few: McInnes's fading composition book, a drawing of the woman in the red coat, a handful of letters. Numbed, I was not writing, either, and time passed unrecorded. In a way, it did not exist at all.

To gather food, Ragno, Zanzara, and I sewed together a crude net, and after much trial and error, we managed to capture a brace of grouse, which we then killed and took home for dinner. The tribe made a ceremony of plucking feathers, tying them in bundles, and wearing them in our hair like the Huron. We dressed the birds and risked our first large fire of the season, allowing us to roast our meal and providing comfort on a cool night. Assembled in a small circle, our faces glowed in the flickering light, signs of anxious weariness in our tired eyes, but the meal would prove revitalizing. As the fire burnt down and our bellies filled, a calm complacency settled upon us, like a blanket drawn around our shoulders by absent mothers.

Wiping his greasy mouth on his sleeve, Béka cleared his throat to summon our attention. The chitchat and marrow sucking stopped at once. "We have angered the people, and there will be no rest for a long, long time. It was wrong to lose that boy, but worse still was bringing him to camp in the first place." We had heard this speech many times before, but Onions, his favorite, played the Fool to his Lear.

"But they have Igel. Why are they so mad?" she asked.

"She's right. They have Igel. He's their Oscar," Kivi said, joining the chorus. "But we don't have ours. Why should they be mad? We are the ones who have lost."

"This is not about the boy. They found us, found our home, and now bury it under asphalt. They know we are here. They won't stop looking for us until they find us and drive us from these woods. A hundred years ago, there were coyotes, wolves, lions in these hills. The sky blackened with flocks of passenger pigeons every spring. Bluebirds lived among us, and the creeks and rivers were fat with fishes and toads and terrapins. Once it was not unusual to see a man with one hundred wolf pelts drying by his barn. Look around you. They come in, hunt and chop, and take it all away. Igel was right: Things will never be the same, and we are next."

Those who had finished their meals threw the bones in the fire, which sputtered and crackled with the new fat. We were bored by doom and gloom. While I listened to our new leader and his message, I noticed some of us did not accept his sermon. Whispers and murmurs ran along the circle. At the far end of the fire, Smaolach was not paying attention, but drawing in the dirt with a stick.

"You think you know better than me?" Béka yelled down to him. "You know what to do, and how to keep us alive?"

Smaolach kept his eyes down, pushed the point into the earth.

"I am the eldest," Béka continued. "By rights, I am the new leader, and I will not accept anyone challenging my authority."

Speck raised her voice in defense. "Nobody questions the rules . . . or your leadership."

Continuing to make his map, Smaolach spoke so softly as to almost not be heard at all. "I am merely showing my friends here our new position, as I estimate it from the time traveled and by calculating the stars in the sky. You have earned the right to be our leader, and to tell us where to go."

With a grunt, Béka took Onions by the hand and disappeared into the brush. Smaolach, Luchóg, Speck, Chavisory, and I huddled around the map as the others dispersed. I do not remember ever seeing a map before. Curious as to how it worked and what all of the symbols represented, I leaned forward and examined the drawing, deducing at once that the wavy lines stood for waterways—the river and the creek—but what to make of the perfectly straight line that crossed the river, the bunches of boxes arranged in a grid, and the jagged edge between one large oval and an *X* in the sand?

"The way I see it"—Smaolach pointed to the right side of the map— "there is what's known and what's unknown. To the east is the city. And I can only guess that the smell of the air means the city is heading our way. East is out. The question is: Do we cross the river to the south? If so, we cut ourselves off from the town." He pointed with the stick to the set of squares.

"If we go south, we would have to cross the river again and again for supplies and clothes and shoes. The river is a dangerous place."

"Tell that," Chavisory said, "to Oscar Love."

Luchóg offered an alternative. "But we don't know that another town might be somewhere over the other side. No one has ever looked. I say we scout for a place on the other side of the river."

"We need to be near the water," I volunteered, and put my finger on the wavy lines.

"But not *in* the water," Speck argued. "I say north and west, stick to the creek or follow the river till it bends up." She took the stick from his hand and drew where the river curved to the north.

"How do you know it bends?" Chavisory asked.

"I've been that far."

We looked at Speck with awe, as if she had seen the edge of the world.

She stared back, defying anyone's challenge or disbelief. "Two days from here. Or we should find a place near the creek. It dries up in August and September some years, but we could build a cistern."

Thinking of our hideaway beneath the library, I spoke up. "I vote for the creek. We follow it from the hills into town whenever we need supplies or anything. If we go too far away—"

"He's right, you know," said Luchóg, patting his chest and the empty pouch beneath his shirt. "We need things from town. Let's tell Béka we want to stay by the creek. Agreed?"

He lay there snoring, slack-jawed, his arm flung over Onions at his side. She heard our approach, popped open her eyes, smiled, and put a finger to her lips to whisper hush. Had we taken her advice, perhaps we would have caught him at a better time, in a more generous mood, but Speck, for one, never had any patience. She kicked his foot and roused him from his slumber.

"What do you want now?" he roared through a yawn. Since his ascension to leadership, Béka attempted to appear bigger than he was. He was trying to imply a threat by rising to his feet.

"We are tired of this life," said Speck.

"Of never having two nights in one bed," said Chavisory.

Luchóg added, "I haven't had a smoke since that man nearly shot off my head."

Béka raked his face with his palm, considering our demands in the haze of half-sleep. He began to pace before us, two steps to the left, pivot, two steps to the right. When he stopped and folded his arms behind his back, he showed that he would prefer not to have this conversation, but we did not listen to such silent refusals. A breeze rattled the upper branches of the trees.

Smaolach stepped up to him. "First of all, nobody respects and admires your leadership more than me. You have kept us from harm and led us out of darkness, but we need a new camp, not this wandering aimlessly. Water nearby and a way back to civilization. We decided—"

Béka struck like a snake, choking off the rest of the sentence. Wrapping his fingers around Smaolach's throat, he squeezed until my friend dropped to his knees. "I decide. You decide to listen and follow. That's all."

Chavisory rushed to Smaolach's defense but was smacked away by a single backhanded slap across her face. When Béka relaxed his grip, Smaolach fell to the ground, gasping for breath. Addressing the three of us still standing, Béka pointed a finger to the sky and said, "I will find us a home. Not you." Taking Onions by the hand, he strode off into the night. I looked to Speck for reassurance, but her eyes were fixed upon the violent spot, as if she were burning revenge into her memory.

I am the only person who truly knows what happened in the forest. Jimmy's story explained for me the mystery of the drowned Oscar Love and his miraculous reappearance several days later. Of course, it was the changelings, and all the evidence confirmed my suspicion of a failed attempt to steal the child. The dead body was that of a changeling, an old friend of mine. I could picture the face of the next in line but had erased their names. My life there had been spent imagining the day when I would begin my life in the upper world. As the decades passed, the cast of characters had shifted as, one by one, each became a changeling, found a child, and took its place. In time, I had come to resent every one of them and to disregard each new member of our tribe. I deliberately tried to forget them all. Did I say a friend of mine had died? I had no friends.

While gladdened by the prospect of one less devil in the woods, I was oddly disturbed by Jimmy's account of little Oscar Love, and I dreamt that night of a lonely boy like him in an old-fashioned parlor. A pair of finches dart about an ironwork cage. A samovar glistens. On the mantelpiece sits a row of leather-bound books gilded with Gothic letters spelling out foreign titles. The parlor walls papered crimson, heavy dark curtains shutting out the sun, a curious sofa covered with a latticed needlework throw. The boy is alone in the room on a humid afternoon, yet despite the heat, he wears woolen knickers and buttoned boots, a starched blue shirt, and a huge tie that looks like a Christmas bow. His long hair cascades in waves and curls, and he hunches over the piano, entranced by the keyboard, doggedly practicing an étude. From behind him comes another child, the same hair and build, but naked and creeping on the balls of his feet. The piano player plays on, oblivious to the menace. Other goblins steal out from behind the curtains, from under the settee; out of the woodwork and wallpaper, they advance like smoke. The finches scream and crash into the iron bars. The boy stops on a note, turns his head. I have seen him before. They attack as one, working together, this one covering the boy's nose and throat, another taking out the legs, a third pinning the boy's arms behind his back. From beyond the closed door, a man's voice: *"Was ist los?"* A thumping knock, and the door swings open. The threshold frames a large man with outrageous whiskers. "Gustav?" The father cries out as several hobgoblins rush to restrain him while the others take his son. *"Ich erkenne dich! Du willst nur meinen Sohn!"*

I could still feel the anger in their eyes, the passion of their attack. Where is my father? A voice pierces the dream, calling "Henry, Henry," and I awaken to a damp pillowcase and twisted sheets. Stifling a yawn, I yelled downstairs that I was tired and that this had better be good. My mother shouted back through the door that there was a telephone call and that she was not my secretary. I threw on my bathrobe and headed downstairs.

"This is Henry Day," I grunted into the receiver.

She laughed. "Hi, Henry. This is Tess Wodehouse. I saw you out in the woods."

She could not imagine the reasons for my awkward silence.

"When we found the boy. The first one. I was with the ambulance."

"Right, the nurse. Tess, Tess, how are you?"

"Jimmy Cummings said to give you a call. Would you like to meet somewhere later?"

We arranged to meet after her shift, and she had me write down directions to her house. At the bottom of the page, I doodled the name: *Gustav.*

She answered the door and stepped straight out to the porch, the afternoon sunlight stippling across her face and yellow sundress. Out of the shadows, she dazzled. All at once, it seems in retrospect, she revealed what I grew to adore: the asymmetrical mottling of the colors in her irises, a blue vein snaking up her right temple that flashed like a semaphore for passion, the sudden exuberance of her crooked smile. Tess said my name and made it seem real.

We drove away, and the wind through the open window caught her hair and blew it across her face. When she laughed, she threw back her head, chin to the sky, and I longed to kiss her lovely neck. I drove as if we had a destination, but in our town there was no particular place to go. Tess turned down the radio, and we talked away the afternoon. She told me all about her life in public school, then on to college, where she had studied nursing. I told her all about parochial school and my aborted studies in music. A few miles outside of town, a new fried-chicken joint had opened recently, so we bought ourselves a bucketful. We stopped by Oscar's to steal a bottle of apple wine. We picnicked on a school playground, abandoned for the summer except for a pair of cardinals on the monkey bars, serenading us with their eight-note song.

"I used to think you were the strangest bird, Henry Day. When we were in elementary school together, you might have said two words to me. Or anyone. You were so distracted, as if you heard a song in your head that no one else could hear."

"I'm still that way," I told her. "Sometimes when I'm walking down the street or am quiet by myself, I play a tune, imagine my fingers on the keys, and can hear the notes as clear as day."

"You seem somewhere else, miles away."

"Not always. Not now."

Her face brightened and changed. "Strange, isn't it? About Oscar Love, that boy. Or should I say two little boys, alike as two pins."

I tried to change the subject. "My sisters are twins."

"How do you explain it?"

"It's been a long time since high school biology, but when an egg divides—"

She licked her fingers. "Not twins. The drowned boy and the lost boy."

"I had nothing to do with either one."

Tess swallowed a sip of wine and wiped her hands with a napkin. "You are an odd one, but that's what I liked about you, even when we were children. Since the first day I saw you in kindergarten."

I sincerely wished I had been there that day.

"And when I was a girl, I wanted to hear your song, the one that's playing in your head right now." She leaned across the blanket and kissed me.

I took her home at sunset, kissed her once at the door, and drove home in a mild euphoria. The house echoed like the inside of an empty shell. The twins were not home and my mother sat alone in the living room, watching the movie of the week on the television. Slippers crossed on the ottoman, her housecoat buttoned to the collar, she saluted me with a drink in her right hand. I sat down on the couch next to the easy chair and looked at her closely for the first time in years. We were getting older, no doubt, but she had aged well. She was much stouter than when we first met, but lovely still.

"How was your date, Henry?" She kept her eyes on the tube.

"Great, Mom, fine."

"See her again?"

"Tess? I hope so."

A commercial broke the story, and she turned to smile at me between sips.

"Mom, do you ever . . ."

"What's that, Henry?"

"I don't know. Do you ever get lonely? Like you might go out on a date yourself?"

She laughed and seemed years younger. "What man would want to go out with an old thing like me?"

"You're not so old. And you look ten years younger than you are."

"Save your compliments for your nurse."

The program returned. "I thought—"

"Henry, I've given this thing an hour already. Let me see it to the end."

Tess changed my life, changed everything. After our impromptu picnic, we saw each other every day of that wonderful summer. I remember sitting side by side on a park bench, lunches on our laps, talking in the brilliant sunshine. She would turn to me, her face bathed in brightness, so that I would have to shade my eyes to look at her, and she told me stories that fed my desire for more stories, so that I might know her and not forget a single line. I loved each accidental touch, the heat of her, the way she made me feel alive and fully human.

On the Fourth of July, Oscar closed the bar and invited nearly half the town to a picnic along the riverbank. He had arranged the celebration in gratitude to all of the people who had helped in the search and rescue of his nephew, for the policemen and firemen, doctors and nurses, all of Little Oscar's schoolmates and teachers, the volunteers—such as myself, Jimmy, and George—the Loves and all their assorted relatives, a priest or two in mufti, and the inevitable hangers-on. A great feast was ordered. Pig in a pit. Chicken, hamburgers, hot dogs. Corn and watermelon trucked in from down south. Kegs of beer, bottles of the hard stuff, tubs of ice and sodas for the youngsters, a cake specially made in the city for the occasion—as big as a picnic table, iced in red, white, and blue with a gold THANK YOU in glittering script. The party began at four in the afternoon and lasted all night. When it became dark enough, a crew of firemen shot off a fireworks display, fading sparklers and candles popping and fizzing when they hit the river. Our town, like many places in America at the time, was divided by the war, but we put Vietnam and the marches behind us in deference to the celebration.

In the languorous heat, Tess looked delicious that evening, a cool smile, and bright lights in her eyes. I met all of her coworkers, the well-heeled doctors, a bevy of nurses, and far too many firemen and policemen, baked tan and swaggering. After the fireworks, she noticed her old sweetheart in the company of a new girl and insisted that we say hello. I could not shake the sensation that I had known him from my former life.

"Henry, you remember Brian Ungerland." We shook hands, and he introduced his new girlfriend to us both. The women slipped away to compare notes.

"So, Ungerland, that's an unusual name."

"German." He sipped his beer, stared at the women, who were laughing in an overly personal way.

"Your family from Germany?"

"Off the boat long time ago. My family's been in town for a hundred years."

A stray string of firecrackers went off in a rat-a-tat of pops.

"Came from a place called Eger, I think, but like I said, man, that was another life. Where are your people from, Henry?"

I told him the lie and studied him as he listened. The eyes clued me in, the set of the jaw, the aquiline nose. Put a walrus mustache on him, age Ungerland a few decades, and he would be a dead ringer for the man in my dreams. The father. Gustav's father. I shook off the notion as merely the odd conflation of my stressful nightmares and the anxiety of seeing Tess's old beau.

Jimmy Cummings crept from behind and nearly scared the life out of me. He laughed at my surprise and pointed to the ribbon hanging around his neck. "Hero for a day," he shouted, and I couldn't help but break into a broad grin. Little Oscar, as usual, appeared a bit dumbfounded by all the attention, but he smiled at strangers who tousled his hair and matrons who bent to kiss him on the cheek. Filled with good cheer, the warm evening passed in slow motion, the kind of day one recalls when feeling blue. Boys and girls chased fireflies in crazy circles. Sullen long-haired teens tossed a ball around with red-faced crew-cut policemen. In the middle of the night, when many had already headed for home, Lewis Love buttonholed me for the longest time. I missed half of what he said because I was watching Tess, who was engaged in animated conversation with her old boyfriend beneath a dark elm tree.

"I have a theory," Lewis told me. "He was scared, right, out all night, and he heard something. I don't know, like a raccoon or a fox, right? So he hides out in a hole, only it's real hot in there and he gets a fever."

She reached out and touched Ungerland on the arm, and they were laughing, only her hand stayed there.

"So he has this real weird dream—"

They were staring at each other, and old Oscar, oblivious to the end, marched up and joined their conversation. He was drunk and happy, but Tess and Brian were staring into each other's eyes, their expressions real serious, as if trying to communicate something without saying a word.

"I personally think it was just some hippies' old camping ground."

I wanted to tell him to shut up. Now Ungerland's hand was on her biceps, and they were all laughing. She touched her hair, nodded her head at whatever he was saying.

". . . other kid was a runaway, but still you have to feel sorry . . ."

She looked back my way, smiled and waved, as if nothing had been happening. I held her gaze a beat and tuned in to Lewis.

". . . but nobody believes in fairy tales, right?"

"You're right, Lewis. I think your theory is dead-on. Only explanation possible."

Before he had the chance to thank me or say another word, I was five strides away, walking toward her. Oscar and Brian noticed my approach and wiped off the grins from their faces. They stared at the stars, finding nothing better to look at. I ignored them and whispered into her ear, and she coiled her arm around my back and under my shirt, tracing circles on my skin with her nails.

"What were you guys talking about? Something funny?"

"We were talking about you," Brian said. Oscar looked down the barrel of his bottle and grunted.

I walked Tess away from them, and she put her head on my shoulder without glancing back. She led me into the woods, to a spot away from the crowd, and lay down in the tall grass and ferns. Voices carried in the soft, heavy air, but their proximity only made the moment more exciting. She slipped out of her shorts and unbuckled my belt. I could hear a group of men laughing down by the river. She kissed me on the stomach, roughly pulled off my shorts. Someone was singing to her sweetheart somewhere far away, the melody on the breeze. I felt slightly drunk and very warm all of a sudden, and thought for an instant I heard someone approaching through the trees. Tess climbed on top of me, guiding us together, her long hair hanging down to frame her face, and she stared into my eyes as she rocked back and forth. The laughter and voices trailed away, car engines started, and people said good-bye, good night. I reached beneath her shirt. She did not avert her gaze.

"Do you know where you are, Henry Day?"

I closed my eyes.

"Do you know who you are, Henry Day?"

Her hair swept across my face. Someone blew a car horn and raced away. She tilted her pelvis and drove me deep inside.

"Tess."

And I said her name again. Someone threw a bottle in the river and broke the surface. She lowered herself, resting her arms, and we lay together, hot to the touch. I kissed the nape of her neck. Jimmy Cummings shouted, "So long, Henry" from the picnic area. Tess giggled, rolled off me, and slipped back into her clothes. I watched her dress and did not notice that, for the first time in ages, I was not afraid of the forest.

CHAPTER 22

We were afraid of what might happen next. Under Béka's direction, we roamed the woods, never camping in the same place for more than three nights in a row. Waiting for some decision from Béka brewed a disease among us. We fought over food, water, the best resting places. Ragno and Zanzara neglected the most basic grooming; their hair tangled in vinelike riots, and their skin darkened beneath a film of dirt. Chavisory, Blomma, and Kivi suffered an angry silence, sometimes not speaking for days on end. Desperate without his smokes and distractions, Luchóg snapped over the tiniest provocation and would have come to blows with Smaolach if not for his friend's gentle disposition. I would often find Smaolach after their arguments, staring at the ground, pulling handfuls of grass from the earth. Speck grew more distant, withdrawn into her own imagination, and when she suggested a moment alone together, I gladly joined her away from the others.

In that Indian summer, the days stayed warm despite the waning of the light, and a second spring brought not only a renewed blossoming of wild roses and other flowers but another crop of berries. With such unexpected bounty, the bees and other insects extended their lives and mad pursuit of sweets. The birds put off their southern migration. Even the trees slowed down their leaving, going from dark saturated hues to paler shades of green.

"Aniday," she said, "listen. Here they come."

We were sitting at the edge of a clearing, doing nothing, soaking in the unusual sunshine. Speck lifted her head skyward to gather in the shadow of wings beating through the air. When they had all landed, the blackbirds fanned out their tails as they paraded to the wild raspberries, hopping to a tangle of shoots to gorge themselves. The glen echoed with their chatter. She reached around my back and put her hand on my far shoulder, then rested her head against me. The sunlight danced in patterns on the ground thrown by leaves blowing in the breeze.

"Look at that one." She spoke softly, pointing her finger at a lone black-bird, struggling to reach a plump red berry at the end of a flexing cane. It persisted, pinned the cane to the ground, impaling the stalk with its sharp hooked feet, then attacked the berry in three quick bites. After its meal, the bird began to sing, then flew away, wings flashing in the dappled light, and then the flock took off and followed into the early October afternoon.

"When I first came here," I confessed to her, "I was afraid of the crows that returned each night to the trees around our home."

"You used to cry like a baby." Her voice softened and slowed. "I wonder what it is like to hold a baby in my arms, feel like a grown-up woman instead of sticks and bones. I remember my mother, so soft in unexpected places— rounder, fuller, deeper. Stronger than you'd expect by looking."

"Tell me what they were like, my family. What happened to me?"

"When you were a boy," she began, "I watched over you. You were my charge. I knew your mother; she loved to nestle you on her lap as she read to you old Irish tales and called you her 'little man.' But you were a selfish boy, constantly wanting more and desperate over any attention shown to your little sisters."

"Sisters?" I asked, not remembering.

"Twins. Baby girls."

I was grateful that she could confirm there were two.

"You resented helping with them, angry that your time was not yours to do with what you pleased. Oh, such a brat. Your mother was taking care of the twins, worrying over your father, with no one to help her. She was worn out by it all, and that made you angrier still. An unhappy child . . ." Her voice trailed off for a moment, and she laid her hand on my arm.

"He waited for you like a fox at the edge of a pond, and he made all sorts of mischief around the farm—a knocked-over fence, a missing hen, the drying sheets torn from the line. He wanted your life, and the one whose turn it is brooks no argument. Every eye was upon you for months, anticipating a moment of petulance. Then, you ran away from home."

Speck drew me closer, ran her fingers through my hair, laid my head in the crook of her nape.

"She asked you to wash up the babies after breakfast, so that she might have a quick bath, but you left them all alone in the house, imagine that. 'Now stay here and play with your dollies. Mom's in the tub, and I'll be right outside, so don't make any trouble.' And out you stepped to toss a ball into the bright yellow sky and watch the grasshoppers scatter across the lawn before your racing feet. I wanted to come play with you, but someone had to watch the toddlers. I slipped inside, crouched on the kitchen countertop, hoping they wouldn't notice me or do themselves a harm. They were at the curious stage and could have been opening cupboards, toying with bleach and furniture polish, fingering rat poison, or opening cutlery drawers to juggle with knives, or getting into the liquor and drinking up all the whiskey. They were in danger, while she was wrapping herself in her robe and singing as she dried her hair.

"Meanwhile, you trolled the woods' edge, hoping to uncover a surprise. Something large stirred among the dried carpet of leaves and shadow of branches, snapping twigs as it ran through the half-light. A rabbit? Perhaps a dog or a small deer? Your mother descended the staircase, calmly calling, and discovered the girls dancing on the tabletop quite alone. You stood blinking into the dappled trails. From behind, a strong hand gripped your shoulder and wheeled you around. Your mother stood there, hair dripping wet, her face a mask of anger.

" 'How could you disappear like that?' she asked. Behind her, you could see the twins toddling across the lawn. In one clenched fist, she held a wooden spoon, and knowing the trouble ahead, you ran, and she gave chase, laughing all the way. At the edge of your world, she pulled you by the arm and smacked you on the bottom so hard, the spoon split in half."

Speck held me tighter still.

"But you have always been an imp. Your bottom hurt, and you'd show her. She fixed lunch, which you refused to touch. Nothing but stony silence. As she carried her babies off for their nap, she smiled and you scowled. Then you wrapped up some food in a handkerchief, stuffed it in your pocket, and slipped out of the house without a sound. I followed you the whole after-noon."

"Was I scared to be alone?"

"Curious, I'd say. A dry creek paralleled the road for a few hundred yards before meandering off into the forest, and you followed its path, listening for the occasional chatter of the birds, watching for the chipmunks skittering through the litter. I could hear Igel signal to Béka, who whistled to our leader. As you sat on the grassy bank, eating one of the biscuits and the rest of the cold eggs, they were gathering to come take you."

"Every time the leaves moved," I told her, "a monster was out to get me."

"East of the creekbed, there was an old chestnut, cracked and dying from the bottom up. An animal had scooped out a large hollow den, and you had to climb inside and see. The humidity and the darkness must have put you right to sleep. I stood outside the whole time, hidden when the searchers al-most stumbled upon you. Skittering flashlights led their dark forms as they shuffled like ghosts through the heavy air. They passed by, and soon their calls receded into the distance and then into silence.

"Not long after the people faded away, the faeries ran in from all direc-tions and stopped before me, the sentinel at the tree. The changeling panted. He looked so much like you that I held my breath and wanted to cry. He scrambled partway into the hole, grabbed you around your bare ankle, and pulled."

She hugged me and kissed me on the top of my head.

"If I changed back," I asked her, "would I ever see you again?"

Despite my questions, she would not tell me more than she thought I should know, and after a while, we set to picking berries. Although the days bore traits of midsummer, there's no stopping the tilt of the globe away from the sun. Night came like a sudden clap. We walked back beneath the emerging planets and stars, the pale ascending moon. Half-smiles greeted our return, and I wondered why the thin children of our temporary quarters were not themselves out watching blackbirds, and dreaming their dreams. Porridge bubbled on the fire, and the troupe ate from wooden bowls with wooden spoons, which they sucked clean. We dumped quarts of raspberries from our shirttails, ambrosia escaping from the bruised fruit, and the others scooped them into their mouths, smiling and chewing, staining their lips red as kisses.

The next day, Béka announced he had found our new home, "a place inaccessible to all but the most intrepid humans, a shelter where we would be safe." He led us up a steep and desolate hill, scrabbling slate and shale from its loose, decaying face, as inhospitable a heap as you'd like to find. No sign of life, no trees or plants of any kind other than a few noxious weeds poking through the rubble. No bird landed there, not even for a moment's rest, nor any flying insect of any sort, though we would soon find out about the bats. No footprints except our leader's. Scant purchase for anything larger than our weary band. As we climbed, I wondered what had possessed Béka to scout out this place, let alone proclaim it home. Anyone else would have taken one look at such devastation and passed by with a shudder. Barren as the moon, the landscape lacked all feeling, and I did not see, until we were nearly upon it, the fissure in the rock. One by one, my cohorts squeezed through the crack and were swallowed up in stone. Moving from the bright heat of Indian summer into the dankness of the entranceway felt as sudden as a dive into a cold pool. As my pupils dilated in the dimness, I did not even realize to whom I addressed my question: "Where are we?"

"It's a mine," Speck said. "An old abandoned mineshaft where they dug for coal."

A pale glow sparked forth from a newly lit torch. His face a grimace of odd, unnatural shadows, Béka grinned and croaked to us all, "Welcome home."

CHAPTER 23

I should have confessed to Tess at the start, but who knows when love begins? Two contrary impulses pulled at me. I did not want to scare her away with the changeling story, yet I longed to entrust all my secrets to her. But it was as if a demon shadowed me everywhere and clamped shut my mouth to hold in the truth. She gave me many opportunities to open my heart and tell her, and I came close once or twice, but each time I hesitated and stopped.

On Labor Day we were at the baseball stadium in the city, watching the home team take on Chicago. I was distracted by the enemy runner at second base.

"So, what's the plan for The Coverboys?"

"Plan? What plan?"

"You really should record an album. You're that good." She attacked a hot dog thick with relish. Our pitcher struck out their batter, and she let out a whoop. Tess loved the game, and I endured it for her sake.

"What kind of album? Covers of other people's songs? Do you really think anybody would buy a copy when they can have the original?"

"You're right," she said between bites. "Maybe you could do something new and different. Write your own songs."

"Tess, the songs we sing are not the kind of songs I would write."

"Okay, if you could write any music in the world, what kind would you write?"

I turned to her. She had a speck of relish at the corner of her mouth that I wished to nibble away. "I'd write you a symphony, if I could."

Out flicked her tongue to clean her lips. "What's stopping you, Henry? I'd love a symphony of my own."

"Maybe if I had stayed serious about piano, or if I had finished music school."

"What's stopping you from going back to college?"

Nothing at all. The twins had finished high school and were working. My mother certainly did not need the few dollars I brought in, and Uncle Charlie from Philadelphia had begun to call her nearly every day, expressing an interest in retiring here. The Coverboys were going nowhere as a band. I searched for a plausible excuse. "I'm too old to go back now. I'll be twenty-six next April, and the rest of the students are a bunch of eighteen-year-olds. They're into a totally different scene."

"You're only as old as you feel."

At the moment, I felt 125 years old. She settled back into her seat and watched the rest of the ballgame without another word on the subject. On the way home that afternoon, she switched the car radio over from the rock station to classical, and as the orchestra played Mahler, she laid her head against my shoulder and closed her eyes, listening.

Tess and I went out to the porch and sat on the swing, quiet for a long time, sharing a bottle of peach wine. She liked to hear me sing, so I sang for her, and then we could find nothing else to say. Her breathing presence beside me, the moon and the stars, the singing crickets, the moths clinging to the porch light, the breeze cutting through the humid air—the moment had a curious pull on me, as if recalling distant dreams, not of this life, nor of the forest, but of life before the change. As if neglected destiny or desire threatened the illusion I had struggled to create. To be fully human, I had to give in to my true nature, the first impulse.

"Do you think I'm crazy," I asked, "to want to be a composer in this day and age? I mean, who would actually listen to your symphony?"

"Dreams are, Henry, and you cannot will them away, any more than you can call them into being. You have to decide whether to act upon them or let them vanish."

"I suppose if I don't make it, I could come back home. Find a job. Buy a house. Live a life."

She held my hand in hers. "If you don't come with me, I'll miss seeing you every day."

"What do you mean, come with you?"

"I was waiting for the right time to tell you, but I've enrolled. Classes start in two weeks, and I've decided to get my master's degree. Before it's too late. I don't want to end up an old maid who never went after what she wanted."

I wanted to tell her age didn't matter, that I loved her then and would love her in two or twenty or two hundred years, but I did not say a word. She patted me on the knee and nestled close, and I breathed in the scent of her hair. We let the night pass. An airplane crossed the visual field between us and the moon, creating the momentary illusion that it was pasted on the lunar surface. She dozed in my arms and awoke with a start past eleven.

"I've got to go," Tess said. She kissed me on the forehead, and we strolled down to the car. The walk seemed to snap her out of the wine-induced stupor.

"Hey, when are your classes? I could drive you in sometimes if it's during the day."

"That's a good idea. Maybe you'll get inspired to go back yourself."

She blew me a kiss, then vanished behind the steering wheel and drove away. The old house stared at me, and in the yard the trees reached out to the yellow moon. I walked upstairs, wrapped up in the music in my head, and went to sleep in Henry's bed, in Henry's room.

What possessed Tess to choose infanticide is a mystery to me. There were other options: sibling rivalry, the burden of the firstborn, the oedipal son, the disappearing father, and so on. But she picked infanticide as her thesis topic for her seminar in Sociology of the Family. And, of course, since I had nothing to do most days but wait around campus or drive around the city while she was in classes, I volunteered to help with the research. After her last class, she and I went out for coffee or drinks, at first to plot out how to tackle the project on infanticide, but as the meetings went on, the conversations swung around to returning to school and my unstarted symphony.

"You know what your problem is?" Tess asked. "No discipline. You want to be a great composer, but you never write a song. Henry, true art is less about all the wanting-to-be bullshit, and more about practice. Just play the music, baby."

I fiddled with the porcelain ear of my coffee cup.

"It's time to get started, Chopin, or to stop kidding yourself and grow up. Get out from behind the bar and come back to school with me."

I attempted not to let my frustration and resentment show, but she had me culled like a lame animal from the main herd. She pounced.

"I know all about you. Your mother is very insightful about the real Henry Day."

"You talked to my mother about me?"

"She said you went from being a carefree little boy to a serious old man overnight. Sweetheart, you need to stop living in your head and live in the world as it is."

I lifted myself out of my chair and leaned across the table to kiss her. "Now, tell me your theory on why parents kill their children."

We worked for weeks on her project, meeting in the library or carrying on about the subject when we went out dancing or to the movies or dinner.

More than once, we drew a startled stare from nearby strangers when we argued about killing children. Tess took care of the historical framework of the problem and delved into the available statistics. I tried to help by digging up a plausible theory. In certain societies, boys were favored over girls, to work on the farm or to pass on wealth, and as a matter of course, many females were murdered because they were unwanted. But in less patriarchal cultures, infanticide stemmed from a family's inability to care for another child in an age of large families and few resources—a brutal method of population control. For weeks, Tess and I puzzled over how parents decided which child to spare and which to abandon. Dr. Laurel, who taught the seminar, suggested that myth and folklore might provide interesting answers, and that's how I stumbled across the article.

Prowling the stacks late one evening, I found our library's sole copy of the *Journal of Myth and Society*, a fairly recent publication which had lasted a grand total of three issues. I flipped through the pages of this journal, rather casually standing there by my lonesome, when the name sprang from the page and grabbed me by the throat. Thomas McInnes. And then the title of his article was like a knife to the heart: "The Stolen Child."

Son of a bitch.

McInnes's theory was that in medieval Europe, parents who gave birth to a sickly child made a conscious decision to "reclassify" their infant as something other than human. They could claim that demons or "goblins" had come in the middle of the night and stolen their true baby and left behind one of their own sickly, misshapen, or crippled offspring, leaving the parents to abandon or raise the devil. Called "fairy children" or changelings in England, "*enfants changés*" in France, and "*Wechselbalgen*" in Germany, these devil children were fictions and rationalizations for a baby's failure to thrive, or for some other physical or mental birth defect. If one had a changeling in the home, one would not be expected to keep and raise it as one's own. Parents would have the right to be rid of the deformed creature, and they could take the child and leave it outside in the forest overnight. If the goblins refused to retrieve it, then the poor unfortunate would die from exposure or might be carried off by a wild thing.

The article recounted several versions of the legend, including the twelfth-century French cult of the Holy Greyhound. One day, a man comes home and finds blood on the muzzle of the hound trusted to guard his child. Enraged, the man beats the dog to death, only later to find his baby unharmed, with a viper dead on the floor by the crib. Realizing his error, the man erects a shrine to the "holy greyhound" that protected his son from the poisonous snake. Around this story grew the legend that mothers could take those babies with "child sickness" to such shrines in the forest and leave them with a note to the patron saint and protector of children: *"À Saint Guinefort, pour la vie ou pour la mort."*

"This form of infanticide, the deliberate killing of a child based on its slim probability of survival," wrote McInnes,

became part of the myth and folklore that endured well into the nineteenth century in Germany, the British Isles, and other European countries, and the superstition traveled with emigrants to the New World. In the 1850s, a small mining community in western Pennsylvania reported the disappearance of one dozen children from different families into the surrounding hills. And in pockets of Appalachia, from New York to Tennessee, local legend fostered a folk belief that these children still roam the forests.

A contemporary case that illustrates the psychological roots of the legend concerns a young man, "Andrew," who claimed under hypnosis to have been abducted by "hobgoblins." The recent unexplained discovery of an unidentified child, found drowned in a nearby river, was credited as the work of these ghouls. He reported that many of the missing children from the area were stolen by the goblins and lived unharmed in the woods nearby, while a changeling took each child's place and lived out that child's life in the community. Such delusions, like the rise of the changeling myth, are obvious social protections for the sad problem of missing or stolen children.

Not only had he gotten the story wrong, but he had used my own words against me. A superscript notation by "Andrew" directed the readers to the fine print of the footnote:

Andrew (not his real name) reeled off an elaborate story of a hobgoblin subculture that, he claimed, lived in a nearby wooded area, preying on the children of the town for over a century. He asserted also that he had once been a human child named Gustav Ungerland, who had arrived in the area as the son of German immigrants in the mid-nineteenth century. More incredibly, Andrew claims to have been a musical prodigy in his other life, a skill restored to him when he *changed back* in the late 1940s. His elaborate tale, sadly, indicates deep pathological developmental problems, possibly covering some early childhood abuse, trauma, or neglect.

I had to read the last sentence several times before it became clear. I wanted to howl, to track him down and cram his words into his mouth. I ripped the pages from the journal and threw the ruined magazine into the trash. "Liar, faker, thief," I muttered over and over as I paced back and forth among the stacks. Thankfully I encountered no one, for who knows how I might have vented my rage. Failure to thrive. Pathological problems. Abandoned children. He gave us changelings no credit at all and had the whole story backward. We went and snatched them from their beds. We were as real as nightmares.

The ping of the elevator chimes sounded like a gunshot, and through the open door appeared the librarian, a slight woman in cats-eye glasses, hair drawn back in a bun. She froze when she saw me, rather savagely disheveled, but she tamed me when she spoke. "We're closing," she called out. "You'll have to go."

I ducked behind a row of books and folded McInnes's pages into eighths, stuffing the packet in my denim jacket. She began walking toward me, heels clicking on the linoleum, and I attempted to alter my appearance, but the old magic was gone. The best I could do was run my fingers through my hair, stand up, and brush the wrinkles from my clothes.

"Didn't you hear me?" She stood directly in front of me, an unbending reed. "You have to go." She watched me depart. I turned at the elevator to wave good-bye, and she was leaning against a column, staring as if she knew my whole story.

A cool rain was falling, and I was late to meet Tess. Her class had ended hours before, and we should have been on our way back home. As I rushed down the stairs, I wondered if she would be furious with me, but such anxieties were nothing compared to my anger toward McInnes. Beneath the streetlight on the corner stood Tess, huddling under an umbrella against the rain. She walked to me, gathered me under its cover, and latched on to my arm.

"Henry, are you all right? You're shaking, baby. Are you cold? Henry, Henry?"

She pulled me closer, warmed us and kept us dry. She pressed her warm hands against my face, and I knew that cold, wet night was my best chance to confess. Beneath the umbrella, I told her I loved her. That was all I could say.

We lived in the dark hole, and the abandoned mine on the hillside proved to be a very bad home indeed. That first winter, I went into a deeper hibernation than ever before, waking only every few days to eat or drink a few mouthfuls, then back to bed. Most of the others dwelt in the narcoleptic state, a haze that lasted from December through March. The darkness enfolded us in its moist embrace, and for many weeks not a peep of sun reached us. Snowfalls almost sealed us in, but the porous entrance allowed the cold to penetrate. The walls wept and froze into slick crusts that shattered under pressure.

In the springtime we slipped into the green world, hungry and thin. In the unfamiliar territory, looking for food became a daily preoccupation. The hillside itself was all slag and shale, and even in high season, only the hardiest grasses and moss clung to a tenuous hold. No animals bothered to forage there. Béka cautioned us not to roam too far, so we made do with what we could scavenge nearby—grasshoppers and grubs, tea made out of bark, robin's breast, a roast skunk. We imagined all we missed by not visiting town.

"I would give my eyetooth for a taste of ice cream," Smaolach said at the conclusion to a mean supper. "Or a nice yellow banana."

"Raspberry jam," said Speck, "on warm, crunchy toast."

Onions chimed in: "Sauerkraut and pigs' feet."

"Spaghetti," Zanzara began, and Ragno finished, "with Parmesan."

"A Coke and a smoke." Luchóg patted his empty pouch.

"Why don't you let us go?" asked Chavisory. "It's been so long, Béka."

The gangly despot sat above us on a throne made from an empty dynamite crate. He had resisted granting liberties every time we had asked, but perhaps he, too, was brightening as the days were on the mend. "Onions, take Blomma and Kivi with you tonight, but be back before dawn. Stay off the roads and take no chances." He smiled at his own benevolence. "And bring me back a bottle of beer."

The three girls rose as one and left without delay. Béka should have read the signs and felt the coming change in his bones, but perhaps his thirst outweighed his judgment. A cold snap rolled over the western hills to meet the warm May air, and within hours a thick fog settled into the woods and clung to the darkness like the skin of a peach. We could see no farther than one giant step ahead, and the invisible cloak stretched between the trees created a general sense of unease about our absent friends.

After the others crawled into the darkness to sleep, Luchóg kept me company at the mine's entrance in a quiet vigil. "Don't worry, little treasure. While they cannot see, they cannot be seen. They'll find a careful hiding place till the sun cuts through this gloom."

We watched and became one with nothing. In the dead of it, a crashing through the trees awakened us. The noise rose in a single frantic wave. Branches snapped and broke, and an inhuman cry resounded and was swiftly extinguished. We peered into the mist, strained in the direction of the commotion. Luchóg struck a match and lit the torch kept at the mine's entrance. The twigs sputtered in the damp, caught hold, and burst into light. Emboldened by the fire, we stepped carefully toward the memory of the noise and the faint scent of blood on the ground. Ahead through the mist, two eyes mirrored our torchlight, and their glowing halted our progress. A fox snapped its jaws and carried away its prey, and we walked over to the killing spot. Fanned out like glass in a kaleidoscope, black-and-white-banded feathers lay strewn on the fallen leaves. Struggling with the heavy turkey, the fox bumbled off into the distance, and above us in the trees, the surviving birds huddled together, churring a comfort to one another.

Onions, Kivi, and Blomma still had not returned when I showed Speck the place where the fox had caught the tom. She chose a pair of the larger feathers and knitted them into her hair. "Last of the Mohicans," she said, and ran whooping into the lightening morn as I gave chase, and so we played away the day. When Speck and I returned late that afternoon, we found Béka angry and pacing. The girls had not come home, and he was torn between sending out a search party or waiting inside the mineshaft.

"What do you mean, keeping us here?" Speck demanded. "You told them be back by dawn. Do you think Onions would disobey you? They should have been back hours ago. Why aren't we out looking for them?" She divided the eight of us into pairs and mapped out four different approaches to town. To keep him calm, she went with Béka on the most direct path. Smaolach and Luchóg circled around our old stomping grounds, and Ragno and Zanzara followed well-worn deerpaths.

Chavisory and I took an ancient artery, blazed by the Indians perhaps, that ran parallel to the river, bending, dipping, and rising as the water twisted in its course. It seemed more likely that Onions, Kivi, and Blomma had taken another trail with better cover, but we stayed vigilant for any movement or other indications they had passed this way—such as fresh footprints or broken branches. The brush sometimes choked off passage, and we stepped out onto the exposed riverbank for short stints. Anyone driving across the high bridge that linked the highway to the town could have spotted us in the half-light, and I often wondered while on this path what we must look like from so far above. Ants, probably, or little children lost. Chavisory sang and hummed to herself a wordless tune at once familiar and strange.

"What is that song?" I asked her when we stopped to get our bearings. Far ahead in the river, a tug pushed a chain of barges toward the city.

"Chopin, I think."

"What is Chopin?"

She giggled and twisted a strand of hair around two fingers. "Not what, silly. Who. Chopin wrote the music, or at least that's what he said."

"Who said? Chopin?"

She laughed loudly, then covered her mouth with her free hand. "Chopin is dead. The boy who taught me the song. He said it is Chopin's mayonnaise."

"What boy is that? The one before me?"

Her demeanor changed, and she looked off in the distance at the receding barges. Even in the dim light, I could see she was blushing.

"Why won't you tell me? Why doesn't anyone ever talk about him?"

"Aniday, we never talk about changelings once they are gone. We try to forget everything about them. No good to chase after memories."

A far-off cry went out, a brief alarm that signaled us to make haste and rendezvous. We dropped our conversation and followed the sound. Ragno and Zanzara found her first, alone and crying in an empty glen. She had been wandering half the day, too confused and distraught to find her way home. The other pairs arrived within minutes to hear the news, and Béka sat down beside Onions and draped his arm around her shoulders. Kivi and Blomma were gone.

The three girls had seen the fog roll in and sped their way into town, reaching the lonesome outer streets as the worst weather fell. The streetlamps and storefront signs cast halos through the misted dark, serving as beacons for the faeries to navigate through the neighborhoods. Blomma told the other two not to worry about being seen by people in the houses. "We're invisible in this fog," she said, and perhaps her foolhardy confidence was their ruin. From the supermarket, they stole sugar, salt, flour, and a netted sack of oranges, then stashed the loot in an alley outside of the drugstore. Sneaking in through the back, they were surprised by all of the changes since their latest visit.

"Everything is different," Onions told us. "The soda fountain is gone, the whole counter and all those round chairs that spin you around. And no more booths. No candy counter, and the big tubs of penny candy are gone, too. Instead, there's more everything. Soap and shampoo, shoelaces, a whole wall of comic books and magazines. And there's a whole row of things just for babies. Diapers made out of plastic that you throw away, and baby bottles and cans of milk. And hundreds of those tiny jars of food, all gooshed up, and on each one the same picture of the cutest baby in the world. Applesauce and pears and bananas. Spinach and green beans. Sweet potatoes that look like red mud. And smooshed turkey and chicken with rice. Kivi wanted to taste every one, and we were there for hours."

I could picture the three of them, faces smeared with blueberries, bloated and sprawled in the aisle, dozens of empty jars strewn across the floor.

A car pulled up outside and stopped in front of the picture windows. The flashlight shone through the glass, slowly swept its beam along the interior, and when it neared, the girls leapt to their feet, slipped on the puddles of peas and carrots, and sent the jars spinning and clattering across the linoleum. The front door opened, and two policemen stepped inside. One of the men said to the other, "This is where he said they would be." Onions shouted for them to run, but Kivi and Blomma did not move. They stood side by side in the middle of the baby food aisle, joined hands, and waited for the men to come and get them.

"I don't know why," Onions said. "It was the most horrible thing I have ever seen. I circled around behind the men and could see Kivi and Blomma when the lights hit them right in the face. They looked as if they were waiting for it to happen. The policeman said, 'He was right. There is someone here.' And the other said, 'Freeze.' Kivi squeezed her eyes shut, and Blomma raised one hand to her forehead, but they didn't look afraid at all. Like they were happy, almost."

Onions wriggled through the door and escaped, not bothering with the stolen goods. Instinct set in, and she ran through the empty streets, heedless of all traffic, never looking back. The fog disoriented her, and she ran all the way through town to the other side. Once she had found a hiding place in a yellow barn, she waited nearly all day to return home, taking a route that skirted the streets. When Ragno and Zanzara found her, she was exhausted.

"Why did the man say that?" Béka asked her. "What did he mean, 'This is where he said they would be'?"

"Somebody must have told the policemen where we were." Onions shuddered. "Somebody who knows our ways."

Béka took her by the hands and lifted her up from the ground. "Who else could it be?" He was looking straight at me, as if accusing me of a heinous crime.

"But I didn't tell—"

"Not you, Aniday," he spat out. "The one who took your place."

"Chopin," said Chavisory, and one or two laughed at the name before catching their emotions. We trudged home in silence, remembering our missing friends Kivi and Blomma. Each of us found a private way to grieve. We took their dolls out of the hole and buried them in a single grave. Smaolach and Luchóg spent two weeks building a cairn, while Chavisory and Speck divided our departed friends' possessions among the nine of us left behind. Only Ragno and Zanzara remained stoic and impassive, accepting their share of clothing and shoes but saying next to nothing. Through that summer and into the fall, our conversations revolved around finding meaning in the girls' surrender. Onions did her best to convince us that a betrayal had occurred, and Béka joined in, affirming the conspiracy, arguing that the humans were out to get us and that it was only a matter of time before Kivi and Blomma would fully confess. The men in the black suits would return, the army men, the police and their dogs, and they would hunt us down. Others among us took a more thoughtful view.

Luchóg said, "They wanted to leave, and it was only a matter of time. I only hope that the poor things find home in the world and weren't sent off to live in a zoo or put under the microscope by a mad scientist."

We never heard of them again. Vanished, as if an airy nothing.

More than ever, Béka insisted we live in darkness, but he did allow us nights away from the diminished clan. When the chance arose over those next few years, Speck and I would steal away to sleep in relative peace and luxury beneath the library. We threw ourselves into our books and papers. We read the Greeks in translation, Clytemnestra in her grief, Antigone's honor in a thin coating of earth. Grendel prowling the bleak Danish night. The pilgrims of Canterbury and lives on the road. Maxims of Pope, the rich clot of humanity in all of Shakespeare, Milton's angels and aurochs, Gulliver big, little, yahoo. Wild ecstasies of Keats. Shelley's Frankenstein. Rip Van Winkle sleeping it off. Speck insisted on Austen, Eliot, Emerson, Thoreau, the Brontës, Alcott, Nesbitt, Rossetti, both Brownings, and especially Alice down the rabbit hole. We worked our way right up to the present age, chewing through the books like a pair of silverfish.

Sometimes, Speck would read aloud to me. I would hand her a story she had never before seen, and almost without a beat, she made it hers. She frightened me from the word *Once* in Poe's "The Raven." She brought me to tears over Ben Jonson's drowned cat. She made the hooves thunder in "The Charge of the Light Brigade" and the waves roar in Tennyson's "Ulysses." I loved the music of her voice and watching her face as she read, season after season. In the summertime her bared skin darkened, and her dark hair brightened in the sunshine. During the cold part of the year, she disappeared beneath layers, so that sometimes all I could see was her wide forehead and dark brows. On winter nights in that candlelit space, her eyes shone out from the circles beneath her eyes. Although we had spent twenty years together, she secreted away the power to shock or surprise, to say a word and break my heart.

CHAPTER 25

I had a name, although at times Gustav Ungerland was no more real to me than Henry Day. The simple solution would have been to track down Tom McInnes and ask him for more details about what had been said under hypnosis. After finding the article in the library, I tried to locate its author but had no more to go on than the address in the magazine. Several weeks after receiving my letter, the editor of the defunct *Journal of Myth and Society* replied that he would be glad to forward it on to the professor, but nothing came of it. When I called his university, the chairman of the department said McInnes had vanished on a Monday morning, right in the middle of the semester, and left no forwarding address. My attempts at contacting Brian Ungerland proved equally frustrating. I couldn't very well pester Tess for information about her old boyfriend, and after asking around town, someone told me that Brian was at Fort Sill, Oklahoma, with the U.S. Army, studying how to blow things up. There were no Ungerlands in our local phone book.

Fortunately, other things occupied my thoughts. Tess had talked me into going back to school, and I was to begin in January. She changed when I told her my plans, became more attentive and affectionate. We celebrated registering for classes by splurging on dinner and Christmas shopping in the city. Arm in arm, we walked the sidewalks downtown. In the windows of Kaufmann's Department Store, miniature animatronic scenes played out in an endless loop. Santa and his elves hammered at the same wooden bicycle. Skaters circled atop an icy mirror for all eternity. We stopped and lingered before one display—a human family, baby in the bassinet, proud parents kissing under the mistletoe. Our own images reflected on and through the glass, superimposed over the mechanicals' domestic bliss.

"Isn't that adorable? Look at how lifelike they made the baby. Doesn't she make you want to have one yourself?"

"Sure, if they were all as quiet as that one."

We strolled by the park, where a ragtag bunch of children queued up to a stand selling hot chocolate. We bought two cups and sat on a cold park bench. "You do like children, don't you?"

"Children? I never think about them."

"But wouldn't you want a son to take camping or a girl to call your own?"

"Call my own? People don't belong to other people."

"You're a very literal person sometimes."

"I don't think—"

"No, you don't. Most people pick up on subtleties, but you operate in another dimension."

But I knew what she meant. I did not know if having a real human baby was possible. Or would it be half human, half goblin, a monster? A horrid creature with a huge head and shrunken body, or those dead eyes peering out beneath a sunbonnet. Or a misery that would turn on me and expose my secret. Yet Tess's warm presence on my arm had a curious tug on my conscience. Part of me desired to unpack the burdens of the past, to tell her all about Gustav Ungerland and my fugitive life in the forest. But so much time had passed since the change that at times I doubted that existence. All of my powers and skills learned a lifetime ago had disappeared, lost while endlessly playing the piano, faded in the comfort of warm beds and cozy living rooms, in the reality of this lovely woman beside me. Is the past as real as the present? Maybe I wish I *had* told everything, and that the truth had revised the course of life. I don't know. But I do remember the feeling of that night, the mixed sensation of great hope and bottomless foreboding.

Tess watched a group of children skating across a makeshift ice rink. She blew on her drink and sent a fog of steam into the air. "I've always wanted a baby of my own."

For once, I understood what another person was trying to tell me. With the music of a calliope harmonizing with the sound of children laughing under the stars, I asked her to marry me.

We waited until the end of spring semester and were married in May 1968 at the same church where Henry Day had been baptized as an infant. Standing at the altar, I felt almost human again, and in our vows existed the possibility for a happy ending. When we marched down the aisle I could see, in the smiling faces of all our friends and family, an unsuspecting joy for Mr. and Mrs. Henry Day. During the ceremony, I half expected that when the double doors opened to the daylight there would be a retinue of changelings waiting to take me away. I did my best to forget my past, to dismiss the thought that I was a fraud.

At the reception, my mother and Uncle Charlie were the first to greet us, and they had not only paid for the party but even made us a gift of a honeymoon in Europe. While we were away in Germany, they would elope together, but that afternoon it was passing strange to see him where Bill Day should have been. Nostalgia for my father was fleeting, for we were leaving behind the past and claiming life. So much would change over the next few years. George Knoll would leave town a few weeks after the wedding to wander across the country for a year, and he ended up in San Francisco, running a sidewalk bistro with an older woman from Spain. With no Coverboys, Oscar would buy a jukebox that fall, and the customers would still flock in for drinks and pop music. Jimmy Cummings took my old job behind the bar. Even my baby sisters were growing up.

Mary and Elizabeth brought their latest boyfriends, a couple of long-haired twins, to the reception, and at the center of the party, Uncle Charlie regaled the crowd with his latest scheme. "Those houses up on the ridge are only the beginning. People are not merely going to move out of the cities; they're going to be moving as far away as they can. My company is sitting on a gold mine in this county."

My mother sidled up to him, and he put his arm around her waist and rested his hand on her hip.

"When I first heard about the trouble up in the woods and sending in the National Guard, well, my first thought was that when the government was through, land would be dirt cheap."

She laughed so willingly at his pun that I flinched. Tess squeezed my arm to prevent me from saying what I was thinking.

"Country living. Moderately priced, safe and secure, perfect for young couples looking to start a family." As if on cue, he and my mother stared right at Tess's belly. Already they were full of hope.

Feigning innocence, Elizabeth asked, "How about you two, Uncle Charlie?"

Tess squeezed my bottom, and I let out a tiny whoop just as Jimmy Cummings stepped up to speak. "I wouldn't want to live up there, man."

"Of course not, Jimmy," Mary said. "After all you went through in those woods."

"There's something up there," he told the party. "Did you hear the rumor about those wild little girls they found the other night?"

The guests began to drift off in pairs and start new conversations. Since his rescue of young Oscar Love, Jimmy had acquired a reputation for tiresome repetitions of the story, exaggerating details until it became a tall tale. When he launched into another yarn, he was bound to be dismissed as merely another storyteller, desperate for attention. "No really," he said to the few of us remaining. "I heard the local fuzz found these two girls, 'bout six or seven, I hear, who had broken into the drugstore in the dead of night and smashed everything in sight. The cops were scared of those girls, said they were spooky as a pair of cats. Man, they could barely speak a word of English or any language known to man. Put two and two together. They were living up in the woods—remember that place I found Oscar? Maybe there are others up there. Put your mind around that. Like a whole lost tribe of wild children. It's a trip, man."

Elizabeth was staring at me when she asked him, "What happened to them? Where are those two girls?"

"Can't confirm or deny a rumor," he said, "and I didn't actually see them with my own two eyes, but I don't have to. Did you know the FBI came and took 'em away? To Washington, D.C., and their secret labs, so they could study them."

I turned to Oscar, who stood slack-jawed, listening to Jimmy. "Are you sure you want this boy tending bar for you, Oscar? Seems like he's been hitting the bottle a bit too much."

Jimmy came right up to my face and said sotto voce, "Know the trouble with you, Henry? You lack imagination. But they're up there, man. You better freakin' believe it."

During the flight to Germany, dreams of changelings interrupted what sleep I could manage on the airplane. When Tess and I landed in damp and overcast Frankfurt, we had two different expectations for our honeymoon. Poor thing, she wanted adventure, excitement, and romance. Two young lovers traveling through Europe. Bistros, wine and cheese, jaunts on motorbikes. I was looking for a ghost and evidence of my past, but all I knew could be written on a cocktail napkin: Gustav Ungerland, 1859, Eger.

Immediately bewildered by the city, we found a small room in a pension on Mendelssohnstrasse. We were dazed by the sooty black elephant of the Hauptbahnhof, disgorging trains by the hour, and behind it the resurrected city, new steel and concrete skyscrapers rising from the ashes of the ruins. Americans were everywhere. Soldiers fortunate enough to have drawn duty guarding against Eastern Europe rather than fighting in Vietnam. Strung-out runaways in the Konstablerwache shooting up in broad daylight or begging for our spare change. Our first week together, we felt out of place between the soldiers and the junkies.

On Sunday we strolled over to the Römerberg, a papier-mâché version of the medieval Alstadt that had been mostly bombed out by the Allies in the final months of the war. For the first time on our trip, the weather was bright and sunny, and we enjoyed a springtime street fair. On the carousel in the middle of the festival, Tess rode a zebra and I a griffin; then we held hands after lunch in the café as a strolling quartet played a song for us. As if the honeymoon had finally commenced, when we made love that night, our tiny room became a cozy paradise.

"This is more like it," she whispered in the dark. "How I imagined we would be together. I wish every day could be like today."

I sat up and lit a Camel. "I was wondering if maybe tomorrow we could go our own ways for a while. You know, have time to ourselves. Just think how much more we'll have to talk about when we're back together. There's stuff I'd like to do that might not be interesting to you, so I was thinking maybe I could get up a bit earlier and go out, and I'd be back, probably, by the time you woke up. See the National Library. You would be bored to tears."

"Cool out, Henry." She rolled over and faced the wall. "That sounds perfect. I'm getting a little tired of spending every minute together."

It took all morning to find the right train, then the right streets, and the address to the Deutsche Bibliothek, and another hour or so to find the map room. A charming young librarian with workable English helped me with the historical atlas and the seemingly thousands of alterations and border changes brought about by hundreds of years of war and peace, from the final days of the Holy Roman Empire through the Hessian principalities' Reichstag to the divisions at the end of both world wars. She did not know Eger, could not find anyone in Reference that had heard of the town.

"Do you know," she finally asked, "if it is East Germany?"

I looked at my watch and discovered it was 4:35 in the afternoon. The library closed at 5:00 P.M., and a furious new wife would be waiting for me.

She scoured the map. "Ach, now I see. It's a river, not a town. Eger on the border." She pointed to a dot that read *Cheb (Eger)*. "The town you are looking for isn't called Eger now, and it isn't in Germany. It's in Czechoslovakia." She licked her finger and paged back through the atlas to find another map. "Bohemia. Look here, in 1859 this was all Bohemia, from here to here. And Eger, right there. I have to say I much prefer the old name." Smiling, she rested her hand on my shoulder. "But we have found it. One place with two names. Eger is Cheb."

"So, how do I get to Czechoslovakia?"

"Unless you have the right papers, you don't." She could read my disappointment. "So, tell me, what is so important about Cheb?"

"I'm looking for my father," I said. "Gustav Ungerland."

The radiance melted from her face. She looked at the floor between her feet. "Ungerland. Was he killed in the war? Sent to the camps?"

"No, no. We're Catholics. He's from Eger; I mean, Cheb. His family, that is. They emigrated to America in the last century."

"You might try the church records in Cheb, if you could get in." She raised one dark eyebrow. "There may be a way."

We had a few drinks in a café, and she told me how to cross the line without being detected. Making my way back to Mendelssohnstrasse late that evening, I rehearsed a story to explain my long absence. Tess was asleep when I came in after ten, and I slid into bed beside her. She woke with a start, then rolled over and faced me on the pillow.

"I'm sorry," I said. "Lost in the library."

Lit by the moon, her face looked swollen, as if she had been crying. "I'd like to get out of this gray city and see the countryside. Go hiking, sleep under the stars. Meet some real Germans."

"I know a place," I whispered, "filled with old castles and dark woods near the border. Let's sneak across and discover all their secrets."

The morning is perfect in memory, a late-summer day when blue skies foretold the coming autumn crispness. Speck and I had awakened next to each other in a sea of books, then left the library in those magically empty moments between parents going off to work, or children off to school, and the hour when stores and businesses opened their doors. By my stone calendar, five long and miserable years had passed since our diminished tribe took up our new home, and we had grown weary of the dark. Time away from the mine inevitably brightened Speck's mood, and that morning, when first I saw her peaceful face, I longed to tell her how she made my heart beat. But I never did. In that sense, the day seemed like every other, but it would become a day unto its own.

Overhead, a jet trailed a string of smoke, white against the paleness of September. We matched strides and talked of our books. Shadows ahead appeared briefly between the trees, a slender breeze blew, and a few leaves tumbled from the heights. To me, it looked for an instant as if ahead on the path Kivi and Blomma were playing in a patch of sun. The mirage passed too quickly, but the trick of light brought to mind the mystery behind their departure, and I told Speck of my brief vision of our missing friends. I asked her if she ever wondered whether they really wanted to be caught.

Speck stopped at the edge of cover before the exposed land that led to the mine's entrance. The loose shale at her feet shifted and crunched. A pale moon sat in a cloudless sky, and we were wary of the climb, watching the air for a plane that might discover us. She grabbed me by the shoulder and spun me around so quickly that I feared imminent peril. Her eyes locked on mine.

"You don't understand, Aniday. Kivi and Blomma could not take it another moment. They were desperate for the other side. To be with those who live in the light and upper world, real family, real friends. Don't you ever want to run away, go back into the world as somebody's child? Or come away with me?"

Her questions poured out like sugar from a split sack. The past had eased its claims on me, and my nightmares of that world had stopped. Not until I sat down to write this book did the memories return, dusted and polished new again. But that morning, my life was there. With her. I looked into her eyes, but she seemed far away in thought, as if she could not see me before her but only a distant space and time alive in her imagination. I had fallen in love with her. And that moment, the words came falling, and confession moved to my lips. "Speck, I have something—"

"Wait. Listen."

The noise surrounded us: a low rumble from inside the hill, zigzagging along the ground to where we two stood, vibrating beneath our feet, then fanning out into the forest. In the next instant, a crack and tumble, muffled by the outer surface. The earth collapsed upon itself with a sigh. She squeezed my hand and dragged me, running at top speed, toward the entrance of the mine. A plume of dirt swirled from the fissure like a chimney gently smoking on a winter's night. Up close, acrid dust thickened and choked off breathing. We tried to fight through it but had to wait upwind until the fog dissipated. From inside, a reedy sound escaped from the crack to fade in the air. Before the soot settled, the first person emerged. A single hand gripped the rim of rock, then the other, and the head pushed through, the body shouldering into the open. In the wan light, we ran through the cloud to the prostrate body.

Speck turned it over with her foot: Béka. Onions soon followed, wheezing and panting, and lay down beside him, her arm roped over his chest.

Speck leaned down to ask, "Is he dead?"

"Cave-in," Onions whispered.

"Are there any survivors?"

"I don't know." She brushed back Béka's dirty hair, away from his blinking eyes.

We forced ourselves into the mine's darkness. Speck felt around for the flint, struck it, and sparked the torches. The firelight reflected particles floating in the air, settling like sediment stirred in a glass. I called out to the others, and my heart beat wildly with hope when a voice replied: "Over here, over here." As if moving through a snowy nightmare, we followed the sound down the main tunnel, turning left into the chamber where most of the clan slept each night. Luchóg stood at the entranceway, fine silt clinging to his hair, skin, and clothes. His eyes shone clear and moist, and on his face tears had left wet trails in the dirt. His fingers, red and raw, shook violently as he waited for us. Ashes floated in the halo created by the torchlight. I could make out the broad back of Smaolach, who was facing a pile of rubble where our sleeping room once stood. At a frantic pace, he tossed stones to the side, trying to move the mountain bit by bit. I saw no one else. We sprang to his aid, lifting debris from the mound that ran to the ceiling.

"What happened?" Speck asked.

"They're trapped," Luchóg said. "Smaolach thinks he heard voices on the other side. The roof came down all at once. We'd be under there, too, if I hadn't the need for a smoke when I woke up this morning."

"Onions and Béka are already out. We saw them outside," I said.

"Are you there?" Speck asked the rock. "Hold on, we'll get you out."

We dug until there appeared an opening big enough for Smaolach to stick his arm through to the elbow. Energized, we pounced, clawing away stones until Luchóg shinnied through the space and disappeared. The three of us stopped and waited for a sound for what seemed like forever. Finally Speck shouted into the void, "Do you see anything, mouse?"

"Dig," he called. "I can hear breathing."

Without a word, Speck left abruptly, and Smaolach and I continued to enlarge the passageway. We could hear Luchóg on the other side, scrabbling through the tunnel like a small creature in the walls of a house. Every few minutes, he would murmur reassurance to someone, then exhort us to keep burrowing, and we desperately worked harder, muscles enflamed, our throats caked with dust. As suddenly as she had disappeared, Speck returned, another torch in hand to throw more light upon our work. Her face taut with anger, she reached up and tore at the stone. "Béka, that bastard," she said. "They've gone. No help to anyone but himself."

After much digging, we made the hole wide enough for me to crawl through the rubble. I nearly landed on my face, but Luchóg broke my fall. "Down here," he said softly, and we crouched together over the supine figure. Half buried under the ruins lay Chavisory, still and cold to the touch. Covered by ash, she looked like a ghost and her breath smelled mortally sour.

"She's alive." Luchóg spoke in a whisper. "But barely, and I think her legs are broken. I can't move these heavy ones by myself." He looked stricken with fear and fatigue. "You'll have to help me."

Stone by stone, we unburied her. Straining under the weight of the last debris, I asked him, "Have you seen Ragno and Zanzara? Did they get out okay?"

"Not a trace." He motioned back toward our sleeping quarters, now buried under a ton of earth. The boys must have been sleeping in when the roof collapsed, and I prayed that they had not stirred and went from sleep to death as easily as turning over in their bed. But we could not stop to think of them. The possibility of another collapse urged us on. Chavisory moaned when we removed the last rock off her left ankle, a greenstick fracture, the bones and skin raw and pulpy. Her foot flopped at a sickening angle when we lifted her, and the blood left a viscous slick on our hands. She cried out with every step and lost consciousness as we struggled up to the tunnel, half pulling, half pushing her through. When he saw her leg, bone piercing the skin, Smaolach turned and threw up into the corner. As we rested there before the final push, Speck asked, "Is anyone else alive?"

"I don't think so," I said.

She closed her eyes for a moment, then issued orders for our quick escape. The most difficult part involved the exit of the mine itself, and Chavisory awoke and screamed as she was pinched through. At that moment, I wished we had all been inside, asleep next to one another, all of us buried for good and out of our own private miseries. Exhausted, we placed her down gently on the hillside. None of us knew what to do or say or think. Inside another implosion shuddered, and the mine puffed out one last gasp like a dying dragon.

Spent and confused by grief, we waited for nightfall. None of us thought that the collapse might have been heard by the people in town or that it might possibly draw the humans to investigate. Luchóg spotted the dot of light first, a small fire burning down by the treeline. With no hesitation or discussion, the four of us picked up Chavisory, our arms linked in a gurney, and headed toward the light. Although worried that the fire might belong to strangers, we decided it would be better, in the end, to find help. We moved cautiously over the shale, causing more pain for poor Chavisory, yet hopeful that the fire would give us a place to stay out of the creeping cold for the night, somewhere we might tend her wounds.

The wind creaked through the bones of the treetops and shook the upper branches like clacking fingers. The fire had been built by Béka. He offered no apologies or explanations, just grunted like an old bear at our questions before shuffling off to be alone. Onions and Speck crafted a splint for Chavisory's broken ankle, binding it up with Luchóg's jacket, and they covered her with fallen leaves and lay next to her all night to share the warmth from their bodies. Smaolach wandered off and returned much later with a gourd filled with water. We sat and stared at the fire, brushing the caked dirt from our hair and clothing, waiting for the sun to rise. In those quiet hours, we mourned the dead. Ragno and Zanzara were as gone as Kivi and Blomma and Igel.

In place of the prior morning's brilliant glow, a gentle rain crawled in and settled. Only the occasional whistle from a lonesome bird marked the passing time. Around midday, a fierce yell of pain punctuated the stillness. Chavisory awoke to her ordeal and cursed the rock, the mine, Béka, and us all. We could not silence her anguished cries until Speck took her hand and willed her through steadfastness to be quiet. The rest of us looked away from her, stealing glances at one another's faces, masks of weariness and sorrow. We were now seven. I had to count twice to believe it.

T ess didn't need to be talked into sneaking across the border, and the very idea of transgression sent an erotic jolt into our honeymoon. The closer we got to Czechoslovakia, the livelier the sex became. On the day we mapped our secret passage to the other side, she kept me in bed until mid-morning. Her desires fed my own curiosity about my hidden heritage. I needed to know where I had come from, who I had been. Every step along the way brought the sensation of returning home. The landscape looked familiar and dreamlike, as if the trees, lakes, and hills lay embedded, but long dormant, in my senses. The architecture of stone and exposed timber was exactly as I had pictured, and at inns and cafés, the people we met bore familial traces in their sturdy bodies, fine chiseled features, clear blue eyes, and sweeping blonde hair. Their faces enticed me deeper into Bohemia. We decided to cross into the forbidden land at the village of Hohenberg, which sat on the German line.

Since it was first dedicated in 1222, the castle at the center of town had been destroyed and rebuilt several times, most recently after World War II. On a sunny Saturday, Tess and I had the place to ourselves except for a young German family with small children who followed us from building to building. They caught up to us outside, near the uneven white walls that ran along the city's rear border, a fortress against attack from the forest and the Eger River beyond.

"Pardon me," the mother said to Tess in English, "you are American, right? Would you a photograph take? Of my family, on my camera?"

I blanched at being so easily recognizable as Americans. Tess smiled at me, took off her backpack, and laid it on the ground. The family of six arranged themselves at the base of one of the original parapets. The children looked as if they could have been my brothers and sisters, and as they posed, the notion that I once was part of such a family lingered and then receded into ether. Tess took a few steps backward to squeeze them all into the frame, and the small children cried out, *"Vorsicht, der Igel! Der Igel!"* The boy, no more than five, ran straight at Tess with a mad expression in his blue eyes. He stopped at her feet, reached between her ankles to a small flower bed, and carefully scooped up something in his small hands.

"What do you have there?" Tess bent to meet his face.

He held out his hands and a hedgehog crawled out from his fingers. Everybody laughed at the minor drama of Tess nearly stepping on the prickly thing, but I could barely light a smoke due to the shakes. Igel. I had not heard that name in almost twenty years. All of them had names, not quite forgotten. I reached out to touch Tess to help put them out of mind.

After the family left, we followed the map to hiking trails behind the castle. Along one path, we came across a miniature cave, and in front, signs of an encampment, what looked to me like an abandoned ring. I led us away quickly, heading east and downhill through the black woods. Our trail spilled out to a two-lane road devoid of traffic. Around the bend, a sign saying EGER STEG pointed to a dirt road to the right, and we came upon mild rapids across a narrow river, no more than a wide but shallow stream. On the opposite bank lay the Czechoslovakian woods, and in the hills behind, Cheb. Not another soul was in sight, and perhaps because of the river or the rocks, no barbed-wire fence protected the border. Tess held my hand and we crossed.

The rocks above the waterline provided safe footing, but we had to watch our step. When we reached the Czech side, a thrill, sharp as a razor, went through me. We'd made it. Home, or as close to it as possible. At that instant, I was ready to convert—or revert—and lay claim to my identity. Tess and I had disguised ourselves as best we could that morning, affecting a European indifference to our hair and clothing, but I worried that others might see through the ruse. In hindsight, I should not have worried so, for 1968 was the year of the Prague Spring, that open window when Dubček tried to bring "socialism with a human face" to the benighted Czechs and Slovaks. The Russian tanks would not roll in until August.

Tess loved the danger of our trespass and skulked along the leafy floor like an escaped prisoner. I tried to keep up with her, hold her hand, and assume an air of silent cunning. After a mile or so on our hike, an intermittent sprinkle fell through the green leaves, and then a shower began in earnest. The raindrops hit the canopy above and dripped down with a steady beat, but underneath that rhythm, an irregular sound of footsteps became audible. It was too dark to make out any figures, but I heard them marching through the brush, circling around, following us. I grabbed her arm and pushed on faster.

"Henry, do you hear that?" Tess's eyes darted about, and she turned her head from side to side. They kept on coming, and we began to run. She took one last look over her shoulder and screamed. Catching me by the elbow, Tess stopped our progress and wheeled me around to face our tormentors. They looked forlorn in the falling rain. Three cows, two brindles and one white, stared back at us, indifferently chewing their cuds.

Soaked, we fled the wet forest and found the road. We must have been a pitiable sight, for a farmer's truck stopped, and the driver indicated with his meaty thumb that we could hitch a ride in the back. Tess shouted "Cheb?" to him through the rain, and when he nodded, we got in and rode atop a mountain of potatoes for a half-hour all the way to the quaint Czech village. I kept my eyes on the receding woods, the winding road, sure that we were being followed.

Like flowers in a spring garden, the houses and stores were painted in pale pastels, the old buildings in white and yellow, taupe and verdigris. While many parts of Cheb seemed ageless, the buildings and landmarks struck no chords in my memory. A black sedan with a red glass siren sat parked at a crazy angle before the town hall. To avoid the police, we walked in the opposite direction, hoping to find someone who could understand our fractured German. We shied away from the pink Hotel Hvezda, spooked by a severe policeman outside who stared at us for a full thirty seconds. Across the square, past the sculpture of the Savage Man, sat a ramshackle hotel near the Ohře River. I had hoped and expected the landmarks to trigger memories of Gustav Ungerland, but nothing was familiar. My vaulted expectations, conjured along the journey, proved too high a hope. It was as if I had never been there before, or as if childhood in Bohemia had never existed.

Inside a dark and smoky bar, we bribed the manager with American dollars to let us dine on sausages and boiled potatoes, and a dank half-bottle of East German wine. After our meal, we were led up a crooked staircase to a tiny room with no more than a bed and a basin. I locked the door, and Tess and I lay on our backs in our jackets and boots on the threadbare covers, too tense, tired, and excited to move. Darkness slowly stole the light, and the silence was broken only by the sounds of our breathing and wild, racing hearts.

"What are we doing here?" she finally asked.

I sat up and began undressing. In my former life, I could have seen her in the dark as clearly as break of day, but now I relied on imagination. "Isn't it a kick? This town was once part of Germany, and before that of Bohemia?"

She took off her boots, slipped out of her jacket. I slid under the woolen blankets and coarse sheets as she undressed. Shivering and naked, Tess moved in close, rubbing a cold foot against my leg. "I'm scared. Suppose the secret police come knocking on the door?"

"Don't worry, baby," I told her in my best James Bond. "I've got a license to kill." I rolled over on top of her, and we did our best to live for the danger.

Waking late the next morning, we hurried over to the grand old Church of St. Nicholas, arriving late for a Mass in Czech and Latin. Nearest the altar sat a few elderly women, rosaries draped in their folded hands, and sprinkled here and there, small families sat in clumps, dazed and wary as sheep. At the entrance-way, two men in dark suits may have been watching us. I tried to sing along with the hymns, but I could only fake the words. While I did not understand the service, its rites and rituals mirrored those long-ago Masses with my mother—icons above candles, rich vestments of the priests and pristine altar boys, the rhythm of standing, kneeling, sitting, a consecration heralded by the bells. Although I knew by then it was just a romantic folly, I could picture my former self done up in Sunday clothes beside her on the pew with my reluctant, sighing father and the twins squirming in their skirts. What struck me most of all was the organ music from the loft above, cascading like a river over rocks.

As the parishioners exited, they stopped to share a few words among themselves and to greet the wizened priest standing in the bright sunshine beyond the door. A blonde girl turned to her nearly identical sister and pointed to us, whispered in his ear, and then they ran hand in hand from the church. Tess and I lingered, taking in the elaborate statues of Mary and St. Nicholas flanking the entrance, and we were the final pair to leave the building. When Tess held out her hand to the priest, she found herself captured in his grasp and drawn closer.

"Thank you for coming," he said, then turned to me, a strange look in his eyes, as if he knew my history. "And God bless you, my son."

Tess broke into a beatific grin. "Your English is perfect. How did you know we are Americans?"

He held her hand the whole time. "I was five years in New Orleans at the St. Louis Cathedral back when I was first ordained. Father Karel Hlinka. You're here for the festival?"

"What festival?" Tess brightened at the prospect.

"*Pražské Jaro.* The Prague Spring International Music Festival."

"Oh, no. We knew nothing about that." She leaned in and said in a low, confidential voice, "We snuck across the border."

Hlinka laughed, taking her remark as a joke, and she swiftly changed the subject, asking him about his American experience and the café life of New Orleans. As they chatted and laughed, I went outside, stood in a corner to light a cigarette, and considered the blue smoke curling to the sky. The two blonde sisters had circled back, this time leading a group of other children gathered from the streets. Like a string of birds on a telephone wire, they stood just beyond the gates, a dozen heads peeking over the low wall. I could hear them babbling in Czech, a phrase that sounded like *podvržené dítě* popping up like the leitmotif of their chattering song. With a glance at my wife, who was holding Father Hlinka in rapt attention, I started to walk over to the children, who scattered like pigeons when I came too close. They flew in again when I showed them my back, and ran off, laughing and screaming, when I turned around. When I stepped outside the gate, I found one girl cowering behind the wall. We spoke in German, and I told her not to be afraid.

"Why is everyone running away and laughing?"

"She told us there was a devil in the church."

"But I am not a devil . . . just an American."

"She said you are from the woods. A fairy."

Beyond the town's streets, the old forest bristled with life. "There are no such things as fairies."

The girl stood up and faced me, hands on her hips. "I don't believe you," she said, and turned to race off to her companions. I stood there watching her go, my mind twisted in knots, worried that I had made a mistake. But we had come too far for me to be frightened by mere children or the threat of the police. In a way, they were no different from other people. Suspicion was a second skin for me, and I felt perfectly capable of hiding the facts from everyone.

Tess bounded through the gates and found me on the sidewalk. "How would you like a private tour, baby?"

Father Hlinka was at her side. "Frau Day tells me that you are a musician, a composer. You must try out the pipe organ here. Best in Cheb."

In the loft high above the church, I sat at the keyboard, the empty pews stretching out before me, the gilt altar, the enormous crucifix, and played like a man possessed. To work the foot pedals and get the right tone from the massive organ, I had to rock and throw my weight against the machine, but once I figured out its complexities of stops and bellows and was in the flow of the music, it became a kind of dance. I performed a simple piece from the *Berceuse* by Louis Vierne, and for the first time in years felt myself again. While I was playing, I became a thing apart, not aware of anyone or anything else but the music, which infused me like hot ice and fell over me like wondrous strange snow. Father Hlinka and Tess sat in the gallery with me, watching my hands move, my head bob, and listened to the music.

When she tired of the violent sound, Tess kissed my cheek and wandered down the staircase to look over the rest of the church. Alone with the priest, I quickly broached the reason for my visit to Cheb. I told him of my research into family history and how the librarian back in Frankfurt had advised me to check the church records, for there was little hope of getting access to the central government archives.

"It's a surprise for her," I said. "I want to trace Tess's family tree, and the missing link is her grandfather, Gustav Ungerland. If I could just find his birthday or any information about him, I will make up a family history for her."

"That sounds like a wonderful thing to do. Come back tomorrow. I'll dig through the archives, and you can play the music for me."

"But you can't tell my wife."

He winked, and we were co-conspirators.

Over dinner, I told Tess about the musical half of Father Hlinka's offer, and she was happy for me to have the chance to go back to the organ loft. On Monday afternoon, she sat below in the middle pew, listening for the first hour or so, but then went off on her own. After she left, Father Hlinka whispered, "I have something for you." He crooked his finger, beckoning me to follow him into a small alcove off the loft. I suspected that he had found some record of the Ungerlands, and my anticipation grew when the priest lifted a wooden chest to the top of a rickety desk. He blew dust off the lid and, grinning like an elf, opened the box.

Instead of the church documents I had expected, I saw music. Score after score of music for the organ, and not just common hymns, but symphonic masterworks that gave life and presence to the instrument—a raft of Handel, Mahler's *Resurrection*, Liszt's *Battle of the Huns*, the *Fantasie Symphonique* by François-Joseph Fétis, and a pair of organ-only solos by Guilmant. There were pieces by Gigout, Langlais, Chaynes, and Poulenc's *Concerto for Organ, Strings, and Timpani*. Record albums of Aaron Copland's *First Symphony*, Barber's *Toccata Festiva*, Rheinberger, Franck, and a baker's dozen of Bach. I was stunned and inspired. To simply listen to it all—not to mention trying my hand at the grand keyboard—would take months or even years, and we had but a few hours. I wanted to stuff my pockets with loot, fill my head with song.

"My only vice and passion," Hlinka said to me. "Enjoy. We are not so different, you and I. Strange creatures with rare loves. Only you, my friend, you can play, and I can but listen."

I played all day for Father Hlinka, who inspected old parish ledgers of baptisms, weddings, and funerals. I dazzled him with incandescence and extravagance, leaning into the extra octave of bass, and hammered out the mad finale from Joseph Jongen's *Symphonie Concertante*. A change came over me at that keyboard, and I began to hear compositions of my own in the interludes. The music stirred memories that existed beyond the town, and on that glorious afternoon I experimented with variations and was so carried away that I forgot about Father Hlinka until he returned empty-handed at five o'clock. Frustrated by his own failure to find any records of the Ungerlands, he called his peers at St. Wenceslas, and they got in touch with the archivists of the abandoned St. Bartholomew and St. Klara churches to help scour through the records.

I was running out of time. Despite the relative freedom, we were still in danger of being asked for our papers, and we had no visa for Czechoslovakia. Tess had complained over breakfast that the police were spying on her when she visited the Black Tower, following her at the art center on the Růžový kopeček. Schoolchildren pointed at her on the streets. I saw them, too, running in the shadows, hiding in dark corners. On Wednesday morning, she groused about spending so much of our honeymoon alone.

"Just one more day," I pleaded. "There's nothing quite like the sound in that church."

"Okay, but I'm staying in today. Wouldn't you rather go back to bed?"

When I arrived at the loft late that afternoon, I was surprised to find the priest waiting for me at the pipe organ. "You must let me tell your wife." He grinned. "We have found him. Or at least I think this must be her grandfather. The dates are somewhat off, but how many Gustav Ungerlands can there be?"

He handed me a grainy photocopy of the passenger list from the German ship *Albert*, departing 20 May 1851 from Bremen to Baltimore, Maryland. The names and ages were written in a fine hand:

| | | | | |
|---|---|---|---|---|
| *212 Abram Ungerland* | *42* | *Musikant* | *Eger* | *Boheme* |
| *213 Clara Ungerland* | *40* | | " | " |
| *214 Friedrich* " | *14* | | " | " |
| *215 Josef* " | *6* | | " | " |
| *216 Gustav* " | *1/2* | | " | " |
| *217 Anna* " | *9* | | " | " |

"Won't she be delighted? What a fine wedding gift."

I could not begin to answer his questions. The names evoked a rush of memory. Josef, my brother—*Wo in der Welt bist du?* Anna, the one who died in the crossing, the absent child who broke my mother's heart. My mother, Clara. My father, Abram, the musician. Names to go along with my dreams.

"I know you said he was here in 1859, but sometimes the past is a mystery. But I think 1851 is right for Herr Ungerland, not 1859," said Father Hlinka. "History fades over time."

For a moment, the six came alive. Of course I did not remember Eger or Cheb. I was a baby, not yet one year old, when we came to America. There was a house, a parlor, a piano. I was taken from there and not from this place.

"No records in the churches, but I thought we should try emigration archives, no? Won't Mrs. Day be thrilled? I cannot wait to see her face."

I folded the paper and stuck it in my pocket. "Of course, Father, yes, you should be the one to tell her. We should celebrate . . . tonight if you like."

The pleasure of his smile almost made me regret lying to him, and I was equally heartbroken to leave the magnificent organ behind. But I hurried from St. Nicholas's, the history in my pocket against my heart. When I found Tess, I made up a story about the police sniffing around the church for two Americans, and we slipped away, retracing our steps to the border.

When we reached the forest near the river crossing, I was shocked to see a young boy, perhaps as old as seven, standing by himself beside a large tree. He did not take notice of us, but remained quite still, as if hiding from someone. I could only imagine what might be in pursuit, and part of me wanted to rescue him. We were nearly upon him before he flinched, and putting a finger to his lips, the child begged us to be quiet.

"Do you speak German?" Tess whispered in that language.

"Yes, quiet please. They are after me."

I looked from tree to tree, anticipating a rush of changelings.

"Who is after you?"

"*Versteckspiel,*" he hissed, and hearing him, a young girl burst from the green background to chase and tag him on the shoulder. When the other children emerged from their hideaways, I realized they were playing a simple game of hide-and-seek. But as I looked from boy to girl, from face to face, I could not help but remember how easily they could alter their appearance. Tess thought them cute and wanted to linger awhile, but I hurried her onward. At the river, I hopped from stone to stone, fording the water as quickly as I could. Tess was taking her time, frustrated and annoyed that I had not waited for her.

"Henry, Henry, what are you running from?"

"Hurry, Tess. They're after us."

She labored to jump to the next rock. "Who?"

"Them," I said, and went back to pull her from the other side.

After our honeymoon trip, life rapidly grew too complicated to continue my research on the Ungerlands or to find another pipe organ. We had one last busy semester of school, and as graduation drew near, our conversations turned to new possibilities. Tess lay in the bathtub, tendrils of steam curling up from the hot water. I leaned on the edge of the hamper, ostensibly reading a draft of a new score, but actually for the sheer pleasure of watching her soak.

"Henry, I've good news. The job with the county looks like it will come through."

"That's great," I said, and turned the page and hummed a few bars. "What is it, exactly, that you'll be doing?"

"Casework at first. People come in with their troubles, I take them down, and then we make all the right referrals."

"Well. I have an interview at that new middle school." I put down the composition and stared at her half-submerged naked form. "They're looking for a band director and music teacher for seventh and eighth grades. It's a pretty good gig and will leave me time to compose."

"Things are working out for us, baby."

She was right, and that was the moment I decided. My life was coming together. Against all odds and despite the interruption caused by my father's death, I would finish school, and a new career was about to start. A beautiful young woman lounged in my bathtub.

"What are you smiling about, Henry?"

I started unbuttoning my shirt. "Move over, Tess, I've got something to whisper in your ear."

CHAPTER 28

The most merciless thing in the world is love. When love flees, all that remains is memory to compensate. Our friends were either going or gone, their ghosts the best our poor minds could conjure to fill love's absence. I am haunted to this day by all those who are missing. Losing Kivi, Blomma, Ragno, and Zanzara proved heartbreaking for Speck, too. She went about her tasks grim and determined, as if by staying busy she could keep phantoms at bay.

After the disaster in the mine, we deposed Béka with his consent, and the diminished clan elected Smaolach our new leader. We lived above ground for the first time in years, bound to one small clearing in the forest by Chavisory's immobility. The impulse to go back home ate at us all. Five years had passed since we had left our camp, and we thought it might be safe to return. The last time anyone had seen our former home, the grounds had been denuded, but surely new growth had begun—where black ash had been, saplings should be inching up amid the wildflowers and fresh grass. Just as nature reclaims its ruins, the people, too, would have forgotten about that boy lost in the river and the two faeries found in the market. They'd want life to remain as they thought it had been.

With it safe to travel again, Luchóg, Smaolach, and I set out, leaving the other three behind at our makeshift camp to watch over Chavisory. Although the wind blew cold that day, our spirits quickened at the prospect of seeing our old haunts again. We raced like deer along the trails, laughing as one passed the other. The old camp shimmered in our imaginations as a promise of bright redemption.

Climbing the western ridge, I heard distant laughter. We slowed our pace, and as we reached the lip, the sounds below piqued our curiosity. The valley came into view through the broken veil of tree limbs and branches. Rows of houses and open lawns snaked and curled along ribbons of neat roadways. On the exact spot where our camp had been, five new houses faced an open circle. Another six sat on either side of a wide road cut through the trees. Branching off from that trail, more streets and houses flowed down the sloping hill to the main road into town.

"Be it ever so humble," Luchóg said.

I looked far ahead and saw bustling activity. From the back of a station wagon, a woman unloaded packages tied up with bows. Two boys tossed a football. A yellow car, shaped like a bug, chugged up a winding road. We could hear a radio talking about the Army-Navy game, and a man muttering curses as he nailed a string of lights beneath the eaves of his roof. Mesmerized by all I saw, I failed to notice as day gave way to night. Lights went on in the homes, as if on sudden signal.

"Shall we see who lives on the ring?" Luchóg asked.

We crept down to the circle of asphalt. Two of the homes appeared empty. The other three showed signs of life: cars in the driveways, lamplit figures crossing behind the windows as if rushing off on vital tasks. Glancing in each window, we saw the same story unfolding. A woman in a kitchen stirred something in a pot. Another lifted a huge bird from the oven, while in an adjoining room a man stared at minuscule figures playing games in a glow-ing box, his face flushed in excitement or anger. His next-door neighbor slept in an easy chair, oblivious to the noise and flickering images.

"He looks familiar," I whispered.

Covered to his toes in blue terrycloth, a young child sat in a small cage in the corner of the room. He played distractedly with brightly colored plastic toys. For a moment, I thought the sleeping man resembled my father, but I could not understand how he could have another son. A woman walked from one room into the other, and her long blonde hair trailed behind like a tail. She scrunched up her mouth into a bow before bending down and whispering something to the man, a name perhaps, and he looked startled and slightly embarrassed to be caught sleeping. When his eyes popped open, he looked even more like my father, but she was definitely not my mother. She flashed a crooked smile and lifted her baby over the bars, and the child cooed and laughed and threw his arms around his mother's neck. I had heard that sound before. The man switched off the console, but before joining the others, he came to the window, cleared a circle with his two hands against the damp panes, and peered out into the darkness. I do not think he saw us, but I surely had seen him before.

We circled back into the woods and waited until the moon was high in the night sky and most of the lights popped off goodnight. The houses in the ring were dark and quiet.

"I don't like this," I said, my breath visible in the violet light.

"You worry your own life away like a kitten worries a string," Smaolach said.

He barked, and we followed him down to the cul-de-sac. Smaolach chose a house with no car in the driveway, where we were not likely to encounter any humans. Careful not to wake anyone, we slipped inside easily through the unlocked front door. A neat row of shoes stood off to the side of the foyer, and Luchóg immediately tried on pairs until he found a fit. Their boy would be dismayed in the morning. The kitchen lay in sight of the foyer, through a smallish dining room. Each of us loaded a rucksack with canned fruits and vegetables, flour, salt, and sugar. Luchóg jammed fistfuls of tea bags into his trouser pockets and on the way out copped a package of cigarettes and a box of matches from the sideboard. In and out in minutes, disturbing no one.

The second house—where the baby in blue lived—proved stubborn. All of the doors and downstairs windows were locked, so we had to shimmy under the crawlspace and into a closetlike room that sheltered a maze of plumbing. By following the pipes, we eventually made our way into the interior of the house, ending up in the cellar. To make ourselves quieter, we took off our shoes and tied them around our necks before sneaking up the steps and slowly opening the door to the kitchen. The room smelled of remembered bread.

While Smaolach and Luchóg raided the pantry, I tiptoed through the rooms to locate the front door and an easy exit. On the walls of the living room hung a gallery of photographic portraits that read mainly as uninteresting shadows, but as I passed by one, illuminated by a white shaft of moonlight, I froze. Two figures, a young mother and her infant child, lifted to her shoulder to face the camera. The baby looked like every other baby, round and smooth as a button. The mother did not stare directly into the lens but watched her son from the corners of her eyes. Her hairstyle and clothing suggested another era, and she, with her beguiling smile and hopeful gaze, appeared hardly more than a child with a child. She lifted her chin, as if preparing to burst out laughing with joy at the babe in arms. The photograph triggered a rush of chemicals to my brain. Dizzy and disoriented, I knew, but could not place, their faces. There were other photographs—a long white dress standing next to a shadow, a man in a peaked cap—but I kept coming back to the mother and child, put my fingers on the glass, traced the contours of those figures. I wanted to remember. Foolishly, I went to the wall and turned on the lamp.

Someone gasped in the kitchen just as the pictures on the wall jumped into clarity. Two older people with severe eyeglasses. A fat baby. But I could see clearly the photograph that had so entranced me, and beside it another which disturbed me more. There was a boy, eyes skyward, looking up in expectation of something unseen. He could not have been more than seven at the time the picture was taken, and had the snapshot not been in black and white, I would have sooner recognized his face. For it was mine, and me, in a jacket and cap, eyes awaiting—what? a snowfall, a tossed football, a V of geese, hands from above? What a strange thing to happen to a little boy, to end up on the wall of this unfamiliar house. The man and woman in the wedding picture offered no clues. It was my father with a different bride.

"Aniday, what are you doing?" Luchóg hissed. "Hush those lights."

A mattress creaked overhead as someone got out of bed. I snapped off the lights and scrammed. The floorboards moaned. A woman's voice muttered in a high, impatient tone.

"All right," the man replied. "I'll go check, but I didn't hear a thing." He headed for the upper stairway, took the steps slowly one by one. We tried the back door out of the kitchen but could not figure out the lock.

"The damned thing won't budge," Smaolach said.

The approaching figure reached the bottom landing, switched on the light. He went into the living room, which I had departed seconds earlier. Luchóg fussed with a rotating bar and unlocked the deadbolt with a soft click. We froze at the sound.

"Hey, who's there?" the man said from the other room. He padded our way in his bare feet.

"Fuck all," said Smaolach, and he turned the knob and pushed. The door opened six inches but hung fast by a small metal chain above our heads. "Let's go," he said, and we changed to squeeze through the gap one by one, scattering sugar and flour behind us. I am sure he saw the last of us, for the man called out "Hey" again, but we were gone, racing across the frosty lawn. The floodlight popped on like a flashbulb, but we had passed its circle of illumination. From the top of the ridge, we watched all his rooms light up in sequence, till the windows glowed like rows of jack-o'-lanterns. A dog began to yowl madly in the middle of the village, and we took that as a sign to retreat home. The ground chilled our bare feet, but, exhilarated as imps, we escaped with our treasures, laughing under the cold stars.

At the top of the ridgeline, Luchóg stopped to smoke one of his purloined cigarettes, and I looked back one last time at the ordered village where our home used to be. This is the place where it had all happened—a reach for wild honey high in a tree, a stretch of roadway where the car struck a deer, a clearing where I first opened my eyes and saw eleven dark children. But someone had erased all that, like a word or a line, and in that space wrote another sentence. The neighborhood of houses appeared to have existed in this space for ages. It made one doubt one's own story.

"That man back there," I said, "the sleeping one. He reminded me of someone."

"They all look alike to me," Luchóg said.

"Someone I know. Or knew."

"Could it be your long-lost brother?"

"I haven't one."

"Perhaps a man who wrote a book you read in the library?"

"I do not know what they look like."

"Perhaps the man who wrote that book you carry from place to place?"

"No, not McInnes. I do not know McInnes."

"A man from a magazine? A photograph in the newspaper?"

"Someone I knew."

"Could it be the fireman? The man you saw at the creek?" He puffed on his cigarette and blew smoke like an old steam engine.

"I thought it might be my father, but that can't be right. There was that strange woman and her child in the blue suit."

"What year is it, little treasure?" Luchóg asked.

It could have been 1972, although in truth, I was no longer sure.

"By now, you must be a young man near the end of thirty years. And how old was the man in the picture window?"

"I'd guess about the same."

"And how old would his father be?"

"Twice that," I said, and smiled like an idiot.

"Your father would be an old man by now, almost as old as I am."

I sat down on the cold ground. So much time had passed since I had last seen my parents; their real age was a revealed mystery.

Luchóg sat down beside me. "After awhile, everyone forgets. I cannot paint you a picture of my dear youth. The old memories are not real—just figures in a fairytale. My mammy could walk right up to me this very minute and say, 'Sonny-boy,' and I would have to say, 'Sorry, I don't know you, lady.' My father may as well be a myth. So, you see, in a way, you have no father or mother, or if you did, you wouldn't know them any longer, nor they you, more's the pity."

"But the fellow falling asleep in the armchair? If I try hard, I can recall my father's face."

"Might as well be anyone. Or no one at all."

"And the baby?"

"They're all one to me. A bother with no teeth but all the time hungry. Can't walk, can't talk, can't share a smoke. You can have them. Some say a changeling's best bet is a baby—there's less to learn—but that's moving backward across time. You should be going forward. And heaven help us if we ever had a baby to look after for a whole century."

"I do not want to steal any child. I just wonder whose baby that is. What happened to my father? Where is my mother?"

To make it through the cold season, we nicked ten blankets and a half-dozen children's coats from the Salvation Army store, and we ate small meals, subsisting mainly on weak teas brewed from bark and twigs. In the dull light of January and February, we often did not stir at all, but sat alone or in clumps of two or three, dripping wet or stone cold, waiting for the sun and the resumption of our lives. Chavisory grew stronger by and by, and when the wild onions and first daffodils appeared, she could take a few steps with bracing assistance. Each day, Speck pushed her one painful pace forward. When she was well enough for us to move, we fled that miserable dungheap of memories. Despite the risks, we found a more suitable hidden home near water, a mile or so north of the new houses. On windy nights, the noises from the families carried as far as our new camp, and while not as secluded, it afforded us adequate protection. As we dug in that first day, restlessness swept over me. Smaolach sat down beside me and draped an arm across my shoulders. The sun was falling from the sky.

"Ní mar a síltear a bítear," he said.

"Smaolach, if I live to be a thousand years, I'll never understand your old language. Speak English to me."

"Are you thinking of our friends, late and lamented? They're better off where they are and not suffering this eternal waiting. Or is there something else on your mind, little treasure?"

"Have you ever been in love, Smaolach?"

"Once and only once, thank goodness. We were close, like every mother and son."

"Luchóg said my mother and father are gone."

"I don't remember much of her. The smell of wool, maybe, and a harsh soap. Mint on the breath. A huge bosom upon which I laid my . . . No, that's not right. She was a rake of a woman, all skin and bones. I don't recall."

"Every place we leave, part of me disappears."

"Now . . . my father, there was a strapping fellow with a big black moustache curled up at the ends, or maybe it was my grandfather, come to think of it. Was a long time ago, and I'm not really sure where it was or when."

The darkness was complete.

"That's the way of life. All things go out and give way to one another. 'Tisn't wise to be too attached to any world or its people."

Mystified by Smaolach's philosophy, I tottered off to my new bed, turned over the facts, and looked at what crawled beneath. I tried to picture my mother and father, and could not recall their faces or their voices. Remembered life seemed as false to me as my name. These shadows are visible: the sleeping man, the beautiful woman, and the crying, laughing child. But just as much of real life, not merely read about in books, remains unknown to me. A mother croons a lullaby to a sleepy child. A man shuffles a deck of cards and deals a hand of solitaire. A pair of lovers unbutton one another and tumble into bed. Unreal as a dream.

I did not confess to Smaolach the reason for my agitation. Speck had all but abandoned our friendship, withdrawing into some hard and lonesome core. Even after we made the move, she devoted herself to making our new camp feel like home, and she spent the sunlit hours teaching Chavisory to walk again. Exhausted by her efforts, Speck fell into a deep sleep early each night. She stayed in her burrow on cold and wet March days, tracing out an intricate design on a rolled parchment, and when I asked her about her drawing, she stayed quiet and aloof. Early mornings, I'd see her at the western edge of camp, clad in her warmest coat, sturdy shoes on her feet, pondering the horizon. I remember approaching her from behind and placing my hand on her shoulder. For the first time ever, she flinched at my touch, and when she turned to face me, she trembled as if shaking off the urge to cry.

"What's the matter, Speck? Are you okay?"

"I've been working too hard. There's one last snow on the way." She smiled and took my hand. "We'll steal off at the first flurries."

When the snow finally came days later, I had fallen asleep under a pile of blankets. She woke me, white flakes gathering in her dark hair. "It's time," she whispered as quietly as the delicate susurrus through the pines. Speck and I meandered along familiar trails, taking care to be hidden, and waited at the edge of the forest nearest the library for dusk to arrive. The snowfall obscured the sun's descent, and the headlights of the few cars on the road tricked us into going too soon. We squeezed into our space only to hear footfall overhead as the librarians began to close for the night. To stay warm and quiet, we huddled beneath a blanket, and she quickly fell asleep against me. The rhythm of her beating heart and respiration, and the heat from her skin, quickly lulled me to sleep, too, and we woke together in pitch black. She lit the lamps, and we went to our books.

Speck had been reading Flannery O'Connor, and I was wading in deep water with Wallace Stevens. But I could not concentrate on his abstractions, and instead stared at her between the lines. I had to tell her, but the words were inadequate, incomplete, and perhaps incomprehensible—and yet nothing else would do. She was my closest friend in the world, yet a greater desire for more had accompanied me around for years. I could not rationalize or explain it away for another moment. Speck was engrossed in *The Violent Bear It Away*. A bent arm propped up her head, and she was lying across the floor, her hair obscuring her face.

"Speck, I have something to tell you."

"Just a moment. One more sentence."

"Speck, if you could put down that book for a second."

"Almost there." She stuck her finger between the pages and closed the novel.

She looked at me, and in one second my mood swung from elation to fear. "I have been thinking for a long, long time, Speck, about you. I want to tell you how I feel."

Her smile collapsed. Her eyes searched my relentless gaze. "Aniday," she insisted.

"I have to tell you how—"

"Don't."

"Tell you, Speck, how much I—"

"Please, don't, Henry."

I stopped, opened my mouth to form the words, and stopped again. "What did you say?"

"I don't know that I can hear that right now."

"What did you call me?"

She covered her mouth, as if to recapture the escaped name.

"You called me Henry." The whole story unraveled in an instant. "That's me, I'm Henry. That's what you said, isn't it?"

"I'm so sorry, Aniday."

"Henry. Not Aniday. Henry Day."

"Henry Day. You weren't supposed to know."

The shock of the name made me forget what I had planned to tell her. Myriad thoughts and emotions competed in my mind. Images, solutions to assorted puzzles and riddles, and unanswered questions. She put down her book, crossed the room, and wound me in her embrace. For the longest time, she held on to me, rocking and soothing my fevered imagination with the lightest touch, caressing away the chaos.

And then she told me my story. The story told in these pages was all she could remember. She told me what she knew, and my recollections of dreams, visions, and encounters filled in the rest. She told me why they kept it all secret for so long. How it is better not to know who you really are. To forget the past. Erase the name. All this revealed in a patient and heavenly voice, until everything that could be answered was answered, no desire left unsatisfied. The candles burned out, we had talked so long, and into darkness the conversation lasted, and the last thing I remember is falling asleep in her arms.

I had a dream that we ran away that night, found a place to grow up together, became the woman and the man we were supposed to be. In the dream, she kissed my mouth, and her bare skin slid beneath my fingertips. A blackbird sang. But in the morning, she was not where I expected her to be.

In our long friendship, she had never written a single word to me, but by my side, where she should have been, lay a note in her handwriting. Every letter is etched on my mind, and though I will not give it all away, at the end she wrote, "Goodbye, Henry Day."

It was time for her to go. Speck is gone.

The first time I saw him, I was too frightened to say anything and too awestruck to touch him. He was not a freak or a devil, but perfect in every way, a beautiful boy. After the long wait to meet him, I found myself overcome by the sudden change, not so much his physical presence, his arrival after being hidden away, but the change in me to something more sublimely human. Tess smiled at my confusion and the look in my eyes as I beheld him.

"You won't break him," she said.

My son. Our child. Ten fingers, ten toes. Good color, great lungs, a natural at the breast. I held him in my arms and remembered the twins in their matching yellow jumpers, my mother singing to me as she scrubbed my back in the bathtub, my father holding my hand when we climbed the bleachers at an autumn football game. Then I remembered Clara, my first mother, how I loved to crawl under the billows of her skirts, and the scent of witch hazel on my father Abram's cheek, his feathery moustache as he pressed his lips against my skin. I kissed our boy and considered the ordinary miracle of birth, the wonder of my wife, and was grateful for the human child.

We named him Edward, and he thrived. Born two weeks before Christmas 1970, he became our darling boy, and over those first few months, the three of us settled into the house that Mom and Charlie had bought for us in the new development up in the woods. At first, I could not bear the thought of living there, but they surprised us on our second anniversary, and with Tess pregnant and the bills mounting, I could not say no. The house was larger than we needed, especially before the baby came, and I built a small studio, moving in the old piano. I taught music to seventh graders and ran the student orchestra at Mark Twain Middle School, and in the evenings and on weekends, when I didn't have to mind the baby, I worked on my music, dreaming of a composition that evoked the flow of one life into another.

For inspiration, I would sometimes unfold the photocopy of the passenger list and study the names. Abram and Clara, their sons Friedrich, Josef, and Gustav. The legendary Anna. Their ghosts appeared in fragments. A doctor listens to my heartbeat while Mother frets over his shoulder. Faces bend to me, speaking carefully in a language I cannot understand. Her dark green skirt as she waltzes. Tang of apple wine, sauerbraten in the oven. Through a frosted window, I could see my brothers approach the house on a winter's day, their breath exploding in clouds as they share a private joke. In the parlor stands the piano, which I touch again.

Playing music is the one vivid memory from the other life. Not only do I recall the yellowing keys, the elaborate twisting vines of the scrollwork music stand, the smoothness of the rosewood finish, but I can hear those tunes again, and feel the sensations he felt while playing—strike these keys, hear these notes resound from the depths of the machine. The combination of notes makes up the melody. Translate the symbols from the score to the corresponding keys, and keep the right time, to make this song. My one true link to my first childhood is that sensation of bringing the dream of notes to life. The song echoing in my head becomes the song resounding in the air. As a child, this was my way of unlocking my thoughts, and now, a century or more later, I attempted to create the same seamless expression through my composition, but it was as if I had found the key and lost the keyhole. I was as helpless as Edward in his preverbal life, learning to communicate my desires all over again.

Being around our tiny speechless boy reminded me of that lost life and made me cherish the memories Edward created every passing day. He crawled, stood, grew teeth, grew hair, fell in love with us. He walked, he talked, he grew up in a moment behind our backs. We were, for a time, the perfect happy family.

My sisters marred that ideal picture. Mary, who had a baby girl, and Elizabeth, who was expecting her first, were the initial ones to point out the curiosity. The extended family had gathered at my mother's house for dinner. Edward was about eighteen months old, for I remember watching him carefully as he waddled up and down the porch steps over and over again. Charlie and the twins' husbands watched the last few minutes of the game before dinner, and my mother and Tess guarded the hot skillets, so I was alone with the girls for the first time in ages, when one or the other led off with her unsolicited opinion.

"You know, he looks nothing like you."

"And hardly a thing like her."

I looked at Edward as he pulled up leaves of grass and tossed them into the still air.

"Look at his chin," Liz observed. "Neither one of you has that cleft."

"And his eyes aren't either of your two colors," said Mary. "Green as a cat's. He didn't get those eyelashes from our side of the family. You have such adorable long eyelashes, yes, you do. Too bad he's not a girl."

"Well, they're not Wodehouse eyelashes either. Take a good look at Tess."

"All mascara."

"And the nose. No so much now, but later, you'll see. That's a beak on him, poor little man. Hope my child doesn't get that nose."

"No Day ever had a nose like that."

"What are you two saying?" My voice was so loud, I startled my son.

"Nothing."

"Kinda odd, don't you think, that he doesn't look like his parents?"

At sunset my mother, Charlie, and I sat on the porch watching the moths dance, and the matter of Edward's appearance arose again.

"Don't listen to those two," my mother said. "He's the spit and image of you, with maybe a little Tess around the eyes."

Uncle Charlie sucked on a pop bottle, burped softly. "The boy looks exactly like me. All my grandchildren do." Eddie tottered across the floor-boards and threw himself at Charlie's legs, and finding his balance, he roared like a tiger.


As he grew older, Edward looked more like an Ungerland than a Day, but I did my best to hide the truth. Maybe I should have explained all to Tess, and perhaps that would have been the end of my torment. But she bore the snide remarks about her son with grace. Days after his second birthday, we had Os-car Love and Jimmy Cummings over for dinner. After the meal, we fooled around with an arrangement that I had written hoping to interest a chamber-music quartet in the city. Of course, we were one player short, with George long gone in California. But playing with them again after a few years was easy and comfortable. Tess excused herself to go to the kitchen to check on a lemon meringue pie. When Edward noticed she was gone, he wailed from his playpen, banging his fists against the slats.

"Don't you think he's getting a bit too big for that?" Oscar asked.

"He can be a bit of trouble after dinner. Besides, he likes it there. Makes him feel safe."

Oscar shook his head and fished Edward from behind the bars, bounced him on his knees, and let him finger the keys of the clarinet. Seeing my single friends react to my son, I couldn't help but feel that they were weighing their freedom against the allure of family. They loved the boy but were slightly frightened of him and all he represented.

"Drawn to the stick," Oscar said. "That's one cool kid. You'll want to stay away from the piano. Too heavy to carry around."

"Sure he's yours?" Cummings asked. "He looks nothing like you, or Tess, for that matter."

Oscar joined the fun. "Now that you mention it . . . look at that split chin and those big eyes."

"C'mon guys, cut it out."

"Chill out," Oscar whispered. "Here comes the old lady."

Tess delivered the dessert, oblivious to the turns of our conversation. I should have brought up my festering doubt, made a joke of it, said something in front of her, but I didn't.

"So, Tess," Jimmy said, balancing his pie plate on his knee, "who do you think Eddie takes after?"

"You have a speck of meringue at the corner of your mouth." She picked up our son and held him in her lap, stroked his hair, and pressed his head against her breast. "How's my little man?"

Edward stuck his hand straight into the pie, pulled up a clump of yellow goo, and crammed it in his mouth.

She laughed. "Just like his daddy."

Thank you, my love. She returned my smile.

After the boys said good night and Edward lay sleeping in his crib, Tess and I washed the dishes together, staring out the kitchen window. The stars shone like pinpricks in the cold black sky, and the hot water in the sink, along with the roaring furnace, gave the room a steamy languor. I put down the tea towel and, from behind, wrapped my arms around her, kissed her damp warm nape, and she shivered.

"I hope you didn't get too mad about Jimmy going on about how Eddie doesn't look so much like either one of us."

"I know," she said. "It's creepy."

For a split second, I thought she suspected something was awry, but she spun herself around to face me and grabbed my face with her rubber gloves. "You worry about the strangest things." She kissed me, and the conversation went elsewhere.

A few nights later, Tess and I were asleep in bed, Edward down the hall in his room. She woke me by shaking my shoulder and speaking harshly in a sort of shouted whisper. "Henry, Henry, wake up. I heard noises downstairs."

"What is it?"

"Would you listen? Someone's down there."

I grumbled that it was nothing.

"And I'm telling you, someone is in the house. Would you go check?"

I rolled out of bed and stood there for a moment, trying to rouse my senses, then headed past Edward's closed door to the top of the stairs. I did not see, but had the sensation, that a light had gone out downstairs and that something moved in a blur from one room to the next. Anxious, I took the steps one by one in a sort of hypnotic trance, sorting through my drifting emotions as it became darker and darker. At the bottom, I turned into the living room and switched on the lights. The room appeared unchanged except for a few photographs on the walls that were slightly askew. We had hung a kind of family gallery, pictures of our parents, images of Tess and me as children, a wedding photo, and a parade of portraits featuring Edward. I nudged the frames back in line and in the same moment heard the deadbolt turn at the kitchen door.

"Hey, who's there?" I yelled, and sped out in the nick of time to see the backside of an imp squeezing through the opening between the door and the jamb. Outside in the cold, dark night, three figures sped across the frosty lawn, and flicking on the floodlights, I called for them to stop, but they had vanished. The kitchen was a mess, and the pantry had been raided of canned goods, cereal and sugar, and a small copper saucepan, but not much else. A bag of flour had burst when they squeezed through the door, leaving a dusty trail dotted with footprints. The oddest sort of break-in by a bunch of hungry thieves. Tess came downstairs and was shaken by the disturbance, but she shoved me out of the kitchen to put it back in order. Back in the living room, I rechecked our belongings, but they were all there—the TV, stereo, nothing of value gone.

I examined the photographs more closely. Tess looked almost exactly the same as she had on our wedding day. Sergeant William Day stared out, frozen in the past in his military dress. From the corners of her eyes, Ruth Day watched her son, hardly more than a child with a child, yet full of love and pride. In the next frame, there I was, a boy again, looking up and full of hope. But, of course, that wasn't me. The boy was too young. And in that instant, I realized who had come and why.

Tess came in and laid her hand on my back. "Shall we call the police? Is there anything missing?"

I could not answer, for my heart was pounding wildly and an overwhelming dread fixed me to the spot. We had not checked on our son. I sprinted up the stairs to his room. He lay asleep, knees drawn up to his chest, dreaming as if nothing had ever happened. Watching his innocent face, I knew at once that he was blood of my blood. He almost looked like the boy I still see in my nightmares. The boy at the piano.

CHAPTER 30

I tucked her letter into my book and went to look for Speck. Panic overwhelmed logic, and I ran out onto the library lawn, hoping that she had left only moments before. The snow had changed over to a cold rain, obliterating any tracks she might have made. Not a single soul could be seen. No one answered when I called her name, and the streets were curiously empty, as church bells began to ring out another Sunday. I was a fool to venture out into town in the middle of the morning. Following the labyrinth of sidewalks, I had no idea which way to go. A car eased around a corner and slowed as the driver spotted me walking in the rain. She braked, rolled down the window, and called out, "Do you need a ride? You'll catch your death of cold."

I remembered to make my voice understandable—a single stroke of fortune on that miserable day. "No, thank you, ma'am. I'm going home."

"Don't call me 'ma'am,'" she said. She had a blonde ponytail like the woman who lived in the house we had robbed months before, and she wore a crooked smile. "It's a nasty morning to be out, and you have no hat or gloves."

"I live around the corner, thank you."

"Do I know you?"

I shook my head, and she started to roll up her window.

"You haven't seen a little girl out here, have you?" I called out.

"In this rain?"

"My twin sister," I lied. "I'm out looking for her. She's about my size."

"No. I haven't seen a soul." She eyed me closely. "Where do you live? What is your name?"

I hesitated and thought it best to end the matter. "My name is Billy Speck."

"You'd better go home, son. She'll turn up."

The car turned the corner and motored off. Frustrated, I walked toward the river, away from all the confusing streets and the chance of another human encounter. The rain fell in a steady drizzle, not quite cold enough to change over again, and I was soaked and chilled. The clouds obliterated the sun, making it difficult to orient myself, so I used the river as my compass, following its course throughout the pale day and into the slowly emerging darkness. Frantic to find her, I did not stop until late that night. Under a stand of evergreens crowded with winter sparrows and jays, I rested, waiting for a break in the weather.

Away from the town, all I could hear was the river lapping against the stony shores. As soon as I stopped searching, the questions I had kept at bay began to assault my mind. Unanswerable doubts that would torment me in quiet moments for the next few years. Why had she left us? Why would Speck leave me? She would not have taken the risk that Kivi and Blomma had. She had chosen to be alone. Though Speck had told me my real name, I had no idea of hers. How could I ever find her? Should I have kept quiet, or told all and given her a reason to stay? A sharp pain swelled behind my eyes, pinching my throbbing skull. If only to stop obsessing, I rose and continued to stumble through the wet darkness, finding nothing.

Cold, tired, and hungry, I reached the bend in the river in two days' walk. Speck had been the only other person from the clan who had come this far, and she had somehow forded the water to the other side. Sapphire blue, the water ran quickly, breaking over hidden rocks and snags, whitecaps flashing. If she was on the other side, Speck had crossed by dint of courage. On the distant shore, a vision appeared from my deep mad memories—a man, woman, and child, the fleet escape of a white deer, a woman in a red coat. "Speck," I called across the waters, but she was nowhere. Past this point of land, the whole world unfolded, too large and unknowable. All hope and courage left me. I dared not cross, so I sat on the bank and waited. On the third day, I walked home without her.

I staggered into the camp, exhausted and depressed, hoping not to talk at all. The others had not worried for the first few days, but by the end of the week, they'd grown anxious and unsettled. After they built a fire and fed me nettle soup from a copper pot, the whole story poured forth—except for the revelation of my name, except for what I had not said to her. "As soon as I realized she was gone, I went to look for her and traveled as far as the river-bend. She may be gone for good."

"Little treasure, go to sleep," Smaolach said. "We'll come up with a plan. Another day brings a different promise."

There was no new plan or promise the next morning or any other. Days came and went. I read every tense moment, every crack and creak, every whisper, every morning light as her return. The others respected my grief and gave me wide berth, trying to draw me back and then letting me drift away. They missed her, too, but I felt any other sorrow a paltry thing, and I resented their shadowy reminiscences and their failure to remember properly. I hated the five of them for not stopping her, for taking me into this life, for the wild hell of my imagination. I kept thinking that I saw her. Mistaking each of the others for her, my heart leapt and fell when they turned out to be merely themselves. Or seeing the darkness of her hair in a raven's wing. On the bank of the creek, watching the water play over stone, I came upon her familiar form, feet tucked beneath her. The image turned out to be a fawn pausing for a rest in a window of sunshine. She was everywhere, eternally. And never here.

Her absence leaves a hole in the skin stretched over my story. I spent an eternity trying to forget her, and another trying to remember. There is no balm for such desire. The others knew not to talk about her around me, but I surprised them after an afternoon of fishing, bumbling into the middle of a conversation not intended for my ears.

"Now, not our Speck," Smaolach told the others. "If she's alive, she won't be coming back for us."

The faeries stole furtive glances at me, not knowing how much I had heard. I put down my string of fish and began to shave the scales, pretending that their discussion had no effect on me. But hearing Smaolach gave me pause. It was possible that she had not survived, but I preferred to think that she had either gone into the upper world or reached her beloved sea. The image of the ocean brought to mind the intense colors of her eyes, and a brief smile crossed my face.

"She's gone," I said to the silent group. "I know."

The following day we spent turning over stones in the creek bed, gathering the hiding newts and salamanders, to cook together in a stew. The day was hot, and the labor took its toll. Famished, we enjoyed a rich, gooey mess, full of tiny bones that crunched as we chewed. When the stars emerged, we all went to bed, our stomachs full, our muscles taxed by the long day. I awoke quite late the next morning and drowsily realized that she had not once crossed my mind when we were foraging the previous day. I took a deep breath. I was forgetting.

Speck's presence was replaced by dullness. I would sit and stare at the sky or watch ants march, and practice driving her out of my mind. Anything that triggered a memory could be stripped of its personal, embedded meanings. A raspberry is a raspberry. The blackbird is a metaphor for nothing. Words signify what you will. I tried to forget Henry Day as well, and accept my place as the last of my kind.

All of us were waiting for nothing. Smaolach never said so, but I knew he was not looking to make the change. And he hatched no plans to steal another child. Perhaps he thought our number too few for the complex preparations, or perhaps he sensed the world itself was changing. In Igel's day, the subject came up all the time with a certain relentless energy, but less so under Béka, and never under Smaolach. No reconnaissance missions into town, no searching out the lonesome, neglected, or forgotten. No face-pulling, no contortions, no reports. As if resigned, we went about our eternal business, sanguine that another disaster or abandonment awaited.

I did not care. A certain fearlessness filled me, and I would not hesitate to run into town alone, if only to swipe a carton of cigarettes for Luchóg or a bag of sweets for Chavisory. I stole unnecessary things: a flashlight and batteries, a drawing pad and charcoals, a baseball and six fishing hooks, and once, at Christmas, a delicious cake in the shape of a firelog. In the confines of the forest, I fiddled with idle tasks—whittling a fierce bat atop a hickory cane, laying a stone ring around the circumference of our camp, searching for old turtle shells and crafting the shards into a necklace. I went up alone to the slag hillside and the abandoned mine, which lay undisturbed, as we had left it, and placed the tortoiseshell necklace where Ragno and Zanzara lay buried. My dreams did not wake me up in the middle of the night, but only because life had become a somnambulant nightmare. A handful of seasons had passed when a chance encounter finally made me realize that Speck was beyond forgetting.

We were tending to delicate seedlings planted on a sun-drenched slope a few hundred yards from camp. Onions had stolen new seeds, and within weeks up came the first tender shoots—snap peas, carrots, scallions, a watermelon vine, and a row of beans. Chavisory, Onions, Luchóg, and I were weeding in the garden on that spring morning, when the sound of approaching feet caused us to rise like whitetail, to sniff the wind, ready to flee or hide. The intruders were lost hikers, off the trail and headed in our direction. Since the housing development had risen, we had a rare traveler pass our way, but our cultivated patch might look a bit peculiar to these strangers out in the middle of nowhere. We disguised the garden under pine brush and hid ourselves beneath a skirt of trees.

Two young men and a young woman, caps upon their heads, huge backpacks strapped at the shoulders, walked on, cheerful and oblivious. They strolled past the rows of plants and us. The first man had his eye on the world ahead. The second person—the girl—had her eye on him, and the third man had his eye on her backside. Though lost, he seemed intent on the one thing. We followed safely behind, and they eventually settled down a hill away to drink their bottled water, unwrap their candy bars, and lighten their loads. The first man took out a book and read something from it to the girl, while the third hiker went off behind the trees to relieve himself. He was gone a long time, for the man with the book had the chance not only to finish his poem but to kiss the girl, as well. When their small interlude ended, the threesome strapped on their gear and marched away. We waited a decent spell before running to the spot they had vacated.

Two empty water bottles littered the ground, and Luchóg snatched them up and found the caps nearby. They had discarded the cellophane wrappers from their snacks, and the boy had left his slim volume of poems lying on the grass. Chavisory gave it to me. *The Blue Estuaries* by Louise Bogan. I leafed through a few pages and stopped at the phrase *That more things move / Than blood in the heart.*

"Speck," I said to myself. I had not said her name aloud in ages, in centuries.

"What is it, Aniday?" Chavisory asked.

"I am trying to remember."

The four of us walked back to the garden. I turned to see if my comrades were following the same path, only to discover Luchóg and Chavisory, walking step by ginger step, holding hands. My thoughts flooded with Speck.

I felt an urgency to find her again, if only to understand why she had gone. To tell her how the private conversations of my mind were still with her. I should have asked her not to go, found the right words to convince her, confessed all that moved in my heart. And ever hopeful that it was not too late, I resolved to begin again.

## · *CHAPTER 31* ·

I would not want to be a child again, for a child exists in uncertainty and danger. Our flesh and blood, we cannot help but fear for them, as we hope for them to make their way in this life. After the break-in, I worried about our son all of the time. Edward is not who we say he is because his father is an imposter. He is not a Day, but a changeling's child. I passed on my original genes, giving him the face and features of the Ungerlands, and who knows what other traits leapt the generations. Of my own childhood, I know little more than a name on a piece of paper: Gustav Ungerland. I was stolen long ago. And when the changelings came again, I began to believe they saw Edward as one of their own and wished to reclaim him. The mess they left in the kitchen was a subterfuge for a more sinister purpose. The disturbed photographs on the wall indicated that they were searching for someone. Wickedness hovered in the background and crept through the woods, plotting to steal our son.

We lost Edward one Sunday in springtime. On that gloriously warm afternoon, we happened to be in the city, for I had discovered a passable pipe organ in a church in Shadyside, and after services the music minister allowed me an hour to experiment with the machine, trying out what new sounds coursed through my imagination. Afterward, Tess and I took Edward to the zoo for his first face-to-face encounter with elephants and monkeys. A huge crowd shared our idea, and the walkways were crammed with couples pushing strollers, desultory teenagers, even a family with six redheaded children, staggered a year apart, a conspiracy of freckles and blue eyes. Too many people for my taste, but we jostled along without complaint. Edward was fascinated by the tigers and loitered in front of the iron fence, pulling at his cotton candy, roaring at the beasts to encourage them out of their drowsiness. In its black-and-orange dreams, one tiger twitched its tail, annoyed by my son's entreaties. Tess took advantage of Edward's distraction to confront me.

"Henry, I want to talk to you about Eddie. Does he seem all right to you? There's been a change lately, and something—I don't know—not normal."

I could see him over her shoulder. "He's perfectly normal."

"Or maybe it's you," she said. "You've been different with him lately. Overprotective, not letting him be a kid. He should be outdoors catching polliwogs and climbing trees, but it's as if you're afraid of him being out of your sight. He needs the chance to become more independent."

I pulled her off to the side, out of our son's hearing. "Do you remember the night someone broke into the house?"

"I knew it," she said. "You said not to worry, but you've been preoccupied with that, haven't you?"

"No, no, I just remembered, when I was looking at the photographs on the walls that night, it made me think of my own childhood dreams—years at the piano, searching for the right music to express myself. I have been looking for the answers, Tess, and they were right under my fingertips. Today in the church, the organ sounded just like the one at St. Nicholas's in Cheb. The organ is the answer to the symphony. Organ and orchestra."

She wrapped her arms around me and pulled herself against my chest. Her eyes were full of light and hope, and in all of my several lives, no one had shown such faith in me, in the essence of who I considered myself to be. I was so in love with her at that moment that I forgot the world and everything in it, and that's when I noticed, over her shoulder, our son was gone. Vanished from the space where he had been standing. My first thought was that he had tired of the tigers and was now underfoot or nearby, ready to beg us to let him in for a group hug. That hope evaporated and was replaced by the horrible notion that Edward had somehow squeezed through the bars and been instantly eaten by the tigers, but a quick glance at their cage revealed nothing but two indolent cats stretched out asleep in the languid sunshine. In the wilderness of my imagination, the changelings appeared. I looked back at Tess and feared that I was about to break her heart.

"He's gone," I told her, moving apart. "Edward."

She spun around and moved to the spot we had seen him last. "Eddie," she cried. "Where in the world are you?"

We went down the path toward the lions and bears, calling out his name, her voice rising an octave with each repetition, alarming the other parents. Tess stopped an elderly couple heading in the opposite direction. "Have you seen a little boy all alone? Three years old. Cotton candy."

"There's nothing but children here," the old man said, pointing a thin finger to the distance behind us. A line of children, laughing and hurrying, chased something down a shady pathway. At the front of the pack, a zookeeper hustled along, attempting to hold back the children while following his quarry. Ahead of the mob, Edward raced in his earnest and clumsy jog, chasing a blackfooted penguin that had escaped his pen and now waddled free and oblivious, heading back to the ocean, perhaps, or in search of fresh fish. The keeper sprinted past Edward and caught up to the bird, which brayed like a jackass. Holding its bill with one hand and cradling the bird against his chest, the keeper hurried past us as we reached our son. "Such a ruckus," he told us. "This one slips out of the exhibit and off he goes, wherever he pleases. Some things have such a will."

Taking Edward's hands in our own, we were determined to never let go.

Edward was a kite on a string, always threatening to break free. Before he started schooling, Eddie was safe at home. Tess took good care of him in the mornings, and I was home to watch him on weekday afternoons. When he turned four, Eddie went in with me on the way to work. I'd drop him off at the nursery school and then swing by from Twain when my music classes were through. In our few private hours I taught him scales, but when he bored of the piano he toddled off to his blocks and dinosaurs, inventing imaginary games and companions to while away lonesome hours. Every once in a while, he'd bring over a playmate for the afternoon, but those children never seemed to come back. That was fine by me, as I never fully trusted his playmates. Any one of them could have been a changeling in disguise.

Strangely, my music flourished in the splendid isolation we had carved out for ourselves. While he entertained himself with his toys and books, I composed. Tess encouraged me to find my own sound. Every week or so, she would bring home another album featuring organ music found in some dusty used record store. She cadged tickets to Heinz Hall performances, dug up sheet music and books on orchestration and instrumentation, and insisted that I go into the city to work out the music in my head at friendly churches and the college music school. She was re-creating, in essence, the repertoire in the treasure chest from Cheb. I wrote dozens of works, though scant success or attention resulted from my efforts—a coerced performance of a new arrangement by a local choir, or one night on electric organ with a wind ensemble from upstate. I tried everything to get my music heard, sent tapes and scores around the country to publishers and performers, but usually received a form rejection, if anything. Every great composer serves an apprenticeship of sorts, even middle-school teachers, but in my heart, I knew the compositions had not yet fulfilled my intentions.

One phone call changed everything. I had just come in the door with Edward after picking him up from nursery school. The voice on the other end was from another world. An up-and-coming chamber quartet in Califor-

nia, who specialized in experimental sound, expressed interest in actually recording one of my compositions, an atonal mood piece I had written shortly
after the break-in. George Knoll, my old friend from The Coverboys, had
passed along my score. When I called him to say thanks, he invited us to visit
and stay at his place so I could be on hand at the recording session. Tess, Edward, and I flew out to the Knolls in San Francisco that summer of '76 and
had a great few days with George and his family. His modest café in North
Beach was the only genuine Andalusian restaurant among a hive of Italian
joints, and his stunning wife and head chef did not hurt business, either. It was
great to see them, and the few days away from home eased my anxieties.
Nothing weird prowling around California.

The pastor of Grace Cathedral in San Francisco allowed us an afternoon to record, and the pipe organ there rivaled in tone and balance the
ancient instrument I had played in Cheb. The same feeling of homecoming
entered me when I pressed the pedals, and from the beginning notes, I was
already nostalgic for the keyboard. The quartet changed a few measures,
bent a few notes, and after we played my fugue for organ and strings for the
seventh time, everyone seemed satisfied with the sound. My brush with
fame was over in ninety minutes. As we said our good-byes, everyone
seemed sanguine about our limited prospects. Perhaps a mere thousand
people might actually buy the record and hear my piece, but the thrill of
finally making an album outweighed any projected anxiety about the size
of its audience.

The cellist in the group told us not to miss Big Sur, so on our last day
before flying home, we rented a car and drove south on the Pacific Coast
Highway. For most of the morning, the sun came in and out between clouds,
but the rocky seascape was spectacular. Tess had always wanted to see the
ocean, so we decided to pull off and relax for a bit at a cove in the Ventana
Wilderness. As we hiked to the sand, a light mist rolled in, obscuring the Pacific. Rather than turn back, we decided to picnic on a small crescent beach

beside McWay Falls, an eighty-foot straight drop of water that plunges from the granite cliff to the sea. We saw no other cars on the way in and thought the place ours alone. After lunch, Tess and I stretched out on a blanket, and Eddie, all of five years old and full of energy, had the run of the sand. A few seagulls laughed at us from rocks, and in our seclusion, I felt at peace for the first time in ages.

Maybe the rhythm of the tides or the fresh sea air did us in after lunch. Tess and I dozed on the blanket. I had a strange dream, one that had not visited me in a long, long time. I was back among the hobgoblins as we stalked the boy like a pride of lions. I reached into a hollow tree and pulled at his leg until he squirmed out like a breached baby. Terror filled his eyes when he beheld his living reflection. The rest of our wild tribe stood around, watching, chanting an evil song. I was about to take his life and leave him with mine. The boy screamed.

Riding the thermals above us, a gliding gull cried, then flew out over the waves. Tess lay sleeping, gorgeous in repose beside me, and a thread of lust wormed through me. I buried my head at her nape and nuzzled her awake, and she threw her arms around my back almost to protect herself. Wrapping the blanket around us, I lay on top of her, removing her layers. We began laughing and rocking each other through our chuckles. She stopped suddenly and whispered to me, "Henry, do you know where you are?"

"I'm with you."

"Henry, Henry, stop. Henry, where's Eddie?"

I rolled off her and situated myself. The fog thickened a bit, blurring the contours of a small rocky peninsula that jutted out into the sea. A hardy patch of conifers clung to its granite skull. Behind us, the waterfall ran down to the sand at low tide. No other noise but the surf against shore.

"Eddie?" She was already standing up. "Eddie!"

I stood beside her. "Edward, where are you? Come here."

A thin shout from the trees, then an intolerable wait. I was already mourning him when he came clambering down and raced across the sand to us, his clothes and hair wet with salt spray.

"Where have you been?" Tess asked.

"I went out on that island as far as you can go."

"Don't you know how dangerous that is?"

"I wanted to see how far you could see. A girl is out there."

"On that rock?"

"She was sitting and staring at the ocean."

"All by herself? Where are her parents?"

"For real, Mom. She came a long, long way to get here. Like we did."

"Edward, you shouldn't make up stories like that. There's not a person around for miles."

"For real, Dad. Come see."

"I'm not going out to those rocks. It's cold and wet and slippery."

"Henry"—Tess pointed out to the fir trees—"look at that."

Dark hair flying behind her, a young girl emerged from the firs, ran like a goat down the sloping face, as thin and lissome as the breeze. From that distance she looked unreal, as if woven from the mist. She stopped when she saw us standing there, and though she did not come close, she was no stranger. We peered at each other across the water, and the moment lasted as briefly as the snapping of a photograph. There and gone at the same time. She turned toward the waterfall and ran, vanishing beyond in a haze of rock and evergreen.

"Wait," Tess cried. "Don't go." She raced toward the girl.

"Leave her," I hollered, and chased down my wife. "She's gone. It looks like she knows her way around this place."

"That's a helluva thing, Henry. You let her go, out here in the middle of nowhere."

Eddie shivered in his damp clothes. I swathed him in the blanket and sat him on the sand. We asked him to tell us all about her, and the words tumbled out as he warmed up.

"I was on an adventure and came to the big rock at the edge. And there she was sitting there. Right behind those trees, looking out at the waves. I said hi, and she said hi. And then she said, 'Would you like to sit with me?' "

"What is her name?" Tess asked.

"Ever heard of a girl called Speck? She likes to come here in winter to watch the whales."

"Eddie, did she say where her parents were? Or how she got all the way out here by herself?"

"She walked, and it took more than a year. Then she asked where was I from, and I told her. Then she asked me my name, and I said Edward Day." He suddenly looked away from us and gazed at the rock and the falling tides, as if remembering a hidden sensation.

"Did she say anything else?"

"No." He gathered the blanket around his shoulders.

"Nothing at all?"

"She said, 'How is life in the big, big world?' and I thought that was funny."

"Did she do anything . . . peculiar?" I asked.

"She can laugh like a seagull. Then I heard you started calling me. And she said, 'Good-bye Edward Day,' like that. And I told her to wait right here so I could get my mommy and dad."

Tess embraced our son and rubbed his bare arms through the blanket. She looked again at the space the girl had run through. "She just slipped away. Like a ghost."

From that moment to the instant our plane touched down at home, all I could think about was that lost girl, and what bothered me about her was not so much her mysterious appearance and disappearance, but her familiarity.

When we settled in at home, I began to see the changelings everywhere.

In town on a Saturday morning for a haircut with Edward, I grew flustered by a towheaded boy who sat waiting his turn, quietly sucking a lollipop as he stared, unblinking, at my son. When school resumed in the fall, a pair of twins in the sixth grade spooked me with their uncanny resemblance to each other and their ability to finish each other's sentences. Driving home from a band performance on a dark night, I saw three children in the cemetery and wondered, for a moment, what they might be plotting at such a late hour. At parties or the odd evening out with other couples, I tried to work in veiled references to the legend of the two feral girls and the baby-food jars, hoping to find someone else who believed it or could confirm the rumors, but everyone scoffed when I mentioned the story. All children, except my own boy, became slightly suspect. They can be devious creatures. Behind every child's bright eyes exists a hidden universe.

The quartet's album, *Tales of Wonder*, arrived by Christmas, and we nearly wore out the groove playing it over and over for our friends and family. Edward loved to hear the dissonance of violins against the steady cello line and the crashing arrival of the organ. Even anticipating its arrival, the movement was a shock no matter how many times one listened to the album. On New Year's Eve, well after midnight, the house quiet as a prayer, a sudden blast of my song startled me awake. Expecting the worst, I came downstairs in my pajamas, wielding a baseball bat, only to find my son bug-eyed in front of the speakers, hypnotized by the music. When I turned down the volume, he began to blink rapidly and shake his head as if awakened from a dream.

"Hey, pardner," I said in a low voice. "Do you know how late it is?"

"Is it 1977 yet?"

"Hours ago. Party's over, fella. What made you put on this song?"

"I had a bad dream."

I pulled him onto my lap. "Do you want to tell me about it?" He did not answer but burrowed closer, so I held him tighter. The last drawn-out note resounded as the song lapsed into silence, so I reached over and shut off the stereo.

"Daddy, do you know why I put on your song? Because it reminds me."

"Reminds you of what, Edward? Our trip out to California?"

He turned to face me until we looked eye-to-eye. "No. Of Speck," he said. "The fairy girl."

With a quiet moan, I drew him closer to me, where I could feel in the warmth of his chest the quickening of his heart.

peck loved to be by moving water. My strongest memory is of her animated by the currents, empathetic to the flow. I saw her once, years ago, stripped to the skin, sitting with her legs tucked beneath her, as the water rolled around her waist and the sunshine caressed her shoulders. Under normal circumstances, I would have jumped and splashed in the creek with her, but struck by the grace of her neck and limbs, the contours of her face, I could not move. On another occasion, when the townsfolk shot off fireworks in the night, we watched the explosions upriver, and she seemed more enchanted by the waterflow than by the loud flowering in the sky. While the people looked up, she watched the light reflecting on the ripples and the sparks as they hissed on the surface. From the beginning, I had guessed where she had gone and why, but I did not act upon that intuition because of a fundamental lack of courage. The same fears that had prevented me from crossing at the riverbend also made me break off the search and come back to camp. I should have followed the waters.

The path to the library never seemed as long and foreboding as on the night of my first return. The way had changed since we had parted. The forest thinned around its edge, and rusty cans, bottles, and other refuse littered the brush. None of us had visited in the years since she left. Books lay where we had left them, though mice had nibbled the margins of my papers, left their scat in our old candleholders and coffee mugs. Her Shakespeare was lousy with silverfish. Stevens had swollen with dampness. By dim candlelight, I spent the night restoring order, pulling down cobwebs, shooing crickets, lingering over what she had once held in her hands. I fell asleep wrapped in the musty blanket that had long ago lost her scent.

Vibrations above announced the arrival of morning. The librarians started their day, joists creaking under their weight and the patterns of their routines. I could picture their goings-on: checking in, saying hello, settling at their stations. An hour or so passed before the doors opened and the humans shuffled in. When the rhythm felt normal, I began to work. A thin film of dust covered my papers, and I spent most of that first day reading the bits and pieces in order, tying the loose pages with entries in McInnes's journal. So much had been left behind, lost, forgotten, and buried after we had been driven away the first time. Reduced to a short pile, the words documented time's passage with deep gaps and yawning silences. Very little existed, for instance, from the early days of my arrival—only a few crude drawings and pathetic notes. Years had gone by without mention. After reviewing all the files, I understood the long chore ahead.

When the librarians left for the evening, I popped open the trapdoor underneath the children's section. Unlike on other forays, I had no desire to pick out a new book, but, rather, to steal new writing supplies. Behind the head librarian's desk lay the treasure: five long yellow pads and enough pens to last the rest of my life. To introduce a minor intrigue, I also reshelved the Wallace Stevens that had been missing.

Words spilled from the pen and I wrote until my hand cramped and pained me. The end, the night that Speck left, became the beginning. From there, the story moved backward to the point where I realized that I had fallen in love with her. A whole swath of the original manuscript, which is thankfully gone, was given over to the physical tensions of being a grown man in a young boy's body. Right in the middle of a sentence on desire, I stopped. What if she wanted me to go with her? I would have pleaded for her to stay, said that

I lacked the courage to run away. Yet a contrary idea pulled at my conscience. Perhaps she never intended for me to find out. She had run away because of me and knew all along that I loved her. I put down my pen and wished Speck were there to talk with me, to answer all the unknowables.

These obsessions curled like parasites through my brain, and I tossed and turned on the hard floor. I woke up in the night and started writing on a clean pad, determined to rid my mind of its darkest thoughts. The hours passed and days drifted one into the other. For the next six months, I divided myself between the camp and the library, trying to piece together the story of my life to give to Speck. Our winter hibernation slowed my progress. I grew tired in December and slept until March. Before I could go back to the book, the book came back to me.

Solemn-eyed Luchóg and Smaolach approached one morning as I crunched a farl of oats and drained the dregs from a cup of tea. With great deliberation, they sat on either side of me, cross-legged, settling in for a long talk. Luchóg fiddled with a new shoot of rye poking through the old leaves, and Smaolach looked off, pretending to study the play of light through the branches.

"Good morning, lads. What's on your minds?"

"We've been to the library," said Smaolach.

"Haven't gone there in ages," said Luchóg.

"We know what you've been up to."

"Read the story of your life."

Smaolach turned his gaze toward mine. "A hundred thousand apologies, but we had to know."

"Who gave you the right?" I asked.

They turned their faces away from me, and I did not know where to look.

"You've got a few stories wrong," Luchóg said. "May I ask why you wrote this book? To whom is it addressed?"

"What did I get wrong?"

"My understanding is that an author doesn't write a book without having one or more readers in mind," Luchóg said. "One doesn't go through the time and effort to be the only reader of your own book. Even the diarist expects the lock to be picked."

Smaolach pulled at his chin, as if deep in thought. "It would be a big mistake, I think, to write a book that no one would ever read."

"You are quite right, old friend. I have at times wondered why the artist dares to bring something new into a world where everything has been done and where all the answers are quite well known."

I stood and broke the plane of their inquisition. "Would you please tell me," I hollered, "what is wrong with the book?"

"I'm afraid it's your father," said Luchóg.

"My father, what about him? Has something happened to him?"

"He's not who you think he is."

"What my friend means to say is that the man you think of as your father is not your father at all. That man is another man."

"Come with us," said Luchóg.

As we wound along the path, I tried to untangle the many implications of their invasion into my book. First, they had always known I was Henry Day, and now they knew I knew. They had read of my feelings for Speck and surely guessed I was writing to her. They knew how I felt about them, as well. Fortunately, they came across as generally sympathetic characters, a bit eccentric, true, but steadfast allies in my adventures. Their line of questioning posed an intriguing concern, however, as I had not thought ahead to how I might actually get a book to Speck, or, more to the point, about the reasons behind my desire to write it all down. Smaolach and Luchóg, ahead on the trail, had lived in these woods for decades and sailed through eternity without the same cares or the need to write down and make sense of it all. They wrote no books, painted nothing on the walls, danced no new dance, yet they lived in peace and harmony with the natural world. Why wasn't I like the others?

At sunset, we stepped out of cover and walked down past the church to a scattering of graves in a green space adjacent to the cemetery enclosed by a stone wall. I had been there once before, many years ago, thinking it a shortcut back to safety, or perhaps merely a good hiding place. We slipped between the iron bars into a tranquil, overgrown garden. Many of the inscriptions on the stones were weathered and faded, as the tenants had lain beneath their vanishing names for many years. My friends took me on a winding path between the graves, and we stopped short among the memorials and weeds. Smaolach walked me to a plot and showed me the stone: WILLIAM DAY, 1917–1962. I knelt down on the grass, ran my finger along the grooves of letters, considered the numbers. "What happened?"

Luchóg spoke softly. "We have no idea, Henry Day."

"I haven't heard that name in a while."

Smaolach laid his hand upon my shoulder. "I still prefer Aniday. You are one of us."

"How long have you known?"

"We thought you should know for the truth of your book. You didn't see your father that night we left the old camp."

"And you understand," Luchóg said, "that the man in the new house with the baby cannot be your father."

I sat down and leaned against the marker to save myself from fainting. They were right, of course. By my calendar, fourteen years had passed since the end date on that gravestone. If he had died that long ago, William Day could not be who I thought he was, and that man was not William Day but his double. I wondered to myself how such a thing could be possible. Luchóg opened his pouch, rolled a cigarette, and calmly smoked it amid the headstones. The stars came out to define the sky—how far away, how long ago? My friends seemed on the verge of revealing additional secrets, but they said nothing, so that I might figure it out for myself.

"Let us away then, lads," Smaolach said, "and think on this tomorrow."

We leapt the gate at the corner and trekked home, our conversation turning to smaller mistakes in my own story. Most of their suggestions escaped scrutiny because my mind wandered down long-neglected lanes. Speck had told me what she remembered, but much remained mysterious. My mother faded in and out of view, though I could now see quite clearly the faces of twin baby sisters. My father was a nearly total void. Life existed before this life, and I had not sufficiently dragged the river of my subconscious. Late that night, while the others slept, I sat awake in my burrow. The image of Oscar Love crystallized before me. We had spent months investigating that boy, finding out in excruciating detail the nature and shape of his life, his family history, his habits of mind—all to assist Igel in the change. If we knew Oscar so well, then the others must have known my history, infinitely better than I knew it myself. Now that I knew my true name, there was no longer any reason for them to hide the truth. They had conspired to help me forget, and now they could help me remember. I crawled out of my hole and walked over to Luchóg's spot, only to find it vacant. In the adjacent burrow, he was wrapped in Chavisory's arms, and for a moment I hesitated to disturb their peace.

"Luch," I whispered. He blinked. "Wake up, and tell me a story."

"Aniday, for the love of—can't you see I'm sleeping?"

"I need to know."

By this time, she was stirring as well. I waited until they disentangled themselves, and he rose to eye level. "What is it?" he demanded.

"You have to tell me everything you remember about Henry Day."

He yawned and looked at Chavisory curled into the fetal position. "Right now, I'm going back to bed. Ask me again in the morning, and I'll help with your book-writing. But now, to my pillow and to my dreams."

I woke Smaolach and Béka and Onions with the same request and was put off by each in much the same way. Despite my excitement, I drew nothing but tired glares at breakfast the next morning, and only after the whole clan had their fill did I dare ask again.

"I am writing a book," I announced, "about Henry Day. I know the broad story that Speck gave me before she left, and now I need you to fill in the details. Pretend I'm about to make the change, and give me the report on Henry Day."

"Oh, I remember you," Onions began. "You were a baby foundling in the woods. Your mother wrapped you in swaddling clothes and laid you at the greyhound's shrine."

"No, no, no," said Béka. "You are mistaken. The original Henry Day was not a Henry at all, but one of two identical twin girls, Elspeth and Maribel."

"You are both wrong," said Chavisory. "He was a boy, a cute, smart boy who lived in a house at the tip of the forest with his mother and father and two baby twin sisters."

"That's right," said Luchóg. "Mary and Elizabeth. Two little curly-tops, fat as lambchops."

"You couldn't have been more than eight or nine," said Chavisory.

"Seven," said Smaolach. "He was seven when we nabbed him."

"Are you sure?" asked Onions. "Coulda swore he was just a baby."

The conversation continued in this fashion for the rest of the day, in contested bites of information, and the truth at the end of the discussion was the distant cousin of the truth at the beginning. All through the summer and into the fall, I peppered them separately and together with my queries. Sometimes an answer, when combined with my prodigal memory or the visual cue of a drawing or a piece of writing, cemented a fact in my brain. Slowly, over time, a pattern emerged, and my childhood returned to me. But one thing remained a mystery.

Before the long sleep of winter, I went off, intent upon climbing the highest peak in the hills surrounding the valley. The trees had shed their leaves and raised naked arms to the gray sky. To the east, the city looked like toy building blocks. Off to the south lay the compact village cut in two by the river. In the west, the riverbend and the big country beyond. To the north, ragged forest, a farm or two hacked out from the trees and stone. I sat on the mountaintop and read, dreamt at night of two Specks, two Days, what we are, what we would be. Save for a flask of water, I fasted and reflected upon the puzzle of existence. On the third day, my mind cleared and let in the answer. If the man who appeared as my father was not my father, who was he? Whom did I meet in the mist? Who was the man by the creek on the night we lost both Igel and Oscar Love? The one who chased us through the kitchen door? He looked like my father. A deer, startled by the snap of my head, bolted through the fallen leaves. A bird cried once; the note lingered, then disappeared. The clouds rolled on and revealed the pale sun. Who had taken my place when they stole me away?

I knew. That man had what had been intended for me. The robber of my name, stealer of my story, thief of my life: Henry Day.

I had been one of them. My son had met one face-to-face on the other side of the country, and there was no telling to what lengths they would go to follow us. The changelings had come for Edward that night years before, and by going downstairs I had scared them off. But they would be back. They were watching us, waiting for my son. He would not be safe as long as they prowled near our home. Edward would not be safe with them in the world. Once they fixed on a child for the change, he was as good as gone. I could not let Edward from my sight, and took to locking our doors and latching our windows every evening. They circled around my imagination, infected my rest. The piano offered my sole relief. By composing, I hoped to steady my sanity. False start followed false start. I struggled to keep those two worlds separate.

Fortunately, I had Tess and Edward to keep me grounded. A delivery truck pulled into our cul-de-sac on my birthday, and Edward, at the window, shouted, "It's here, it's here!" They insisted that I remain in the bedroom with the shades drawn until my gift could be brought into the house, and I dutifully complied, mad with love at my son's jumpy exuberance and Tess's sexy, knowing smile. On the bed in darkness, I closed my eyes, wondering if I deserved such love in return, worrying that it might be stolen should the truth ever be revealed.

Edward bounded up the stairs and hammered on the closed door. Grabbing my arm with his two small hands, he pulled me to the studio. A great green bow stretched across the door, and with a curtsey, Tess presented me with the scissors.

"As mayor of this city," I intoned, "I'd like my distinguished son to join me in the honors." We cut the ribbon together and swung open the door.

The small organ was not new or elaborate, but it was beautiful from the love given. And it would prove enough for me to approximate the sounds I was after. Edward fiddled with the stops, and I took Tess aside and asked how she could afford such a luxury.

"Ever since San Francisco," she said, "or maybe since Czechoslovakia, I've been wanting to do this for you. A penny here, a dollar there, and a woman who drives a hard bargain. Eddie and I found it for sale at an old church up in Coudersport. Your mom and Charlie put us over the top, you should know, but we all wanted you to have it. I know it's not perfect, but—"

"It's the best gift—"

"Don't worry about the cost. Just play the music, baby."

"I gived my allowances," Edward said.

I embraced them both and held tight, overcome by fortune, and then I sat down and played from Bach's *The Art of the Fugue*, lost again to time.

Still enamored with the new machine days later, I returned with Edward from kindergarten to an empty and quiet house. I gave him a snack, turned on *Sesame Street*, and went to my studio to work. On the organ keyboard sat a single sheet of folded paper with a yellow sticky note affixed to the surface. "Let's discuss!" she had scribbled. She had found the passenger list with the names of all the Ungerlands, which I had hidden and locked up among my papers; I could only imagine how it wound up in Tess's hands.

The front door swung open with a screech and banged shut, and for a dark moment the thought danced through my mind that they had come for Edward. I dashed to the front door just as Tess inched her way into the dining room, arms laden with groceries. I took a few bags to lighten her load, and we carried them into the kitchen and danced around each other in a pas de deux, putting food away. She did not seem particularly concerned about anything other than the canned peas and carrots.

When we were done, she brushed imaginary dust from her palms. "Did you get my note?"

"About the Ungerlands? Where did you get the list?"

She blew her bangs out of her eyes. "What do you mean, where did I get it? You left it on the sideboard by the phone. The question is: Where did *you* get it?"

"In Cheb. Remember Father Hlinka?"

"Cheb? That was nine years ago. Is that what you were doing? What possessed you to investigate the Ungerlands?"

Total silence gave me away.

"Were you that jealous of Brian? Because honestly, that's a little crazy, don't you think?"

"Not jealous, Tess. We happened to be there, and I was simply trying to help him trace his family tree. Find his grandfather."

She picked up the passenger list and her eyes scanned it to the end. "That's incredible. When did you ever talk to Brian Ungerland?"

"This is all ancient history, Tess. I ran into him at Oscar's when we were engaged. I told him we were going to Germany, and he asked me if I had the time could I stop by the National Archives and look up his family. When I didn't find them there, I thought maybe his people were from someplace else, so I asked Father Hlinka when we were in Cheb. He found them. No big deal."

"Henry, I don't believe a word you're saying."

I stepped toward her, wanting to enfold her in my arms, desperate to end the conversation. "Tess, I've always told you the truth."

"But why didn't Brian just go ask his mother?"

"His mother? I didn't know he had a mother."

"Everyone has a mother. She lives right here in town. Still does, I think. You can tell her how jealous you were."

"But I looked her up in the phone book."

"You're kidding." She crossed her arms and shook her head. "She remarried years ago when Brian was in high school. Let me think. Her name is Blake, Eileen Blake. And she'd remember the grandfather. He lived till he was a hundred, and she used to talk about that crazy old man all the time." Giving up, she headed for the staircase.

"Gustav?" I shouted after her.

She looked over her shoulder, scrunched up her face, found the name in her memory. "No, no . . . Joe. Crazy Joe Ungerland is Brian's grandfather. Of course, they're all crazy in that family, even the mother."

"Are you sure we're not talking about Gustav Ungerland?"

"I'm going to start calling you Crazy Henry Day. . . . You could have asked me all about this. Look, if you're so interested, why don't you go talk to Brian's mother? Eileen Blake." At the top of the stairs, she leaned over the railing, her long blonde hair falling like Rapunzel's. "It's sweet you were so jealous, but you have nothing to worry about." She flashed her crooked smile and set free my worries. "Tell the old girl I said hello."

Buried to her neck in fallen leaves, she stared straight ahead without blinking, and the third time I passed her I realized she was a doll. Another had been lashed with a red jump rope to a tree trunk nearby, and dismembered arms and legs poked up at odd angles from the long, unmowed grass. At the end of a string tied to a chokecherry limb, a head hung and rotated in the breeze, and the headless body was stuffed into the mailbox, anticipating Saturday's postman. The masterminds behind this mayhem giggled from the porch when I stopped the car in front of their house, but they looked almost catatonic as I walked up the sidewalk.

"Can you girls help me? I seem to be lost," I said from the bottom step. The older girl draped a protective arm across her sister's shoulder.

"Is your mommy or daddy home? I'm looking for someone who lives around here. Do you know the Blakes' house?"

"It's haunted," said the younger sister. She lacked two front teeth and spoke with a lisp.

"She's a witch, mister." The older sister may have been around ten, stick-thin and raven-haired, with dark circles around her eyes. If anyone would know about witches, it was this one. "Why do you want to go see a witch, mister?"

I put one foot on the next step. "Because I'm a goblin."

They both grinned from ear to ear. The older sister directed me to look for a turn before the next street corner, a hidden alleyway that was really a lane. "It's called Asterisk Way," she said, "because it's too small to have a real name."

"Are you going to gobble her up?" the smaller one asked.

"I'm going to gobble her up and spit out the bones. You can come by on Halloween night and make yourself a skeleton." They turned and looked at each other, smiling gleefully.

An invasion of sumac and overgrown boxwood obscured Asterisk Way. When the car began to scrape hedges on both sides, I got out and walked. Half-hidden houses were scattered along the route, and last on the left was a weathered foursquare with BLAKE on the mailbox. Obscured by the shrubs, a pair of bare legs flashed in front of me, racing across the yard, and then a second someone rustled through the bushes. I thought the horrid little sisters had followed me, but then a third movement in the brush unsettled me. I reached for my car keys and nearly deserted that dark place, but having come so far, I knocked on the front door.

An elegant woman with a thick mane of white hair swung open the door. Dressed simply in crisp linen, she stood tall and erect in the doorway, her eyes bright and searching, and welcomed me into her home. "Henry Day. Any trouble finding the place?" New England echoed faintly in her voice. "Come in, come in."

Mrs. Blake had an ageless charm, a physical presence and manner that put others right at ease. To gain this interview, I had lied to her, told her that I had gone to high school with her son Brian and that our class was organizing a reunion, tracking down classmates who had moved away. At her insistence, we chatted over a lunch she had prepared, and she gave me the full update on Brian, his wife and two children, all that he had accomplished over the years. Our egg-salad sandwiches lasted longer than her report, and I attempted to steer the conversation around to my ulterior motive.

"So, Mrs. Ungerland . . ."

"Call me Eileen. I haven't been Mrs. Ungerland for years. Not since my first husband passed away. And then the unfortunate Mr. Blake met with his strange accident with the pitchfork. They call me 'the black widow' behind my back, those awful children."

"A witch, actually . . . I'm so sorry, Eileen. About both your husbands, I mean."

"Well, you shouldn't be. I married Mr. Blake for his money, God rest his soul. And as for Mr. Ungerland, he was much, much older than I, and he was . . ." She pointed to her temple with a long, thin finger.

"I went to Catholic elementary school and only met Brian in ninth grade. What was he like growing up?"

Her face brightened, and she stood up so quickly that I thought she would topple over. "Would you like to see pictures?"

At every stage of his life—from the day he was born through grade school—Brian Ungerland looked as if he could be my son. His resemblance to Edward was uncanny, the same features, posture, even the way they ate corn on the cob or threw a ball. As we paged through the album, my conviction increased with each image.

"Brian used to tell me pretty wild family stories," I said. "About the Ungerlands, I mean, the German ones."

"Did he tell you about Opa Josef? His grandpa Joe? Of course, Brian was still a baby when he passed away, but I remember him. He was a crazy loon. They all were."

"They came over from Germany, right?"

She sat back in her chair, sorting through her memories. "It is a sad, sad story, that family."

"Sad? In what way?"

"There was Crazy Joe, my father-in-law. He lived with us when we were first married, ages ago. We kept him in a room off the attic. Oh, he must have been ninety, maybe one hundred years old, and he would rant and rave about things that weren't there. Spooks, things like that, as if something were coming to get him, poor dear. And muttering about his younger brother, Gustav, claiming that he wasn't really his brother at all and that the real Gustav had been stolen away by *der Wechselbalgen.* Changelings. My husband said it was because of the sister. If I remember, the sister died on the passage over from Germany, and that plunged the whole family into grief. And they never recovered. Even Josef, still imagining spirits after all those years."

The room began to feel unusually warm, and my stomach churned. My head hurt.

"Let me think, yes, there was the mama, and the papa, another poor man. Abram was his name. And the brothers. I don't know anything about the older one; he died in the Civil War at Gettysburg. But there was Josef who was a bachelor until he was pushing fifty, and then there's the idiot brother, the youngest one. Such a sad family."

"Idiot? What do you mean, idiot?"

"That's not what they call it nowadays, but back then, that's what they said. They went on and on about how wonderfully he could play the piano, but it was all a trick of the mind. He was what they would call an idiot savant.

Gustav was his name, poor child. Could play like Chopin, Josef claimed, but was otherwise quiet and extremely introverted. Maybe he was autistic, if they had such a thing back then."

The blood rushed to my head and I began to feel faint.

"Or maybe highly strung. But after the incident with the so-called changelings, he even stopped playing the piano and completely withdrew, never said another word for the rest of his life, and he lived to be an old man, too. They say the father went mad when Gustav stopped playing the music and started to let the world just drift right by. I went out to see him once or twice at the institution, poor dear. You could tell he was thinking something, but Lord only knows. As if he went off to live in his own little world. He died when I was still a young newlywed. That was about 1934, I think, but he looked older than Moses."

She bent over the photo album and flipped through to the front of the book. She pointed to a middle-aged man in a gray fedora. "There's my husband, Harry—that's crazy Joe's son. He was so old when we married, and I was just a girl." Then she pointed to a wizened figure who looked as if he was the oldest man in the world. "Gustav." For a brief moment, I thought that would be me, but then I realized the old man in the photograph was no relation at all. Beneath him there was a scratched image of an elderly woman in a high collar. "*La belle dame sans merci*. Gone well before my time, but were it not for his mother holding things together, that would have been the end of the Ungerlands. And then we wouldn't be sitting here today, would we?"

"But," I stammered, "but how did they manage to go on after so much misfortune?"

"The same way that all of us do. The same way that I went on after losing two husbands and Lord knows all that's happened. At some point, you have to let go of the past, son. Be open to life to come. Back in the sixties, when everybody was lost, Brian used to talk about going off to find himself. He used to say, 'Will I ever know the real me? Will I ever know who I am supposed to be?' Such foolish questions beg straight answers, don't you think, Henry Day?"

I felt faint, paralyzed, destroyed. I crawled off the sofa, out the front door, all the way home and into bed. If we made our good-byes, they evaporated quickly in the residual shock of her story.

To rouse me from deep slumber the next morning, Tess fixed a pot of hot coffee and a late breakfast of eggs and biscuits, which I devoured like a famished child. I was sapped of all strength and will, confounded by the news of Gustav as an idiot savant. Too many ghosts in the attic. We sat on the veranda in the cool morning, swapping sections of the Sunday newspaper. I pretended to read, but my mind was elsewhere, desperately trying to sort through the possibilities, when a ruckus arose in the neighborhood. Dogs started howling one by one as something passed in front of their homes, a chain reaction of maddening intensity.

Tess stood and peered down the street both ways but saw nothing. "I can't stand it," she said. "I'm going inside until they knock it off. Can I freshen your coffee?"

"Always." I smiled and handed her my cup. The second she vanished, I saw what had driven the animals mad. There on the street, in the broad light of Sunday morning, two of the devils zigzagged across the neighborhood lawns. One of them limped along as she ran, and the other, a mouselike monster, beckoned her to hurry. The pair stopped when they saw me on the porch, two houses away, and stared directly at me for an instant. Wretched creatures with hideous holes for eyes, bulbous heads on their ruined bodies. Caked with dirt and sweat. From downwind, I could smell the feral odor of decay and musk. The one with the limp pointed a bony finger right at me, and the other quickly led her away through the gap between houses. Tess returned with the coffee too late to see them go, and once the creatures disappeared, the dogs quieted, settled back in their kennels, and relaxed their chains.

"Did you figure out what all the commotion was about?"

"Two things running through the neighborhood."

"Things?"

"I don't know." I took a sip. "Little monsters."

"Monsters?"

"Can't you smell their awful odor? Like someone just ran over a skunk."

"Henry, what are you talking about? I don't smell a thing."

"I don't know what set those dogs off. Mass hysteria, a figment of their doggy brains? A mouse and a bat? A couple of kids."

She put her cool hand on my forehead. "Are you feeling okay, Henry? You don't seem yourself today."

"I'm not," I said. "Maybe I should go back to bed."

As I drifted off to sleep, the changelings haunted my dreams. A dozen crept out of the woods, stepping out from behind each tree. They kept on coming, a band of hollow children, surrounding my home, advancing toward the doors and windows. Trapped inside, I raced from floor to floor and looked out through peepholes and from behind curtains as they silently marched and assembled in a ring. I ran down the hall to Eddie's room, and he was a baby again, curled up in a ball in his crib. I shook him to wake him up and run away with me, but when the child rolled over, he had the face of a grown man. I screamed and locked myself in the bathroom. From the tiny window I could see the monsters begin to climb up the porch rails, scale the walls like spiders, their evil faces turned to me, menace and hatred in their glowing eyes. Windows were shattered in other rooms; the glass exploding and hitting the floor in an oddly gentle crescendo. I looked into the mirror, saw my reflection morph into my father, my son, Gustav. Behind me in the mirror, one of the creatures rose and reached out its claws to wrap around my neck.

Tess sat on the edge of the bed, shaking my shoulder. I was drenched with sweat, and though I felt hotter than hell, she said I was clammy and cold. "You've had a bad dream. It's okay, it's okay." I buried my face on her breast and she stroked my hair and rocked me until I gained my full senses. For a moment, I did not know where I was, did not know who I was now or ever.

"Where's Edward?"

She looked perplexed by my question. "At my mother's, don't you remember? He's spending the weekend. What's wrong with you?"

I shivered in her embrace.

"Was it that mean old Mrs. Ungerland? You need to concentrate on what's important and stop chasing after what's past. Don't you know, it's you I love. And always have."

Everyone has an unnameable secret too dire to confess to friend or lover, priest or psychiatrist, too entwined at the core to excise without harm. Some people choose to ignore it; others bury it deep and lug it unspoken to the grave. We mask it so well that even the body sometimes forgets the secret exists. I do not want to lose our child, and I do not want to lose Tess. My fear of being found out as a changeling and rejected by Tess has made a secret of the rest of my life.

After hearing the true story of Gustav, it is no wonder that I remembered so little from those days. I had been locked inside my own mind with music as my only means of self-expression. Had I not been stolen, I would never have lived among the changelings, never had the chance to become Henry Day. And had I not changed places with the boy, I would never have known Tess, never had a child of my own, and never found my way back to this world. In a way, the changelings gave me a second chance, and their reappearance—the break-in at our home, the encounter in California with Edward, the pair dashing across the lawn—was both a threat and a reminder of all that was at stake.

When I had first started seeing the changelings again, I attributed it to the stress of discovering my past. They seemed hallucinations, nightmares, or no more than a figment of my imagination, but then the real creatures showed up and left their signs behind. They were taunting me: an orange peel on the middle of the dining room table; an open bottle of beer on top of the television; cigarette butts burning in the garden. Or things went missing. My chrome-plated piano trophy from the statewide competition. Photographs, letters, books. I once heard the fridge door slam shut at two in the morning when we were all asleep, went downstairs and found a baked ham half-eaten on the countertop. Furniture that hadn't been moved in ages suddenly appeared next to open windows. On Christmas Eve, at my mother's house, the younger children thought they heard reindeer tramping on the roof, and they went outside to investigate. Twenty minutes later, the breathless kids came back in, swearing they had seen two elves hopping away into the woods. Another time, one of them crawled through a gap no bigger than a rabbit hole under a gate in our backyard. When I went outside to catch it, the creature was gone. They were becoming brazen and relentless, and I wanted only for them to go away and leave me at peace.

Something had to be done about my old friends.

CHAPTER 34

I set out to learn everything that could be known about the other Henry Day. My life's story and its telling are bound to his, and only by understanding what had happened to him would I know all that I had missed. My friends agreed to help me, for by our nature we are spooks and secret agents. Because their skills had lain dormant since the botched change with Oscar Love, the faeries took special delight in spying on Henry Day. Once upon a time, he was one of them.

Luchóg, Smaolach, and Chavisory tracked him to an older neighborhood on the far side of town where he circled round the streets as if lost. He stopped and talked to two adorable young girls playing with their dollies in their front yard. After watching him drive off, Chavisory approached the girls, thinking they might be Kivi and Blomma in human form. The sisters guessed Chavisory was a faery right away, and she ran, laughing and shrieking, to our hiding place in a crown of blackberry stalks. A short time later, our spies spotted Henry Day talking to a woman who seemed to have upset him. When he left her old house, Henry looked haunted, and he sat in his car for the longest time, head bent to the steering wheel, shoulders heaving as he sobbed.

"He looked knackered, as if the woman sapped his spirit," Smaolach told us afterward.

"I noticed as well," said Luchóg, "that he has changed of late, as if he is guilty of the past and worried of the future."

I asked them if they thought the older woman had been my mother, but they assured me she was somebody else's.

Luchóg rolled himself a smoke. "He walked in one man, came out another."

Chavisory poked at the campfire. "Maybe there are two of him."

Onions agreed, "Or he's only half a man."

Luchóg lit the cigarette, let it dangle from his lower lip. "He's a puzzle with one piece missing. He's a tockless clock."

"We'll pick the lock of his brain," Smaolach said.

"Have you been able to find out more about his past?" I asked them.

"Not much," said Luchóg. "He lived in your house with your mother and father, and your two little sisters."

"Our Chopin won lots of prizes for playing music," said Chavisory. "There's a tiny shiny piano on the mantel, or at least there was." She reached behind her back and held out the trophy for us to admire, its facade reflecting the firelight.

"I followed him to school one day," said Smaolach. "He teaches children how to play music, but if their performance is any indication, he's not very good. The winds blow harsh and the fiddlers cannot fiddle."

We all laughed. In time, they told me many more stories of the man, but large gaps existed in the tale, and singular questions arose. Was my mother living still, or had she joined my father under the earth? I knew nothing about my sisters and wondered how they had grown. They could be mothers themselves by now, but are forever babies in my imagination.

"Did I tell you he saw us?" Luchóg asked. "We were at our old stomping grounds by his house, and I am sure that he looked right at Chavisory and me. He's not the handsomest thing in the world."

"Tell the truth," Chavisory added, "he's rather fearsome. Like when he lived with us."

"And old."

"And wearing out," said Smaolach. "You're better off with us. Young always."

The fire crackled and embers popped, floating up in the darkness. I pictured him snug in his bed with his woman, and the thought reminded me of Speck. I trudged back to my burrow, trying to find comfort in the hard ground.

In my sleep, I climbed a staircase of a thousand steps carved into the side of a mountain. The dizzy view below took my breath away, and my heart hammered against my bones. Only blue skies and a few more steps lay in front of me. I labored on and reached the top, and the stairs continued down the other side of the mountain, impossibly steep, even more frightening than the way up. Paralyzed, I could not go back and could not go on. From the side, from nowhere, Speck appeared, joining me on the summit. She had been transformed. Her eyes sparked with life; she grinned at me as if no time had passed.

"Shall we roll down the hill together? Like Jack and Jill?"

I could not say a word. If I moved, blinked, opened my mouth, she would disappear and I would fall.

"It isn't as difficult or dangerous as it appears."

She wrapped me in her arms and, next thing, we were safe at the bottom. The dreamscape shifts when she closes her eyes, and I fall deep into a well. I sit alone waiting for something to happen above my head. A door opens, light floods the space. I look up to find Henry Day looking down at me. At first he appears as my father, and then becomes himself. He shouts at me and shakes his fist. The door slams shut, erasing the light. From beneath my feet, the well begins to fill with water flowing in like a river. I kick in panic and realize a strong gossamer rope binds my limbs. Rising to my chest, to my chin, the waters wash over me, and I am under. Unable to hold my breath any longer, I open my mouth and fill my lungs.

I woke gasping for breath. A few seconds passed before the stars came into view, the reaching branches, the lips of my burrow an inch or two above my face. Throwing off the blanket, I rose and stepped out of that space onto the surface. Everyone else was asleep in their dens. Where the fire had been, a faint orange glow was visible beneath the black kindling. The starlit woods were so quiet that I could hear the steady breathing of the few faeries left in this place. The chilly air robbed me of my bed-warmth, and a film of nervous perspiration dried and evaporated off my skin. How long I stood still, I do not know, but I half expected someone to materialize from the darkness either to take me or to embrace me.

I went back to work on my book, stuck mid sentence at the point where Igel is about to switch with little Oscar Love. During my first visit beneath the library, I re-read the pages in light of what we had discovered about Henry Day, and all that had been revealed to me through the other clan members about my former life and circumstances. Needless to say, my first story reeked of false impressions. I gathered my papers and the error-riddled manuscript and thought through the problem. In my original version, I had assumed that my parents lived still and that they had spent their lives missing their only son. Of the few chance encounters with my natural father, only one could possibly be true. And, of course, the first story had been written with no real knowledge of the fraud and imposter who had taken my place.

We started watching him again and found a troubled man. He carried on conversations with himself, his lips mouthing a violent argument. Ages ago, he'd had a number of other friends as well, but as his strangeness increased, they vanished from the story. Henry spent most of his time locked away in a room, reading books or playing a booming organ, scrawling notes on lined paper. His wife lived in the margins, working on her home, every day driving away and returning hours later. Onions thought that a telltale unhappiness weighed heavily on the woman's mind, for when she was alone, she often stared into the distance, as if to extract from the air the answer to her unuttered questions. The boy, Edward, was ideal for the change, alone and distanced from the rise and fall of life, caught up in his own thoughts, and wandering through his parents' house as if looking for a friend.

Waking in the middle of a full-moon night, I overheard Béka and Onions whispering about the boy. Cozy in their den, they expected a degree of privacy, but their conspiracy hummed along the ground like the faraway sound of an approaching train.

"Do you think we'd be able to, ourselves alone?" Onions asked.

"If we can catch him at the right moment. Perhaps when the father is distracted or drowning out every known sound on that infernal organ."

"But if you change with Edward Day, what will happen to me?" Onions said, never more plaintive. I coughed to alert them to my presence and walked over to where they huddled, feigning sleep, innocent as two newborn kits. They might be brazen enough to try, and I resolved to keep closer watch and crack any plots before one might hatch.

In the past, the faeries refused to spy on one who had quit the tribe. The changeling was left alone, forgotten, and given a chance to live out his human life. The danger of being exposed by such a person is great, for after they make the change, they grow to resent their time among us and fear that other humans will discover their dark secret. But such concerns, once great, became less important to us. We were disappearing. Our number had diminished from a dozen to a mere six. We decided to make our own rules.

I asked them to find my mother and sisters, and at Christmas they were discovered at last. While the rest of us dozed, Chavisory and Luchóg stole away to town, which glowed with blinking lights as carolers sang in the streets. As a gift to me, they decided to explore my boyhood home, hoping to find missing clues that might give my past more meaning. The old house stood in the clearing, not as solitary as it had once been. Nearby farms had been sold off one by one, and the skeletons of new houses rose in all directions. A handful of cars parked in the drive led them to believe that a celebration was taking place at my former house, so they crept to the windows to see the assembled crowd. Henry Day, his wife, and their son were there. And Mary and Elizabeth. At the center of the festivities, a gray-haired woman sat in an easy chair by a sparkling fir tree. Her mannerisms reminded Luchóg of my mother, upon whom he had spied many years ago. He climbed a nearby oak and leapt from its outstretched limbs to the rooftop, scrambling over to the chimney, its bricks still warm to the touch. The fire below had gone out, making it easier for him to eavesdrop. My mother, he said, was singing to the children in the old style, without instrumentation. How I would have loved to hear her again.

"Give us a song, Henry," she said when they were through, "like you used to do."

"Christmas is a busman's holiday if you play the piano," he said. "What'll it be, Mom? 'Christmas in Killarney' or some other blather?"

"Henry, you shouldn't make fun," said one of the daughters.

" 'Angels We Have Heard on High,' " said an unfamiliar, older man who rested his hand on her shoulder.

Henry played the song, began another. When Luchóg had heard enough, he jumped back to the oak and climbed down to rejoin Chavisory. They stole one last look at the party, studied the characters and scene for me, then returned home. When they told the story the next day, I was deeply pleased to hear about my mother, as puzzling as the details might be. Who was this old man? Who were all these other children? Even the tiniest scrap of news brought back that past. I hid in a hollow tree. She was angry with me, and I would run away and never come back. Where are your sisters? Where are my babies? I remembered that I had sat in the V made by her legs, listening to the story of the wanderings of Oisín in Tír na nÓg. It is not fair to have to miss someone for so many years.

But this is a double life. I sat down to work on the true story of my world and the world of Henry Day. The words flowed slowly, painfully, sometimes letter by letter. Whole mornings escaped without a single sentence worth saving. I crumpled and threw away so many pages that I was forever popping up into the library to steal more paper, and the pile of trash in the corner threatened to consume the whole room. In assembling my tale, I found myself tiring easily, early in the day, so that if I could string together five hundred words, writing had triumphed over uncertainty and procrastination.

At times I questioned my reasons for written proof of my own existence. When I was a boy, stories were as real as any other part of life. I'd hear Jack climb the beanstalk, and later wonder how to climb the tall poplars outside my window. Hansel and Gretel were brave heroes, and I shuddered at the thought of the witch in her oven. In my daydreams, I fought dragons and rescued the girl trapped in her tower. When I could not sleep for the wild doings and extravagant deeds of my own imagination, I'd wake my father, who would invariably say, "It's only a story." As if such words made it less real. But I did not believe him even then, for stories were written down, and the words on the page were proof enough. Fixed and permanent in time, the words, if anything, made the people and places more real than the ever-changing world. My life with the faeries is more real to me than my life as Henry Day. And I wrote it down to show that we are more than a myth, a tale for children, a nightmare or daydream. Just as we need their stories to exist, so do the humans need us to give shape to their lives. I wrote it to create meaning for my change, for what happened with Speck. By saying *this* instead of *that*, I could control what mattered. And show the truth that lies below the surface life.

I finally decided to meet the man face-to-face. I had seen Henry Day years before, but I now knew that he had once been a changeling who had kidnapped me when I was a boy of seven. We had uncovered him, followed him everywhere, and learned the outlines of his daily routine. The faeries had been to his house, taken a random score of the music he wrote, and left him with a sign of their mischief. But I wanted to confront him, if only to say goodbye, through him, to my mother and sisters.

I was on my way to the library to finish my story. A man stepped out of a car and marched through the front door of the building. He looked old and tired, worn by care. Nothing like me, or how I imagined I would be. He walked with his head down, eyes on the ground, a slight stoop to his shoulders, as if the simplest things gravely distracted him. He dropped an armful of papers and, bending down to gather them, muttered a stream of curses. I considered pouncing out of the woods, but he looked too fragile to spook that night, so instead I squeezed through the crevice to go about my craft.

He had begun frequenting the library that summer, showing up several days in a row, humming snatches of the symphony we had stolen from him. On hot and humid afternoons, when sensible people were swimming or lying in bed with the shades drawn, Henry was often reading alone at a sun-splashed table. I could sense his presence above, separated only by the thin ceiling, and when the library closed for the night, I climbed through the trapdoor and investigated. He had been working in a quiet spot in the back corner. Upon a desk, a stack of books lay undisturbed, with neat slips of paper sticking out like tongues between the leaves. I sat where he had sat and looked at the mishmash of titles on everything from imps and demons to a thick book on "idiots savants." Nothing connected these titles, but he had scribbled diminutive notes to himself on bookmarks:

*Not fairy but hobgoblin.*

*Gustav—savant?*

*Ruined my life.*

*Find Henry Day.*

The phrases were discarded pieces to different puzzles, and I pocketed the notes. In the morning, the sounds of his dismay penetrated the floor. Henry muttered about the missing bookmarks, and I felt a guilty pleasure at having nipped them. He ranted at the librarians, but eventually he collected himself and went about his work. I welcomed the peace, which gave me the time to finish writing my book in the quiet hours. Soon I would be free of Henry Day. That evening, I packed the sheets in a cardboard box, placing a few old drawings on top of the manuscript, and then folded Speck's letter carefully and tucked the pages in my pocket. After a quick trip home, I planned on returning one last time to collect my belongings and say my final goodbyes to the dear old space. In my haste, I neglected to think of the time. The last hour of daylight held sway when I pushed out into the open. Considering the risk, I should not have chanced it, but I stepped away from the back staircase and began to walk home.

Henry Day stood not a dozen feet ahead, looking directly at me and the crack beneath the library. Like a cornered hare, I reacted instinctively, running straight at him and then veering off sharply into the street. He moved not a single step. His dulled reflexes failed him. I ran through town with complete disregard for any people, crossed lawns with sprinklers spritzing the dry grass, leapt chainlink fences, tore in front of a moving car or two. I did not stop until deep in the woods, then collapsed on the ground, panting, laughing until tears fell. The look of surprise, anger, and fear on his face. He had no idea who I was. All I had to do was go back later for the book, and that would be the end of the story.

The monster never breathes," the composer Berlioz supposedly said about the organ, but I found the opposite to be true. When I played, I felt alive and at one with the machine, as if exhaling the music. Tess and Edward visited the studio to hear the lengthening shape of my composition, and at the end of the performance my son said, "You were moving the same as I was breathing." Over the course of a year, I worked on the symphony during what hours I could steal, regenerating it constantly from the desire to confess, seeking to craft a texture that would allow me to explain. I felt that if she could but hear my story in the music, Tess would surely understand and forgive. In my studio, I could take refuge at the keyboard. Lock the door and draw the curtains to feel safe and whole again. Lose myself, find myself, in the music.

By the springtime, I had secured a small orchestra—a wind ensemble from Duquesne, timpani from Carnegie-Mellon, a few local musicians—to perform the piece when it was completed. After Edward had finished first grade in June, Tess took him for a two-week visit to her cousin Penny's to give me time alone in the house to finish my symphony—a work about a child trapped in his silence, how the sounds could never get out of his own imagination, living in two worlds, the internal life locked to all communication with outside reality.

After struggling for years to find the music for that stolen child, I finally finished. The score lay spread out across the organ, the scrawled notes on the staves a marvel of mathematical beauty and precision. Two stories told at the same time—the inner life and the outer world in counterpoint. My method was not to juxtapose each chord with its double, for that is not reality. Sometimes our thoughts and dreams are more real than the rest of our experience, and at other moments that which happens to us overshadows anything we might imagine. I had not been able to write fast enough to capture the sounds in my head, notes that flowed from deep within, as if half of me had been composing, and the other half acting as amanuensis. I had yet to fully transcribe the musical shorthand and to assign all of the instrumentation—tasks that might take months of rehearsal to perfect—but the initial process of setting down the bones of the symphony had made me giddy and exhausted, as if in a waking dream. Its relentless logic, strange to the ordinary rules of language, seemed to me what I had been hoping to write all along.

At five o'clock that afternoon, hot and wrung-out, I went to the kitchen for a bottle of beer, and drank it on the way upstairs. My plan was a shower, another beer with dinner, and then back to work. In the bedroom closet, the empty spaces where her clothes had been reminded me of Tess, and I wished she had been there to share the sudden burst of creativity and accomplishment. Moments after stepping into the hot shower, I heard a loud crash downstairs. Without turning off the water, I stepped out, wrapped a towel around my waist, and hurried to investigate. One of the windows in the living room had been broken, and glass lay all over the rug. A breeze flapped the curtains. Half naked and dripping wet, I stood there puzzled, until a sudden discordant hammering of the piano keys frightened me, as if a cat had walked across it, but the studio was empty and silent. I took a long look around.

The score was gone—not on the table where I had left it, not fallen to the floor, not anywhere. The window gaped open, and I ran to look at the lawn. A solitary page fluttered across the grass, pushed along by a thin breeze, but there was nothing else to see. Howling with anger and pacing the room, I stubbed my toe on the piano leg and began hopping up and down across the rug, nearly impaling my foot on a piece of glass, when another crash sounded upstairs. Foot throbbing, I climbed the steps to the landing, afraid of what might be in my house, worried about my manuscript. My bedroom was empty. In our son's room another window had been broken, but no glass littered the floor. Shards on the roof meant the window had been shattered from the inside out. To clear my head, I sat for a moment on the edge of his bed. His room looked the same as the day he'd left for the vacation, and thoughts of Edward and Tess filled me with sudden sorrow. How would I explain the missing symphony? Without it, how could I confess my true nature? I pulled at my wet hair till my scalp ached. In my mind, my wife, my son, and my music were wound together in a braided chain that now threatened to unravel.

In the bathroom, the shower ran and ran. A cloud of steam billowed out into the hallway, and I stumbled through the fog to shut off the water. On the cabinet mirror, someone had fingered words on the fogged surface: *We No Your Secret.* Copied above, note for note, was the first measure of my score.

"You little fuckers," I said to myself as the message vanished from the mirror.

After a restless and lonesome night, I drove to my mother's house as a new day began. When she did not immediately answer my knock, I thought she might still be asleep, and went over to the window to look in. From the kitchen, she saw me standing there, smiled, and waved me to her.

"Door's never locked," she said. "What brings you here in the middle of the week?"

"Good morning. Can't a guy come and see his best girl?"

"Oh, you're such an awful liar. Would you like a cup of coffee? How about I fry you a couple of eggs?" She busied herself at the stove, and I sat at the kitchen table, its surface pocked with marks left from dropped pots and pans, nicked by knives, and lined with faint impressions of letters written there. The morning light stirred memories of our first breakfast together.

"Sorry I was so long in answering the door," she said above the sizzle. "I was on the phone with Charlie. He's off in Philadelphia, tying up loose ends. Is everything all right with you?"

I was tempted to tell her everything, beginning with the night we took away her son, going back further to a little German boy snatched away by changelings, and ending with the tale of the stolen score. But she looked too careworn for such confessions. Tess might be able to handle it, but the story would break my mother's heart. Nonetheless, I needed to tell someone, at least provisionally, of my past errors and the sins I was about to commit.

"I've been under a lot of pressure lately. Seeing things, not truly myself. Like I'm being followed by a bad dream."

"Followed by troubles is the sign of a guilty conscience."

"Haunted. And I've got to sort it out."

"When you were a baby, you were the answer to my prayers. And when you were a little boy, remember, I used to sing you to sleep every night. You were the sweetest thing, trying to sing along with me, but you could never carry a tune. That certainly changed. And so did you. As if something happened to you that night you ran away."

"It is like the devils are watching me."

"Don't believe in fairy tales. The trouble is inside, Henry, with you. Living in your own head." She patted my hand. "A mother knows her own son."

"Have I been a good son, Mom?"

"Henry." She rested her palm against my cheek, a gesture from my childhood days, and the grief over losing my score abated. "You are who you are, for good or ill, and no use torturing yourself with your own creations. Little devils." She smiled as if a fresh thought had entered her mind. "Have you ever thought whether you're real to them? Put those nightmares out of your head."

I stood to go, then bent and kissed her good-bye. She had treated me kindly over the years, as if I had been her own son.

"I've known all along, Henry," she said.

I left the house without asking.


I resolved to confront them and find out why they were tormenting me. To flush out those monsters, I would go back into the woods. The Forest Service provided topographical maps of the region, the areas in green indicating woodland, the roads drawn in meticulous detail, and I laid a grid over the likely areas, dividing the wilderness into manageable plats. For two days, despite my loathing for the forest and my aversion to nature, I explored a few of those squares, looking for their lair. The woods were emptier than when I lived there—the occasional hammering of a woodpecker, skinks sunning themselves on rocks, the raised white flag of one deer running away, and the lonesome hum of greenbottle flies. Not much life, but plenty of junk—a swollen copy of *Playboy*; a four-of-hearts playing card; a tattered white sweater; a small mound of empty cigarette packages; a canteen; a tortoiseshell necklace on a pile of stones; a stopped watch; and a book stamped *Property of County Library*.

Aside from the dirt on its cover and the slight musty odor to its pages, the book was intact. Through the mildewed pages, the story revolved around a religious fanatic named Tarwater or Tearwater. I gave up reading novels in childhood, for their artificial worlds mask rather than reveal the truth. Novelists construct elaborate lies to throw off readers from discovering the meaning behind the words and symbols, as if it could be known. But the book I found might be just the thing for a fourteen-year-old hellion or some religious misfit, so I took it back to the library. Virtually nobody was there on that mid-summer day, except for a cute girl behind the counter.

"I found this in the woods. It belongs to you."

She looked at the novel as if it were a lost treasure, brushed off the grime, and opened the back cover. "Just a minute." She leafed through a stack of stamped cards. "Thank you, but this has not been checked out at all. Did you forget?"

"No," I explained. "I found it, and wanted to return it to the rightful owners. I was looking for something else."

"Maybe I can help you?" Her smile reminded me of so many other li-brarians, and a small twinge of guilt poked me in the ribs.

I leaned close and smiled at her. "Do you have any books on hobgob-lins?"

She skipped a beat. "Hobgoblins?"

"Or fairies. Imps, trolls, sprites, changelings, that sort of thing?"

The girl looked at me as if I were speaking a foreign language. "You shouldn't lean on the desk like that. There's a card catalog right over there. Alphabetical by subject, title, or author."

Rather than providing shortcuts to useful information, one search begat another, and the curiouser and curiouser I got, the more rabbit holes popped open. My search for fairies resulted in forty-two titles, of which a dozen or so might be useful, but that search branched off into goblins and hobgoblins, which in turn branched off to abnormal psychology, child prodigies, and au-tism. Lunchtime had come and gone, and I felt lightheaded and in need of some air. At a nearby convenience store I bought a sandwich and a bottle of pop, and I sat on a bench by the empty playground, contemplating the task before me. There was so much to know, so much already forgotten. In the relentless sunshine I fell asleep, waking up three hours later with a nasty sun-burn on one arm and the left side of my face. From the library's bathroom mirror stared a person divided in two, half of my face pale, the other half crimson. Exiting past the young librarian, I tried to keep my profile two-dimensional.

My dream returned in full detail that night. Tess and I spoke quietly on the deck of a local pool. A few other people milled about in the background, sunning themselves or diving into the cool water. As wallflowers: Jimmy Cummings, Oscar Love, Uncle Charlie, Brian Ungerland. All the librarians in bikinis.

"How have you been, my love?" she teased. "Still chased by monsters?"

"Tess, it's not funny."

"I'm sorry, but no one else can see them, sweetheart. Only you."

"But they're as real as you and me. What if they come for Edward?"

"They don't want Eddie. They want you." She stood up, tugged at the bottom of her suit, and jumped in the pool. I plunged in after her, shocked by how cold the water felt, and frog-kicked my way to the middle. Tess swam to me, her body becoming more streamlined and graceful, and when the top of her head broke the surface, her hair was plastered against her scalp. As she stopped and stood, the film of water ran off her face, parting like a curtain to reveal not her face at all, but a hobgoblin's face, horrid and frightening. I blanched and hollered involuntarily; then she changed right back again to her familiar self. "What's the matter, love? Don't you know I know who you are? Tell me."

I went back to the library, hunted for a few of my titles, and sat down at a corner table. The research, especially on hobgoblins, was wrong in virtually every particular and no better than myth or fiction. Nobody wrote accurately about their habits and customs, how they lived in darkness, spying on human children, looking for the right person with whom to make the change. There was not one single word about how to get rid of unwanted visitors. Or how to protect your child from every chance and danger. Lost in these fairy tales, I became hypersensitive to the stillness of my surroundings, jarred by the sounds that penetrated the silence. At first the noises appeared to be the random shufflings of another patron languidly turning pages, or one of the librarians, bored out of her mind, pacing the corridors or sneaking outside for a smoke. Soon every minute sound intensified in the mind-numbing quiet.

Someone breathed deeply and regularly, as if asleep, the noise emanating from an indeterminate direction. Later I heard a rasping in the walls, and when I asked the cute librarian, she said it was only mice, but the scrabbling was scratchier, like a fountain pen racing across a pad of paper. That evening, someone began singing tunelessly to himself from the lower depths. I followed the melody to a spot in the children's section. Not a soul around, I lay down, pressed my ear to the floor, and ran my fingers along the ancient carpet, catching my thumb on a hard bump, like a hinge or a bent nail. Carefully cut and nearly indiscernible, a carpet square had been glued to the spot, covering a panel or hatch below, and I would have pried it open, but the passing librarian startled me by clearing her throat. With a sheepish grin, I stood up, mumbled an apology, and went back to my corner. Convinced that something lived beneath the building, I brooded over how to catch him and make him talk.

Next morning, my books were in disarray, titles scrambled out of alphabetical order and all my bookmarks missing. They had been spying on me again. For the rest of the day I pretended to read, while actually listening for any noises from below, and once I wandered back to the children's section. The carpet square had been slightly raised above the surface. On my hands and knees, I tapped on the panel and realized that a hollow space existed beneath the floorboards. Maybe one or more of the fiends toiled below, hatching plots and tricks to further savage my life. A slight red-haired boy whistled behind my back, and I quickly stood, stamped down on the lid, and went away without a word.

That boy made me anxious, so I went out and stayed on the playground until the library closed. The young librarian noticed me on the swing set, but she turned away and pretended not to care. Alone again, I searched the grounds for evidence. If they had followed me to the library, they must have dug a hole or found a secret entranceway into the building. On my third trip around the building, in the shadows of the sun, I saw him. Behind the back stairs, he squeezed out through a crack in the foundation like a baby being born and stood there for a moment, blinking in the fading light. Afraid that he might attack me, I looked left and right for an escape route. He ran directly at me, as if to seize my throat in his jaws, and then darted away as quickly as a bird in flight, too fast for me to see him clearly, but there is no doubt who it was. A hobgoblin. When the danger passed, I could not keep from laughing.

Nervous for hours, I drove around and found myself at my mother's place near midnight. While she slept upstairs, I crept through the house gathering supplies: a carpet knife, an iron crowbar, and a coil of strong rope. From the old barn, I stole my father's ancient kerosene camping lamp, its wire handle dusty and cold to the touch. The wick sputtered when I tried to light the lamp, but it came to life and suffused the long-neglected corner with an unearthly glow.

Insomnia gripped me those last few hours, my mind and body refusing rest until the deed was done. In the predawn gloom, I went back and memorized the layout of the building, figuring out step by step what I was going to do. Patience nearly deserted me. The goblin might have been spooked, so I went about my business as if nothing had ever happened. I spent the day reading a book about remarkable children, gifted savants whose minds were damaged in such a way that they could see the world only through a sole window of sound or mathematics or another abstract system. I would press the hobgoblin for the story of what had really happened to Gustav Ungerland and to me.

But more than any explanation, I simply and desperately wanted my symphony back, for I could not write a note knowing it was gone. Nothing would stop me from making him return the score. I would reason if I could, beg if I must, or steal it back if need be. By now, I was no longer something wild and dangerous, but I was committed to restoring my life.

Unmistakable noises stirred beneath the floor all day. He was back. As the library emptied, I napped in the front seat of my car. Sultry August heat poured in through the windows, and I dozed off longer than intended. The stars had risen, and that short nap had energized me. I slung the rope around me like a bandolier, took out the tools, and skulked over to the side window. There was no telling how far below lay their underworld. Wrapping my fist in a towel, I punched through the glass, unlocked the window, and crawled through the opening. The stacks loomed like a maze of tunnels, the books watching my every movement through the darkness as I crept to the children's section. Anxious, I spent three wooden matches attempting to light the kerosene lantern. The oily wick smoked and at last caught flame. My shirt clung to my sweaty back, and the heavy air made breathing difficult. With the knife, I cut away the carpet square and saw that it had been glued atop a small trapdoor, easily pried open with the crowbar. A perfect square separated our two worlds.

Light filtered up from below and revealed a cramped room strewn with blankets and books, bottles and dishes. I bent down for a closer look and stuck my head through the hatchway. As quick as a striking snake, his face appeared in front of mine, not inches from my nose. I recognized him at once, for he looked exactly as I had as a young boy. My reflection in an old mirror. His eyes unmasked him, all soul but no substance, and he did not move but stared back silently without blinking, his breath mingling with mine. He expressed no emotion, as if he, too, had been waiting for this moment and for it all to be over.

This child and I were bound together. As boys dream of growing into men, and men dream of the boys they once were, we each took measure of the other half. He reminded me of that nightmare long ago when I was taken, and all at once my long-held fears and anger broke through the surface. The lantern ring bit into my fingers, and my left eye twitched with tension. The boy read my face and flinched. He was afraid of me, and for the first time I regretted what I had taken from him and realized that, in feeling sorry for him, I grieved for my own stolen life. For Gustav. For the real Henry Day. His unknowable life. For all I could have with Tess and with Edward. My dream of music. And who was I in this equation but the product of my own division? What a terrible thing to have happened to such a boy.

"I'm sorry," I said, and he vanished. Years of anger dissipated as I stared at the space where he used to be. He was gone, but in that brief moment we'd faced one another, my past had unspooled deep inside my mind, and I now let it go. A kind of euphoria raced through my blood, and I took a deep breath and felt myself again.

"Wait," I called out to him, and without thinking I turned and slid feet first through the opening, and landed in the dust. The space below the library was smaller than anticipated, and I bumped my head on the ceiling when I stood. Their grotto was but a murky shadow, so I reached up for the lantern to better see. Hunched over, I searched with the firelight for the boy, hoping he might answer a few questions. I wanted nothing more than to talk to him, to forgive and be forgiven. "I'm not going to hurt you," I cried out in the darkness. Wrestling free of the rope, I laid it and the carpet knife on the ground. The rusty lantern creaked in my hand as the light swept the room.

He crouched in the corner, yapping at me like a trapped fox. His face was my own fear. He trembled as I approached, eyes darting, searching for an escape. Candlelight illuminated the walls, and all around him on the ground lay stacks of paper and books. At his feet, tied in a strand of twine, a thick sheaf of handwritten pages sat next to my purloined score. My music had survived.

"Can't you understand me?" I held out my hand to him. "I want to talk to you."

The boy kept eyeing the opposite corner as if someone or something were waiting there, and when I turned to look, he rushed past me, knocking into the lamp as he ran. The rusted wire snapped, sending the lamp flying, shattering the glass on the stone wall. The blankets and papers ignited at once, and I snatched my music from the flames, beating it against my leg to extinguish the wisps of fire along the margins. I backed my way to the overhead entrance. As if fixed to the spot, he stood gazing up in amazement, and just before climbing out of the hole, I called for him a final time: "Henry—"

His eyes went wide, searching the ceiling as if discovering a new world. He turned to me and smiled, then said something that could not be understood. By the time I got upstairs, a fog of smoke rose through the hole below. It followed me through the broken window just as the flames began to lick the stacks of books.

After the fire, Tess saved me. Distraught over the damage I had done, I moped about the house for days. The destruction of the children's section was not my fault, although I deeply regretted the loss of all the books. The children will need new stories and fairy tales to see them through their nightmares and daydreams, to transfigure their sorrows and fears at not being able to remain children forever.

Tess and Edward arrived home from her cousin's just as the police were leaving. It seems I was regarded as a person of suspicion, for the librarians had reported my spate of frequent visits and "erratic behavior." The firemen had discovered the lantern in the ashes, but there was no way to link back to me what had once been my father's. Tess accepted my feeble explanations, and when the police came around again, she told them a little white lie, saying that we had spoken over the phone on the night of the fire and she remembered quite clearly having woken me from a deep sleep. Without any proof, the matter faded. The arson investigation, as far as I know, proved inconclusive, and the blaze passed into local lore, as if the books themselves had suddenly burst into flames.

Having Tess and Edward back home those few weeks before school started was both reassuring and unnerving. Their mere presence in the house calmed my fragile psyche after the fire, but there were times when I could barely look Tess in the eye. Burdened with guilt over her complicity, I searched for some way to tell her the truth, and perhaps she guessed the reasons for my growing anxiety.

"I feel responsible, in part," Tess told me over dinner. "And helpless. As if we should do something about rebuilding." Over our lamb chops, she outlined a plan to raise money for the library. The details arrived in such waves that I knew Tess had been contemplating the matter since the day of her return. "We'll start a book drive, too, and you can make your concert a benefit for the children."

Stunned and relieved, I could raise no objection, and over the next weeks, the bursts of activity overwhelmed my sense of decorum and privacy. People boxed up their fairy tales and nursery rhymes, and swarmed through the house at all hours with cartons of books, stacking them in the studio and garage. What had been my hermitage became a beehive for the well-intentioned. The phone rang constantly with offers to help. On top of the hubbub over the books, planning for the concert interrupted our peace. An artist came by to show poster designs for the concert. Advance tickets were sold from our living room. On a Saturday morning, Lewis Love and his teen-aged son, Oscar, showed up with a pickup truck, and we loaded the organ in the back to install it in the church. Rehearsals were scheduled for three nights a week, and the students and the musicians constructed it measure by measure. The giddy pace and hum of life left me too exhausted to consider my conflicted emotions. Swept up in the motion Tess had created, I could only truly function by concentrating on the music as the date for the performance drew near.

From the wings, I watched the crowd file into the church for the benefit premiere of *The Stolen Child* on that night in late October. Since I was performing on the organ, I had passed the conductor's baton to Oscar Love, and our old Coverboys drummer Jimmy Cummings was on timpani. Oscar had rented a tuxedo for the occasion and Jimmy had cut his hair, and we seemed much too respectable versions of our former selves. A few of my fellow teachers from Twain sat together in the back rows, and even one of the last remaining nuns from our grade school days attended. Ebullient as ever, my sisters showed up in formal wear, pearls at their collars, and they flanked my mother and Charlie, who winked at me as if to impart a dose of his abundant confidence. I was most surprised to see Eileen Blake escorted by her son Brian, who was in town for a visit. He gave me a momentary fright when they arrived, but the more I studied him, the less he could be compared rationally with Edward. My son after all, and thank goodness, he takes after his mother in every respect but appearance. With his hair tamed, and dressed up in his first suit and tie, Edward looked like another boy altogether, and seeing the foreshadowing of the man my son will become one day, I felt both pride and regret over the brevity of childhood. Tess could not stop grinning that crooked smile of hers, and rightfully so, for the symphony I had promised to write long ago was nearly hers.

To let in some fresh air on the crisp autumn night, the priests had cracked the windows, and a light breeze crossed the altar and the nave. The organ had been positioned at the apse because of the acoustics, and my back was to the audience and the rest of the small orchestra as we took our positions; from the corner of my eye, I could see only Oscar as he tapped and tensed the baton.

From the very first notes, I was determined to tell the story of how the child is stolen and replaced by someone else, and yet both the child and the changeling persist. In place of the usual distance and separation from the audience came a sense of connection through performance. They were stilled, hushed, expectant, and I could feel two hundred pairs of eyes watching. I concentrated to the point where I could let go and play for them rather than satisfy myself. The overture teased out the symphony's four movements: awareness, pursuit, lamentation, and redemption, and at the moment when I lifted my hands from the keys and the strings took up the pizzicato to indicate the arrival of the changelings, I felt his presence nearby. The boy I could not save. And as Oscar waved me in for the organ's interplay, I saw the child through an open window. He watched me play for him, listened to our music. As the tempo slowed in the second movement, I took more chances to watch him watching us.

He was solemn-eyed, listening intently to the music. During the dance of the third movement, I saw the pouch slung over his shoulder, as if he were preparing for a journey. The only language available to us was the music, so I played for him alone, forgot myself in its flow. All through the movement, I wondered if anyone else in the church had seen that strange face in the window, but when I looked for him again, there was nothing but black night. At the cadenza, I realized he had left me alone in the world and would not return.

The audience rose as one when the last notes of the organ expired, and they clapped and stomped for us. When I turned from the window to the thundering of friends and family, I scanned the faces in the crowd. I was almost one of them. Tess had lifted Edward to her side to join in joyful bravos, and caught off guard by their exuberance, I knew what must be done.

By writing this confession, Tess, I ask for your forgiveness so that I might make it all the way back to you. Music took me part of the way, but the final step is the truth. I beg you to understand and accept that no matter what name, I am what I am. I should have told you long ago and only hope it's not too late. My years of struggle to become human again hinge upon your belief in me and my story. Facing the boy has freed me to face myself. As I let go of the past, the past let go of me.

They stole me away, and I lived for a long, long time in the forest among the changelings. When my time to return came at last, I accepted the natural order. We found the boy Day and made the change. I did my best to ask his forgiveness, but perhaps the child and I are too far gone to reach each other anymore. I am no longer the boy I was once upon a time, and he has become someone else, someone new. He is gone, and now I am Henry Day.

CHAPTER 36

Henry Day. No matter how many times uttered or written, those two words remain an enigma. The faeries had called me Aniday for so long that I had become the name. Henry Day is someone else. In the end, after our months of watching him, I felt no envy for the man, only a sort of restrained pity. He had become so old, and desperation bowed his shoulders and marked his face. Henry had taken my name and the life I could have lived, and let it run through his fingers. How passing strange to settle on the surface of the world, bound to time and lost to one's true nature.

I went back for my book. Our encounter outside the library spooked me, so I waited overnight, and before dawn, through the cranny, I slid into the old darkened room and lit a single candle to show the way. I read my story and was satisfied. Tried to sing the notes of Henry's song. Into one bundle went my manuscript, papers from when I first arrived, and the letter from Speck; and into another, Henry's score. The last of these I planned to leave at his corner table. Our mischief over, the time had come to make amends. Above me, glass crashed, as if a window broke and shattered. An obscene exclamation, a thud to the floor, then the sound of footsteps approaching the hidden trapdoor.

Perhaps I should have run away at the first chance. My emotions drifted from dread to excitement, a sensation not unlike waiting at the door long ago for my father's daily return from work to wrap me in his arms, or those first days in the forest when I expected Speck to show up suddenly and relieve my lonesomeness. No such illusions with Henry Day, for he would doubtless not befriend me after all these years. But I did not hate him. I planned my words, how I would forgive him, present his stolen music, give him my name, and bid him farewell.

He sawed away at the carpeting to figure out how to get into the crawlspace, while I paced beneath, pondering whether to come to his aid. After an eternity, he found the door and swung it back on its hinges. A spotlight flooded in from above, like sunshine piercing a dark forest. A perfect square separated our two worlds. All at once, he stuck his head in the frame and peered into the blackness. I darted over to the opening and looked him straight in the eyes, his nose not six inches from my own. The sight of him disconcerted me, for no sign of kindness or recognition marked his features, no expression but raw disgust, which twisted his mouth into a snarl, and rage beat out of his eyes. Like a madman, he clambered through the hole into our world—a torch in one hand, a knife in the other, a coil of rope unspooling across his chest—and chased me into the corner. "Keep your distance," I warned. "I can send you from this world in a single blow." But he kept coming. Henry said he was sorry for what he was about to do and lifted the lantern above my head, so I ran right past him. He threw the fire at my back.

The lantern glass broke and a blaze spilled out like water over a pile of blankets, and the wool smoldered and burned, flames racing straight for my papers. We faced each other in the smoldering light. As the fire roared and burned brighter, he rushed forward and picked up all the papers. His eyes widened at the sight of his score and my drawings. I reached for the book, anxious only for Speck's letter, and he threw it into the corner for me to retrieve. When I turned around, Henry Day was gone, and his weapons—the rope, the knife, the iron bar—were on the floor. The trapdoor banged closed, and a long, thin crack opened overhead. The flames burst upward, brightening the room as if sun bore through the walls.

On the ceiling a picture began to emerge in the intense light. In the ordinary darkness, the surface lines seemed nothing more than random cracks and pockmarks in the foundation, but as the fire reached more fuel, the outlines flared and flickered. The shapes puzzled me, but once I perceived the pieces, the whole became apparent: the ragged East Coast of the United States, the fishlike contours of the Great Lakes, the broad and empty plains, the Rockies, and on to the Pacific. Directly above my head, the black brushstroke of the Mississippi divided the nation, and somewhere in Missouri, her trail crossed the river and raced west. Speck had marked her escape route and drawn a map of the trail to follow from our valley to the western ocean. She must have worked alone in the dark for months or years, arms arched to the ceiling, chipping away at the stone or painting with a rough brush, not showing a soul, hoping for the day her secret would be discovered. Around the outline of the country, she had etched and painted on that rough concrete a constellation of drawings invisible these many years. Hundreds of inscriptions, primitive and childlike, images laid over other images, each story told on top of its ancestor. Some of the drawings looked ancient, as if a prehistoric being had been here and left memories like paintings on a cave wall: a flock of crows lighting from a tree, a brace of quail, deer at a stream. She had drawn wildflowers, oxlips, violets, and thyme. There were creatures from her dreams, horned men with rifles and fierce dogs. Sprites and imps and goblins. Icarus, Vishnu, the angel Gabriel. Others as modern as cartoons: Ignatz throws the brick at Krazy Kat, Little Nemo slumbers in Wonderland, Koko jumps out of the inkwell. A mother with a child in her arms. A pod of whales arcing through the waves. Spirals roped into knots, a garland knitted from morning glory vines. The pictures unwrapped themselves in the dancing flames. The temperature rose as in an oven, but I could not save myself from her wild designs. In the darkest corner, she had painted a left hand and a right hand, thumbs overlapping. Her name and mine in a dozen fonts. Two figures raced over a hill; a boy with his hand caught in a beehive; a pair of readers sat back to back on a mountain of books. On the ceiling above the entrance to the outer world, she had carved *Come with me and play*. The fire sucked in the oxygen, and the rush of air caught my heart and blew it open. I had to leave.

I studied Speck's passage west, hoping to commit it to memory. Why had I never before thought to look up? A cinder popped and flew like the devil up under my eyelid. Smoke and heat filled the room, so I gathered McInnes's book and a few other papers and ran to the exit, but my bundle would not fit through the crack. Another pile of blankets ignited, sending a wave of heat that knocked me to my knees. I tore open the package, scattering papers to the floor. Close at hand were Speck's letter and a few stray childhood drawings, which I pressed against my chest; then I squeezed through the opening and into the fresh night.

The stars had come out and the crickets were fiddling madly. My clothing smelled of soot, and many of the pages had been scorched at the edges. The ends of my hair had been singed off, and every inch of bare skin throbbed, red, as if sunburned. Pain shot through the soles of my bare feet with each step, but I knew enough to get away from a burning building, dropping a few more pages at the door as I ran toward the woods. The library groaned once, and then the floor collapsed upon the grotto and thousands of stories went up in flames. From a green hideaway I heard the sirens of the fire engines coming to fight the bonfire. Tucking the papers into my shirt, I started the long trip home, remembering the mad look in Henry's eyes and all that had been lost. In the complete darkness, fireflies flashed their semaphores of longing.

Speck made it, I am sure, from here to there, and lived on a rocky shore, the bright Pacific her daily companion as she gathered mussels and clams and crabs from tidal pools, slept on the sand. She would be brown as a berry, her hair a tangle of knots, her arms and legs strong as ropes from swimming in the sea. In one long breath, she would exhale the story of her journey across the country, the pines of Pennsylvania, the cornfields and wheatfields and soybeans of the Midwest, sunflowers of Kansas, up the steep pitch of the Divide, summer snow in the Rockies, Painted Desert beyond, and finally ocean in view, oh joy! And then: What took *you* so long? And I would give her my story, this story and Henry Day's, until in her arms again I slept. Only through imagining could I bear the pain. Such a dream drew me homeward step by tortured step.

The other faeries took kind care of me upon my return to camp next morning. Onions and Béka scoured the woods for balm to soothe my blistered feet. Chavisory limped off to the cistern and drew a jug of cool water to quench my thirst and wash the ash from my skin and hair. My old friends sat beside me to hear the adventure and to help me salvage my literary remains. Only a few scraps from the past survived to prove that it had once existed. I told them all I could remember about Speck's map on the ceiling and the art she had left behind, hoping to store it in the collective consciousness of the tribe.

"You'll simply have to remember," said Luchóg.

"Rely upon the mind, for it is a complicated machine inside your skull," Smaolach said. "I can still recall exactly how I felt when I first saw you."

"What the memory loses, imagination re-creates." Chavisory had been spending far too much time with my old friend.

"Sometimes I don't know whether life's strange turns happened or I dreamed them, or if my memory remembers what is real or the dream."

"A mind often makes its own world," said Luchóg, "to help pass the time."

"I'll need paper. Do you remember when you first got me some paper, Luchóg? That kindness I'll never forget."

From memory, I transferred Speck's map on the ceiling to the back of her letter, and in the weeks that followed, I asked Smaolach to find me a detailed map of the country and any book he could about California and the Pacific Ocean. She might be anyplace along the northern coast. There was no certainty that I would find her in the large, wide land, but the possibility sustained me as I began again. My feet healed as I sat quietly in our camp, writing every day outdoors while the heat of August gave way to the cool weeks of early autumn.

As the maples flamed to yellow and red, and the oaks to crispy brown, a strange sound drifted now and again from the town and over the hills to our camp. Emanating from the church on still nights, the music arrived in starts and fits, broken now and again by other sounds—traffic on the highway, crowds roaring at Friday night football games, and the chatter of noise that intrudes upon modern life. Running like a river, the music forked through the forest and spilled down from the ridge into our glen. Entranced by the sudden sound, we would stop to listen, and mad with curiosity, Luchóg and Smaolach set out to find its source. They came back breathless with news one late October night.

"Stay just a short while, *a stoirín*, and it will be ready."

By the light of the fire, I was lashing a leather strap to my travel pouch. "And what will be ready, my friend?"

He cleared his throat, and when he still did not get my attention, he coughed again, but louder. I looked up to see him grinning and Luchóg holding an unrolled poster almost as big as himself. All but his hands and feet had disappeared behind the broadside.

"You have it upside down, Luch."

"Surely you can read it any which way," he complained, and then he righted the poster. The concert at the church was scheduled for two days hence, and I was struck by not only the title but, underneath it, a small woodcut engraving of two figures in flight and pursuit.

"Which one is the faery, and which is the child?"

Smaolach considered the artwork. "No matter what you think, you're just as likely to be right as wrong. But you'll stay for the symphony? Composed by Henry Day, and him playing the organ as well."

"You can't miss that," Luchóg argued. "Another day or two, and the journey is just as long."

We footed our way through the dark forest, a last bit of mischief together, taking bold delight in coming close yet not being seen. On the night of the concert we hid in the graveyard as the people filed into the church, and the opening notes of the symphony soared through the windows and echoed among the stones. The prelude announced his grand themes, ending in a long solo on the organ. He played beautifully, I'll admit, and we were drawn closer, rising one by one from behind the gravestones to stand next to the church windows. Béka wrapped his arms around Onions, and whispered in her ear. When she began to laugh at his joke, he clamped a hand against her mouth till she sputtered for breath and then kept still. Chavisory mimed the role of conductor, her hands tracing arcs and waves in the sky. My old cronies, Luchóg and Smaolach, leaned against the church wall and smoked, staring at the night stars.

Cinching my bag across my shoulders—I carried my book in it everywhere now—I made my way around to a rear window and dared look in. Henry had his back to the audience and rocked as he played the organ, fierce concentration written on his face. When he closed his eyes and moved in time with the rise and fall of the notes, he was lost. The strings alone took up the next measures, and he saw me through the window, but the peaceful look never left his face. Henry was transformed, younger than before, more like a man than a monster. I would think on him no longer and soon be gone, but whether or not he realized I intended to leave, I can never know.

The crowd in the pews was transfixed by the small orchestra, and I am quite sure that had anyone spotted me looking through the window, they would have rushed past the altar and out into the churchyard. So I had the rare chance to study their faces from afar, recognizing at once Henry's wife and son, Edward, in the front row. Thank goodness I had convinced Béka and Onions to leave that child alone. Most of the other people were strangers to me. I kept hoping to see my sisters, but, of course, they are still ageless children in my memory. An older woman, holding her fingers against her lips as she listened, seemed to glance my way once or twice, and when she did so, she reminded me of my mother, the last I shall see of her. Some part of me desired to crawl through the opening and run to her, to feel her hand against my cheek, to be held, to be known by her, but my place is not among them. Goodbye, my dear, I whispered to her, sure that she could not hear, but hoping that somehow she understood.

Henry kept smiling and playing, and like a book the music told a story that seemed, in part, a gift—as if, in our only common language, he was expressing what beat in his heart. Some sorrow, perhaps, some remorse. It was enough for me. The music carried us in two directions, as if above and below; and in the interludes, the spaces between the notes, I thought he, too, was trying to say goodbye, goodbye to the double life. The organ breathed and laid sound upon sound, and then exhaled into silence. "Aniday," Luchóg hissed, and I shrank from the window to the ground. A beat or two, and the crowd burst like a thunderstorm. One by one, we faeries rose and disappeared into the falling darkness, gliding past the gravestones and back into the forest, as if we had never been among the people.

Having made amends with Henry Day, I am ready to leave come tomorrow. This version of my story has not taken nearly as long to re-create. I have not been concerned with putting down all the facts, nor a detailed explanation of the magic, as far as I understand such things, of the people who lived in secret and below. Our kind are few, and no longer deemed necessary. Far greater troubles exist for children in the modern world, and I shudder to think of real and lurking dangers. Like so many myths, our stories will one day no longer be told or believed. Reaching the end, I lament all those lost souls and those dear friends left behind. Onions, Béka, Chavisory, and my old pals Smaolach and Luchóg are content to remain as they are, indifferent children of the earth. They will be fine without me. We all go away one day.

Should by chance any of you see my mother, tell her I cherish her every kindness and miss her still. Say hello to my baby sisters. Kiss their chubby cheeks for me. And know that I will carry you all with me when I leave in the morning. Heading west as far as the waters to look for her. More beats than blood in the heart. A name, love, hope. I am leaving this behind for you, Speck, in case you return and we somehow miss each other. Should that be so, this book is for you.

I am gone and am not coming back, but I remember everything.

# *ACKNOWLEDGMENTS*

Thank you to Peter Steinberg and Coates Bateman. I am also happily indebted to Nan Talese, Luke Epplin, and everyone at Doubleday, to Joe Regal and the redoubtable Bess Reed. To Melanie for her insightful reading and suggestions and for years of encouragement. To all my children.

For their advice and inspiration, Sam Hazo, David Low, Cliff Becker, Amy Stolls, Ellen Bryson, Gigi Bradford, Allison Bawden, Laura Becker, and Sharon Kangas. And for the swift kick at Whale Rock, thank you to Jane Alexander and Ed Sherin.

Sarah Blaffer Hrdy's *Mother Nature: A History of Mothers, Infants, and Natural Selection* inspired the journal article on the anthropological roots of the changeling myth.

*Keith Donohue* lives in Maryland, near Washington, D.C. For many years, he was a speechwriter at the National Endowment for the Arts, and now works at another federal agency. *The Stolen Child* is his first novel.